I, Alexandra

A Legacy of Stehle's Door

William M. O'Brien Jr.

I, Alexandra

A Legacy of Stehle's Door

By William O'Brien

This book is a work of fiction. Names, characters, places, and incidents are a product of the author's imagination or are used fictitiously. Any resemblance to actual events, locales, or persons, living or dead, is coincidental.

Cover Design: Linda Boulanger
Interior Design: Jennifer McMurrain/Linda Boulanger
www.TreasureLineBookServices.weebly.com

Published by TreasureLine Publishing
www.TreasureLinePublishing.weebly.com

ISBN: 978-1-61752-150-8

Also available in eBook publication

PRINTED IN THE UNITED STATES OF AMERICA

To my wife and daughter
for their love, support, and
dedication to my work

Prologue

Galveston, Sept 8, 1900
Late Evening

The holes in the floor were not working. Now the water was rising quickly, through the holes and from the outside through smashed windows. Houses on each side had gone down, the Taylor house only thirty minutes before. A constant howling wind and pouring rain seemed only to increase and what daylight there was at this hour had turned to blackness. A frightened group of people huddled together at the top of the stairs.

"Mama, your new rug," the six-year-old blurted, through tears. "It's all wet. All our stuff is wet."

"Quiet, Baby. Try to sleep." The mother gently stroked the forehead of the frightened child. Lantern in hand, the father stepped cautiously down the stairs to gauge the depth of the water filling the house.

"If this doesn't last too much longer," he said over his shoulder, "I think we'll be all right. The fierce wind, however, beat harder against the house, trying to turn it over, like it had all houses around.

The two older children, Phoebe and her friend, Johanna, from Houston, huddled together in the bedroom atop the stairs. Both girls were terrified. They had planned a pleasant weekend together, but now this storm had destroyed everything. Furthermore, the neighbors were all gone. To them it seemed only a question of time before they would be gone, too.

A piece of wreckage smashed into the front of the house, shaking the entire building. The children screamed and the father, on the stairs, grabbed the railing and hurried to the top.

"Katie, get Mary and the girls into the back bedroom!" He stopped and turned again toward the front of the house. "I think that wall's going to give way," he said to himself, not to frighten his family any more than they were.

The mother clutched the little girl to her and hurried down the hall, beckoning the two older girls in the room to follow. The father remained at the top of the stairs and watched the front wall. The front door, with a heavy chair barring it, rattled loudly as surging water rushed against it.

"Katie, if that wall gives, we're going to be flooded to the second floor," he yelled to the back of the house. He thought about opening his back door to allow the water to rush through the house, but he worried that water in the house, now four feet deep and rising rapidly, would not allow him to get to the back door and still return to the stairs. He figured the rear windows were still closed, so if he could open these, the rushing water could flow through the house and keep it stable. If the incoming water were blocked, the house would surely be pushed off a foundation that consisted only of sunken posts, four feet from the packed sand. The water was not supposed to reach even the four-foot level in an overflow, which was what this was supposed to be.

Again, a heavy piece of wreckage crashed against the house, this time on the side. What was left of a windowpane smashed inward, raining broken glass into the water.

Now the father realized the only thing he could do was comfort his family. He stared at the water swirling in and out of the light of his lantern and knew there was nothing left to do on the first floor.

The noise still rose with scores of small bits of debris slamming against the house, even knocking out slats from the windows the father had had time to board up. One roof shingle smashed between two slats and, with bullet-like velocity, embedded itself in the opposite wall.

The father made his way to the top of the stairs and toward the back bedroom where his family sheltered. At the door, he was met by a spray of water through a window that was completely gone. In the darkness, he made out four people huddled in a corner as far as they could get from the smashed window. Hurriedly, he lit another lamp and joined them. In the corner, he noticed a piece of debris sticking in the far wall.

Apparently, the outside air was filled with deadly missiles.

"My God, Kate, this storm just keeps getting worse," he whispered to his wife, trying not to let the children hear.

Although they had two lanterns lit, the darkness was overpowering. Helplessly, the family huddled around them, hoping the house, now creaking and weaving in the wind, would stay erect.

The father was now sure the front wall was gone for the house moved in the wind more violently than ever. Water had to be lapping at the top of the stairs. However, he dared not leave the room.

"God, when is this going to end?" the mother wailed beside her husband.

"Just stay still. We're going to be all right." The father turned to his wife and then to the girls. The small child's face showed in the dim light an urgency and at the same time a resignation that he hadn't expected.

My God, if I could only be as placid as she is, he thought.

Outside the storm roared on, ever increasing in intensity. It seemed now to be much worse than it had been when the neighbor's houses had blown down. The father wondered what had happened to his neighbors. Had they heeded an early warning and gone to high ground? Had they swam to safety? He remembered the earlier warning and his reaction that his house was stout enough to withstand anything. In his mind he knew that his neighbors had probably heeded the warning he had ignored.

The house now swayed so strongly in the violent wind that he knew it would surely collapse. And the darkness was more overwhelming than ever. Any gust of wind getting to them would surely blow out both lanterns.

The house began to move. Slightly, at first, and then a jolt that the father knew was the building moving on its foundation.

Dear God, he thought. *It's going over now.* He said a silent prayer and then put his arms around his wife and the little girl. The two older girls huddled nearby, just inside the lantern light.

He thought about putting his family through a nearby window upon floating wreckage. It had occurred to him that they might be safer in the water, flattened out on floating debris.

But the flying missiles terrified him. And they were everywhere. At least in the house they were safe from these.

Again the house moved on its post foundation. This time, the family stood and braced themselves against the wall.

The girl from Houston pulled away from the older daughter and ran for the door.

"I'm going to die!" she screamed. "Oh God, I don't want to die! Jesus Christ! Jesus Christ, I'm going to die!"

The father caught her in his arms and pulled her to him. "Johanna. Johanna," he said in a high whisper. "Quiet down. You're not going to die. You're going to be safe with the rest of us." He clutched the girl tightly to him.

As he did, the house suddenly shifted once again, this time off its foundation. The walls disintegrated and the force of the water deposited the frightened family into the swirling, wreckage-choked waters.

Chapter One

"There are more things in Heaven and Earth, Horatio, than are dreamt of in your philosophy." So says Hamlet to his friend, Horatio, after visiting with the ghost of his father. This was no idle observation meant to entertain sixteenth century theater goers.

The terrifying realities of Shakespeare's time are alive and well today. And capable of the gravest harm. When I encountered these things years ago, I knew that they aimed at no less than my life itself. Years later, these images have faded; they don't even interrupt my sleep anymore. But they are there. Because of Joseph Stehle's hideous door, they will always be there. I haven't forgotten them. Now, years after encountering the horror of Stehle's door, I should be safe from them. But I wonder, for I know about them and most people don't. Because of this I, Alexandra Elizabeth Zunker, know too much.

--Journal entry by Alex Zunker, written upon her graduation from high school.

"There, finally. I think I got it." The tall, blond girl put her pencil down and sat up. "Alex, you'll have to look over number ten. I'm still kind of hazy about that one, but I think the others are right."

Alex Zunker sat up, blinking from her interrupted movie. "Roomie, do you have all fifteen of them?" she asked.

"Yeah. But like I said, number ten is probably screwed up. I worked and worked on that one and still don't think I have the right answer."

"Okay. I'll look it over."

"God, I've got to go to bed." Stephanie Helsing, Alex's roommate, stood up from the table, pulled her shirt down, and swept her long, blond hair away from her face. "It's after midnight and I've got class in the morning. Time sure goes fast when you're having fun. Right?"

"You betcha." Alex rose and stretched, her hands thrusting upwards from her shapely six-foot frame almost reached the light fixture. She blew a wisp of strawberry blond hair out of her face. "And single variable calculus is some of the best. Is it still raining? I must have dozed off."

"Yes. Another shitty night. I can't wait to get in that rack. I swear the only thing you can do in this weather is sleep." Stephanie was tall herself, but her five feet eleven inches fell short of Alex's six. Their classmates at Rice playfully referred to them as "those amazons."

"I'll be up in a minute. I'm going to give Henrietta and Sabrina a little more food." She stopped and looked around. "Where are they? I don't remember seeing them this evening."

"I don't know. I haven't seen them either." Stephanie began to get her things together for next morning's class.

"They're probably upstairs. When I pour out the food, they'll come running. They always do." After one more stretch, Alex turned and went into the kitchen where she poured out two bowls of dry cat food. Then, after shaking the canister vigorously, she put both bowls on the floor and waited, hands on hips.

But no cats came.

After a few minutes, she reentered the living room and looked around.

"Where the hell are they?" she asked herself, irritated. She noticed her roommate had gone upstairs. "Stephanie, do you see them up there?" she yelled.

"No. They're not in my room. You want me to look in yours? You know how they love your bed."

"Yes, would you? I have their food ready down here." Not waiting for her roommate's reply, she ran up the stairs and down the hall to her room.

Neither cat could be found, however, in their usual spot on

her bed.

Alex turned to Stephanie, a look of alarm on her face. “Surely they didn’t get out earlier.” Now, she began to panic. Declawed cats didn’t need to be running loose in the Houston Heights.

While Alex looked in her closet and around the bed, Stephanie left the room. A few moments later, Alex was startled by her roommate’s voice.

“Alex, come in here and look.” Stephanie was now in the bathroom, stripped to her underwear. “I knew those two couldn’t have gotten out.”

Alex joined her where both girls stared at two cats huddled together in the bathtub, feline fear stamped plainly on both faces.

“What in the name of God is this all about?” Alex, relieved, but puzzled and still a bit irritated, stepped to the tub, but neither cat made a move. They just followed her with their eyes. “Stephi, you’re the one who grew up with cats. What are they up to?”

“I don’t have any idea, Alex, but they look scared. Yesterday, they were staring at the wall and arching their backs. Remember?”

“That was probably a rat in the wall.”

“Jesus. I hate rats!”

“That’s what was happening yesterday. But what is this?” She squatted down by the tub and reached out to the cat nearest her. “Sabrina, what’s the matter, kitty?” The large orange tabby craned her head toward Alex’s hand and she rubbed her under her head. “What are you two up to?” she asked, gently.

Stephanie picked up Henrietta, a part Siamese, and clutched her to her. The cat emitted a low whine. “Come on, Henry, you and I are going to bed.”

She took the cat into her room and put her on the bed. “You know, Alex, these two are aware of something,” she said from her room. “There’s something around here that scares them”

“That’s rather obvious, Stephi. But what is it?”

“I don’t know. It might be a dog, although I haven’t seen one around.” She walked to her bedroom door, Henrietta making a nest for the night on the bed behind her.

In the meantime, Alex picked up Sabrina and carried her into the hall. "But why would they act that way to a dog. Any dog would be outside."

"I have no idea. Maybe they heard it." Stephanie slowly walked into the hall and followed Alex to her room, her arms crossed over her chest. "I think we would have heard a dog if there were one around. Mrs. Frank hasn't mentioned any dog except the Warner's dachshund across the street. And I don't think these two are going to be afraid of a dachshund."

"It beats me." At her bedroom door, Alex let the large cat down and she immediately ran downstairs. "Well, whatever it is, it isn't going to get in."

"The boogey-man maybe?" Stephanie grinned and turned back toward her door.

"I'm going down and check the doors." Alex followed her roommate down the hall and then turned toward the staircase. "I'm sure Sabrina is down there gorging herself so she can puke in the night."

"Come off it, Mama. She just had a scare." Stephanie bent over the stair rail and laughed, a somewhat coarse laugh that Alex didn't think belonged to so pretty a girl.

At the bottom of the stairs, Alex switched on the living room light. Then, she stopped cold and listened. From the kitchen the sound of Sabrina attacking her food was the only thing she could hear. Placing her hands on her hips, she thought about going outside and looking around.

"Stephanie, I'm going outside and look around the back and the driveway," she called up the stairs. "I'll be back in a minute."

Outside, there was no sound except the distant noise of a few late night cars. Mrs. Frank's house, which soared up in front of her was dark. Apparently, she was not keeping one of her late night vigils in front of the TV set.

Alex walked around the large garage apartment and then down the driveway by Mrs. Frank's house. Nothing could be found. A single light lit up most of the street but she could see nothing. There was no sign of a dog or anything else. In what she could see in the porch light, she looked over the walls of the apartment for any evidence of an entrance a rat might have made. She had seen a rat on the power lines just after she had moved in last fall, but since then she had seen nothing. Besides, weren't cats supposed to keep rats away?

The girl, sighing, re-entered the apartment. "There's nothing outside, Stephi."

"Is Mrs. Frank still up?"

"No, she's in bed. The house is dark."

In her pajamas, Stephanie appeared at the top of the stairs. "Well, I'm going to bed. Wake me at seven, will you? I don't want to be late for Swarthmore's class again."

"Sure. Why don't you set your alarm?"

"Because I roll over too easy, Roomy Dear." She chuckled. "Besides, you know that."

"Yes, I do. What are you going to do when you have to get to a job?"

"Oh, that's easy. Turn the radio up full blast." The girl retreated to her room and turned off the light.

Alex checked the doors and climbed the stairs, followed by Sabrina, stomach full and heading for Alex's bed for the night.

What an occurrence, she thought. *The bathtub, for God's sake. I could think about cats for a thousand years and not envision anything like that.*

When she reached her room, she turned her light off at the door. "Good night, Stephi. Seven o'clock, like you said."

"Good night, Alex. Thanks. Remember to look over number ten in the morning."

"Right." After changing her clothes in the dark, Alex lay in her bed and stared at the ceiling. She could feel the presence of her cat apparently already asleep at the foot of the bed. Since it was late, she dispensed with the usual bedtime contemplations and rolled over on her side and closed her eyes.

At four o'clock, she was awakened by a truck turning around in Mrs. Frank's driveway. Cursing, she rolled over on her other side, afraid she might not get back to sleep.

She had no trouble going to sleep. However, this time she began to dream, a terrifying dream of darkness and confusion. In a haze, she couldn't see anything but she could hear screams and the roaring sounds of water and wind.

A strong wind pressed her against an unseen wall like a giant hand. She could not tell what the wall was but she could feel it moving. Pieces of things she could not identify, along with water spray, struck her all over her body, stinging momentarily but quickly blowing away.

Slowly she began to make out things nearby in the darkness, things she could not readily identify. She tried to move down the wall to ball up at its base, but the wind was too strong. Water and water spray was everywhere. But when she clutched herself, she felt dry! She should be soaked but she was dry!

Turning her head away from the wind, she spotted a large object, like a roof beam, coming straight at her out of the darkness.

Oh God, this is it, she thought. With all her might, she jerked her body to the right to move out of the way of the oncoming object. The effort landed her on the floor of her room, dazed and blinking.

"Oh, my God, Roomy, what in hell happened?"

Alex turned over on the floor to see Stephanie standing in the door, eyes wide with alarm.

"I…I had a bad dream and…and…I guess I just fell out of bed." She smiled slightly and rubbed sleep out of her eyes, then turned over on her back. "What're you doing up?"

"Call of nature. All those sodas and iced tea yesterday evening, I guess." Stephanie backed out of the doorway to let Alex make her way to the bathroom. "But look at you. You look like crap."

"God, Stephi, I had one hell of a nightmare. And just before dawn."

"What brought that on?"

"I have no idea." Alex turned back to her room and looked around. "By the way, where are the two little paranoids?" She smiled faintly.

"They're not up here. They're probably downstairs scorfing the rest of the food Sabrina left."

"That's odd. Sabrina usually doesn't go downstairs until I do."

"Speaking of food, I'm going downstairs to get breakfast.

I've got time this morning." Stephanie bounded to the staircase. "Thanks to my bladder, I'll have no trouble getting to Swarthmore's class this morning."

In the bathroom, Alex studied the circles under her eyes in the mirror. Sighing, she wet her face and hands. From downstairs, she could hear Stephanie getting the skillet ready to cook scrambled eggs.

"That sounds good," she said to herself. "I think I'll have some of that myself." She thought about changing clothes but decided against it because it was still early. There will be a lot of time for that later.

Then, she thought about the strange dream. It was clearly one which she had never had before. *A damned flood,* she thought. *I was in a damned flood.* It occurred to her that the dream may have been the result of yesterday's rain. A continual rain had fallen on Houston for days, and sure, such a distressing phenomenon could cause bad dreams. Again she wondered. The weather had never affected her like this before.

"Alex, you want yours scrambled like mine?" Stephanie yelled from downstairs. "I can fry a couple if you want. I got a load of time."

Shaken from disturbing thoughts, Alex walked calmly to the stair rail and leaned over. "Just make mine scrambled, Steph. Are the two kids down there?"

"Oh, Henrietta and Sabrina have full bellies, now. Any moment they ought to be on their way up."

Stephanie returned to the kitchen while Alex slowly walked to her bedroom to find something to wear to class.

Although she had two classes that day, English literature and organic chemistry, both of which she liked and was prepared for, she didn't want to go. She wanted to get back in her bed and stay there. Oddly, she felt threatened, by whom or what she did not know. This new sensation and the strange, oppressive dream weighed on her like a curse.

I guess I better get dressed, she thought. *Stephanie's probably going to need some prodding to get to calculus on time. I know how she piddles around so I don't need to be dragging my feet.*

She had just slipped on her second shoe when she heard the

shower come on in the bathroom.

"Wow, Steph, finished cooking already?" Quickly, she made her way to the bathroom where she noted that the door was open. Stephanie always made sure it was closed when she took her shower. But now it was open and the shower faucet was on full blast.

Puzzled, she cut it off, and ran to the stairs. "Stephi!" she yelled. "Why'd you turn the shower on?"

"What, Roomy? The eggs are ready." Stephanie stood in the middle of their small living room, a plate of eggs and sausage in her hand.

"The shower was on. Didn't you turn it on?"

"No. I've been down here cooking breakfast."

"Jeez. That's just plain weird. The shower just came on. By itself." Alex put her hands on her hips and cast concerned glances about the landing.

"Come on, Alex. Something's got to have turned the water on. It's never…"

"Stephanie, I was in my room getting dressed. And the water came on." She turned and walked back to the bathroom. Nothing seemed out of the ordinary. She tightened both water spigots for the shower as much as she could, thinking they probably came on by themselves because they were not turned off all the way.

Boy, this has never happened before, she thought, realizing now that her roommate couldn't have possibly turned on the upstairs shower while in the middle of cooking the morning meal. *Maybe we need to get a plumber. What if it comes on while we're gone?*

She dismissed the shower as an unusual circumstance, one of the many quirks of modern appliances in old houses. But in the back of her mind, she knew that no matter how insignificant she made it out to be, the shower incident was somehow connected with her strange dream.

Chapter Two

A few days later, the weekend found Alex preparing for Easter Sunday. She and Stephanie would take Mrs. Frank across town to church for the eight-thirty service and Bible Class. Then, joined by Alex's parents, all would go out for lunch. Alex looked forward to Easter Sunday as it was always a convivial holiday.

Coming in from Good Friday services the previous evening, the girls had found the upstairs lights on in their apartment. At the time they had thought nothing of it as they had left for church in broad daylight and figured they had just thoughtlessly left the lights on. But then, Mrs. Frank, who had gone with them, noticed that some of her lights were on also. The old lady feared a burglary from the start but an examination of the apartment and the house found nothing amiss.

"It's not like Mrs. Frank to leave lights on," Stephanie remarked the next day. She sipped on a glass of pink Chablis while lounging against Alex's bedroom door. Her brother had brought her six bottles of this wine in March and she and Alex and assorted friends had already drank four of them. "I mean I can see us leaving lights on. We're space cadets. But her? You know how precise she is."

"When we left yesterday, Steph, the sun was still way up in the sky." Alex had laid out five good dresses on her bed and was examining them for something to wear to Easter services the next day. "We probably switched the lights on and didn't notice they were on before we left. She probably did the same thing."

"In that dark house?" Stephanie took another sip of wine. "Parts of that place are like a damned cave at high noon."

"I know, but she's entitled to a couple of mistakes, too, isn't she?" Alex turned toward her roommate and smiled. "And if you pour me a glass of that hooch, I'll be forever grateful."

Stephanie disappeared downstairs to get more wine while Alex continued to examine dresses. She was not satisfied with any of them. Arms crossed over her chest, she was thinking of calling her mother, Elizabeth, to meet her at Baybrook Mall to buy her a new dress when she noticed her window, behind the curtains, was wide open.

She stared at it momentarily, incredulously. She never opened the window because any gust of wind would blow the curtains around. Besides, because of the humidity, the girls had just begun running their window-unit air conditioners.

What in the name of God, she thought. It occurred to her that the window had not been open last night because the curtains had remained still and the window air conditioner had been on low cool. But when she had cut if off this morning, she hadn't noticed the open window.

She hurried to the window and shut it, locking it at the top. Stephanie appeared at the door behind her, a full wine glass in each hand.

"What are you doing there, Roomy," she said, with a giggle that suggested she had already drunk more than one glass.

"Steph, I just noticed the window was open. Did you by chance open it?"

"No."

"Well, somebody did. It was wide open." Alex turned toward her roommate and took her glass of wine.

"Alex, that's really freaky." Stephanie suddenly became serious, almost alarmed. "That's the window we tried to open last fall, remember? That night we wanted the breeze. And it wouldn't budge then."

"Yes, I remember that. It was this window." Alex walked slowly back to the window. "We couldn't open it. But why is it open now?"

Stephanie took another sip and followed her to the window. "Did you by chance get it open last night?" she asked. "You know how we've been forgetting things around here."

"Stephanie, I swear to God I didn't touch it." Alex put her hands on her hips and turned toward her roommate. "You know, there's been a lot of weird things going on around here. The shower the other morning, the lights, the window now and then there's the cats. All, all of a sudden."

"I didn't do any of those things, Alex."

"Roomy, I know you didn't. You were downstairs cooking the other morning and you couldn't do anything with that window last fall." She sighed and turned again to the window. An image of her strange dream suddenly appeared in her mind and she shuddered. "I just wish I knew what the hell was going on around here."

"Maybe it's gravity." Stephanie giggled again, this time more forcefully.

"You better not get too potted on that stuff. We have to get up early tomorrow and drive Mrs. Frank to church, as you know." Alex turned and walked to the telephone table on the hall landing at the head of the stairs. "I'm going to call Mama and have her meet me at Baybrook Mall. I need a dress for tomorrow."

"What about the ones you usually wear to church?"

Alex paused, momentarily, before dialing the phone. "I don't know, Steph, I just feel like something new. You know."

She called her home but there was no one there. "I guess I'm stuck with my usual church clothes," she said as she hung up the receiver. "You better go fix me another one of those things." She smiled as she passed her roommate and returned to her room.

"Sure. You got anything to do tonight?"

"No. Josh is helping his family get ready for the usual Easter deluge of relatives and my family is nowhere to be found."

"Good. We don't have to put a stopper in the bottle."

"Stephi, the last thing I need now is a wine drunk."

"Why not? You have congenial company, all evening by ourselves, and a damn good alarm clock to wake you up in the morning."

"Yeah, with a throbbing…"

Alex stopped in mid sentence when the cat Sabrina slipped through the door and silently jumped on her bed. Ordinarily such an act would elicit only a glance, but now she noticed the animal's eyes were wide and staring in alarm.

"What in the name of God," she said in a half whisper. "Steph, look at this animal. She looks like something, or someone, scared her to death."

"Or mad, as if someone kicked her."

"She's been downstairs, hasn't she?"

"I don't know. I didn't notice her when I went down for the drinks."

"Sabrina, what's the matter, kitty?" Alex said gently. She reached over and petted the animal which turned its head away toward the wall.

"I'm thinking she and Henrietta got into a fight." Stephanie walked over to the cat and rubbed its back.

"We would have heard it, wouldn't we?"

"Not necessarily. Particularly if it happened downstairs." Stephanie turned toward the hall. "Let's go find the other one."

The search was over before it started. Henrietta sat at the top of the stairs, the same wide-eyed expression on her face.

"I knew it." Stephanie said, walking toward the animal. "They got in a fight, probably over food. Alex come here and look."

"Oh, those two." Alex again put her hands on her hips. "I'm going back in and hang my stuff up before Sabrina gets cat hair all over them."

"Great. And I'll get refills for both of us."

While Alex carefully hung her clothes up in her closet, Sabrina never took her eyes off her. Silently, the animal followed her every move. When she had finished, Stephanie appeared at the door.

"One more round, Roomy Dearest. And there's another one left in the bottle." This time Stephanie chuckled under her breath. "And another whole unopened bottle to go with it."

"Great. We can get snockered." Alex took the glass and raised it in a mock toast. "What if Mrs. Frank wants to go out to eat tonight? Have you thought about that?"

"Sure. We'll let her drive. She likes to drive."

"God, you've thought of everything. Typical drunk."

"Absolutely. Especially on Saturday when there's nothing better to do."

"Except get ready for Easter."

The two were startled by the ringing of the phone. Alex was first to it so she picked it up.

"Hello, Sis," a low voice sang into the other end of the line.

"Pauli? Where's Mama. I wanted to meet her at Baybrook Mall to get an Easter dress for tomorrow."

"I'm doing fine, Sis. How are you?"

"Oh, Pauli, I don't mean to sound pissed. I'm just a tad bit irritated. I've been going through my good clothes and can't seem to find anything exciting to wear tomorrow. Some of my stuff is so threadbare." Alex thought again about her five dresses lying on the bed but now hanging up.

"Well, you know what Papa says about that."

"Yes, Pauli, I know. Wear what you have until it rots off you."

Paul laughed on the other end of the line. He was getting ready to graduate from high school and, at seventeen, felt like he was ready for anything, especially his sister's roommate. "How's that beautiful roomy of yours?"

"Ornery as ever." Alex chuckled.

"Anyway, I told Papa I'd call you as soon as I got home this afternoon. He wants us all to go to Kima to eat seafood after Bible class tomorrow."

"Sounds good to me."

"Yeah. Papa's reserved a table outside and everything." Paul paused a moment. "I think he mentioned something about these plans to Mrs. Frank last night, but I guess she just forgot to tell you about them."

"She didn't mention them, if he did."

Something in Alex wanted her to tell her little brother about the weird occurrences, but something else told her not to mention them. She decided on the latter, thinking she could mention them later, maybe tomorrow.

"Well, I got to get off the phone now. There's a couple of things I promised Mama I'd do before she got home and I haven't even thought about them before now."

"O.K. Pauli. Tell Papa and Mama I love them."

"Sure. You tell Mrs. Frank hello and Beautiful Body I love her."

"Oh, sure, everyday."

When Alex hung up, she heard a voice behind her.

"I bet I know who that was." Stephanie had gone into her room and come out on the landing during the phone conversation.

"Yep. Little brother Paul. Papa and Mama weren't home. We're all going over to Kima tomorrow after church to eat."

"Sounds great to me."

Alex smirked. "He said for me to tell you, quote, Beautiful Body, unquote, that he loves you."

"Oh, wow, it's great to be loved!" Stephanie pressed her hands against her chest dramatically.

"I think he actually has a crush on you, Steph."

"Do you? Alex, your little bro is cute but just a tad bit on the immature side."

"Don't we both know it?"

At that, both girls laughed and descended the stairs. In the small living room they sipped their wine and talked quietly about a variety of things, nothing of pressing importance. They seemed, at least momentarily, to have put aside the odd events of the past few days.

Later, they found a good movie on T.V. during which they opened the last of Stephanie's wine bottles. The wine continued to warm both of them and made the movie that much more entertaining.

When the movie ended, Alex went to the restroom downstairs while Stephanie made for the bathroom upstairs. Alex was in the kitchen, pouring another glass, when her roommate returned.

"Hey, Roomy, there's a little girl in Mrs. Frank's backyard."

"What?"

Neither girl was slurring her words yet but both had become a bit unsteady.

"I said I saw a little girl in Mrs. Frank's backyard. I walked out on that little balcony thing off the back room and there she was."

"Who was it?"

"How should I know?" Stephanie set her empty glass on

the counter and eyed the bottle which now was only one third filled.

"There are no little girls around here, Steph. Except Old Man Winslow's granddaughter. Was it her?"

"Alex, I know her. She's twelve years old. This is a little girl. About five or six years old."

"A little girl five or six years old?"

"Yeah. You want to come and see for yourself?" She turned toward the door and Alex followed her through the living room and up the stairs. At the back of the landing, they entered a small bedroom that both of them had turned into an extra closet. This room led to an outside staircase but now, with the stairs long gone, was only a make shift balcony. But if afforded a view of Mrs. Frank's closed backyard as well as the street and neighborhood beyond.

"Now, she was right down there by the birdbath." Stephanie pointed with one hand and braced herself with the other.

Alex looked where her roommate was pointing but saw nothing. "I don't see anything, Steph."

"She was right down there just a few minutes ago, I tell you. Just a few minutes ago." She jabbed her finger downward in emphasis and then bent over the rail to examine the whole backyard. "Now, where the hell did she go?"

Alex laughed quietly and then put her hand on Stephanie's shoulder. "You're drunk, Baby."

"No, I'm not, damn it! I saw a little girl just a few minutes ago. She had on a white dress and…and…"

"A white dress?"

"Yeah, Alex. A white dress. It…It…looked more like a nightie or something, not like an ordinary dress."

Now Alex laughed out loud. "God, Stephi, seeing things and it's not even dark yet. What's it going to be like when it gets dark?"

"You think I'm drunk? I came up here to go to the bathroom. Afterwards I came out on this balcony to get a breath of fresh air. And I saw this kid, running around in Mrs. Frank's backyard." She was breathing hard and Alex knew now that she was more than a little irritated.

"O.K. Steph. We'll ask Mrs. Frank tomorrow who she is. She probably had some company and they brought a little girl along."

"Yeah. A kid we've never seen before." Stephanie turned toward the doorway to the makeshift closet. "I need another drink. I hope to God we're not out."

"Nope. Looks to me like about four or five drinks left."

Alex followed her roommate to the landing and then paused at the top of the stairs. She thought about what Stephanie said she had seen. It certainly was strange because whenever Mrs. Frank had company before she had told the girls ahead of time about it, in case they needed to move their cars. She hadn't mentioned anything about company today. A strange little girl in the backyard. Something told Alex that if this wasn't a figment of Stephanie's imagination, it belonged in the same realm with the open window and the other strange events.

Chapter Three

Mrs. Lila Frank, age seventy-six, had lived in the huge, old house on Harvard Street for over forty years. It had been in her husband Leo's family for over a century. In 1905, the Franks had bought it from a family named Diehls. Much later, Leo and his family had moved in after a grandparent had died. And since Leo Frank had been a genius at building and carpentry, the house had been kept in continual good condition. Leo had even modified the garage apartment, adding an upstairs bedroom and a kitchen and bathroom downstairs. After Leo died, Lila stayed on in the house alone.

Later, Thomas and Elizabeth Zunker, feeling the old woman needed someone to look out for her, had offered to have their daughter, Alexandra, and her college roommate, Stephanie Helsing, move into the garage apartment. Lila was delighted. Since her own two sons had grown up and left years before, here were the daughters she never had. Not a weekend went by without the three of them, provided neither girl had anything else to do, going out to eat, with Lila picking up the tab, of course.

This Easter Sunday would be a typical Sunday in that the two girls would take Mrs. Frank to St. John's Lutheran Church, almost an hour's drive across town. Afterwards, if there was a Zunker get -together, Lila and anyone else Alex or Paul would bring along would be welcome. This Easter, all would go to lunch in Kima, a small community on the Houston ship channel.

At seven o'clock Easter morning, Alex, with just a little bit of a hangover, waited somewhat impatiently for her roommate to appear. After Stephanie locked their apartment, Alex would knock on Mrs. Frank's back door. But since Stephanie had not yet put in an appearance, she reentered the apartment.

"Steph, we need to get going," she yelled up the stairs.

"Just a moment!" an impatient answer resounded from somewhere at the top. "Go ahead and get Mrs. Frank; I'll be along in a couple of minutes."

Shrugging her shoulders, Alex turned toward the door, but before she could leave, Stephanie appeared at the top of the stairs, wearing only her underwear.

"Hey, Roomy, where's the Extra Strength Tylenol?"

"It's downstairs in the kitchen. And why aren't you dressed? We have to leave in a few minutes."

"I'll be ready. I've just got to get something for this damned headache."

"Hangover, Honey."

"Okay, hangover, Dearest Mother confessor." She descended the stairs and sped past Alex toward the kitchen.

"And hurry up and put something on your bare ass, too," Alex laughed. "I'll go across and get Mrs. Frank."

Alex was still chuckling when she walked up the back steps to Mrs. Frank's door and knocked. As always the old lady appeared, dressed and ready to go.

"My, you look nice this morning, Alexandra," she said as she descended the back steps. Alex thought Mrs. Frank had the energy of someone thirty years younger than she was. "Is that a new dress?"

"Oh, no. I've had this for about a year, Mrs. Frank."

"Where's my other lovely young boarder this morning?"

"Well, Mrs. Frank, she's still getting dressed, but she had better be out here in a couple of minutes."

"My, my. Sometimes we all take a little bit longer," Mrs. Frank said, at the foot of the steps. "My Leo used to get so impatient when I was late."

Alex couldn't visualize Mrs. Frank ever being late for anything.

"When he would fuss about my not being ready, I would remind him of the times he was late. He had a habit of oversleeping." The old lady looked at Alex and winked.

A minute later, Stephanie appeared at the apartment door, adjusting her skirt and picking at her hair.

"We were just about to leave without you, Roomy," Alex said, grinning.

"Funny." Stephanie locked the apartment door and walked over to the car. "Hello, Mrs. Frank."

"Hello, Honey." The old lady suddenly looked down from left to right. "Oh, my stars. I left my umbrella in the house. Now I'm going to make us all late."

"Oh, that's all right, Mrs. Frank," Alex said. "Let me go in and get if for you."

"That's all right, Honey. It's just inside the door." She retraced her steps up the back stairs and in the back door.

"Boy, did you get dressed fast," Stephanie said to Alex's back with a smirk. "Did you remember to put your skivvies on?"

"You bet. A long time before you put yours on." Alex turned and faced her roommate. "That Tylenol's not going to do you any good. It never helps me."

"Well, I had to have something and as far as I know that's the only thing we had in the house. What I really need is hair off the dog." At that, she guffawed so loud Alex was afraid Mrs. Frank would hear it.

"Oh, God. You're still drunk."

"No, I'm not. I'm as sober as you are."

Mrs. Frank suddenly appeared at the back door, this time moving a little faster than before. "Leave it to an old woman to make everybody late," she said.

"You're just in time, Mrs. Frank. All aboard."

Just after leaving the house, Stephanie leaned forward over the center console.

"Mrs. Frank, who was that little girl in your backyard yesterday evening?" she asked.

"Little girl?" The old lady screwed up her face in puzzlement. "In my back yard?"

"Yes. Yesterday evening there was a little girl running around in your backyard. About six or seven o'clock, I'd say."

Alex was surprised her roommate had remembered anything about the little girl. She had put it down as a figment of Stephanie's juiced-up imagination.

"I don't know why any little girl would be in my backyard," Mrs. Frank said. "I had no company. I was alone all day yesterday."

"Stephi, don't you think that might be just a figment of your overactive imagination?"

"No, it wasn't, Alex." Stephanie turned abruptly toward Alex, a frown upon her face.

"You might mean the little Winslow girl, Stephanie. But I don't know why she would be in my…"

"No, Mrs. Frank. I know that girl and it wasn't her. This girl was about five or six years old and she had on a white dress."

"Stephanie, I'm afraid that's someone I don't know." Mrs. Frank wrinkled her forehead in concern.

"Stephi, I think we have a kid from somewhere down the block who just happened to have gotten in the backyard. Probably a little girl from across the alley somewhere."

Alex still wondered at her roommate's fixation on this subject.

"Oh, Lord. Folks have to watch their children like hawks nowadays." Mrs. Frank turned her head back toward the front and leaned back. "No telling what's going to happen to them. Why, in my day, we were walking all over town when we were six years old. Not anymore."

"Mama watched my every move," Alex said, keeping both hands on the wheel and her concentration on her driving.

Later, after church, everyone drove to the little community of Kima as planned, in two cars. Since they were early at eleven o'clock, they got to sit on the porch in the restaurant, a Zunker favorite. They had all placed their orders and were sipping their drinks when Stephanie once again broached the subject of the little girl.

"I just think it's weird that there was a little girl in Mrs. Frank's back yard yesterday evening and no one around knows who she could belong to," she said.

Alex sat her tea glass down and stared at her roommate who was sitting across the table from her. "Stephi, why don't you give it a rest. After all, we're not even sure you saw what you say…"

"Alex, I saw her. How many times do I have to tell you that?"

"Okay, Stephanie, a little girl in the backyard, as you say,"

Thomas Zunker said, noting the girl's impatience. "It was probably someone new to the neighborhood and the little girl was just out exploring."

"That's what I said earlier, Papa." Alex tried to smile across the table at her roommate who looked at her and frowned.

"It is absolutely amazing how many people nowadays do not watch their children," Elizabeth Zunker, who had listened carefully to every word said, now joined the conversation. "And when something happens to them, it is such a tragedy."

"That is certain," Thomas replied. "There's such a price to be paid for neglect and now it's more than ever."

Paul, who sat next to Stephanie, leaned over to her and whispered. "Never mind Sis. She's always been somewhat of a Doubting Thomas."

"Thanks, Paul. I think I'm beginning to see that." She smiled. "When we go out to eat, she's always questioning if something will make her sick or not." Now she laughed.

"Out to eat?" Thomas quickly broke into the conversation. "Lila Frank, have you been treating these two to meals out again. That becomes so expensive after awhile."

"Tom Zunker, you know better than that." The old lady turned her head in Thomas' direction. "An old woman living alone. I thank God everyday that these two lovely girls are right there near me. Why, my James and my Raymond have been grown and gone years ago. Now, I have two daughters."

At that everyone chuckled as the food was delivered.

Later that evening, Alex and Stephanie both attacked their schoolwork back at the apartment. Alex had some organic chemistry which she found easy while her roommate struggled once again with calculus. After helping Stephanie with one of her problems, Alex went up to her room to get her purse she had left on the bed. When she bent over to retrieve her handbag, she noticed that the window was open again. Staring incredulously at the curtains which had been pulled back from where she always kept them, she put her hand to her mouth with a gasp.

"Now, what is it this time?" she said, alarmed, out loud. "What the hell is going on here now?"

Then she realized that Stephanie had gone upstairs earlier

to change clothes. Had she opened the window, believing the apartment to be stuffy? Alex wouldn't put it past her since Stephanie tended to be hot even with the air conditioners on this time of the year.

Alex was still pondering this possibility when her roommate appeared in the door behind her.

"Hey, did you hear the thunder," she said. "It's going to rain again."

"Stephi, did you open this window again?" Alex turned and, facing Stephanie, moved away from the window.

"No, I haven't been in here."

"Well, it's open again." She indicated the window with a hand gesture. "Just like it was yesterday."

"Wow, that's weird, Roomy."

"Damned right it's weird. Like the little girl in white from out of nowhere. And the shower the other day. And the cats. Stephanie, all this crap has just started in the last week or so. Why now? What's going on?"

"You got me." She raised both hands in puzzlement. "We explained the little girl at lunch. Kinda. And as for the window, this is an old house. Old houses have weird things going on in them all the time."

"Stephi, this is not the house. This is the apartment."

"Yeah, but wasn't it built about the same time? Your room was not the part Leo Frank added."

"I don't know, Stephanie. A window suddenly starts opening for no reason at all. A window that was hard as hell to open last fall."

"Maybe the place is haunted." Stephanie giggled.

Alex froze. A sudden wave of breath-taking horror swept over her. Memories flooded her mind, all horrifying, some painful. She had never told her roommate about the paranormal events in her past because she felt certain she would not be believed. Until this moment, the events had seemed like they had occurred a hundred years ago.

"This house is not haunted," she replied, regaining her composure. "You know better than that. There's a logical explanation for all this crap. There are laws of physics, you know."

"Excuse me from that, Roomy Dearest, but I don't get physics until next semester."

"You had it in high school, stupid."

Stephanie was taken aback by Alex's abruptness and wondered what was going on.

"Maybe if we nailed the window shut, it couldn't open by itself," she said in a meek tone.

"I'm sorry, Stephi. This business is wearing me out. And we have finals coming up in a few weeks."

"How well I know," Stephanie replied.

Alex turned and shut the window. Before pulling the curtains back in their proper place, she made sure the latch at the top of the window pane was fully in place. "I've got a feeling that this latch hasn't been secure at all," she said. "And that might enable the window, for some weird reason, to come open by itself."

Later, the two girls joined Mrs. Frank in her kitchen for home-made peach cobbler. The old lady loved to cook and made meals for her two boarders often. And desserts were her specialty. "Luby's cafeteria couldn't even begin to top this," she would say with a wink.

While she helped Mrs. Frank put things away for the night, Alex mentioned the odd circumstances of the window, but the old lady replied that old houses always had such things like this going on.

"Something to do with shrinking boards," she said, closing the cabinet where the dessert bowls were kept.

"Mrs. Frank, that window couldn't be opened at all last fall," Alex replied. "In fact, we thought it had been nailed or cemented in place."

"Well, like I said, Honey, odd things like that happen in old houses, even old apartments behind them. I have several doors that won't close. And one that won't stay closed for anything. It is always ajar. Yet, not too long ago, it was always closed. And it stayed closed."

Alex wanted to tell her about the shower as well as about the strange behavior of the cats but decided there would be a logical explanation for those as well.

Back in the apartment Alex and Stephanie prepared for the

next day. Alex was delighted to find the window shut and the curtains in place as she had left them. Sabrina was even in her usual place on Alex's bed. *Great,* she thought. *Nothing odd to disturb tonight.*

She descended the stairs to watch the news with Stephanie before going to bed. On the sofa, Stephanie had Henrietta, stroking her fur.

"You know, this thing keeps waking me up in the middle of the night," she said.

Alex turned to her roommate in interest. "She never did that before."

"I know. I don't know what's wrong with her." Stephanie put the large cat down and she walked slowly into the kitchen to eat. "There's something upsetting them. I'm sure of it."

"Well, Sabrina's asleep on my bed for now." Alex thought about what her roommate had said about Henrietta and tried to remember if Sabrina had done anything odd in the past few days. There was nothing.

"What do you suppose it could be?" Alex asked. Then she remembered the past. "You'll remember the other night they disappeared and we found them in the bathtub together."

"I remember." Stephanie settled back in her chair and focused her eyes on the TV. "I have no idea what it is," she said in an offhand manner. "Sometimes the weather affects them. At other times, it's a person they don't like. I don't see either one of those here now, though."

"It's probably the shitty weather," Alex replied. "No sooner do you think the rain's gone for a while then it comes back again."

"You're probably right." Stephanie tossed her left leg over the arm of the large easy chair and concentrated on the TV.

Although there had been thunder earlier, there had been no rain, but now an announcement at the beginning of the newscast told of a thunderstorm that had moved into the area and, before the newscast had ended, had moved over the apartment. With the lights flickering on and off and the rain hammering against the roof, the storm lasted a little less than an hour. The girls, terrified, thought about joining Mrs. Frank in her large house but balked at the prospect of getting drenched running to her back door. Instead, they sat in their easy chairs until the storm abated about a quarter to midnight. Then, they checked outside to see about any damage and to see if Mrs. Frank was still up.

"I'm glad that damned thing ended before we went to bed," Stephanie remarked while ascending the stairs behind her roommate. "I can't sleep while that crap is going on."

"I can't with the thunder and lightning," Alex said over her shoulder. "But the rain puts me to sleep every time."

After darkening the downstairs and locking all doors, each girl retired to her bedroom to get ready for the night.

"Too bad we didn't have any of that wine left," Stephanie called from her room. "It would have gone great with that storm."

"It wouldn't have gone great after it, though," Alex answered. "What with acid indigestion and having to get up and pee during the night."

"Details, details." Stephanie laughed out loud. "I've got this monster on the bed here. Do you have yours?"

Alex glanced at her bed to see the large, orange tabby curled up at her pillow. "Yeah. Sabrina's here. God knows where they were during the storm."

"Probably in the bathtub again."

"Well, they seem pretty settled now." Her pajamas now on, Alex reached over and stroked the cat which closed its eyes in contentment. "I think Sabrina's ready for the night."

"Good," Stephanie answered, now from the bathroom. "If Henry wakes me up again, I'm going to throw her out and close the door."

"Oh, wonderful. Then she'll come in here." Alex laughed as she visited the bathroom after her roommate. Then both girls settled in bed for the night.

It was now after twelve and Alex went to sleep immediately. But then, she began to dream.

She stood in a road facing a beach at, from what she could tell, just before dawn. She could barely make out a wall with a ruined top at her left and a large, weedy field to her right. The weeds, she noticed, were pressed down as if a giant hand had crushed them.

Walking very slowly, her eyes fixed on the beach and the

incoming surf in the distance, she made her way toward the end of the road. In the sand where the road ended was a telephone pole bent at a sharp angle almost to the ground, its wires cut short and spread all around it.

The surf rolling lazily in was a sight that should have filled Alex with joy and anticipation but now it froze her in terror. She didn't know what was out there and she didn't know what lay beyond the road.

She reached the sand and walked to the side of the downed telephone pole. Where beach sand had always been so soft she sank in it, this sand was hard and wet. She looked down the beach toward the first vestiges of sunlight. All she could see immediately was sand and what was left of a long pier off in the distance.

The sun rose slowly behind a bank of clouds on the horizon. In the growing light she could see an object down the beach, still in shadows. The beach was deserted and there was no sound, only the surf breaking on the shore.

Where are the sea birds? she thought. *And why is everything so wet?* Again she focused her attention on the object down the beach. It seemed to move.

She turned and walked toward it. The closer to it she got, the more she could tell that it wasn't an object at all, but a small cluster of figures squatting in the sand. As she got closer, she could make out four or five children, seemingly playing on the beach.

How odd, she thought. *Why would kids be out here this time of day?*

She yelled out but could not hear her voice. She walked even closer but the little figures in the group were oblivious to her. They were seemingly digging a large hole in the beach.

"What are these little twerps up to so early in the morning?" she asked herself.

Just before she walked up on the group, she noticed that each child was wearing a white garment that was soaking wet, so wet that it clung to their skin. Also, their hair seemed to be wet and full of sand.

Finally, she reached the group and craned her neck to see over the squatting figure just in front of her. She could see easily down into the hole they were digging and at the bottom, about a foot from the surface, was a corpse, still half buried with mouth and eyes wide open.

Alex screamed as loud as she could but now, seemingly, the little group had heard her. They rose to their feet and turned toward her.

She gagged in utter horror. There before her were what was left of five children, their bodies battered and torn, their mouths open and pouring water. Some had glazed over eyes but a few eyes were missing. All were hideously animated as they began to walk toward her.

“Oh, Jesus! God! Help me!” Alex thrust both hands out in front of her and turned to run. The effort in the dream woke her.

My…My God, she thought as she lay in the quiet darkness. A tear rolled down her cheek. Sabrina, startled awake by her mistress’ animation, curled up again at the foot of the bed.

Alex sat up and looked around the room. Nothing moved. She could see just a hint of light from the outside but most of the room was in inky blackness. Clasping her hands to her chest and breathing heavily, she thought about turning on her light but she still didn’t move.

Finally, she moved quickly above the covers and reached her cat which she could just make out in the dimness. Grasping the animal, she clutched it to her. It whined momentarily at being disturbed.

She still breathed heavily and felt fear in the dark. Trembling, she held the cat tightly to her breast. There was no sound from anywhere in the house, or even from outside. She wanted to wake Stephanie and tell her about the hideous dream but remembered how much difficulty her roommate had in getting back to sleep.

After ten minutes, she released the cat and rolled on her side to see the clock. A quarter to four.

“Shit,” she whispered. She wanted it to be five or five-thirty so she could get up but now she had over an hour to lie in bed and think about the dream.

Then she remembered the dream she had a little over a week before. It had been a nightmare, too. Like this one, it had been disturbing; in fact, it had deposited her on her bedroom floor. She had experienced bad dreams all her life but they were relatively rare. Except for one time in her life. A time when she was much younger and more vulnerable. It had been a time of utter horror which she had put out of her mind as a psychological necessity. She had reached the utter brink of madness as a young girl in several encounters with the paranormal which had left her in a Memphis hospital with a serious bullet wound. Now, she found herself comparing the present to then and found frequent nightmares in both places.

But she knew the gist of the dreams back then. They had fit in with what she had been experiencing while awake. What about now?

Just a coincidence? she thought.

She looked for Sabrina but the cat wasn't there; probably gone to the kitchen for food or prowling downstairs.

Suddenly, she thought of the window and, trembling again, moved the curtains to the side.

"Thank God," she whispered when she found the troublesome window firmly in its place. "There's no way I could take that."

The dreams, the window, the cats, the shower, what else? she thought. All of these things were mere nuisances. But did they add up? Her intuition told her they did, but where were they going? She shuddered as she leaned back, pulled the cover up over her, rolled over and tried to go back to sleep.

Chapter Four

Despite everything, Alex returned to sleep to be awakened by her alarm at six o'clock. She had experienced no dreaming after dozing off and even had trouble getting up with her alarm. After she rolled over, it was Stephanie's prodding her instead of the usual vice versa.

Alex didn't tell her roommate about this latest dream because she convinced herself the nightmares were only a fluke brought on by some physiological or psychological reason. What else could they possibly be?

Nothing out of the ordinary occurred that week as the girls attended class and prepared for their final exams. Alex was in a good mood when Friday came and she had no classes to attend.

She rose early, though, in order to see that her roommate was up in time to get to calculus. *Fridays are hell for her,* she thought to herself and laughed while frying eggs downstairs. When she opened the refrigerator to get sausage, she found she had none. The only solution for this predicament was to borrow some from Mrs. Frank.

Covering the eggs to keep them fairly warm and free of feline incursions, she started for the front door. Noise from above told her Stephanie was already getting dressed without her usual foot-dragging.

"Glory hallelujah, she's going to be early," she muttered as she exited the apartment, the key to Mrs. Frank's back door in her hand. The old lady had left the day before to visit relatives out of town and she never minded the girls coming into her house to borrow anything they needed as long as they told her what they took.

At daybreak Alex let herself into Mrs. Frank's back door. She flipped a light switch and started for the kitchen but stopped when she glimpsed two silhouettes in the office off the parlor.

One she recognized was a lamp; the other was bigger, taller. The light was poor in the parlor and the office was in total darkness except for light from a window against which these two figures appeared.

The unfamiliar figure took the vague form of a human. Alex thought she had encountered the old lady who had apparently not left after all. It wouldn't be unusual for Mrs. Frank to change her mind at the last minute.

"Mrs. Frank," she said, walking slowly toward the office door.

A faint gleam emanated from the head of the tall figure. Alex stopped abruptly.

She stood for a full two minutes and studied the large silhouette. Then she started forward again, but stopped, startled by a commotion behind her.

Stephanie had come in the back door, a large black and white cat under her right arm.

"What the hell? You scared the crap out of me." Alex put both hands on her hips and bent forward.

"Ah, so we're up to something, huh." Stephanie grinned. "I got up before you did because my loving bedmate bit me."

"I heard you thumping around up there before I left. I came over here to borrow some sausage." Alex pointed at the cat. "Where did you find her?"

"Under Mrs. Frank's back steps." Stephanie looked down at the cat and stroked its back. "And it's not a she; it's a he."

"You don't mean…"

"Yep. This is what's commonly called a tomcat."

"You mean to tell me he's what's been going on with our cats all along?"

"I'm sure of it."

"But…But how can that be? Our cats are fixed. They don't even have any front claws so they can't go out."

"Yes, but they still know when there's a male around."

"Well, I guess that settles that, doesn't it." Alex walked over and stroked the fur of the large tom. "He sure seems friendly enough."

"He's just a great big purring ball of fur."

"Wonderful. A third cat." Alex laughed.

"Not this baby. All kinds of crap will happen with him in the house."

"Then what are you going to do with him?"

"Feed him and put him back under the steps in the hope that maybe Tom will keep Jerry away."

"At least now we'll know what's going on with our cats."

"Yes."

Alex turned back toward the office, but the large silhouette was gone. "Stephi, I thought I saw someone in that office over there."

"I don't know who it could be." Stephanie, now scratching the back of the cat's neck, walked up next to Alex. "It couldn't have been Mrs. Frank. Oh, she didn't leave yesterday after all. She left early this morning. I heard her just after Henry did a number on my big toe."

"But I saw someone in there." Alex walked to the office door and switched on the light. "A figure was silhouetted against the window over there." She pointed at an area above the desk across the room.

"You saw a lamp in the window, Roomy Dear." Stephanie, who had moved up to the desk, reached out and tweaked the lampshade.

"I'm positive someone was there." Again Alex pointed, this time at the area beside the desk. "Standing right there."

"It's awfully early in the morning," Stephanie replied in a sing-songy voice. "Are we still dreaming perhaps?"

"Maybe so." Alex looked once more around the room. Nothing was disturbed. In fact, everything had a thin coat of dust that said this room had not been cleaned for quite some time. "Let's go see if we can find Thomas some food. There are fried eggs getting cold in the kitchen." Alex turned back toward the door. "I better get that sausage. We could use some jam, too. We're about out."

The girls found what they needed in Mrs. Frank's refrigerator and returned to their apartment. Stephanie got ready for class while Alex finished cooking breakfast.

After her roommate left, Alex sat at the breakfast table sipping a second cup of coffee. She couldn't get the strange experience of that morning out of her mind. Although

Stephanie's discovery of the tomcat should be a relief by way of an explanation, she thought more about the odd silhouette in Mrs. Frank's house. She was positive it had been there. But upon investigation, nothing had been disturbed. Everything was intact, even the dust and dirt.

She wanted to talk to someone about it but didn't know whom. Stephanie was gone to class and wouldn't return until after lunch. Her brother was in school. He had a little more than a month of high school left before graduation so he would be in class all day. Her parents? She didn't want to worry them.

She decided to put the episode out of her mind and work on a chemistry project due the following week but it never entirely left her consciousness. *What is it that keeps bothering me,* she thought. *I thought I saw something that obviously wasn't there.* She put down her pencil and shoved her papers aside.

"I'm going to look again," she said to herself. "I'm going to make sure there was nothing there. Far too much strange crap has been going on around here to let this one incident go without further investigation."

She retrieved Mrs. Frank's key from the kitchen and made her way to the back door of the old house. Mrs. Frank wouldn't return until the early evening so she should be alone. After unlocking the back door, she went straight to the office where she thought she had seen the figure.

A musty smell filled her nostrils while she looked carefully around the desk for any sign of a disturbance. The only thing she could find was vague footprints made by Stephanie and her that morning. And nothing was disturbed anywhere around the desk. She ran a finger through the thin covering of dust and left a distinct mark across the top of the desk. Then, she dragged a toe through the dust where the figure supposedly had stood and left much the same mark. No one but she and her roommate had been there. That much was obvious.

She turned toward the door and listened for any sound she could hear in the old house. All was silent. Since she was alone, she got the idea to have a look around.

She had never been upstairs and the parts of the downstairs she was familiar with were only the back parlor, the office, the kitchen, the large living room and the entrance hall. When she and Stephanie had eaten at home with Mrs. Frank, they had always eaten in the kitchen, so, although she had been in the dining room, she was unfamiliar with it. Also, the old lady kept a good many rooms closed off for the purpose of climate control.

She made her way down the hall toward the front of the house and discovered a large storage closet under the stairs. Then, she wandered through the living room and dining room and peeped into a closed room that Mrs. Frank had earlier referred to as a music room.

Nothing seemed amiss in these parts of the house but here everything was clean. Mrs. Frank had a cleaning lady, Martha, who came every Tuesday and stayed all day. But why hadn't she cleaned in the office?

At the base of the main staircase, Alex gazed upwards with curiosity. The old lady still slept upstairs. Alex had always found it fascinating that Mrs. Frank at seventy-six still drove her car and climbed stairs. But she still spent most of her time in the downstairs portion of her house and joked about eventually installing some kind of lift on her staircase.

Alex made her way up the stairs and into a hallway that led through the house from front to back. Across the front of the second floor was a large bedroom with accompanying bathroom that was obviously where Mrs. Frank slept. Its size indicated a master bedroom.

No wonder we never see any lights on, she thought. *She's at the other end of the house from us.*

The other bedrooms were all closed off but a second large bathroom toward the back of the second floor was open. Alex peeped into each bedroom and then went into the back bathroom. It seemed this bathroom still retained its old fashioned features.

It had a claw-foot bathtub with accompanying shower, an old time sink that was much water stained and a wicker laundry hamper darkened from age. Even the commode was stained and old. Also, the window above the tub had been closed for years because it seemed sealed shut.

"It's obvious no one comes in here," Alex said to herself. "How quaint. I've always wondered what an old fashioned bathroom looked like."

At the end of the hall were the back stairs that led from the first floor to the attic. Looking up the last flight to the attic, Alex wondered if she should go up there.

It's probably all closed off, she thought. *And that door up there is probably locked.*

However, curiosity got the better of her and she made her way up the stairs to the door which was not only unlocked but ajar. Very slowly, she pushed the door open to a gentle cloud of dust that wafted out and made her cough.

"This door was open but it's obvious no one has been up here for quite some time," she muttered.

The attic had a short hall which fed into a cross hall at its end. Standing in the door to the stairs, Alex noticed that the doors she could see were all open and, unlike the rooms on lower floors, everything seemed lit by sunlight.

She headed for the room at the end of the hall, thinking it might be the biggest. When she reached the end of the hall, she looked to her right to see that the door to the bigger room was closed. To her left was another door to the same room which was also closed.

Puzzled as to why these doors were closed where the others were open, she chose the door to her right. She tried the knob and it opened, almost on its own accord. This room was also lit by sunlight, a flood of which struck her as the door opened wider.

She started to enter but stopped immediately, seized by an overpowering sense of dread. Something was in the room; something that was powerful, totally menacing and hateful to the point that it froze her in the doorway. She wanted to turn and run but instead stepped softly backwards through the doorway. The icy feeling of coldness and malice enveloped her from head to toe so that she wanted to cry out.

Her instinct was to get out of there but she was at a loss as to how to do it. She knew she couldn't run because the presence in the room would surely come after her.

Carefully, trembling, she tiptoed backwards into the main hall and then turned toward the back staircase, all the time watching the end of the hall. Her heart felt like it would burst.

Tears filled her eyes when she finally got to the door of the landing. Then she turned and hurried down the back stairs all the way to the first floor, all the time looking back expecting something to be behind her. At the ground floor she made her way through the back parlor and out the back door. Only when she was out on the driveway did she turn back to the old house.

Nothing was there. Nothing made noise; all was silent. All Alex could hear was her heavy breathing. It seemed that even the cicadas that usually filled the trees with a raucous noise this time of day were silent.

She scanned the back of the house all the way to the roof where she could see a single window jutting out from the roof slant, dark and foreboding. Expecting to see something appear in that window, she watched it closely. Nothing appeared.

For a full five minutes she stood and studied the old house. Then she thought about what had happened in the attic and the terror returned, churning her stomach to the point that she felt like throwing up. She pressed both hands against her mid-section and sobbed, trying to put the attic out of her mind. She had not been so frightened in years.

After entering her apartment she locked the door behind her and sat down in an easy chair where she could see the door. There she realized she had the same problem she had earlier. She needed to talk to someone but there was no one around and no one to call. In the middle of the day she was alone and she didn't want to be.

She looked at her watch; it was almost noon. Stephanie would be home by one o'clock if she didn't stop to pick up something for lunch. Feeling a bit better in that she wouldn't be alone for long, she sat back in the chair to wait.

God, what a morning, she thought. *What the hell is wrong with me? I didn't see anything in that attic. What was in that room?* The thought of that room brought the horror back again. *I shouldn't even have been snooping around in Mrs. Frank's house.*

She closed her eyes momentarily but something told her not to sleep while she was alone in the apartment. When Stephanie returned, she would tell her what happened and get her opinion about the morning's events. "I hope to God she believes what I tell her," she said to herself. "Oh, Jesus. What if she wants to go snooping up there?"

A few minutes later, Alex was making a glass of iced tea when she heard a car on the driveway.

"What's she doing home so early?" she asked out loud. Again she looked at her watch. "It's just twelve fifteen." Entering the living room from the kitchen, she met her roommate coming in the door.

"I was going to stop and get us something for lunch," she said. "But I am so damned pissed I could chew nails."

"What…What's up, Stephi?" Alex was amazed at the emotion in her roommate's face, an unusual manifestation.

"Killebrew. Killebrew's what's up! That bastard assigned us a paper due the day of the final. Six to eight thousand words, documentation, with a full works-cited page.

Caught aback by her roommate's outburst, Alex was at a loss for something to say.

"As if we had nothing to do but work on his goddamned course," Stephanie continued. She threw her books on the couch and plopped down in a nearby chair.

"I would say, Stephi, that a trip to the library is in your near future." Alex tried to smile but couldn't. She couldn't believe she had been one-upped by her roommate's temper.

"He cut his damned lecture short today and passed out topics and assignment sheets. I got *Lyndon Johnson and the Escalation of the Vietnam War.* Where the hell am I supposed to find that? Other people got topics like the media and the times and the cold war. Then we were told the paper would count heavily on the final exam. Where the hell was that in his syllabus?" Stephanie made an angry flipping gesture with her hand and settled back in her chair. "Six to eight thousand words, goddamn it! And here I am with a bunch of calculus shit I don't understand."

"I can help you with that, Stephi."

Stephanie turned toward Alex. "But you have a chemistry project due Tuesday. And all that English to read."

"I finished that the other night." Alex put her hands on her knees and regarded her roommate across the room. Obviously, now was not the time to tell her about her morning. She wondered when her roommate would calm down.

Stephanie suddenly sprang to her feet and headed for the kitchen. “I’m going to have to get up early tomorrow morning and head for the library to start getting that shit together. He isn’t going to let us use any on-line sources.”

Still edgy, Alex wanted to talk to her roommate about her morning, but didn’t see any way now with this outburst. She would have to wait until later but she didn’t know if she could.

“Too bad you don’t have some of that wine we drank the other day,” Alex said. She settled back in the chair and watched the door to the kitchen.

“No shit!” Stephanie reentered the room, a glass of iced tea in her hand.

“You have your ID. Why don’t we go to the store and get some. At the same time we can get something for lunch.”

“God, Roomy, you’re a genius! I’m living with a genius!” Stephanie took a big swig from her glass and settled back against the door frame. “After I get some lunch in me, I’ll be set for a glass of wine or two before Mrs. Frank gets home. Oh, that reminds me. Howie’s going to make a beer run for us on Monday. From the looks of things, we’ll need it.”

“Stephi, all this hooch. We’re going to drown along with our sorrows.”

“Roomy, finals are coming up. I’m pissed off. I have all kinds of crap to do. With that in mind, I don’t mind going to bed drunk a night or two next week. At least I’ll be calmed down.”

Alex laughed. “Drink up and let’s go. La Fiesta is the place to go. They didn’t even ask you for your ID that last time you were there.”

“Right. And be sure to lose yourself while I’m checking out.”

On the way to the grocery store, Alex couldn’t wait until her roommate had a drink or two in her so she brought the subject up. Seemingly, Stephanie had calmed down quite a bit already.

“Stephi, this morning I took a little tour of Mrs. Frank’s house,” she said while they sat at a traffic light.

“You went through Mrs. Frank’s house?” Stephanie answered, an incredulous look on her face. “I love Mrs. Frank dearly, but her old house gives me the creeps."

"Yes, I did." Alex turned in the passenger seat, facing her roommate as she drove. "I thought I saw something in there this morning before you left. After you left I got to thinking about it. I went back over and went all through the house. I found something in there, Stephanie; something evil, something malign, something hateful that would have harmed me if I hadn't gotten out of there."

"Alex, what are you talking about?"

"In the attic, there is a presence. A force that I believe is capable of doing great harm to anyone who disturbs it. I felt it almost envelop me. I'm sure if I hadn't gotten out of there it would have been on me."

"Roomy, when I said the place was haunted the other day, I was only joking. You remember we were…"

"We were in the apartment, Stephi. This morning I was in the house. The attic."

Stephanie turned to her roommate. "That's weird, Alex. I've never heard Mrs. Frank mention anything like that. Don't you think she would have mentioned it if…"

"She never goes up there, Stephanie. That was obvious. There was dust everywhere. But you know, every door in that attic was open except two. Isn't that odd? From what I could see, there are three rooms at least, the biggest in the front. That was the room with closed doors; when I opened one of them, I was overcome."

"Well what…what do you think it was?"

"I don't know. I just don't know."

"What's really strange, Alex, is that Mrs. Frank has never said anything about the attic. After all, she's lived in that house for God knows how long by herself and a long time before that with her husband."

"I think what's there hasn't been there very long, Stephanie. You know Leo Frank used the attic. Then after he died, Mrs. Frank just closed everything up and left it."

"I believe what you say, Alex, because I've never known you to make things up. But God, this is the strangest thing I've ever heard."

Alex thought about what she could tell her roommate about

her experiences years before. Something told her she would eventually have to tell her what had happened when she was fourteen.

"I know for a fact Mrs. Frank doesn't know what's up there." Alex turned again to her roommate. "Whatever it is, it doesn't seem to be bothering her. And she sure isn't going up there to bother it."

Stephanie seemingly had more to say but they had reached their destination. Nothing was said as the two entered the store and went their separate ways. Alex picked out some microwave meals while Stephanie chose a large bottle of St. Genevieve. When they checked out, Stephanie, her fake out-of-state ID close at hand, would pay for everything while Alex waited for her outside.

Walking to the car, Stephanie brought the subject up again. "You know Mrs. Frank is going to want to eat out tonight. Are you going to tell her what happened to you in her attic today?"

"No. I'm not even going to mention it. Why should I? Like I said, this thing doesn't seem to be bothering her. Besides, what's she going to think about my snooping around?"

"Well, you might have disturbed it or something. What if it comes downstairs?"

"I don't think it will, Stephi. I don't know what the hell it's up to or why it's even there, but I don't think it's going to harm Mrs. Frank."

Stephanie had no answer to that and decided to continue her litany of complaints about school. When they arrived home, Alex fixed the microwave lunches while her roommate got things together to complete the homework she had.

"I don't know what that damned thing was you saw in the attic," Stephanie said while looking over her history assignment again. "But it doesn't hold a candle compared with my man Killebrew and his impromptu bullshit."

"Well, you're just going to have to live with him and his assignment for the next week."

"Yeah, starting tomorrow. What a way to poop off a Saturday."

After Alex finished preparing the meals, they ate in silence. In the back of her mind, Alex still thought about her morning's experience. It seemed the terror was there to stay and it was still very real. And most terrifying of all was that she didn't know what she could do about it. It had caught her completely off guard.

They finished their meals and Alex started upstairs to lie down, but she was stopped by her roommate, newly poured wine glass in hand.

"You're not starting on that, are you?" Alex said, leaning over the banister. "You're going to be potted when Mrs. Frank gets home. She's going to know you've been drinking."

"Alex, I want to see it." Stephanie's wide eyes and smile told Alex something was up.

"What?'

"The attic. I want to go up in the attic."

"No, Stephanie." Alex was emphatic.

"Why not? You went up there. I want to go up there, too."

"Stephanie, there's something up there that's very dangerous. I don't want to go back up there." Alex began breathing heavily again. The last thing she wanted was to go back to Mrs. Frank's attic. She knew if she went again she might not return.

"What could that be, Alex? After all, you didn't see anything."

"Damn it, Roomy. Something up there scared the shit out of me. I'm not going back up there and neither are you."

Stephanie turned away and Alex knew she was going to pout. What else could she do. Alex knew something was waiting up there. Waiting for someone like Stephanie, who didn't really believe anything was there.

She thought about hiding Mrs. Frank's house key but felt that would be petty because she knew Stephanie was not the type who would venture up there alone. But she felt sorry for her roommate who obviously felt a trip to the attic would be only an adventure.

Later, lying on her bed, Alex thought about calling her brother. It would be an hour and a half before he would be home, but more and more, she needed to talk to him. He had handled the problem years ago after she had nearly been killed. And now, more than ever, she needed his advice.

Without much effort, Alex fell asleep and slept peacefully, but at half past four, Stephanie shook her awake.

"Roomy, how about a glass of hooch?"

"Yeah. Is Mrs. Frank home?"

"No, I haven't heard her." Stephanie straightened up and Alex was glad to see she was cold sober. "I got busy downstairs. Would you believe I got started on that paper. You had a book on the Vietnam War and that's going to be my first source."

"That's great, Steph." Alex looked at her watch. "I'm going to try to call Pauli. I'll be down in a few minutes."

"Okay. I'll wait until you get down to pour another one." She turned and left while Alex dialed her home phone number.

She was surprised when her brother picked up the phone right away.

"Hi, Sis. The new caller ID kicked in again."

"Pauli, you got a minute or two?"

"Yeah. Hey, I'm glad you called. I was going to call you. I wanted to ask you if the Galveston trip is still on."

Alex was taken aback by her brother's starting the conversation. "Yeah…Yes. Josh says he can go with us so everything's on go." Alex thought a minute. "But aren't you going to Port Aransas with your buddies right after graduation?"

"Yes, but the Galveston trip is the next week, isn't it?"

"Yeah, Pauli. Sure. I'm looking forward to it."

"Me, too. I can't wait to see your Roomy Dearest in a bikini."

"Oh, brother." Alex sighed.

"Sis, you know what is so wonderful about your roommate besides her beautiful body and her delightful demeanor?"

"I give up, Pauli. What?"

"She has no boyfriend. Isn't that great? I think that's best of all."

"Great, huh. What if I told you she was engaged to be married."

"I'd say bullshit. If she was engaged, she would have told us a long time ago."

"You're right. She's all by her lonesome. But that's not what I wanted to talk to you about."

"Oh, yeah?"

"Pauli, some things around here have come up and have been downright frightening. Things have happened that remind me of what happened to us years ago."

"Oh?"

"Yes. For instance, I don't know if they have a bearing on anything or not, but I've even had a couple of nightmares. One of them put me out of bed."

"Oh God, Sis."

"Pauli, think back to what happened years ago. What happened first?"

"Well, hell, Sis. I bought those letters and the shit hit the fan."

"Think, Pauli. What happened first?"

"It started that day on the way home from the flea market. We encountered that horse, remember?"

"Yeah, the horse. Then everything got worse after that."

"Yeah, that's right."

"Now, things have started again, it seems." In as much detail as she could, Alex related the events of the last few weeks, beginning with the behavior of the cats, which supposedly had been resolved. Paul was silent and Alex could tell he was thinking. And remembering. When she was finished, she asked him what he thought."

"I don't know, Sis," he answered. "It seems like an awful lot of things that could be only circumstance. But don't you remember? A trigger brought on all that stuff years ago."

"Yes, I do, Pauli. And there doesn't seem to be anything like that now."

"Still there seems to be a lot of stuff going on. And that bit about the attic is downright frightening."

"I know. I told Stephanie about that earlier. And she knows what's been going on around here. She doesn't know anything about what happened years ago, though."

"Yeah. And I remember that bit about the little girl from nowhere."

The little girl. Alex hadn't mentioned that because she had forgotten about it. But now it jostled a memory in her that she couldn't quite pinpoint.

"I…I think we resolved that one, Pauli. That and the one

about the cats."

"I hope so, Sis." Paul chuckled softly on the other end. "And stay out of Mrs. Frank's creepy old house."

"Really." She heard her brother sigh into the phone. She wanted to ask him again about the possibility of a trigger but she knew the answer would be the same. There was none. There was nothing to physically bring any of the new stuff around.

After a few minutes, Paul spoke again. "Sis, I got to go. I promised Papa I'd get the back lawn mowed since he doesn't get off until late. And you know the rain around here. If I don't get to it, it'll pour down."

"Okay, Pauli. I feel a lot better now that I've talked to you."

"I'm glad, Sis. But I'm still a big shaky about what you told me. Let me know if anything else happens."

"Will do. See you later."

Downstairs, Alex and Stephanie sat quietly and drank their wine. Alex told her roommate about her conversation with her brother, but she wanted to get her mind off Mrs. Frank's house.

"Stephi, Pauli says he can't wait to see you in a bikini." Alex laughed and took another sip.

"Wonderful. That's the signal to wear a one-piece."

"He'll be crushed."

"Did you tell him about today?"

"Yes. He reacted about the same way you did. He even wanted to see for himself also but there's no way he's going up there either."

A car door slam outside told the girls Mrs. Frank was home. Since she didn't like to drive at night, the old lady tried to return from her visits to Conroe well before twilight, usually around five o'clock or shortly thereafter. She didn't like to drive in traffic either, so the earlier she came home, the better.

"Right on time, Steph," Alex said, peering out a front window. She turned and grinned. "And well before we had a chance to get snockered."

"Good old Mrs. Frank to the rescue." Stephanie got to her feet and set her empty glass on the table. "Are you going to tell the old gal about your excursion to her house?"

"Hell, no. You asked me that earlier. What she doesn't

know won't hurt her."

"Are you sure?"

"If she has anything to say about her house, I'm sure she'll tell us."

The two girls showered, changed their clothes and then met Mrs. Frank for supper at seven o'clock. The decision was made to go to Ferrugio's for Italian food but when they got there they found they had a thirty-minute wait. Therefore, it was almost eight thirty when they were finally served.

Arriving home well after nine o'clock in the dark, Mrs. Frank offered the girls some banana pudding for dessert. "Something tasty before bed," she said.

Since Stephanie drove, Alex helped the old lady out of the car. As she took Mrs. Frank's arm, she happened to look up at the attic window in the back of the house and there was, as she somehow knew there would be, a light on in that window.

"Mrs. Frank, look. There's a light on up there."

The old lady looked up immediately. "A light on? Where?"

"In the attic." When Alex looked up again, the light was gone. In fact, she couldn't even see the window in the dark.

"Oh, Honey, there's nothing up there." Mrs. Frank made a vague pointing gesture upward. "It's all closed up. I haven't been up there since my Leo died."

"I could have sworn there was a light on up there." Alex looked over at Stephanie, who stood, wide-eyed, on the other side of the car.

Although she was annoyed, Alex knew that no one beside her would see the attic light.

She knew now that whatever was up there was meant only for her. Whatever was there certainly knew her now. Now, she wished she had never seen Mrs. Frank's old house.

Chapter Five

That night Alex slept uneasily. Three times she awoke and walked to her bedroom window to check for a light in Mrs. Frank's attic. Also, the older matter of her own window was a concern so she made sure it was tightly closed. Nothing, of course, happened. No lights. No open windows.

The next morning Alex awakened Stephanie so she could get to the library on Rice campus. While her roommate was away, Alex would stay at home and finish her chemistry project. After preparing a light breakfast and feeding the cats, Alex shuffled into the living room and settled down to her work.

Even though she was alone, she found that if she kept busy she couldn't think about what might be going on around her. However, she finished her project early and went fast to sleep.

In a dream she wandered in a high wind in a city she did not recognize. In fact, it seemed strangely deserted as if she were the only one not sheltering from the wind. Directly in front of her rose a tall edifice that seemed strange and out of place at first. It was not a building at all but a monument, complete with statuary, about three stories high. She wanted to approach it but she couldn't. Some unseen force held her back.

She turned away from the monument to see houses along the street begin to fly apart. Then, the rain began, a deluge that quickly filled the gutters and street in which Alex stood. Panicking, she started to seek shelter on a nearby porch but again something held her back. The noise of the rain was deafening and the immensity of it should have saturated her, but she wasn't even wet.

She turned to run down the street but a wall of water forced her to seek a higher elevation. However, now she found she couldn't even move. Horror and panic growing rapidly within her, she made an effort to move her body forward and in the process awoke. Outside, there was the sound of driving rain.

Holy shit, what's going on, she thought, breathing heavily and lying still to get her bearings. She rose and walked to the window. Now she was afraid. Another nightmare and a hard rain that seemed to have followed her out of it were two things that could easily unnerve her.

The clock on the wall read twelve-thirty so she had slept longer than she had thought. Stephanie was due back around noon but was probably held up by the rain. In the meantime, Alex would call and check on Mrs. Frank, but before she could reach the phone, it rang. Quickly, she snapped up the receiver.

"Hi, Roomy," a voice on the other end chirped. "I'm held up here by this crap outside."

"Hello, Steph. You kind of caught me off guard. I just woke up."

"God, did you go back to bed?"

"No. I finished up the chemistry project and took a nap. Now I'm sorry I did."

"Not another nightmare."

"Yep. Another one."

"Oh Jesus, Alex. This is getting serious."

"I'm going to put this one aside, too, Steph. After all, nightmares won't hurt you."

"But in the middle of the day?"

"They can come anytime."

"Well, as I was saying, I'm going to finish what I've got here and get something to eat. Then, I'll come on home. Did you check on Mrs. Frank?"

"No. I was going to do that when you called. But I will."

"Okay. I'll see you pretty quick."

After hanging up, Alex found Sabrina and took her up to her bedroom to lie down. In the pouring rain, the large orange cat would be a great comfort and companion. She would not sleep. She could also call Mrs. Frank from upstairs and check on her.

But the rain reminded her of her dream. She hoped there wasn't any wind with it. Putting the cat down beside her, she dialed Mrs. Frank's number. The thought occurred to her that the old lady might not be home but she answered on the second ring.

"My goodness, Honey. Stephanie is out in this?"

"She just called, Mrs. Frank. She's in the library at Rice. She'll probably make her way home after this has passed. How are you doing?"

"I'm okay. I'm tired of all this rain like I'm sure everyone else is."

"Yes, me too." Alex suddenly wanted to tell her what had happened in her house but didn't know how to broach the subject. Instead, she tried a circuitous question. "Mrs. Frank, does Martha clean all of your house or just that part you occupy?"

"She tries to clean all of the first and second floors. Why? Would you like for her to clean your apartment?"

Alex suddenly didn't know where to go next. "Oh…Oh, no, Mrs. Frank. I was just wondering that your house seems to be an awful lot to clean."

"Oh, yes, Honey. And she often doesn't get to a lot of it. In fact, I have to do a little cleaning myself, but I don't mind that."

"Well, I was just curious about that, Mrs. Frank."

When she hung up, Alex thought about the attic and its seeming neglect. But where she had noticed the dust in the office on the first floor, she hadn't noticed too much dust or dirt in the attic. Perhaps she had been just too preoccupied to pay any attention.

She settled down to read a few minutes before making her lunch and became so interested in what she was reading she didn't notice the rain had stopped. In fact, it was an hour before she went downstairs to prepare a sandwich for lunch.

In the kitchen, spreading mayonnaise on a piece of bread, she heard Stephanie come in the door.

"Alexandra, I'm back," she called from the front room. "God, I'm up to my butt in this junk. I'm going to have a hell of a time organizing this stuff." She tossed her books on the sofa. "Oh, my little friend is back. And this time, I'm sober as a judge."

"What? Who?" Alex stood in the kitchen door and chewed on a bit of sandwich.

"The little girl. She's in Mrs. Frank's yard."

"Stephi, let's go find out who she is. Come on." Alex put her sandwich in a dish by the kitchen door and raced for the door, Stephanie turning to follow her.

To get to Mrs. Frank's back yard, all they had to do was go through a chain link gate and a hedge. But when they arrived, there was no little girl to be seen.

"I don't get it, Roomy. She was here just a minute ago. She was standing right over there." Stephanie pointed to a corner of the yard that had an old slide swing in it. "She had her back to me like before or I would have waved to her."

"Her back to you? You've never seen her face?"

"No, I don't think so. I don't remember seeing her from the front the other day."

"Well, she sure made a fast exit this time."

The girls looked around the back yard to find it completely enclosed by a chain-link fence overgrown by plants and a board fence bordering the alley. The only gate was the one they had just entered. They even looked around for possible hiding places but there were none. There was a slide swing, a birdbath and a garden built up around two trees. They even searched down the alley but found no trace of the girl.

The girls never came into the backyard and Mrs. Frank had come only to plant a few irises and daisies along the back fence. Because of the frequent rains she had never needed to water them. Now Alex and Stephanie were both puzzled about how a little girl could possibly get in and out of this yard so fast.

"That kid must have taken off right after I went inside the apartment," Stephanie said as they filed back into the back yard.

"I don't know, Stephi. Wouldn't she have left the gate open? It was closed when we arrived, remember?"

The girls made one more cursory look around and then turned and walked out again, to be confronted by Mrs. Frank.

"My, my, what are you two up to?" She smiled at both girls.

"Stephanie saw that little girl again just a few minutes ago, Mrs. Frank."

"Yes. She was in the backyard, about in the same place she was before."

"Girls, I don't know who that is, but I'll try to find out."

The old lady screwed up her face in puzzlement. “It seems so odd, though, that she should be here.”

“Yes, it does.” Alex crossed her arms over her chest and looked again at the back yard. “I think it would be a good idea if you did find out who she is. A parent needs to be alerted.”

“A very sensible idea, Alexandra.” The old lady led the two girls up to her back steps to find the large black and white tomcat lounging on the bottom step.

“Oh, that thing.” Mrs. Frank put her hands on her hips. “I saw that thing around here the other day.”

“That’s Thomas, Mrs. Frank,” Stephanie piped up. “He lives under the back steps.”

“Oh, I hope he’s not getting with your cats.” Mrs. Frank turned back to the girls.

“He’s not.” Alex looked down at the sleepy cat and grinned. “He’s been stirring them up some, though.”

A little later, the girls began to get ready for a party that night near Rice University. Alex chose her clothes and laid them out on the bed, all the time checking through the window for the appearance of the little girl. She could see most of the yard from her bedroom window and she thought if she saw her she could rush downstairs and find out who she was and where she lived.

No one, however, appeared in Mrs. Frank’s backyard all the rest of the afternoon. More and more Alex believed the little girl was somehow related to all of the other things that were happening. How the mysterious tyke was related she couldn’t figure. Alone upstairs before getting dressed, she thought about the little girl and shivered.

The next morning Alex picked up the Sunday paper on Mrs. Frank’s driveway at five thirty. She checked Mrs. Frank’s bedroom windows to make sure she was up. Lights on there and downstairs meant she was. Also, she checked the attic. No lights on there this morning. Now she wondered if she had imagined the light Friday night, but she knew for a fact there was something in the attic. She clutched herself and shivered.

Later, after church, the girls had put their school work aside and were discussing the little girl.

“Stephi, I don’t know but I swear that gate looked like we

were the first to use it in a long time, at least since Mrs. Frank was last in there to tend her plants. I mean there was ivy growing across it and everything." Alex reclined on the couch and played with her hair.

"She might have climbed the fence." Stephanie crossed her arms over her chest and leaned back in the easy chair in front of the TV. "You know, kids do that all the time."

"She might have, Steph. But wouldn't we see some evidence of that? Like trampled plants or something. I swear to God nothing in that yard looked disturbed."

"Alex, I saw that kid, damn it. This is the second time. And this time, I hadn't had anything to drink."

"Stephi, I don't doubt that you did. But I'm just at a loss to explain her presence. I can't explain shit anymore." Alex rose up from the couch and put both feet on the floor. "The window and shower the other week. I'm not so sure Tom's the answer for the cats. Whatever is in that attic. And now the little girl." She made a gesture of futility with both hands.

"Roomy, don't get upset. I'm sure there's a logical explanation for this stuff. You know a little kid can go places an adult can't."

"Stephanie, tell me this. What did that little girl look like? You mentioned it before but tell me again."

"She…Alex, I've never seen her face. I've always seen her from behind."

"What did she look like from behind, then?"

"From what I could see, she looked like she was maybe five or six years old. She had on a white dress that came down to her calves. It looked like a hospital type thing to me."

"A hospital type thing?"

"Yeah, it looked like one of those nightshirt-type things you wear in the hospital. But what the hell would a kid wearing a nightshirt be doing in Mrs. Frank's backyard in the middle of the day?"

"A night shirt." Alex put her hand to her mouth in thought. Vivid in her mind was her second dream, the one of the beach. In it there had been children wearing white. The children had been horribly dead, though, and their white clothes soaked and torn. She looked up again at her roommate. "It was probably some kind of dress, Steph."

"I'm sure it was. I haven't seen anything like it before, though."

"It's odd that you never saw her face."

"Neither time. It looked like she had blond hair, though. It was almost white."

Alex stared into her roommate's face. She knew Stephanie wasn't lying any more than she had been lying about the attic on Friday. She was positive the little girl was somehow connected to the thing in Mrs. Frank's house as well as the other disturbances.

Figuring how, though, she knew, would drive her crazy.

"Stephanie, that little girl, and whatever is in Mrs. Frank's house, and that window and everything else that has been going on are somehow related. Even my nightmares are related in some way." Alex opened her eyes wide and threw her hands up in exasperation. "One of my bad dreams had dead kids in it. Dead kids wearing white."

"White? What are you saying Alex?"

Alex put her hands on her hips and watched for a further reaction from her roommate.

"God…God, Alex. This little girl was alive. As alive as you and me."

She didn't reply to Stephanie. Instead, she backed away a moment and thought.

"Alex, when you told me about Mrs. Frank's attic the other day, I thought about a ghost or something. But this little girl couldn't have been anything like that."

"Why, Stephi?"

"Well…Well, she just couldn't have. If I could have been in the yard with her, I could have touched her. And they say you can't touch…"

"You could have touched her. Or she could have touched you."

Stephanie's blue eyes grew wider. "Touched me?" she said, her voice trembling.

"Yes. And you probably would have seen her face. And then you would know."

"I would know? I…I would know what?"

"You would know what she was." Alex's voice had gone down to whisper. "Alive or dead. There are animated dead people, Stephanie. I have seen them. Years ago. Even one whose body was burned to a crisp. That one hurt me on two different occasions."

"Oh, my God, Alex. You can't be…"

"Telling the truth? I wish to God I wasn't. I told Pauli the other day that some of the same crap is happening now that happened back then, and as for the veracity of what I am saying, you can ask him. He was right there with me all the time." Alex remained perfectly still, staring at her roommate who, with eyes like saucers, was now breathing heavily.

"I…I don't believe in ghosts, Alex."

Alex detected a sob in the bottom of Stephanie's throat. She looked down at the floor and softened. "There's so many things that can't be explained, Stephi. Or explained logically." Suddenly she felt sorry for her roommate. She obviously didn't understand any of it and Alex was at a loss to explain it any better to her.

The next evening, Monday, brought to the apartment Howard Simmons, known affectionately as "Howie" to his fellows at Rice. Although winning a full scholarship to college, Howard had chosen to lay out of school a few years and work before his higher education. Hence, after those years in the world of work and a full knowledge of meager pay checks, he was now an engineering student. His vibrant personality and short, peppy stature endeared him to anybody he met. Tonight, he was on an errand.

Stephanie was first to the door.

"Is this where the amazons hang out?" Howard stood in the door, wide grin on his face and both hands full.

"Come on in, Howie." Stephanie turned and yelled at the kitchen. "Howie's here and he's carrying a full load!"

Alex appeared quickly and stood, grinning, just behind Stephanie.

"You betcha. Two twelve packs of Coors Light. As ordered." He set the beer packs down in front of him. "I wouldn't study organic chemistry without them."

"Absolutely right." Alex picked up both packs and headed

for the kitchen.

“Won’t you stay and have one with us?” Stephanie grinned down into Howard’s face.

“No, thanks. I’ve got to go out to the Medical Center.”

“Where? Methodist?”

“No. M. D. Anderson. My first boss from back in Beaumont, Art Tisdale, is out there with cancer and it doesn’t look too good.”

“I’m sorry, Howie.”

“Yeah, me, too. Art was a peach of a fellow. Put up with a ton of shit from us.”

Howard looked briefly around the room. “How are you doing, Blondie? Getting along all right with Swarthmore?”

“Yes, with Alex’s help. I’ve been able to stay on top of all the crap in that class. I’m worried about the final, though.”

“Ah, don’t. I hear it’s easy.”

Alex re-entered the room with two open beers for her and Stephanie. “I heard you say you weren’t going to be able to have a sip with us tonight, Howie.”

“Yeah. I’ve got to run out to M.D. Anderson.”

“Howie’s probably going to have one on the way home, though.” Stephanie looked at Alex and laughed.

“Are you kidding? That’s not even a one beer trip.” Howard scratched his nose and glanced at each girl in turn. He suddenly turned to Alex. “Hey, introduce me to your friend upstairs. She looks more my size.”

“What?” Alex replied, a quizzical look on her face.

“The girl upstairs.” Howard pointed toward the ceiling. “I saw her silhouette in the window when I drove up.”

“Howie, no one’s been upstairs.” Alex set her beer down and crossed her arms over her chest. “Stephi, have you been upstairs?”

“No. Not all evening.”

“Ladies, I swear to God. I saw someone in the window when I drove up.”

“Well, then,” Alex replied, “let’s go look. She turned toward the stairs, her beer back in her hand.

“Yeah. It might be a burglar.” Stephanie grinned at Howard.

The three of them started upstairs with Howard trailing.

"You know, female burglars are the worst," Stephanie joked over her shoulder. "You got a pistol in your car, Howie?"

"Pistol, hell," Howard chuckled. "Either one of you could whip Xena's ass. You don't need any pistol."

When they arrived at Alex's room, the one with the window in question, it was, of course, empty. Alex thought she caught a whiff of a smell that was vaguely familiar.

"Well, you haven't been drinking, Howie. So what have you been doing, smoking?" Stephanie positioned herself behind Howard. "What's going on with you, Howie?"

"Boy, I don't know." Howard slowly shook his head. "I could have sworn there was someone at that window." He pointed at the window opposite the head of the bed, not the one which they had trouble with earlier.

Alex turned to Howard. "Howie, we've been seeing a strange little girl in our yard. You don't suppose…"

"Too Tall, Dear, I know what a little girl looks like. This was a big girl." Howard turned to Stephanie and sniggered. "What would I want with a little girl, anyway?"

"Well, they're about your size, Howie." Stephanie beamed down at Howard.

"Naw, Blondie. I need something five-foot two, eyes a-blue and about twenty-five years of age."

Howard and Stephanie laughed but Alex was lost in thought. Just what did Howard see?

"Well, ladies, I feel a good time coming on around here real quick, but I still need to get out to the hospital." Howard turned toward the door and the two girls followed him out of the room, he and Stephanie chatting away but Alex still silent.

At the front door, Howard turned to the two girls. "Well, we'll see you later. Good luck with Swarthmore, Stephanie."

"Thanks, I'll need it." Stephanie caught the door when he opened it. "Thanks for getting the beer. I think we're both going to have one more before we hit the sack."

"Sounds great. Goodbye Alex." Howard turned to Alex and winked. "You can tell your mysterious friend upstairs what she missed. When I come again, I want to meet her."

After Howard left, the two girls, beer cans almost empty,

positioned themselves in the living room.

"Well, Roomy, what do you suppose Howie saw?" Stephanie pulled her feet up and tucked them underneath her.

Alex just shrugged her shoulders. "Our mysterious friend upstairs."

"Alex, you weren't up there when Howie drove up, were you?"

"No, Steph. I was downstairs in the kitchen, remember?"

"Well, I know he didn't see the little girl. How would she have gotten in the house in the first place." Stephanie looked away, a thoughtful expression on her face. "Besides, it's kind of late. What would she be doing out this time of night, anyway?"

Alex had no reply to this. She knew Stephanie didn't believe anything she had told her earlier. What real evidence did she have? Just strange things going on that eventually would be explained. Alex guessed Stephanie really believed that Tom had stirred up the cats, the window had been an architectural fluke, the little girl was someone's kid running loose and what Alex had experienced in Mrs. Frank's house was a figment of her imagination. For her, there was no evidence to the contrary. But the incidents were piling up.

She looked across the room at her roommate. *She's really trying to think of some explanation for what Howie saw,* she thought. But Alex had none either. She could only surmise, with dread, what that was.

Chapter Six

The following week brought finals and the end of the term but no more occurrences. The girls threw themselves into their course work and temporarily forgot the odd events that had occurred since the beginning of April. The rain, however, continued.

On Tuesday, the week after her finals, Alex lay on her bed and thought about dropping a note to Coach Bill Abernathy, her high school chemistry teacher. She had just found out her grade in organic chemistry was an "A," the second she had made in a chemistry class since she had been in college and she knew that Coach Abernathy would still be teaching chemistry class to high school students. She had gotten out her note pad and a pen when Stephanie appeared at her bedroom door, a Coors Light in her hand.

"Roomy, there's seven more of these in the fridge. You want to have one with me?" She grinned and leaned against the door frame. "It's late enough. Three o'clock."

"Sure. I've got to write a quick note, though." She rolled over on her back and turned her head in Stephanie's direction. "I'm dropping a line to Coach Abernathy back at Clear Lake to tell him about my two "A's" in chemistry. He'll love it."

"Sounds like a winner. My chemistry teacher in high school laid tons of work on us and half of what we learned, we had to learn on our own."

"Not Bill Abernathy…"

"Oh, Roomy," Stephanie interrupted. "I just talked to Mom. I've a 9:00 AM flight to Topeka on Thursday morning." Stephanie took a big swig of beer.

"Great. I'll take you to Bush Intercontinental."

"Come down quick." She suddenly turned toward the hall. "I'm celebrating the end of Swarthmore's class and bullshit papers at the last minute and there's no telling where I'm going to wind up."

"I know where you're going to wind up. Single variable calculus two." Alex laughed and rolled back over on her side.

"That's not until the fall," Stephanie said from the head of the stairs.

Alex started her note and wrote in a single paragraph how much she appreciated Coach Abernathy's teaching and the two "A's" it had brought her in college. She had just started a second paragraph in which she would ask about next year's football team when, for no reason, she looked up.

Through the window, she spotted a small figure, clad in an off-white garment, standing, back to her, at the bird bath in Mrs. Frank's back yard. She hesitated momentarily, but then realized *that's the little girl.*

She put down her pen and started to rise when, from out of the bottom of the window, appeared Stephanie, quickly tiptoeing toward the gate.

Alex jumped up and ran downstairs to the front door. When she opened the door, she heard her roommate say "gotcha" from the back yard. This was followed in a few seconds by a piercing scream that startled Alex to the point that she knew Stephanie surely was in some kind of danger.

She began running toward the gate but before she got there Stephanie appeared, bent over and clutching her stomach. Just beyond the gate, the girl retched violently and lost the contents of her stomach.

"Oh, my God, Stephi," she shouted, hurrying to the girl who couldn't stop vomiting. Alex caught her in her arms and clasped her to her. "Stephi…Stephi."

Now Stephanie was sobbing, thick, heavy sobs from the bottom of her throat. Alex held her as tight as she could.

Stephanie finally began to calm as she realized Alex had her in her arms.

"Jesus Christ, Alex, that…that…" she sobbed, shaking her head back and forth.

"What, Stephanie, what? I've got you. You're okay."

Stephanie breathed in and out deeply now, still sobbing. "That thing…That thing in there…had no eyes. She had no eyes."

"She was a corpse, Stephi."

"Oh, dear God, Alex, how…how…" Stephanie still choked and sobbed.

"Stephi, Stephi, the little girl is dead. She's not of this life. She's a presence here. She's…"

Stephanie suddenly pulled away from Alex, face deeply flushed and tears streaming down. "You're…You're trying to tell me she's a ghost?"

Alex looked straight into her wide, tear-filled eyes. "Yes, Stephanie, if you want to call her that."

Stephanie's chest heaved as she tried to choke back her tears. "Alex…Alex, her face was torn open, her clothes were ripped and…and liquid kept coming out of her mouth."

"Did it look like blood?"

"No, it looked like water. Dirty water."

Alex still held Stephanie's left arm at the elbow. Now she turned and gently prodded her toward the apartment. "Come on. Let's go in," she said gently. "There's something I want to tell you."

Stephanie bowed her head and sobbed again. "Alex, I wet my pants. I…I never wet my pants before."

"I did that, too," Alex whispered. "Years ago."

She guided her roommate into the apartment and Stephanie went immediately upstairs to change clothes. The girl was so upset, Alex wanted to cry with her but somehow she kept from doing it. Instead, she would try to remain calm with an explanation.

When Stephanie returned to the living room, they settled in easy chairs, Stephanie, still sniffling and breathing deeply, by the fireplace and Alex across from her. In a soft level voice, Alex told her everything that had happened to her years ago. She went into detail and explained each event in sequence. Stephanie said nothing, sitting wide-eyed and wiping away tears with a Kleenex.

"I know I've told you some things before," Alex said in finishing. "But now you have the whole story. I know it's very hard to believe. Some of the things that happened I can hardly believe myself. But now you have first hand evidence that these things do exist."

"But you're talking about dead soldiers, Alex. This is a little girl. Why a little girl?"

"I don't know, Steph. That I have no answer for."

"That thing out there was so horrible." Stephanie choked back a sob. "I…I thought it was going to come after me. I peed all over myself." Stephanie's voice trailed off as she stared at the floor and Alex thought she was going to start crying again.

"Stephi," Alex started in a gentle voice. "That thing couldn't have been half as horrible as what I went up against years ago. I was only fourteen then. And I encountered a hideous burned-up thing that hurt me bad."

Stephanie suddenly straightened up. "Alex, what would something like that be doing here?"

"I told you, Stephi, I don't know." Alex tried to be as gentle as she could with her roommate. "I'm sure she's here for a reason but I don't know what it is." Alex thought for a minute. "Maybe Mrs. Frank knows something about a little girl that died sometime in the past."

"Tell her her goddamn house is haunted," Stephanie blurted.

"I doubt if she would believe any of this, Stephi." Alex crossed her legs, bent forward and rested her chin on her hand. "I don't really know what a little girl would be up to around here, but I'm sure she's really quite harmless."

"She just scares the shit out of you." Stephanie had calmed down and regained most of her composure. Alex could tell, though, that she was trying hard not to believe what she had seen.

After a lengthy period of silence, Stephanie looked up at her roommate. "Do you think that little girl is what Howie saw the other night?" she asked Alex, who had settled back in her chair.

"Yes, I do. What else could it be?" Alex reached up and began playing with her hair. "From what I know about these things, she's probably around here right now."

"But Alex, Mrs. Frank has never seen the little girl."

"That's right. She's appeared to us, particularly you. And there's probably a reason for that." Alex rose to her feet and started for the kitchen "I'll take that beer, now. I'll bring you another, too."

"Thanks. I need it," Stephanie replied. At last, she leaned back in her chair and relaxed. "Stomach ache or no stomach ache, I really need it."

In the kitchen, Alex poked around in the refrigerator. "Whatever that reason is," she said, loud enough for Stephanie to hear in the other room. "I think we need to find it out pretty quick."

Two days later, Stephanie flew to Topeka, Kansas, from which she would drive to her home in Lawrence. Nothing had happened in the meantime and Alex began to think that maybe Stephanie had somehow scared the little girl away. She was glad the disturbances had ceased, however, if for no other reason, Stephanie's state of mind. Her roommate had been badly shaken by her encounter with the little girl. Alex wondered how she would have fared had she run into the things she had encountered years ago.

Friday evening after Stephanie had left on Thursday brought a visit from Josh Hamilton, a boy from Katy whom Alex had been dating. They had known each other since elementary school since they attended the same church and after Josh's family had moved to Katy when he was in the sixth grade, they had never lost touch. Now, Josh, who, like Paul Zunker, was just finishing high school, was the closest thing Alex had to a boyfriend.

They had gone to dinner together and talked about Josh's plans for the future as well as a forthcoming trip to Galveston to be made accompanied by Paul and Stephanie. When they returned to the apartment, Mrs. Frank was on her back steps with a message from Alex's mother, Elizabeth. Naturally, the old lady invited the couple in for dessert.

After a large helping of cherry cobbler, Alex and Josh excused themselves and, since he had to be at school early the next morning to turn in equipment, Josh left after making plans for a movie the next night. As he drove out of the driveway, Alex glanced at the attic window, which, of course, was dark.

Shortly after feeding the cats, she prepared for bed. She thought about checking on Mrs. Frank, but decided the old lady was probably already in bed and fast asleep. She read for about thirty minutes and then, at a quarter to twelve, turned off the lights and went to sleep.

At a little past three o'clock, she awoke, with the feeling that something, or someone, was in the apartment. She looked down in the vague light from the window at the cat Sabrina, dozing peacefully at the foot of her bed.

Trying not to disturb the animal, she got up and groped her way into the hall where she turned on a light. Nothing appeared to be upstairs. She wondered now if she had forgotten to lock the front door.

She peeked into Stephanie's room to find that Henrietta was not at her usual place on the neatly made bed. *She probably went downstairs to eat or prowl,* Alex thought. *Maybe she made a noise that woke me up.*

Gingerly, Alex crept down the stairs and turned on a light in the living room. By the kitchen door crouched Henrietta, wide eyes staring and tail fluffed out.

"Henry, what's the matter, kitty?" Alex asked gently.

The animal did not move, but just crouched and stared, straight at Alex.

"What the hell is the matter with her?" Alex whispered.

She checked the front door to find it locked and then looked in the kitchen to find nothing amiss. Then, she thought about looking outside. She started for the front door but was startled to hear a soft footfall from upstairs.

Alex froze in horror. She had just come from up there. Who could be up there, now? She hurried into the kitchen, took a butcher knife from a drawer and then cautiously made her way upstairs.

Almost at the top of the staircase, she was suddenly stopped by Sabrina, darting, snarling, in front of her down the staircase. Alex froze on the stairs. She listened. All she could hear was her own heavy breathing. There seemed to be nothing that could have frightened her cat.

"God help me," she said under her breath. Then she reached the top of the stairs and started down the hall, all the time listening for the slightest sound. Just outside her bedroom door, she stopped.

"Little girl?" she said aloud, and then listened. All was silent.

Quickly, Alex reached through the doorway and switched on the light. Then, quickly, she entered her room.

Nothing was there. Nothing was disturbed. The room was just as she had left it only a few minutes earlier.

"But what happened to the cat?" Alex, exasperated, exclaimed. Whatever had frightened Sabrina had surely frightened Henrietta downstairs.

"Little girl?" Alex said again, louder this time. Surely that was what was in the apartment for she couldn't think of anything else. She thought of Howard seeing a silhouette of something in her room the other night.

This is where she's got to be if she's here, Alex thought. Then, she remembered the smell. It was here the other night, but now it wasn't.

It occurred to her to check the window but she found it secured and un-tampered with. Thinking of another bad experience earlier, she pressed her cheek to the window to look up at Mrs. Frank's attic window. Again, she froze in terror. The light was on, just as it had been that night she saw it. She stared at it for what seemed like a lifetime until it went off.

"My God," Alex whispered to herself. "Could the little girl be up there? And if she is, how could she have exerted such a hideous influence on me when I was up there?"

It crossed her mind to awaken Mrs. Frank and tell her someone was in her attic, but somehow this idea wasn't feasible. She looked again at the rooftop window to make sure it was still off.

"Damn it, what's going on here?" she cried. She turned and went downstairs to find Sabrina, knowing the large, old orange tabby would be a comfort to her alone in the dark.

A few minutes later in bed, the cat nestling at her feet, she thought about what had just happened.

"That little girl was in the apartment," Alex whispered in the dark. "I know she was. What in the name of God does she want?" For some reason, she couldn't place the little girl in the attic. There something had overpowered her; something had wanted to hurt her, maybe even kill her. And a little five or six-year-old girl just didn't fit. No, there was something else. There had to be. Alex began reviewing what had been happening around the apartment since Easter, but the effort soon put her into a deep sleep.

She awoke at eight o'clock, one whole hour later than she had wanted to. Even though rain had fallen earlier before dawn, now sunlight flooded her bedroom.

Alex had planned to take a large load of laundry, hers and Stephanie's, to her parents house to wash them and she had told Elizabeth she would be there at eight-thirty. Now she would have to call and tell her she wouldn't be there until nine-thirty. Before she could make the call, however, the phone rang.

"Hi, Roomy. Just wanted to get you up," a voice chirped on the other end.

"Stephi? Hi, how are you doing?"

"Great. Visiting is wonderful. And I'm renewing old friendships, like old boy friendships."

"Boy friendships?"

"Yeah. His name is Luke and he goes to school in Wichita. We dated some in high school."

"Well, I'm glad you're having so much fun."

"Yep. I'm thinking about bringing Luke back to Houston with me. Ha! Just kidding. He'd go great with Josh, though."

"Yeah. Josh and I went to dinner last night."

"Oh, yeah?"

"Uh huh. Dinner and some of Mrs. Frank's cherry cobbler. He had to go home early because he had something to do early this morning."

"Oh, too bad."

"Something else, Stephi. That little girl was in the apartment last night."

There was a silence on the other end that made Alex wonder if Stephanie was still there.

"My God," Stephanie finally said. "Did you see her?"

"No. I just felt her. I woke up around three with a feeling that something was in the apartment. I investigated and found nothing. I think Henrietta saw something, though. She was wild-eyed with a fluffed-out tail. And Sabrina was scared of something upstairs."

"Oh, Jesus, Alex. What are you going to do?"

"Nothing. There's nothing I can do." Alex paused momentarily and took a deep breath. "I'm going over to my parents' house this morning to do laundry."

"Why don't you stay over there?"

"I can't, Steph. Who would take care of the cats? Besides, what can a little girl do?"

"Scare the piss out of you. Alex, I've never been so frightened in all my life."

"Yeah, that's for sure. That attic light was on, too."

"Oh, Alex, you know they're connected."

"I know they are, somehow. But I don't think it's the little girl in the attic. There's something else."

"What could that be?"

"Again, I don't know, but I'm going to find out. And if I can get a hand on our little kinder-gardener friend, I'm going to find out about her, too."

"Alex, I wouldn't even touch her. I don't even want to be near her."

"Well, sometimes that has to be done, especially to get rid of them before they drive you nuts." Alex paused and breathed deeply again. "Well, Steph, I've got to go and get across town before mama gives up on me."

"Now, Alex, I'm going to worry about you staying there by yourself."

"I'll be okay, Stephanie. You're still coming back next week?"

"Yeah. Tuesday."

"Good. I'll see you then."

After hanging up the phone, Alex gathered the laundry, which wasn't as much as she had thought. In fact, she would get it to her car in only one trip. Carrying the laundry in front of her bundled up in a sheet, she made her way through the front door.

Beyond the door, she noticed the absence of Thomas, who always slept on Mrs. Frank's back steps. He only left them in the daytime when Mrs. Frank ran him off or he was hungry. But Alex had not heard Mrs. Frank this morning and Tom should be sound asleep after a night of prowling.

"That's pretty peculiar," Alex said to herself. "I wonder

where he is." She scanned the area under the back steps as she carried the load to her car.

She had just tossed the load in her backseat when she turned to her left.

Squatting on the first floor roof over the single garage was a girl, or a young adult, dressed in a shredded white dress, badly scarred, pale and missing eyes. Unlike the little girl, this figure was hideously animated, its head swiveling to and fro and coming to rest in a position staring straight at Alex.

Alex's first reaction was to say "Hi," but the sudden, icy chill, slicing razor-like through the early morning Houston humidity told her immediately she was in the presence of her worst fears.

The thing's mouth opened and a liquid, like dirty water, poured out of it. Then, the figure moved its right hand into sight and Alex could see it had nails, grown in death, over an inch long. The hand moved over its leg as the figure started to rise.

In revulsion and terror, Alex backed up. She started to urinate but checked herself. Her next impulse was to run but she was afraid the thing would come after her. And she felt like she was going to retch although there was nothing in her stomach.

She stepped slowly toward the front door of the apartment, all the time keeping an eye on the thing on the roof. Its head moved in her direction, but every other part of it was still.

When she got to the front door, she darted inside and immediately locked the door, securing it with the night security lock. Then, she made for the restroom and once inside, locked that door as well. There, she bent over the toilet and retched, coughing up a bit of phlegm. When she brought her stomach under control, she turned and sat on the toilet.

She began to breathe a bit easier but suddenly there was a heavy crash against the bathroom door, like someone had thrown himself against it.

Alex screamed and stood up, her clothes disarrayed, and turned toward the door.

"That thing is out there," she whispered loudly. She began to cry. In the dark, breathing slowly, trying not to make a sound, she remembered locking the front door soundly. The back door was never used.

If that thing got through the front door, it damn sure can get through this one, she thought, tears streaming down her face. She pressed her body firm against the opposite wall and waited for the worst.

Silence. Nothing could be heard outside the bathroom door. Alex didn't even breathe. She had stifled her sobs but she still shook. Closely, she listened for any noise. There was none.

She wondered if the thing was gone but she dare not open the door. The memory of the thing squatting on the roof caused her to be sick again but she tried desperately to control her stomach. Then, she couldn't control herself. She kneeled by the toilet and cried again, loud gasping sobs that shattered the silence.

In the darkness, she remained sitting by the toilet for fifteen minutes, not daring even to stand. She thanked God there was no window in the bathroom for that thing to get through or look in.

Finally, when the downstairs phone rang, she got up. Carefully, she opened the door to be met by the sickening smell of putrefaction.

"Oh, Jesus," she said, aloud. "That thing's still here." Her immediate thought was to run back into the bathroom but, looking around, she could tell that nothing was there. Then, she realized it was not the little girl that had been in her room the night of Howard's visit. It was the thing she'd just seen. The thought froze her in horror.

By now, the phone had quit ringing and everything was silent again. She noticed the front door was still securely locked. There was no sign of forced entry anywhere. Remembering the upstairs window, she hurried up to her bedroom and checked it. Securely locked, the latch in place where she had put it.

"How? For God's sake, how did that thing get in?" she asked herself, fiercely. A cold wave of terror came over her as she remembered the other-worldliness of the thing on the roof and its obvious malign intentions. Almost in panic, she wondered where it was now.

At the head of the stairs, she stood, hugged herself, and stared at the front door. Did she dare open up and go out? In all probability, that thing was outside waiting for her. This thought unnerved her so much her stomach churned and she was afraid she was going to be sick again.

"Goddamn it, why me?" she choked. Tears blurred her eyes as she sat down on the top step. Aside from her fear, she was frustrated by not knowing what to do now. Even a loud scream would relieve at least some of her tension. But what would be the use. Who would hear it?

Slowly descending the staircase, she was determined to open the front door and go out but the thought of coming face to face with that thing unnerved her again. At the foot of the stairs, she looked through a window but saw nothing between the apartment and Mrs. Frank's back door. She was peeking out another window when the phone rang again.

Her mother on the other end gently chided her about not being over there to do laundry earlier. Alex wanted to blurt out what had just occurred but decided not to, giving oversleeping as the excuse for her tardiness. Even though her mother had been a party to the events of the past, Alex could still see her not believing her now. No, the only family member to be told about the recent goings-on was her brother, whom she asked about and was told he had gone up to Huntsville for the day to visit an old soccer friend.

Oh, fine, Alex thought as she hung up the phone. *I get to live with this crap all day long.*

She longed for Stephanie, who would not be back until next week. Although she wanted her company, she shuddered when she thought about how Stephanie would react to what she had seen that morning. *God, she went to pieces over the little girl,* she thought.

After garnering enough nerve to open the front door, Alex carefully searched around the outside but found no trace of the manifestation from that morning. Nor was there any indication of entry in the apartment from the outside, natural or unnatural. Still, the crash against the bathroom door rang in Alex's ears for it was obviously an attempt by something inside the apartment to get into the bathroom to her. The thought of those hideous claws on her body made Alex sick again.

Later, after gaining control of herself, she thought about the two manifestations she had seen at the apartment. Obviously they were related? But how? The little girl didn't seem to mean any harm, but the other was just the opposite—malicious and foreboding. Both figures' bodies and clothing were ripped and torn, like they had been in some sort of explosion. Both figures regurgitated a light, brown liquid, like dirty water.

What did this mean? Were these two victims of something or someone? Using logic to figure out the paranormal was one way they had solved their problems years ago. But now, nothing seemed to fit. Two manifestations, one of them obviously malign, had appeared at her apartment. Alex didn't need her small degree of ESP to know that both figures were up to something.

She spent the rest of the day at her parents' house doing laundry, watching TV and just relaxing. Although she tried to put the morning's events out of her mind, she couldn't. Her thoughts kept going back to the figure on the roof. Was it back there waiting for her?

It was obvious that figure wanted her. She tried to figure out why but couldn't come up with a satisfying answer. What she needed was her brother but when she inquired again when he would be home, she learned he wouldn't return until late. Alex left for home that evening at six o'clock. After all, she could call Paul early the next morning. And she needed to take care of the cats.

At a little before seven, she arrived at her apartment to find Mrs. Frank and the large tomcat on the back steps. Silently, Alex thanked God she was there. When she saw Alex drive up, Mrs. Frank walked toward her car.

"Don't let this thing in your apartment, Honey," she said. "He'll squirt all over the place."

"Oh no, Mrs. Frank. We wouldn't think of it." Alex got out of her car and closed the door behind her. "Our cats are fixed and they've been de-clawed." She chuckled. "Stephanie found him under the back steps and she's been feeding him ever since." Her mind went back to Thomas' mysterious absence that morning. She wondered where he'd been.

"Well, I guess that's all right." Mrs. Frank turned to the cat, now sitting up on the top step. "They do keep rats and mice away."

"Mrs. Frank, I have a question for you." Alex wondered if she was going to annoy the old lady. After all, she had broached the subject before. "When was the last time anyone used your attic?"

"Oh, Honey, not since my Leo died." Her face screwed up in thought. "He didn't use the attic except for a place to store things he was afraid to throw away. Like boxes full of old bank statements, old income tax returns, stuff like that. Like I told you, I haven't been up there since he died."

Alex believed that, remembering the thin layer of dust that pervaded everywhere. "Did you ever know if anyone ever lived up there?"

"Well, Raymond and James never lived up there but they played up there." The old lady suddenly chuckled. "That's about as close as anyone ever got to living up there as far as I know."

"The reason I asked, Mrs. Frank, is that lately I've noticed the light on up there at night." Alex stared at her intently.

"The…The light on up there?"

"Yes, Mrs. Frank, I've seen it a couple of times." Now the old lady was genuinely concerned. "The only thing I can think of is a short or something in that light. There certainly hasn't been anyone up there to turn it on."

Alex knew there was something up there turning on that light and she had a good idea what it was. She wished, though, that Mrs. Frank had seen it, too.

"Well, I guess I better get an electrician up there to look at it," the old lady added. "That certainly is strange, though. How could a light come on by itself?"

"I don't know, Mrs. Frank." Immediately, Alex was ashamed of her lie because she wanted to admit more.

Later, in her apartment, Josh called and broke their date. She thought about going out alone but decided to watch TV instead. She wondered where various college friends were, including Howard, who had probably gone home to Beaumont. Mrs. Frank's presence just across the driveway was reassuring, but she felt she would be imposing if she went over there tonight. Usually, it was Mrs. Frank who did the inviting.

Settling on TV for the night's entertainment, she lay down

to watch a movie, but was soon in a deep sleep in front of it.

In a dream she floated on what seemed like a platform, but a closer look revealed it was part of a wooden floor, broken away from a house. Although it kept her afloat, her weight caused it to sink one to two inches below the surface of the water, which was relatively calm. Water reached her certainly, and dampened her legs but she didn't feel like she was wet. She turned about on her platform to look in all directions but could see nothing around but a few objects that looked like wreckage. There was also something in the water that appeared to be bundles gently bobbing up and down amid the wreckage. At one point she could see land but it was far away and seemingly barren. In another direction was land also, but this was even farther away.

When she turned again, she noticed one of the bundle-like objects very close to her platform. Stretching out carefully, she tried to shift the platform closer to it. When she was able to see it, however, she stopped, in terror. The object was not a bundle of any kind but a corpse, face down, bobbing gently up and down in the water. Instinctively, she drew back and almost fell over backwards off her platform. Quickly recovering her balance as best she could, she tried to paddle away from the object with her hands but did not have much success at it.

She turned around quickly to try to give some momentum away from the horrid object but found another "bundle" floating at the other end of the platform. Her piece of wreckage was between two of these things, but she could barely see the new object in the water. Curiously wanting a closer look, she edged carefully to the other end to find that this object was also a corpse, but this one was face up. Choking in horror, she immediately recognized the figure from that morning, still in the water, eyes closed. The hideous nails were spread wide on either side of it. Suddenly, eyes that had not been present that morning, opened and the head moved slightly in Alex's direction.

Drawing back, like to avoid the strike of a deadly snake, Alex screamed as loud as she could.

She came to, breathing heavily, on the floor in front of the couch, her knee sore from having struck the coffee table when she fell off. She lay still on the floor; the only sound she could hear was her own breathing and a man announcing baseball scores on TV.

"Jesus Christ," she sobbed. "What's going on here?"

She rolled over on her side and looked at the clock on the mantel to see the current hour of ten o'clock, three hours after she had started watching the movie. Carefully, she got back on the couch, looked in all directions and wondered if anyone had heard her scream. From past experience she knew she had screamed out of her dream.

But nothing moved. Everything was silent, except for the drone of the TV.

When the phone rang, she jumped clear off the couch, catching herself to sprint toward the phone stand by the stairs.

"Hi, Sis. Mama said you were looking for me today. I thought you had a date tonight?"

Alex, almost delirious with joy, clutched the phone with both hands. "I did, but Josh got called into that job he has. My God, Pauli, am I ever glad to hear from you."

"Yeah? When does…"

"Pauli, I've just had one hell of a dream, lying here on the couch."

"What? Again?"

"Yes, and it's even more awful than the others I told you about. In this one, there's a difference, a bad difference." As clear and detailed as she could, she related the early morning's events and details of her dream to her brother. Then she told him about what had happened to Stephanie with the little girl. Returning to the horrible figure from that morning she described it again in much more detail and included her associating it with Mrs. Frank's attic. When she had finished, there was silence as she knew Paul was thinking on the other end.

Finally, he spoke. "It sounds like we got another Caleb, Sis."

"Pauli, this thing is much worse than Caleb. It's like Elizabeth Merriwether coming out of a dream to hurt me."

"It hurt you?"

"No, but I sense the malice in that thing and it's deadly. I know I'm going to be attacked. I just don't know when."

"When does Stephanie get back?"

"Tuesday. She and I have to register for that humanities seminar on Wednesday. I haven't told her about the stuff recently yet. When I do, she's liable to go all to pieces. She was a basket case over her encounter with the little girl."

"Still, two of you against these things are better than one."

"How well I know."

"Do you expect anything else to happen tonight?"

"I don't think so. I don't sense anything around. I'm just going to go to bed and hope for the best."

"Well, good luck, Sis. If you need anything, call. Anytime."

"Thanks, Pauli, I just may do that."

After she hung up the phone, she felt better. What she told her brother was correct; she didn't expect anything else to happen that evening. But there was always tomorrow and she knew, even from the recent experiences, that her problems had only just begun.

Chapter Seven

Three days later, Alex picked Stephanie up at Bush Intercontinental Airport. Despite her apprehension, nothing had occurred since Saturday. During the day, she had been wary leaving the apartment, and she spent the evenings with Mrs. Frank, even playing Scrabble until late Monday night.

She knew these manifestations were on and off; they had been that way years ago. But for almost two months they had grown worse and worse, like they had years ago. Now Alex feared that somehow these new things were worse than those when she was younger, more malign and more dangerous. At least one of them was. Thus although nothing had happened for three days, she wondered what was next.

Driving across town from the airport, Stephanie chattered away about Kansas, her resurrected boyfriend, and various other things. She did not mention the little girl. Alex wondered why not.

When they turned on Yale Street into the Heights, Stephanie suddenly grew quiet. When Alex turned to ask a question, Stephanie suddenly cut her off.

"Well, did you see our little friend again?" she asked.

"I didn't see her at all, Stephanie."

"You said on the phone the other day that you thought she was in the apartment."

Alex turned onto Heights Boulevard and headed for the apartment a short distance away. "I said I thought she was in the apartment, Stephi. I didn't see her."

Alex pulled up to a red light and turned full to her roommate. "That morning, right after I talked to you, I did see something else, though." Now Alex worried about how Stephanie was going to react to what she was going to tell her.

"You saw something else? What?"

Alex had turned back toward the front but glanced at her momentarily to see Stephanie's eyes as big as saucers. "Well, it wasn't the little girl I saw. It was something worse."

"Something worse, Alex? Oh, Jesus, what?" Stephanie sounded like she was going to cry.

"An older girl, about our age. Just like the little girl. She was on the garage roof when I was loading the car."

"She had vacant eyes and…and she…?"

"Yes, Stephanie, and she regurgitated a dirty looking liquid."

"Oh, shit, Alex."

"Yes. And I was petrified, of course. I went back into the apartment and locked myself in the downstairs bathroom. She followed me."

"She followed you?"

"Yes. And she…I guess she threw her body against the door. Something heavy hit the door. I'm sure she was trying to get to me."

"Oh, God," Stephanie choked. "Now I can really piss my pants and puke with the best of them." Stephanie breathed heavily and Alex was sure she regretted leaving Kansas.

"No, Stephi." Alex turned momentarily in her seat and stared at her roommate.

"We're not going to show these things we're afraid. That's the worst thing we can do. These damned things thrive on fear. I know that for sure."

"But Alex. What can we do when that thing shows up again?"

For this question, Alex had no immediate answer. While she had waited for the older girl for three days, there had been nothing. But she knew it was only a matter of time. Although Stephanie was obviously disturbed about the news, Alex was glad that she was going to be with her now. She started to reply to her roommate but Stephanie beat her to it.

"Alex, that goddamned thing means us harm. You know it does."

"Probably so," Alex replied, remembering the hideous claws, which she had not mentioned to Stephanie yet. "We're going to have to be wary. We're going to have to watch for it.

And others if they show up."

"Others?"

"Yes, others. The cats have been sensitive to these things for months. We're going to have to keep an eye on them."

There was a silence during which Alex wondered what her roommate was thinking. After all, this was all new to her.

"I don't think that little girl means us any harm," Stephanie finally said.

"Probably not, Stephi. But the other thing does." Alex pulled into the driveway and pulled up close to the garage door. "At least to me."

They entered the apartment, Alex carrying one of Stephanie's bags. That night, they were supposed to attend Paul Zunker's graduation so they would not be home all evening. But arriving home late that night caused Alex some apprehension because she knew Stephanie would be terrified.

The rest of the afternoon was spent getting Stephanie settled and getting ready for the graduation ceremonies later. Neither girl mentioned what was on both of their minds. Would something be waiting for them when they got home?

Later they drove to Clear Lake to arrive at the Zunker home at seven o'clock. From there they would all go to the ceremonies together. Alex secretly wanted to pull her brother aside and ask him what to do about Stephanie, but she didn't get a chance all evening. After the ceremonies, Paul left with some friends for Port Aransas, leaving his sister with her worries.

Not a word was said all evening, but, driving home, Stephanie broached a subject Alex knew she had been thinking about during the whole outing.

"Alex, what are we going to do if that thing is there when we get home?" she asked, in a matter-of-fact tone.

"I don't think it will be, Steph." Alex replied, watching the road straight ahead. "These things don't jump out at you from behind a curtain. If we're going to hear from our friends, I imagine it will be after we're settled in."

"You're awfully damned nonchalant about this. It's going to be after midnight when we get home."

"I'm not going to worry about them, Stephanie." Alex was emphatic but gentle. "I told you earlier we should not show them fear."

"These things scare the shit out of me, Alex." Stephanie choked on a sob and turned away.

Oh, God, Alex thought. *What do I do now?*

"Look, Stephi," she said. "I'm going to be right there with you. If something appears, just call out and I'll come running." Alex thought a minute. "And you can do the same for me."

"What…What should I do?"

"You can be there with me. You ever heard of safety in numbers?" Alex turned her head momentarily and smiled.

At twelve thirty, they reached the apartment. Since there was some beer in the refrigerator and both girls were too keyed up to go to bed, they settled down with beers in the living room. There, they listened closely for any noise in the apartment.

Their vigil producing no results by a little after one, they went to bed. Alex wondered if her roommate would sleep tonight.

"How about a sleep aid, Stephi?" she asked, appearing at her roommate's bedroom door. "There's some Sominex in the bathroom cabinet."

"Thanks. That might help." She brushed past and Alex followed her to the bathroom.

"If something wakes you up, come get me," Alex said, now standing in the doorway.

"Damn right."

Stephanie took her pill and went to her bedroom while Alex went to hers. Lights were out almost immediately and both girls settled in their beds, Alex hoping the night would not produce any dreams. She turned over in the bed and petted Sabrina a few minutes. "I hope your sister's going to look after her mistress tonight," she said to the animal, which by now was purring.

Before she went to sleep, Alex rose and checked the attic window. Dark. *I wonder if anything is up there tonight,* she thought. After she got back in bed, she thought about checking on her roommate but before she could act, she fell into a deep sleep.

In a dream, she stood on a playground and watched several children playing on swings and slides. Strange, she thought.

Some of them were naked, some had torn clothes, all of them ignored her. Then, she was awakened by someone nudging her.

"Alex, Henrietta's gone," Stephanie whispered at her ear.

"What?" Alex rose up and rubbed the sleep out of her eyes.

"I said Henrietta's gone. I woke up having to pee and she wasn't there. She was there when I went to sleep."

"Stephanie, she's probably gone downstairs to eat. Or prowl. What's so unusual about that?"

"But I'd hear her down there, Alex. I always do." Now, she sounded genuinely frightened.

Alex looked around the bed and found Sabrina. Gathering the orange tabby in her arms she rose from the bed. "Come on, Stephi, let's go find her."

They found Henrietta in the kitchen, pressed against the back door they never used. The cat appeared terrified.

"Come on, Henry. Let's go to bed." Stephanie squatted in front of the animal and reached out for her.

The cat reacted immediately and sank her teeth in Stephanie's right hand.

"Shit! Damn it! What in hell is the matter with you?' she screamed.

The animal shrank back against the door, hissing and snarling.

"Stephanie, something's happened down here. That animal's scared to death." Alex turned toward the back door and searched each dark corner in the kitchen. Then, cautiously, she stepped to the kitchen door.

The living room, lighted by two lamps, showed nothing unusual. There was obviously no one beside the two girls around.

Alex entered the living room and Stephanie appeared in the door behind her, holding her injured hand.

"That cat's supposed to be sleeping peacefully in bed with me, not biting the shit out of me," she sobbed.

"I know that, Stephi." Alex reached back and cut the kitchen light off. Then she cast another cursory look about the living room and dining room. "Whatever scared Henrietta is long gone. Come on. I'll fix your hand. We've got to get to bed. We're supposed to be at Rice at eight-thirty."

Alex bandaged Stephanie's hand, happy to learn that she was current on her tetanus shots, then returned to bed.

A few minutes later, after studying Sabrina closely, Alex lay in the dark and wondered if her roommate was going to sleep at all the rest of the night.

Poor Stephi, she thought. *She's starting to get a full dose of this crap and she doesn't have any earthly idea what it's all about.*

When Alex went to sleep, the dream she had been having did not return, nor did Stephanie awaken her again. What had been in the apartment indeed was gone. At least for now.

The next day, the two girls registered for their humanities seminar and then took Mrs. Frank to a movie in the afternoon. It was only late evening that they settled down in the apartment, the inevitable rain pouring down outside.

Stephanie had made a glass of iced tea and settled into an easy chair in the front room. Alex was busy making a tossed salad for supper.

"Stephi, you want chicken in the salad tonight?" Alex called from the kitchen.

"Yeah, Roomy. If these cats go crazy tonight, I'm going to ignore them." Stephanie leaned back in her chair and glared at Henrietta on the stairs with her head poking through the railing.

"If you're referring to Henrietta, something scared her last night. Scared the hell out of her."

"It would seem so." Stephanie took a slow sip of her tea glass. "She was all cozy and hugs this morning, purring and rubbing up against me. I swear to God, I felt like throwing her across the room."

"She's just an animal, Stephi. They have feelings, too. They get scared, too."

To this Stephanie had no reply. Instead, she watched Henrietta make her way into the kitchen to the food dish next to Alex's foot.

Later, Alex was getting ready for bed when Stephanie appeared at the door.

"Alex," she said in a timid voice. "If something happens tonight, I'm coming in here. Okay?"

"Sure, Stephi. I think we're going to be all right, though."

"What makes you say that?"

"Well, it seems these things come and go, with time in between them. Since something was here last night, I don't think anything will be here tonight. Of course, I could be wrong."

"Oh, wonderful."

"Stephi, try to put if out of your mind." Alex sat down on the bed hard and crossed her arms over her chest. "That will help. Trust me. Do you want something to help you sleep?"

"No. I don't want to get dependent on that." Stephanie breathed heavily and turned back toward her room. "Just what I was looking forward to, spending another night in a genuine haunted house."

Alex jumped up and ran to the door. "Stephanie, consider the facts. The only thing you've trafficked with is the little girl, and she's harmless. All the other stuff has come at me, including my latest friend who, if you don't mind my saying so, scares the shit out of me." Alex's voice grew in impatience. "So, from where I stand, I'm the target, not you."

Stephanie turned in her doorway. "I'm sorry, Roomy. But this stuff is so weird. I didn't even tell anyone in Kansas about the little girl. They would have thought I was nuts."

Alex calmed a bit. "It's weird all right. And might get weirder. We just have to take it one day at a time and hope for the best."

"But how do you stop it, Alex?"

"I don't know. You have to find a key. There's always a key somewhere. Like the triggers I told you about."

"Yeah. But now there's no trigger."

"Not that we can see." Alex smiled a little. "We just have to keep alert. Our eyes and ears open." She looked down at the floor and then back at her roommate. "And like I said, hope for the best."

They said good night and each went to her own bed. Alex settled in and cuddled Sabrina. "Nothing seems to bother you," she whispered to the animal and then let her go to settle in at the foot of the bed. Thirty minutes later, she was asleep and dreaming vividly again.

This time, she was lying in bed and watching the windows.

Suddenly, the little girl appeared at the window she had trouble with earlier.

She had not seen the little girl's face; she had only heard Stephanie describe it. But she knew at once who she was. The girl, completely naked, opened the window latch. Then, she threw the window wide open and hopped into the room at the foot of the bed.

Without seeming to move, she grabbed Sabrina by a hind leg and, holding the writhing animal up above her head, turned to face Alex.

Alex started to scream but woke up instead. Sitting up in bed, she saw nothing and heard nothing. She felt around the darkest portions of the bed for the cat and found her, waking up with a whine. Comforted that she had found the animal, she petted her and then threw her legs off the bed to get up. Before she could arise, she heard the downstairs clock faintly chime one.

Disappointed that it wasn't later, she slowly arose and made her way into the bathroom. Then she checked on her roommate. She was sound asleep, the cat Henrietta, now awake but at peace, beside her.

"Thank God for that," she whispered to herself. Slowly, in the dark since a light would awaken Stephanie, she descended the stairs into the darkness of the living room. Away from the staircase, she lit a lamp and looked around the living room-dining room area. She couldn't see anything out of the ordinary. Nor was there anything to be heard.

Sighing deeply, she turned to switch off the light when she heard a sound from just outside the apartment. At first, she couldn't tell what it was but soon it was unmistakable, the sound of a child running in bare feet across the driveway toward the garage. From what Alex could tell, it stopped in the vicinity of her car.

She froze and listened attentively. Now all was silence again. For five minutes, all she could hear was the sound of her own breathing.

Of course she knew it was the phantom little girl, but she didn't know what to do. She wondered if it was still there by her car. Or was it completely gone? Or, an even worse scenario, was the other one with it?

On tiptoes she crept to the front window and looked out but she couldn't see anything. Then, as carefully as she could, she made her way to the front door and unlocked it. Slowly, she pulled the front door open and looked out through the screen door.

She couldn't see anything immediately, not even in the vicinity of her car which she could see most of from the front door. To the right, she couldn't see anything in the backyard where the little girl had appeared earlier. She would be sure, however, that nothing was there.

As quiet as she could, she pushed open the screen door and stepped forward to go just out front like she always did when she heard something outside.

Out of nowhere, the tiny phantom appeared just in front of her. Without seeming to move, a small hand latched painfully onto Alex's inner thigh, between the knee and the hip. Crying out in pain, Alex peered down into a face long dead with vacant eyes and a vicious open gash in its cheek. Tears came to Alex's eyes when she realized the hideous thing was locked on to her. Reeling in horror, she closed her eyes and tried to think of what to do.

She tried to regain at least some of her composure; after all, this was the little girl, not the other one. She opened her eyes and looked again on the monstrous thing still clasped painfully to her and noticed the girl was completely naked, as she had been in her dream.

Closing her eyes again, she tried to grasp the child to push her away but before she could touch her, she released Alex and pulled away. When Alex opened her eyes, it was gone.

Now breathing heavily and gently rubbing the spot where she had been grasped, she looked around for any vestige of the little girl but nothing could be seen. Again, the tears came.

"What in hell do you want," she sobbed. She closed the door and locked it in two places. Then, through teary eyes, she looked around the living room to make sure that, by some trick, the little girl had not gotten into the apartment.

Now she knew the phantom child was truly gone. Alex sat on the bottom step of the stairs and put both hands on her leg. A large bruise was beginning to form where she had been held. The child's grasp had been like steel but, Alex thought, the child had meant no harm. In fact, she thought the child might have wanted to communicate. But the little phantom had vanished when she had tried to touch her.

She thought about waking Stephanie but decided not to since her roommate would only be stirred up all the more. After all, when Stephanie had looked the little girl in the face, she had become a basket case. *I don't need that again,* Alex thought.

Slowly, she made her way back to bed, checking for a light in Mrs. Frank's attic before she lay down. It was now clear to Alex that the little girl and the other thing were connected, but how? And Alex knew the other thing was in Mrs. Frank's attic.

Lying in the dark, she again envisioned the little girl directly in front of her, her hand fixed firmly on her leg. "What in hell does that little bitch want?" Alex whispered, tearfully, rubbing the inside of her thigh.

Perhaps she's trying to warn me, she thought. *Perhaps against the other manifestation. But how can I be sure?*

Although Alex was keyed up, she eventually did get back to sleep and slept undisturbed and dreamless until Stephanie shook her awake at eight o'clock the next morning.

"I woke up in the night and couldn't get back to sleep," she said, in a groggy tone that hid the real reason for her sleeplessness.

"Well, you're going to have to hustle," Stephanie said. "We're supposed to be on campus at nine thirty.

"I know. I know." Alex, awake, now remembered the night's events.

I wonder if I dare tell her, she thought. She arose finally and began gathering her clothes for the day. *I guess I better later. The next occurrence she's liable to have a ring-side seat for.*

Downstairs after breakfast, the girls divided up the books they had bought for the seminar and prepared to leave. While putting her books and purse in the car, Alex was startled by Tom, back from an absence of several days, scratching around on the garage roof in the exact location where the horrid apparition had squatted that day it had confronted her. Cursing under her breath, Alex turned from the car, almost colliding with her roommate on her way with her stuff.

"Stephi, your buddy's back," Alex said, tossing her thumb over her shoulder. "He's on the garage roof."

"You mean Tom? I thought he was gone for good." Stephanie looked up to see the large cat, now squatting on its haunches watching the two girls.

"Yeah. He scared the shit out of me." Alex quickly thumbed through her keys to find the one for the front door. "He's exactly where I saw that thing the other day."

"Well, better him than it."

"Really." Alex locked the front door and joined Stephanie in the car.

Later, over lunch at a restaurant near Rice campus, the two girls' quiet conversation about the morning's seminar suddenly ended when Alex realized now would be a good time to tell Stephanie about the previous night's events. She began with a question "out of the blue."

"Stephanie, have you ever seen the little girl without any clothes on?" Alex propped her head on her clasped hands. She knew the answer to that question.

"What? You mean…You mean naked? No. No, every time I've seen her she's always had on the same off-white dress, or smock, or whatever it is." Stephanie's expression turned to a quizzical frown. "What brought this on all of a sudden?"

"I did last night," Alex answered in a matter-of-fact way. "I first had a dream about the little girl, completely naked, entering my room. Then, after I woke up, I went downstairs to check things out and heard footsteps outside the apartment. When I opened the front door to investigate, there she was. Completely in the buff, like in my dream. She grabbed my leg and held on so tight I thought she was going to pinch it off, but when I tried to grab her she vanished. Gone!" Alex made a flipping motion with her hand.

"She grabbed your leg, Alex?" Stephanie's eyes, wide and staring, moved across the table.

"Yeah. I have a great big bruise there. It's so horrible looking, I'm wearing pants today."

"Jeez, Alex. I didn't notice."

"I know you didn't."

Stephanie remained silent, in thought for a few moments; then, she looked up, wilting.

"Alex, you said the little girl didn't mean any harm."

"I don't think she does, Stephanie. I'm pretty sure now she was trying to communicate with me somehow."

"But why wouldn't she have any clothes on?"

"I don't know, Steph. Maybe she was naked when she died."

"When she died? God, this is weird. I still can't believe I'm having a conversation like this."

Alex ignored her roommate's exclamation. "Stephanie, I'm pretty sure that what we have here are two girls who died at the same time, maybe in an accident of some kind. They're both pretty scuffed up."

"Oh, Christ. What kind of accident, Alex?"

"That, I don't know. A good guess would be an explosion of some kind. I think something like that would cause the kinds of injuries I've seen on both of them. And an explosion could blow the little girl's clothes off." Alex sat, pensive, stirring her iced tea and staring at her roommate who, she could tell, was still fighting to believe that what was happening at the apartment was true.

Finally, Stephanie spoke up. "Nobody, Alex, nobody would believe what you've just said to me."

"Of course not, Stephi. Nobody believes stuff like this until they've experienced it themselves, firsthand. As a kid, I quit believing in ghosts and monsters about the same time I quit believing in Santa Claus. And then, later, when I experienced those things, I still couldn't believe what was going on until it occurred to me that I was menaced by supernatural manifestations and I not only had to believe in them but I had to combat them. Their motives, although vague, clearly meant danger to me and those around me. Things progressed until I almost died and then my brother, with others, was finally able to get rid of them. But you know all of this, Stephanie. I've told you about it before."

"I know, but I'm still having trouble believing it."

"You're going to have to. These things are there. Like I

said before, the little girl clearly wants to communicate and in doing so, she may man-handle you."

"Oh, Jesus," Stephanie choked. "What am I supposed to do?"

"You're supposed to try to communicate with her. If she comes back to me, that's what I'm going to try to do."

"This haunted house shit's going to drive me crazy."

"Stephi, understanding them and then communicating with them are the first steps in getting rid of them."

"But what do you think she's trying to communicate?"

"Again, I don't know. I thought about that earlier. The only clear idea I have about that is that she's trying to warn us against something. Maybe even against the other thing I saw."

"The girl on the roof."

"The other girl. On the roof. It was very clear when I saw her she wasn't exactly Casper the Friendly Ghost. And furthermore, she came into the apartment after me."

"But…But who do you suppose the other one is. Or the little girl for that matter?"

Alex shrugged her shoulders. "They could be sisters, but you couldn't really tell that with the shape they're in. Or they could be non-related. Two victims of something. That's another aspect of understanding, finding out who they are. Or what they are."

"Alex, if that horrid little thing comes at me, I'm going to run like hell."

"Where to, Stephi? She'll be right there with you. One thing I've learned is that it's difficult to run from these things. If they want something of you, they're going to stay with you."

Stephanie stared down into her iced tea glass and seemed to be lost in thought. Alex could tell she was trying to think of what to say next.

"They're very determined." Alex continued. "Whether that determination is to communicate with you or to harm you, or whatever, remains to be seen. You just have to take things one day at a time."

"I think I'm beginning to find that out." Stephanie looked up and wrinkled her nose. "They're horrible, Roomy. And they stink."

"They're dead, Stephi."

"Yes," Stephanie exclaimed. "That's what so mind-blowing."

Alex couldn't help giggling at her roommate's outburst, but then she turned serious again.

"I know Mrs. Frank's house plays some role in all of this," she continued. "I don't know how and I don't know why, other than seemingly a dwelling spot for one of them. However, this is one thing we need to find out more about. I guess the best thing to do right now is go right back to the source."

"The source?"

"Yes. Tonight would be a good night to take Mrs. Frank to supper. Or at least some dessert. Her delicious cherry cobbler or apple pie, or whatever."

"And we grill her about the house."

"Bingo."

"What kind of things are you going to ask her?"

"Well, for starters, who lived there before her and her husband. I seem to remember her saying something about this earlier but I'm still going to ask her anyway." Alex quickly polished off her iced tea. "Then, we need to inquire into anything out of the ordinary concerning the house; for example, an explosion."

"Or a fire."

"These things don't appear to be burned, Stephanie. I can tell that. I'm thinking a gas explosion could do a minimum amount of structural damage to the house and still take out a couple of girls."

"Alex, a gas explosion could blow the whole house up."

"Or only a part of it. If the whole house was blown up, it would have been rebuilt. Therefore, it wouldn't seem to be as old as it obviously is. It's obviously the original house." Alex turned and signaled her server for the check.

Driving home through steady rain, both girls remained quiet; Alex thinking of exactly what questions to present to Mrs. Frank and Stephanie seemingly lost in thought. Just before they reached the Heights, though, Stephanie propounded another question.

"Alex, if something drastic had happened to that house,

don't you think Mrs. Frank would have mentioned it before now. You know how old ladies are."

"Yes, forgetful. Whatever happened might never have occurred to her while in our company. Also, what happened might have occurred before she came into the picture. I do know that Leo's family did not build that house. Someone else did."

"Yes, I do remember her saying something like that."

Slowly, Alex turned into the Heights. "She may have no knowledge of what happened there before Leo's family came along. But we're going to find out just what she does know."

When they reached home, both girls were in good spirits. Their attempt to find Mrs. Frank to present that evening's invitation came to naught when they found her not at home.

"I hope she comes home pretty soon," Alex commented, dumping her books on the dining room table. "You know how she likes to have a lot of time before we do anything together."

Stephanie plopped down in an easy chair in the living room. "I could use a beer. But since we're hopefully going out with Mrs. Frank later…"

"We don't have any, anyway, Steph."

"Oh no. Howie, where art thou?" Stephanie made a summoning motion with her hand.

"Beaumont."

"Oh crap. Now I'm going to have to use that fake ID again. I hate to…"

Stephanie was interrupted by the sound of a definite footfall upstairs just in front of her bedroom door. Both girls suddenly became deathly quiet for one minute and then looked upwards.

"Dear God in Heaven, what is that?" Stephanie whispered.

"That's someone upstairs, Stephi." Silently, Alex turned and began walking toward the staircase.

"Alex, you're not going up there!" Stephanie, now in tears of terror, grabbed Alex with both hands.

"Stephanie, I'm going to find out who, or what, is up there in the middle of the afternoon."

"Oh, Jesus. Please don't go up there."

Alex put her hands on her roommate's shoulders. "Stephi, I'm going up there. I don't know what I'm going to find. The footfall's kind of heavy so I suspect the other girl. All I want is a glimpse of her and then I'm going to come right back down. If something happens up there, I'll yell out. When you hear me, come up as fast as you can. I don't want to go one-on-one with that thing."

"Oh, Alex, no."

Alex looked into her roommate's face and reconsidered leaving her, she was in such bad shape. Tears streaming down her face, she was bawling like a baby. But Alex knew she must find out what was in the house.

She turned and quickly mounted the stairs. She could not see anything on the landing in the area where they had heard the footfall, so she slowed down and carefully crept the rest of the way to the top of the stairs.

"Oh, God, I've got to go to the bathroom," she whispered to herself as she reached the top step. "I don't hear anything. Hopefully, what was up here is gone." But the air at the head of the stairs was freezing cold, telling her there very much was a presence near.

She took one large step forward from the stairs and looked to her left into Stephanie's room. Nothing. Then, she looked to her right.

At the end of the hall, in front of her bedroom door, stood a man. He had his back toward the hall, but when Alex turned, he turned toward her. His face was just like the girls', dead and vacant. His eye sockets were empty. His shirt, torn and ragged, hung on his frame and his pants had great gashes in both legs. He didn't move but seemed to stare at Alex. Suddenly, slowly, he raised his left arm and, without moving his head, pointed into Alex's room. When he dropped his arm, he turned and walked into Alex's room.

Carefully, Alex followed, but before she could reach her door, the air turned back to the warmth and humidity the apartment always had before the girls turned on their window unit air conditioners. Alex knew he was gone.

Breathing easier, she quickly descended the staircase to find her roommate overjoyed to see her.

"My God, did you find anything?" Stephanie asked in a breathless tone that still showed signs of her sobbing.

"Yep." Alex smiled at her roommate and went directly to the downstairs bathroom. Inside, she kept talking. "It wasn't who I thought it was, Steph. God, if it had been her, I would have been changing my underwear and my pants. I've had to pee ever since I went up there."

"Well, what was it then?"

"It was a man."

"A man?"

"Yes, a man. A man in the same shape as the girls. But this time the thing pointed."

"Alex, that means…"

"Yes, dear. A definite sign he wanted to communicate."

"Communicate what?" Stephanie blurted without thinking.

"Of that, I'm not sure, Steph. He pointed toward Mrs. Frank's house. Upwards, like toward the attic."

"That means…that sounds like he was trying to warn you, Alex."

"Yes, warn me. Warn me against whatever is in that attic. And I know exactly what's in that attic." Alex emerged from the bathroom, straightening her clothes. "Now, there's no doubt about it," she continued. "We've got to talk to Mrs. Frank about her house again. If she doesn't know anything, then we're going to have to see if she can show us anything that would shed some light on the house's past. Like an old newspaper article her husband's family might have saved, or something like that. I think the key to our problem is right there in that house." Alex put her hands on her hips and looked around the living room. Then, she turned and went upstairs to take a nap. Not to be left alone downstairs, Stephanie followed.

Basically, Alex was right. The key to their problems was the old house, one of the oldest in the Heights. But it was only one key; there were others. No real solution was to be found in the house; no real answer except that the danger posed by the problem was coming nearer all the time.

Chapter Eight

That night over Mexican food, Alex and Stephanie entertained Mrs. Frank with stories about their school experiences before they began the questioning which was the real reason for the evening. The old lady enjoyed herself, rejoining the two girls with tales of her own two sons in their school days. Alex thought that Mrs. Frank seemed to be wide open, a good time to find out necessary details about the house. So, after ordering dessert, Alex changed the subject.

"Mrs. Frank, I know you've mentioned something along these lines before," she said, stopping a moment to think. "But when did you say your husband Leo's family acquired your house?'

The old lady looked up, a bit startled, and thought a minute. "Leo's family bought the house in 1905, I believe. I still have the bill of sale somewhere, I think. Why do you ask that, Honey?"

"Oh, I was just curious." Alex sat back in her chair and smiled. "We've got a book about interesting old architecture for our humanities seminar and that got me to thinking about your house. It certainly is interesting." Alex had not lied. One of her texts had fired her interest in the old house, especially when she had found a reference to old buildings always having secrets. And Mrs. Frank's house certainly did.

"Well, the Franks had the house years before either Leo or I were born," Mrs. Frank glanced at Alex and then at Stephanie. "They bought it from a man named Diehls who had built it in 1895. His children were all gone. I understand he and his wife wanted to move to a smaller place. My Leo mentioned once where they went but I don't remember that."

"Mrs. Frank, do you remember your husband mentioning anything unusual about the house, like storm damage, or an explosion, or anything like that?" Now, Alex leaned forward across the table.

"Oh no, Honey. I don't remember anything like that." The old lady screwed up her face in perplexity. "I don't recall Leo saying anything along those lines. The Diehls were interested in a smaller place. That's why they moved. And as far as I know, nothing ever happened to the Franks in the house."

"What was the name of Leo's relatives who first moved into the house." Alex moved a bit farther across the table.

"Let me see." Mrs. Frank put her hand to her chin in thought. "Eldon...Eldon Frank and his wife, and their children. Eldon was Leo's uncle, since Leo's father was his youngest brother. They still lived here after Leo was born and later."

"I see." Alex thought a moment and then smiled. "You mentioned children. What children did they have?"

"Two boys and a girl. The girl was the youngest. She used to baby-sit Leo when he was a baby. He used to talk about her a lot. A pretty, blonde girl."

A vision of light hair on the garage roof flashed through Alex's mind.

"...All the young men were interested in her," the old lady continued.

"Uh, what happened to her, Mrs. Frank?" Now Alex glanced at Stephanie.

"Oh, she died of pneumonia when she was seventy-two years old. Leo and I went to her funeral." Mrs. Frank shook her head slightly. "You know, that man cried over her like she was his own sister. I never will forget that."

Alex smelled a dead end. Stephanie had excused herself to the rest room so Alex looked around the crowded restaurant. After a few minutes, she came back to the subject.

"Mrs. Frank, do you remember anything about the Diehls?"

"Not too much, Honey. I haven't thought about them in years."

"You mentioned they had children, too. Children who were gone when they sold the house."

"Yes." The old lady lowered her head in concentration. "I believe Leo said they had four children. There were originally two boys and two girls; one of the girls died when she was quite young. One of the boys moved to St. Louis as a young man and later became mayor of that city. I remember Leo telling me about that soon after we were married."

Alex was a bit flustered. Nothing that Mrs. Frank had said lent itself to violent death. And there was nothing so far about a dead little girl.

"Mrs. Frank, you mentioned one of the Diehls children was a girl who had died young. Do you remember how old she was?"

"Oh, goodness, Honey, not off hand. I understand she was pretty young, though. Teens, maybe early twenties. I sure don't remember."

Stephanie suddenly returned to the table and smiled at her roommate. "Well, have you learned all about Mrs. Frank's interesting example of late Victorian architecture?" she asked.

"Oh, boy. I got so wound up about the tenants, I completely forgot about the architecture." Alex smiled sheepishly at Mrs. Frank. "It just seems that houses like that always have many stories to tell. You want to know them all."

"Oh Lord, Honey. As long as I've lived in that house, I've never heard much of anything about any stories." Mrs. Frank chuckled and the two girls laughed. "Nothing dramatic has ever happened there as far as I know. But I think that's fortunate, isn't it?"

Alex smiled wide and sat back in her chair. "Oh yes, Mrs. Frank. Disasters and emergencies do disrupt the quiet of daily life." *Damn it,* she thought. *Nothing. She's told me absolutely nothing.*

"Well, Mrs. Frank, I guess your house has led a fortunate existence," she commented, finishing off her glass of iced tea.

"I believe you're right, Honey." Mrs. Frank chuckled again. "As far as I know, nobody has even died in that house. My Leo passed away in the hospital."

"You know, we never did find out where that little girl belonged," Stephanie interrupted before Alex could reply to Mrs. Frank's statement. "We still see her from time to time."

"Oh, you do?" Now Mrs. Frank seemed concerned. "I don't have any idea where she belongs. I remember you said something about her around Easter."

"Yes. And she popped up just the other day." Stephanie glanced over at Alex, who eyed her suspiciously.

"My stars. Still?" Mrs. Frank shook her head again. "I just can't believe some parents would let a little thing like that run wild."

"Some just don't seem to care, Mrs. Frank." Alex shook her head slightly at Stephanie to tell her to leave off the conversation.

After they had arrived home and Mrs. Frank had turned in for the night, Alex and Stephanie sat in their living room, an action film about Viet Nam blaring from the TV. Suddenly, Alex reached the TV control and turned the volume down.

"We didn't get a damned thing from her tonight," she said. "And I'm sure now that her house figures into our problems someway. It has to. It plays a big role."

"She sure didn't know much about it, did she?"

"No, she didn't." Alex clasped her hands in front of her mouth, her elbows on the chair arms. "There's a skeleton or two in a closet over there and we've got to find it."

"Well, what can we do now?" Stephanie asked in a worried tone.

"For one thing, I can go up to that attic again the next time Mrs. Frank isn't around."

"Oh, God, Alex. Don't go up there." Stephanie abruptly set both feet on the floor and sat up straight in alarm.

"It might be the only thing we can do." Alex, however, remained calm. "Tomorrow, Pauli comes back from Port Aransas. I think I'm going to meet him some place and tell him what's been going on in the meantime. He's been thinking about our situation and he might be able to shed some light on this since he handled that crap years ago."

"Can I come, too."

"Sure. You can even put in your two-cents worth." Alex slowly looked about the room and rose from the chair. "I'm going upstairs and read a while. You coming up or are you going to watch some tube?"

"I think I'll stay down here and see if I can find something on TV." Stephanie smiled up at her roommate. "I don't feel like going to bed right now."

Alex left her and went up to her bedroom. Although she wasn't sleepy, she really didn't feel like reading. She kept thinking about what Mrs. Frank had said about the Diehls and their children. Particularly, about the daughter who had died prematurely.

She and Mrs. Frank had been talking about this girl when Stephanie had interrupted them.

She put on her night clothes and lay down on top of the bed covers. *She never did say what the girl died of,* she thought. *I wonder.*

The thought came to her to check the attic window and she rose and swung her legs off the side of the bed to check it out. All windows, however, including that in the attic of Mrs. Frank's house, were dark. Coming up the driveway at a slow gait was Tom, back from prowling most likely. *Nothing is wrong in this world,* Alex thought.

Sighing, she drew the bedcovers back and got into bed. Now, she felt sleepy. She could hear the TV downstairs so she wondered if she should put Sabrina out and close her door. Stephanie, though not really a night owl, could stay up late if she found something to watch on TV. She decided to close the door to block out the little bit of noise and light from below.

Later, after dozing off for an hour, she was on her way to the bathroom when she realized the TV was no longer on and all the lights downstairs were turned off.

"Well, I guess she couldn't find anything on TV after all," she said to herself. Then, she heard it.

"Alex! Alex, help me! Oh God, help me!"

Momentarily, Alex froze in terror. Then, summoning the strength to move, she dashed out into the hall toward the stairs, turning on lights in the upstairs hall and landing as she went.

Bounding down the stairs, she immediately noticed her roommate pressed against the front wall in the corner by the big picture window. She looked frantically around the room and then switched on the living room light.

"Stephanie, what on earth happened?" She felt no change in temperature and there was no smell, but something was amiss. She could tell.

"I...I don't know." Stephanie remained against the wall,

one hand on her breast and the other on her stomach. "I was watching TV when all of a sudden, it went off. Then, the lights all went off."

Alex walked into the living room and turned toward the TV. "Well, it couldn't be a power-out and come back on this quick. She put her hands on her hips and turned again to her roommate.

She was about to say something else when she heard it, the distinct sound of childish footsteps running across the driveway away from the front door.

"That's our little friend, Steph." Alex slowly turned and walked toward the front door. "It looks like you were on tap for a little visit." When she reached the door, she put out her hand for the knob.

"For Christ's sake, Alex. Don't open the door!"

"Well, I think our little friend is gone for now, Stephi." She pulled the door open and looked out through the screen. There was nothing. She even walked outside and looked up and down the driveway but the little girl was gone.

Alex turned back toward the front door to find Stephanie, the look of terror still on her face, standing behind the screen.

"Alex…Alex, how did that hideous little thing do all that?"

"That, I don't know, Steph." She looked at her roommate's pitiful countenance and couldn't help feeling sorry for her. "She wanted to communicate with you, though. Like the other time, she had something to tell you."

"For God's sake," Stephanie cried. "I saw that bruise on your leg. That thing's horrible, Alex." Her chest heaved and Alex wondered if she was going to break out sobbing.

"Well, she's gone, now," Alex said, calmly locking the front door behind her. "Let's go to bed. Nothing's going to bother us now."

"How the hell do you know?" Stephanie folded both arms over her chest. "What if that thing comes to me while I'm in my bed?" Stephanie's voice rose almost to a screech.

"She won't, Stephanie." Alex enunciated each word, like she was talking to a child. "She's gone."

"Shit." A tear rolled down Stephanie's face. "Alex, oh Alex, what are we going to do?"

"We're going to go to bed and sleep." She sighed and turned again to her distraught roommate. "Look. If it will make you feel better, you can get the sleeping bag and sleep in my room on the floor."

"No. No. I'll sleep in my own room, but if anything happens, I'm going to scream like hell."

"Nothing's going to happen, Stephanie. And if it does, I'll be in there like a shot."

Alex looked deep into her roommate's still-worried face. "One thing I learned about these damned things years ago is that one episode at a time is about it."

"I hope you're right." Stephanie followed Alex up the stairs and both girls prepared for bed. When they were ready, they turned off the lights but Stephanie had a night light she kept on. Nothing disturbed them after they had both fallen asleep around ten PM.

About five o'clock the next morning, Alex was awakened by a fierce cry of a cat nearby. Although she couldn't clearly pin-point it, the noise sounded like it had come from the alley. Alex thought about Tom and wondered if he'd gotten into a fight. But after another sharp cry, all was silent. Alex turned to see Sabrina's head perked up.

"I'm worried that your boyfriend is having problems out there," she whispered to the sleepy cat, now settling down beside her.

She couldn't go back to sleep so, after checking on Stephanie, she went downstairs and made coffee. Since it would be a long time before Stephanie got up, she made more than usual, an extra two cups for her at least.

She loved the early morning in the apartment. Everything was quiet and the disturbances of the earlier hours seemed far away. She could sip coffee and watch the news on TV without any interference from anything. Stephanie was a late riser so on days when there was nothing doing, she had the apartment to herself. This morning was no exception.

But she still thought about Tom. The loud noise out back had stopped abruptly and not trailed off, as it would in a typical cat fight. The more she thought about it, the more she came to the reasoning that it might not even have been Tom. However, since he was the only tomcat in the neighborhood, as far as she knew, it stood to reason that the night shattering noise was his. *Oh well,* she thought. *I'll investigate later.*

Alex was settled on the couch with coffee and toast before the TV news when her sleepy roommate came down just before eight.

"God, I can't believe I slept so soundly," she said, yawning. "After last night. Henrietta didn't even wake me up like she usually does."

"Stuff for toast is out and there's some eggs in there." Alex motioned toward the kitchen.

"I've got to get some coffee, first." Stephanie ambled toward the kitchen. "What's on the weather?"

"More damned rain."

"So, what else is new?" After a minute or two, Stephanie appeared at the kitchen door, steaming coffee cup in her hand.

"You were right about last night," she said, taking a sip. "Nothing happened."

"Well, I chalk that up as typical, Steph." Alex glanced at the TV, distracted by a last minute news item. Then she turned again to her roommate. "I think I heard Tom in a fight early this morning. I've never heard such a caterwaul. It came from the alley, I think."

"Tom? That's typical. Tomcats fight all the time. They even fight when they mate."

"Isn't it kind of odd, though, Steph, that I just heard one cat? If he was mixing it up with another, wouldn't I have heard both cats?"

"Sure, I suppose so." Stephanie cocked her head. "You sure you just heard one?"

"Only one. And it was a hell of a racket."

"That's weird, Roomy."

"Yep." Alex took another sip of coffee and turned back to the TV. Stephanie settled into the easy chair across from her.

Alex was about to say something else when the phone rang.

She jumped up and grabbed the phone, thinking it was a call from her mother concerning her brother.

"Hello, Big Sister," a chirpy voice sang on the other end. "I was thinking about you when I got up and I thought I'd give you a call. I hope I didn't get anybody out of bed."

"Pauli? My God! What are you doing home? You weren't supposed to be back until this afternoon."

"I got back last night. Terry had to get back. He starts a new job today."

Alex was ecstatic. "I'm so glad you're back."

"Yeah. Papa's already started bugging me about what I'm going to do for the summer. He asked me point blank last night before I'd even settled in if I had any prospects."

"Prospects?"

"Yeah. For work, I suppose." Paul paused a bit and then changed the subject. "Hey, Sis, is the Galveston trip still on? I've been looking forward to that for a long time."

"Yes. This coming weekend."

"Absolutely great. Did you talk to Josh?"

"Not yet. I'll probably call him this afternoon."

"He might not be there. I seem to remember him telling me something about baseball tryouts before I left."

"Well, if he's not there, I'll call later." Alex paused a moment to collect her thoughts. "Pauli, I want to meet with you about something of great importance. Since you left, some things have been happening. In fact, things seem to have escalated somewhat."

"Oh? Things like what you told me about before I left?"

"Yes. I want to meet you for lunch so we can talk privately. Maybe tomorrow…"

"I can meet you today, Sis," Paul interrupted. "I told Mr. Bigelow I'd come over and see if he needed another loader on his docks this summer. So I can probably meet you somewhere for lunch."

"Fantastic. Let's try to meet somewhere between us."

"How about Smokey Joe's on Forty-Five over near old Gulfgate? That's almost halfway between you and me."

"Smokey Joe's? Great. Stephanie wants to come too, and put in her two-cents worth." Now Alex was excited. "We'll be there about eleven, before everyone else gets there. I want it kind of quiet."

"Right. I'll be there."

After Alex hung up the phone, she turned to Stephanie, who had just poured a second cup of coffee.

"That was my little brother. We're to meet him at eleven at Smokey Joe's"

"Paul? He's back already?"

"Got back last night." Alex picked up her coffee and took it to the kitchen. "I'll shower first while you finish your coffee and breakfast," she said, leaving the kitchen and heading for the stairs.

"Okay. Don't use all the hot water."

While in the shower, Alex thought about what she was going to tell her brother. She'd told him about the little girl and even about the other thing, but now she wanted his input about the communication idea. She had turned off the water and was reaching for a towel when the light flickered and went out.

She froze. Was this just the light or was something in the bathroom with her? She turned and backed away from the shower door, pressing herself against the opposite wall. Her question was answered quickly with the appearance of the unmistakable smell, the odor of death she had experienced so many times before.

"Oh, Jesus," she whispered to herself. "Something's in here with me." She stared at the door, trying to see through the frosted glass with the little light from the small bathroom window. She could see nothing. Then, just as suddenly as it had gone off, the light came back on. And the smell vanished.

Knowing it was safe to get out of the shower, Alex opened the door and grabbed a towel. Immediately, she began to dry off and look around the bathroom. When she got to the mirror across from the shower, she froze in terror. There, etched in the steam film on the glass was the word, *Alexandra.*

She felt sick. Her stomach heaved and she knew she was going to throw up. In an effort to take control of herself, she pressed both hands to her stomach and bent over. A tear rolled down her face. "What the hell's going on now," she whispered.

Taking the towel she had dried off with, she wiped her name off the mirror and began getting dressed. She decided not to tell Stephanie about this latest episode but she would tell her brother about it later that morning. Stephanie would be safe taking her shower but she would be close by if something happened. Her roommate didn't need anything else to upset her after last night. And, of course, she could find out later with Paul, what had happened to her that morning in the bathroom. For the remainder of the morning, Alex was watchful, knowing that whatever had been in the bathroom was close by.

At ten minutes after eleven, Alex and Stephanie settled into a booth off by itself at Smokey Joe's Barbecue, a "Ma and Pa" owned restaurant just off Highway Forty-Five. After ordering tea, Alex turned to her roommate. "Pauli's late as usual. If he's not here in the next ten minutes, I'll order for him." However, before their drinks came, Paul Zunker was there.

He greeted his sister and then Stephanie and settled in the booth across from the girls.

"Mr. Bigelow's going to give me a job," he said, turning to scan the menu on the wall. "But not for another two weeks."

They exchanged small talk for a few minutes but Alex wanted to get to the subject at hand.

"Pauli, I'll get right to the point." Alex crossed her arms in front of her. "Some things have been happening, even in the last twenty-four hours, that have been downright frightening."

"Oh?" Paul turned to his sister, his face, eyebrows raised, showed genuine concern. "Is this more of the same stuff you told me about before?"

"Yes and no." Alex leaned forward and put her elbows on the table. "The little girl appeared again. To me. This time she grabbed me on the leg. I believe this was an effort of hers to communicate something but we really can't pinpoint what. Last night she was going to visit Stephanie, but Stephi grew alarmed and I think I broke that affair up." Alex paused and took a deep breath. Then she glanced at her roommate. "Stephi's really come unglued over all this and I really can't blame her. This crap's new to her and even I still have trouble believing some of it."

"Even after that stuff years ago?" Paul leaned back when a server arrived with the iced tea and then took their lunch orders. When she left, Paul leaned forward again. "You say the little girl was trying to communicate with you? You don't have any idea what she wants?"

"Yes, Pauli, I do." Alex stared directly into her brother's face. "I think she was trying to warn me against the other one. I told you about her right before you left."

"Yes, I remember." Paul took a drink of iced tea and glanced at Stephanie. "Roomy, have you seen this other playmate?" he asked, half-jokingly.

"No, thank God!" Stephanie's face turned dark. "Paul, that little girl makes my skin crawl. This other one means real harm. I firmly believe what Alex says about the communication thing, though."

Now Paul turned back to his sister. "Sis, have you given any more thought to a trigger. You'll recall things like this don't happen unless there's a trigger."

"Pauli, I've thought and thought about that. But there is nothing, absolutely nothing like that, that I can see. They seem to vanish into thin air. They come and go randomly and the only hint of their motivation is the communication thing. Except for the malice and pure hatred I feel from that one thing. And it scares the shit out of me, I don't mind telling you."

"Alex saw a man, too," Stephanie chimed in. "He seemed to be doing the same thing as the little girl, but this time he pointed."

"Pointed?" Paul cast quizzical looks at both Stephanie and his sister.

"Yes, pointed." Stephanie continued. "At Mrs. Frank's house."

"Pauli, here's a capper for you." Alex glanced at both her brother and roommate to see both had their eyes fixed on her. "I was taking a shower this morning when I felt the usual coldness come over me. The light went off just like it did last night. I felt something come into the bathroom and abruptly leave while I was still in the shower stall. The hideous smell was there, too."

Stephanie's hand came to her mouth and her eyes became saucers.

"When I left the shower stall," Alex continued, "I found, written in the mist on the mirror, my name, *Alexandra.*

Stephanie gasped and Paul grew fully alert, but Alex continued. "Don't ask me what that means because I do not know. As terrifying as it seems, I don't think I'm in any real danger. Yet." Alex paused and took a sip of tea. "There's only one of these things that intends me any real harm as far as I know and I am fully alert for her. And like I said earlier, right now I'm pretty convinced the others are warning me of her."

"Sis, that seems pretty strong stuff. *Alexandra?*"

"Well, Pauli, we've been attacked before. You and I both." Alex smiled at Paul and then at Stephanie, who was still speechless. "I'm pretty sure I can fend for myself."

"Alex, how do you…how do you fight off something like that?" Stephanie's voice cracked with emotion.

"By going about our business and acting like nothing happened, Steph." Alex spoke slowly and softly. "And when they come around, you avoid them if you can."

A silence followed while each of the young people at the table thought about what Alex had said. Alex was afraid Stephanie was going to cry and she didn't know what her brother was thinking. She wished she had more answers but these could only be provided by the manifestations themselves. *Oh God,* she prayed. *Poor Stephanie. Please help her to understand.*

"Alex," Paul suddenly interjected. "If anything else happens, anything! I want you to call me."

"I will, Pauli." Alex turned to her roommate again and smiled. "In the meantime, I'll be looking out for myself and my good buddy here."

"Yes," Stephanie choked.

"She got kind of unnerved by the little girl."

"She scared the piss out of me." Stephanie combined a sob and a chuckle.

The remainder of the lunch was spent in small talk until the trio parted at one o'clock, Alex and Stephanie returning to their apartment and Paul to his parent's house.

Later, at home, Alex couldn't get the early morning scream of a cat out of her mind.

"Did you see Tom when we drove off this morning?" she asked Stephanie as they settled down to work on a humanities assignment for which they had the week off. "I didn't see him when we came back."

"No, as a matter of fact, I didn't." Stephanie shot her

roommate a quizzical look. “I saw him eating yesterday.”

Alex suddenly rose and laid a book on the table. Then she headed for the front door. “I’m going to see if he’s under the steps,” she said, heading out the door.

She found no trace of the tomcat anywhere around Mrs. Frank’s back steps. *Odd,* she thought. *He’s usually asleep this time of day. Maybe Mrs. Frank ran him off.* However, Alex knew this was not the case.

“He’s not anywhere around here,” she told Stephanie, who stood just outside the apartment door.

Then, Alex headed for the alley, followed by her roommate some distance behind. They hadn’t gone far past their apartment when they found the scattered remains of a black and white cat. The animal had been torn apart and its pieces scattered over a fifteen foot area.

“Oh, my God,” Alex choked. She bowed her head and stifled a sob. “What in the name of…” But she knew what had happened.

“Jesus Christ. What happened?” an elevated voice next to her asked.

“It’s Tom. What’s left of him.”

“Did a dog…”

“No, Stephanie. A dog didn’t do this. What kind of dog would do this? A Great Dane? A Doberman? A German Shepherd? A goddamn Pit Bull? No dog could do something like this.” Tears began rolling down Alex’s cheeks.

“Tom,” Stephanie sobbed beside her.

“That damned thing was in the bathroom with me this morning.”

“The…The little…”

“No, goddamn it, the other one! The one that’s vicious as hell.” Alex, breathing heavily, could not take her eyes off the remains. “And it did this earlier this morning.” She closed her eyes and sobbed. Then she turned to her roommate who now was crying audibly. “Come on,” she said gently. “Let’s bury him. We’ll put him in the garden.” She sniffed heavily and then, putting her arm around Stephanie, led her around the apartment to the garage.

Together, they dug a hole in Mrs. Frank’s backyard garden

where plants were scarce and, gathering the remains in a towel, buried them. When they had finished, they put a flat stepping stone over the place. Then, they returned to the apartment, Stephanie still quietly sobbing and Alex visibly upset.

"The little girl must know what that goddamned thing is capable of," Alex said, crossing her arms over her chest and sitting down on the bottom step. Alex sniffed again. "She's been trying desperately to communicate with us."

"Alex…Alex, what are you saying?" Stephanie turned a red, tear stained face downward toward her roommate.

"I saw that thing the other morning," Alex continued in an even voice. "It's hideous. And grotesquely strong. And it can go anywhere and do anything it wants. And it's just shown us a sample of what it's capable of. I expected something like this. Unfortunately, it had to involve a poor old cat, a furry clown that only wanted a little human love." A sob rose once again in Alex's throat.

"Alex…Alex," Stephanie said in a low tone. "Which of our cats is next? And if not them, which one of us?"

Alex stood up rapidly and turned to her roommate. "None of us, Stephi," she said, emphatically. "We're going to proceed as planned. We're going to watch out for that goddamned thing and, if possible, try to communicate with the little girl." Alex paused a moment. "And, if he's still around, maybe the man."

"The man. I'd forgotten about him until I remembered him today at lunch."

"Yeah, the man. He just may be our best bet."

Chapter Nine

Three watchful days passed, but nothing out of the ordinary occurred. On Friday morning, Alex lay in bed, staring at the ceiling.

She had had a nightmare where a frightful surf had engulfed a series of piers and seaside buildings. The towering water had smashed everything and when it withdrew, there was nothing but barren beach and dunes as far as the eye could see. When she awoke, she had wondered what the dream meant but had remembered similar dreams in the immediate past. She was ready to discard it as maybe something spawned by her approaching beach trip when Stephanie appeared at the door.

"Are you awake?" she asked. "Josh called. He's on his way."

Alex turned a sleepy face toward the doorway. "Great. He might even be on time for a change." She rose and threw both legs off the bed. "Did you watch the weather this morning?"

"Yes. Sunshine and partly clouds. No rain. Can you believe it?"

"No, I can't." Alex shook her head and blew hair away from her face. "I thought we'd get rained on at least part of the way down there."

"Nope. Partly cloudy for the whole area."

Alex began getting her clothes together for the whole day while Stephanie cooked breakfast. She couldn't get the previous night's dream out of her mind. Since she was going to the seashore, she'd automatically thought that this had inspired such a dream. But if it had, wouldn't it have been more pleasant? And what about the others? Like those others, this dream had been grossly disturbing.

After breakfast, the girls were loading Stephanie's car when Josh Hamilton drove up. Josh, always with a smile on his face, stood six feet four and weighed well over two hundred pounds. A football and baseball player, he had a tremendous good nature. However, Alex figured he'd have the usual complaints about his mother and his future plans.

"You want to ride up front with Alex and me or sit in the back with your lonesome?" Stephanie addressed Josh as he walked up. She was in high spirits for the first time in several days. Enough time had passed so that her worries were seemingly over. Alex knew better, however.

"I'll sit up front with you girls 'til we pick up Boy Wonder." Josh placed an overnight bag and a backpack in the back end.

"There's some eggs in the kitchen if you want some breakfast." Stephanie pointed toward the apartment. Then she turned to her roommate. "Boy, you seem down in the dumps. What's wrong?"

"Oh, just another bad dream." Alex turned toward Josh and smiled at him. "Now that my knight in shining armor is here, I guess I should be glad."

"Yeah," Stephanie replied. "And you better call the other one and make sure he's ready."

"Definitely. There's nothing like getting there and finding him still in bed."

"Oh, Paul's ready," Josh piped up. "He should be ready to go. He told me on the phone last night he was going to set his alarm for school time." He turned to Stephanie and winked. "He said for you to be ready for him."

"Oh, he did, did he?" Stephanie laughed. "What's that supposed to mean?"

Thirty minutes later they were on their way to Highway Forty-Five, the Gulf Freeway, the road to Galveston. Since Paul was close by, they would swing by the Zunker house and pick him up. Then, they expected to be in Galveston in less than an hour.

When he piled in the car twenty minutes later, Paul was in high spirits. He joked with Josh and Alex and then sat himself in the front seat next to Stephanie. As a matter of fact, Paul seemed so elated, Alex wondered if he had forgotten the interview just three days before.

Paul turned toward the back seat. "I've got a coupon from Wendy's." He laughed and waved a piece of paper around over his head. "First gal to strip down gets it."

"Oh, wow," Stephanie chuckled as she pulled out on Highway Forty-Five access road. "Free hamburgers by the sea and all you have to do is go naked."

"Steph, I've got two of them." Paul laughed again. "You get two of them if you do it."

"Make that dinner for all four of us at Guido's and I'll do it." Alex smiled in the back seat.

"How about that, Josh?" Paul turned from Stephanie to Alex and then back again. "Your lady's compromising us."

"Pauli has such high hopes for things that are so improbable." At that the four of them roared.

Galveston lies on an island at the end of the Gulf Freeway. The city is old, one of the oldest in Texas, but it has grown considerably in the last forty years, stretching out east to west for miles along Galveston Island.

Alex had made reservations at a hotel along the seawall, the boys in one unit, the girls next door. She had spent a little more and gotten a splendid view for both units of the Gulf of Mexico across Seawall Boulevard.

After they crossed a high bridge and entered Galveston, Alex told Stephanie to turn on Sixty-First Street and head for Seawall Boulevard. Then they would be at the beach.

"Boy, it's good to get back to the coast again after only a few days." Paul said, turning around in the front seat and laughing.

"Yeah. You went to Port Aransas." Josh leaned back in the back seat and put his hands on his knee. "I've been trying to get a baseball tryout but not having much luck."

"Your Mom know about that, Josh?" Alex turned in the seat toward him.

"No, but my Dad does, though. He thinks it's great. Yes, my English-Scottish father is all for my sports aspirations, but my German-Czech mother is totally against them. She wants me to go to medical school. She thinks ball players are bums."

"Maybe you could do both," Paul suggested from the front seat.

"She doesn't see it that way."

At that point they had reached the beach and the blue-green

Gulf of Mexico stretched out in front of them. In the backseat, Alex felt a twinge of recognition as they turned on Seawall Boulevard. Everyone else perked up.

"All right, Paul. Heads up," Josh rang out. "Bathing beauties to the right."

"'Kinis' galore, Josh." Paul's head swiveled to and fro from the sidewalk along the seawall to Josh.

"And maybe a few topless, too." Josh laughed.

"You two clowns, I guess, are too dumb to know that's against the law." Stephanie smirked, and turned her head once or twice in Paul's direction but she had to concentrate on Seawall traffic.

Alex, however, was hearing none of it. Her instance of recognition had turned into a feeling of horror so overpowering she felt like she was going to pass out. She kept her face pointed out the window but pressed her hands to her stomach and chest.

"That's all right, Steph," Josh rejoined from the back seat. "Paul and I are going to find a few violators."

"Look real hard, Josh." Stephanie guffawed. She turned her head quickly toward the back seat as far as it would go and then back again. "I'll give you fifty dollars for every bare boob you see, Josh Hamilton."

Paul roared at this. "All right, Josh. With that fifty bucks, maybe we would get Stephi to buy us some beer."

"Bullshit, gents!" Stephanie, working on a piece of gum, intentionally smacked it at Paul. "No hooch for the kiddies. Besides, Alex and I are going to do a little watching of our own. We're going to eyeball hunks. Isn't that right, Roomy?" Stephanie turned quickly to Alex and then back again.

Alex, hearing her roommate, somewhat recovered and turned her gaze back into the car.

"Yes…Yes, that's right." She was breathing deeply but trying to act normal. "Keep an eye out for the Comfort Inn, Stephi." She managed a small smile.

"These two yahoos are already starting to badger me about getting beer for them."

Stephanie suddenly smacked her gum again.

"Oh, they're just blowing smoke, Stephi." Now, Alex felt better.

"Blowing smoke is right." Stephanie chomped her gum and turned to Paul and smiled. "They might have just graduated but they're still right back in high school. What d'ya say, boys, about tenth grade?"

"Hey, that's cruel, Steph," Paul snickered. "We're just trying to fit in with you college types. You know. Party hardy all the time."

Josh laughed in the back seat along with Stephanie who had just driven up to the Comfort Inn. She turned into the office driveway, stopped , and she and Alex went in to register.

Their rooms were on the sixth floor with the prescribed view of the Gulf across the street. They were delighted to find each room had a small balcony.

They had agreed after checking in, each person was responsible for his own luggage, such as it was. The girls quickly placed their stuff in their room and went directly out on the balcony to sit. After fifteen minutes, they came back into the room to put their clothes away and prepared to go to the beach.

Alex was still bothered by the episode earlier. She remembered with horror how these things could follow her anywhere. She could not leave them in Houston. At least the dreams would follow her. And now this other thing. Of course, she realized, that even down here, everything could still be connected.

After they came back into the room, Alex lay down on the bed for a moment while Stephanie headed for the bathroom.

On the bed, she felt sleepy, but focused her attention on a full- length mirror at the foot of her bed. But suddenly, it wasn't a mirror at all, but a window looking out on a deserted beach. In the distance was a large pier with a building on it that looked curiously like a castle. Fascinated, Alex started to rise from the bed but her concentration was broken by a sharp scream from the bathroom.

What now? She thought. Then it came to her. *On no, not greasy butt. Pauli.*

Stephanie appeared at the bathroom door, fuming, holding her clothes up with one hand.

"Your damned little brother needs to go back and repeat the second grade," she barked at Alex, now off the bed.

"Oh Stephanie, I warned you about Pauli's practical jokes."

"Some practical joke. I peed on the floor. I peed on my clothes." Stephanie's face glowed with anger. "He greased up the whole goddamned seat."

"I'm sorry, Stephi. We should have locked the door when we went out on the balcony." Ordinarily, Alex might have found the scene comical but she was in no mood to laugh. She thought a moment about what to do and then picked up the phone.

Josh answered next door, caught off guard.

"Uh…Uh," he stammered. "Paul wanted to grease down the toilet. I…uh…started to talk him out of it…"

"Uh…Uh…Uh…! Yeah, right! Josh, put Pauli on."

"Hello, Sis," a giggly voice on the other end said.

"Okay, Pauli. Let's have the Vaseline."

"What?"

"You heard me. Stephanie here is very pissed. She's coming next door to kick your ass." She could hear the two of them talking on the other end.

Stephanie, who had cleaned herself up and hurriedly changed clothes, appeared just behind Alex.

"Let me talk to that twerp," she hissed.

"Okay, boys, here she is." Now Alex laughed.

"Paul Zunker, your ass now belongs to me!"

There were paroxysms of laughter on the other end.

"I'm coming over there." Stephanie put the phone down and turned toward the door. Alex placated her, momentarily, before she moved any more.

"Wait a minute," she said. "We'll get back at them some way. I'll think of something and it's going to be worse than a greasy rear end."

Stephanie sighed, turned, and sat on the bed. Alex sat on hers across from her.

"I don't think there's going to be anymore of this crap this trip," she said. "I knew Pauli would pull something but I never dreamed it would be the grease. He hasn't done that since he was a kid."

"Alex, from the looks of things, he's still just that. A kid!" Stephanie sighed again and then clasped her hands around her knee. "Jesus Christ, Alex. They're middle school turds. They might have just graduated from high school, but emotionally they're in about the sixth grade.

"Oh, Stephi, I agree." Alex smiled. "But let's hope this is the end of it. Otherwise, they're going to be high and dry. For instance, you and I enjoying a beer and them with none." She winked and then smiled again.

"Oh, my God, Alex, you're a genius. I didn't even think of that. They've already started badgering me about that."

Stephanie, giggling, got up to finish putting her stuff away and Alex turned and lay back down on her bed. The mirror across the room was now just that, a mirror. Now she wondered if she really saw what she saw. What would have appeared if Stephanie hadn't broken things up with her scream? She hadn't imagined her feelings earlier and partly, deep down, they were still with her. She decided she would tell Stephanie about her apprehensions.

She turned and rose from the bed, but before she could speak, there was a knock at the door.

"Now, who's that knocking at my door?" Stephanie sang, loud enough to be heard outside. "Someone who needs his ass kicked, I bet." She marched to the door and flung it wide open.

Standing at the door were Paul and Josh, wearing bathing trunks with beach towels thrown over their shoulders.

"We're going to the beach," Paul announced in a timid voice. "Would you two ladies like to join us?" Paul seemed a bit subdued but Josh grinned.

"Not with you two creeps." Stephanie put her hands on her hips and squared herself in front of both boys. "Alex and I are going down to that little grocery down the block and get a little beer. Then we're going to have one and then go to the pool downstairs. But since you two teenyboppers seem to have never got out of the eighth grade, you will not be joining us."

"Oh, Stephi, can't you take a joke?" Paul seemed genuinely repentant.

"Oh, sure, I can take a joke. But for now, I've got enough of the grease off my ass so you can kiss it."

"Paul, I think you screwed up, buddy," Josh said, now serious. "I think she's really pissed.

"Damn right!" Stephanie exclaimed.

Alex appeared at the door next to Stephanie. “Pauli, let’s drop the teenybopper bullshit, okay?” She looked down at her brother and frowned. “I want to have a good time down here and so does Stephanie.”

“All right, ladies. I’m sorry for the prank.” Paul seemed genuinely contrite. “The opportunity was there and, I guess, I just couldn’t resist.”

“Paul just can’t turn down a chance for a joke,” Josh said, in an apologetic manner,.

“Turn down a chance for a joke?” Alex’s voice rose in emotion. “Josh, I’ll have you know that Stephanie has no boyfriend, would probably go out with him if he was to ask her, but he chooses to act like a middle school shithead when he does get a chance to be around her.”

“God, Sis, I said I was sorry.” Now, Paul sounded like a scolded child.

“No more!”

“All right, already.”

For the rest of the day, they went swimming in the surf, but the girls soon got out, cleaned up and went shopping while the boys stayed in. Alex did not think about what had occurred earlier, before Paul’s prank. She kept it, however, in the back of her mind, knowing full well that neither manifestation was a figment of her imagination.

After supper at a restaurant down Seawall Boulevard, they found a pool table in a game room at a nearby hotel and played until ten o’clock that night. Then they listened to music from a club on the beach until half past eleven. Only close to midnight did they return to their rooms. Very shortly they retired, Alex wondering if anything waited in her sleep. She could handle bad dreams, but Galveston had shown more than bad dreams already. Hence, she went to sleep with a sense of dread.

A sound sleep, though, was that night’s offering. Stephanie nudged her awake at nine o’clock, announcing she wanted a morning swim in the surf.

“All right,” Alex said, sleepily. “Call the guys and tell them we want a morning swim.”

“Right.” Stephanie, dressed only in underwear, headed for the phone. “There’s coffee and a doughnut from downstairs over on the table," she said.

Stephanie, who had to be dragged out of bed on school days, was always the first one up on holidays. Her good mood made Alex wonder if now would be a good time to tell her what had happened the previous day. She decided not to.

"They're up and ready to go," she said, hanging up the phone.

In the meantime, Alex had risen and was drinking the coffee left on the table. "Well, are you going to put your suit on or are you going to go over there in your skivvies?" she said, managing a smile in a sleepy face.

"Oh, they'd both love that, I'm sure." Stephanie put her hands on her hips and turned toward the window. "Better still, I won't wear anything at all. How about that?"

"That would get a standing ovation from those two, to say the least."

"Oh, Roomy, I wanted to tell you," Stephanie suddenly turned serious. "I had a dream about this place last night."

"Oh?"

"I guess it was this place. There was this beach with a bunch of kids on it."

"Oh, yeah?" Now dread came in waves.

"There was the water coming in and these kids were playing in the sand. I started to walk over and see what they were doing but then I woke up."

Oh, dear God, I know exactly what they were doing, Alex thought. *I had the same goddamned dream.*

"What do you suppose that means, Roomy?"

"I don't know, Stephanie," Alex answered, fixing the horrid nightmare she had in her mind. But then, Alex needed to pull away from it. "What woke you up, anyway?"

"The people over here coming in last night." She motioned toward the unit next door. "It was after two o'clock. They sounded drunk. God, do the bars around here stay open past two AM?"

"I wouldn't know." Alex looked away toward the mirror opposite her bed. "I didn't hear them come in, though. I slept like a log. One thing about this place is that it's very conducive to sleep."

It suddenly occurred to Alex to tell Stephanie about her dream, but she decided to wait and see if anything else happened to either one of them. After all, it could spoil the trip.

There was a knock at the door and Stephanie yelled. "Wait a minute. We're putting our suits on."

Quickly the girls changed, put on beach tops and then met the boys outside to go to the beach.

They stayed on the beach until eleven o'clock when Alex's observation about too much sun brought the four back up to the rooms. Alex and Stephanie were deep in conversation when they reached their door.

"Yes, I saw that little whore down there," Stephanie giggled. "If I had gone out wearing something like that at her age, my dad would have seen to it that I wouldn't have lived to reach ninth grade."

"Boy, who do you suppose she was trying to impress?" Alex snorted, and turned to the boys.

"Whom are you talking about, Sister Dear?"

"You know good and well whom I'm talking about. I saw you down there ogling her. You looked like Kermit the Frog."

Josh roared with laughter while Paul grinned again, this time sheepishly.

"I don't go in for tweeners, Sissy Dearest," he said. "Maybe Josh does, but I don't."

"Watch what you say, soccer man." Josh edged up next to Paul.

"Naw. She's just about your little brother's speed, roomy." Stephanie smirked at Paul.

"No. Nasty little bitches are a bit much for him, Steph." Alex laughed. "He needs to stick to greasing up the potty in the first grade girls' room."

All but Paul roared.

Josh, however, put his hand on Paul's shoulder. "Hey, I got an idea. Let's go down to the Strand and look in a few of those neat shops. Then we can get something to eat down there."

"That's a good idea, Joshua," Alex said. "We'll meet you out here in about thirty minutes."

After the girls took quick showers and changed their clothes, they settled in the room for a few minutes before they met the boys.

Again, Alex wanted to talk to Stephanie about her dream and tell her about the one she had which was like it; indeed, she wanted to tell her about yesterday's events, but something held her back. Nervously she checked the mirror but everything was the same. What bothered her most now was that the events of the last few months seemed to have followed her to Galveston. And from what Stephanie had said about her dream, they were affecting her, too.

Finally, Alex made up her mind.

"You know, Stephi, I had a dream much like yours back at the apartment a while back," she said in a matter-of-fact way. She looked deep into Stephanie's wide-open blue eyes. Then she continued. "There were kids in it, too. They were digging on a beach. They were either digging up a corpse or burying one and they were all dead."

"Oh, Jesus Christ, Alex..."

"Yes. That was one of my nightmares." Alex breathed deeply.

Stephanie leaned toward Alex. "You mean if it hadn't been for those drunks next door, that's what I would have seen?"

"Probably so, yes."

"I don't...Why?"

"Because the dreams are part of what's going on back at the apartment, Stephi. One thing I learned about this crap years ago was that you can't run away from it." Alex again looked toward the mirror. "Any more dreams or even monkey business, I need to know about it."

"Jesus, you can't even get away from that crap down here," Stephanie whined.

"No, we can't. But like I've told you, we need to try to ignore it as much as we can. If it's not anything other than dreams, we're okay." She grinned at her roommate. "What's a nightmare or two as long as you wake up?"

To this Stephanie said nothing. She just stared at the floor and fidgeted with her hands.

Alex went on. "Besides, you seem to have an advantage. You have potted folks next door to come in and interrupt them." Her solace, it seemed, had no effect on her roommate, however.

Stephanie just looked up at her, a concerned frown on her face. Finally, Alex, who was ready to go, rose and quietly walked out the door. At the end of the hall was a window looking out on the heart of Galveston. As Alex stood and looked out on the panorama of the city, the sense of dread returned. Only this time it ripened into a full sense of horror, the horror of something lying in wait.

Chapter Ten

Alex returned to her room in time to meet the boys at her door. Together they collected Stephanie and set off for downtown Galveston.

It occurred to her to continue her conversation with Stephanie but, given the boys' jocular mood, she decided against it. In the meantime, she would smile and try to act as normal as she could. After all, she had to set an example for her roommate whose sudden turn to seriousness would surely be noticed by the boys.

In the car, however, the friendly badinage stopped, momentarily, when Josh announced he was thirsty.

"We can stop at an ice house on the way to town," Paul said. "There's surely some place, a gas station or something, where you can get a soft drink."

They found an ice house on Broadway, a long thoroughfare that essentially bisected the island. A wide, divided street, it provided the best way to get from one end of the city to the other.

Stephanie pulled up in front and all piled out of the car, but Alex was stopped suddenly by something that appeared in her peripheral vision. She turned full to her left and confronted it.

Standing across the street, in the median of Broadway, was an edifice which had appeared in one of her recent nightmares. Only it wasn't a building at all, but a tall, over two-story monument, crowned by a standing figure that seemed to point north.

The terror returning, Alex stood and stared while the others filed into the little store.

"What in the name of God is this, now?" she asked under her breath. Slowly, she walked toward the structure, down the little parking lot and across the street.

The monument stood in the middle of an intersection, so she had to watch traffic coming from more than one direction. As if in a trance, however, she continued to the base of the structure.

When she reached the base, she studied the figure at the top. At the bottom were seated bronze figures on either side.

Why this thing? She thought. *Why did I dream about this thing? I've never even seen it, that I know of.*

The monument, commemorating the Texas Revolution, seemed harmless enough, but something about it threatened her. Slowly, she walked around to the opposite side, to the other seated bronze figure. Again, she looked up at the figure at the top. Was she seeing things or had it moved? From this new position, it seemed that the figure had shifted its body around toward her. She walked a few steps back and then looked again. Then, she stepped up very close to the structure.

When she did, the bottom figure lifted its head up and turned its face in her direction.

"Jesus Christ!" Alex exclaimed and stepped backward, stumbling and falling on her backside. Wild with terror, she rolled over and started to get to her feet to run when she felt two hands on her waist.

She screamed and tried to get out of the grasp when she heard Josh behind her.

"Alex…Alex…What's wrong? What the hell?"

She turned to look him straight in the face. Breathing in and out heavily, she pressed herself against him and put her arms around him.

"My God, Josh, that statue," she choked.

"Statue? This statue?" He turned toward the monument, Alex still in his arms.

"That statue." Alex, still with one arm around him, turned to the side toward the monument.

The seated statue at the base was in its original position. Seemingly, it had never moved at all.

"Josh, that figure at the bottom moved its head toward me." Alex swallowed hard and felt a tear roll down her cheek. "I swear to God it moved."

"Alex, that thing's made of metal, bronze or something.

How could it move?"

She stared at the figure at the base, now totally lifeless and immovable. Taking her arm away from Josh, she moved up to it.

The covered head looked slightly downward to its left, and the weathering and dust on the figure seemed to show that it couldn't possibly have moved or been moved.

"What's the matter with me?" Alex muttered to herself. Then she remembered the monument, which she had never seen before to her knowledge, had appeared to her in her dream. *But why?* she thought.

Josh stepped up behind her. "Are you all right?" he asked gently. "You were giving all this traffic a good show."

"Yes…Yes, Josh. I'm okay." She turned toward him. "I must have freaked out at this thing."

"This? This is the Texas Victory Monument, Alex. The figure at the top, they say, points toward the battlefield of San Jacinto."

Alex looked again at the figure at the top, terrified that it might make a move. Then, she leaned her head to Josh's chest.

"I'm going nuts, for God's sake," she said.

"Come on. We're ready to go." He put his arm around her shoulders and guided her around the structure and into the street. Running, they beat a red light across the street.

"I got you a Dr. Pepper. Is that okay? It's what you usually get when we're out."

"That's okay." She felt somewhat better in Josh's presence but something told her he had reached her just in time.

The Strand is the major street of Galveston's business district. Just two blocks over from the old harbor on the bay, most of the buildings have stayed the same for over a century. In Galveston, most old buildings are not torn down; they are renovated and protected so that the city appears not to have changed over the years. A few modern buildings appear here and there, however, and it was in front of one of these that Stephanie found a parking place.

"I hope everyone remembered to bring spending money," she said as she pulled the keys out of the ignition. "And that includes some money for the parking meter."

"And gas, too. Isn't that right, Sexy?" Paul grinned from ear to ear, getting out of the car.

"That's right. And I'll take ten bucks from everyone at the next fill-up."

Alex, still shaken from the event at the monument, got out of the car in silence. She looked over at Josh and tried to smile while they gathered on the sidewalk but a cold sense of fear had settled within her and wouldn't move. It kept her out of the banter she had always enjoyed entering. And the deeper into Galveston she went, the greater this fear grew.

"Hey Josh, Steph's going to show us most of it during the swim this afternoon." Paul laughed and deposited two quarters into the parking meter.

"Bullshit. Your turn, Josh." Stephanie put one hand on her hip and the other on the meter.

Alex fished into her purse for some change while Stephanie smiled at her. A weak smile on her face, she put some change into the meter.

"Thanks, Roomy. Now were set for almost two hours." Stephanie turned to Josh. "Okay, one who knows all about this place, lead on."

In the first store they entered, Stephanie pulled Alex off to the side. "What's wrong, Roomy? Did you get into something with Josh?"

"No. No, Stephi. Josh pulled me away from something." As succinctly as she could, Alex told her roommate about the incident at the monument. When she was finished, Stephanie was flabbergasted.

"My God, Alex, alive? You've got to be seeing things."

"I hope to God I was, Stephi. And that I'm not going crazy. Oh Stephanie, when these things come on and on, they make you doubt your own sanity. It was like that years ago."

"But Alex, how can a bronze monument come alive?"

"I don't know. I really don't know." She was on the verge of tears.

The two were interrupted by the incursion of Paul, an insinuative leer on his face. "Is this a private party or can anybody join? Hey, Steph. Josh and I have found the ultimate bathing…"

"Pauli, this crap has followed us down here," Alex said abruptly. She turned full facing her brother. It was about time.

"What…What?"

"I said this stuff has followed us down here. You remember what we talked about earlier this week?"

The smile, even the high color, evaporated from Paul's face. He looked from Alex to Stephanie, then back to Alex. "You mean those things you've been seeing around the apartment have followed you down here?"

"No. No. Not those things. Other things have happened. Different things."

"Other figures? Or what?"

"No Pauli. Weird occurrences. Yesterday and today."

Josh walked up on them, smiling, a tiny, stretch bikini bottom in his hand.

Paul turned toward him. "Go put that back, Josh. We got a problem here."

Suddenly shocked, Josh turned to do as he was told.

"It wouldn't fit me, anyway," Stephanie said, quietly, a weak smile on her face.

When Josh returned to the group, Alex told all of them what had occurred since they had gotten to Galveston. Then Alex and Paul filled Josh in on what had been happening at the apartment.

"I knew something was wrong," he said. "Alex looked like she'd seen a ghost back at the monument."

"I may have, Josh. I may have."

The revelation to all present made Alex feel much better. Now all four of them were in it together, and, as always, there was safety in numbers.

Each trying to put the strange events in the back of his mind, the four ate lunch at a place on the Strand and then looked into some of the shirt and souvenir shops, Alex all the time uneasy and the others checking on her from time to time. At four o'clock, they returned to their car to go back to the hotel; Alex was relieved at this as she had been haunted by a nagging fear all the time she was in downtown Galveston. She felt like something evil, something truly malign, was very near and it was biding its time until it had a chance to reveal itself and cause harm. Indeed, in one store on the Strand, Alex felt like she was in the company of hundreds of dead bodies.

"I think a swim in the surf is just what your doctor would order." Josh leaned across the back seat and smiled at Alex who smiled back.

"Along with a little beer," Paul chirped in the front seat. "How about it, Steph? Budweiser, maybe?"

"Sure. Maybe for Alex and me." Stephanie had put a piece of gum in her mouth and was now smacking it. "I haven't forgotten about your little incident yesterday."

"O, come on, Stephi. That's a thing of the past." Paul whined. "Alex, talk some sense into your roomy, would you?"

"Stephanie, I think something stronger than soda pop would hit the spot." Alex settled back in the backseat. "With everything else that's been going on, I'd completely forgotten about his elementary school antics."

"So you think I should include these two clowns?"

"Yeah!" The boys provided a chorus in agreement.

Stephanie had reached Broadway when Alex told her to turn left and head down toward the end of the street, away from the Texas Victory Monument.

"You'll probably find an ice house near where the street ends," she said.

They did find a small store and Stephanie, using her Kansas ID, bought one six pack of beer.

"Only one," Paul exclaimed.

"Only one. I don't want certain people getting shit-faced." Stephanie looked at Alex in the backseat and winked. "You and I get the extra ones, Roomy."

"What's this one beer bullshit, Blondie?" Paul barked.

"Just what I said it was. If you're good boys, I might get some more later." Stephanie chomped on her gum and headed for the hotel. "We drink the stuff in the hotel room," she said. "We don't take it to the beach." Suddenly, she blew a bubble and popped it.

"You call me a little kid. Look at you," Paul muttered beside her.

Alex finally became amused by the banter in the car. "We can have a beer while we put our suits on," she said. "Then we can sit out on the balcony and finish them."

"Sounds great." Paul, suddenly serious, turned to his sister in the back seat. "Sis, I want you to tell me what exactly is going on in these dreams."

"From what I can see, Pauli, they have to do with some kind of storm, or flood, or something like that. That is, all of them except maybe the one about the dead kids."

"I had that one, too," Stephanie remarked. "Or at least part of it."

"That's right." Alex turned from Paul to Josh. "From what I can tell, it's the same dream. But Stephanie was awakened before she could get to the really bad part."

"Years ago, Sis, things came out of dreams. Remember?"

"How well I do, Pauli. And I've been expecting something like that but it hasn't happened. At least not yet. But the monument freaked me out. I dreamed about it over a month ago and as far as I know, I've never seen it before today. I've been to Galveston before, many times, and I guess I just never noticed it. But what happened there today was straight out of a nightmare."

"You said the thing came alive?" Paul glanced over at Stephanie and then back at Alex.

"It either did or I have a hell of an imagination." Alex briefly looked over at Josh, who so far had contributed nothing to the conversation.

Now, however, he spoke up. "Alex, you mentioned a storm," he said. "You know, Galveston once had a bad storm. It killed thousands of people."

"Oh yeah?" Alex muttered, expressing sudden interest. "When?"

"I don't remember, really. It was a long time ago, though."

"That might be interesting to look into, Pauli." She leaned forward and put her forearms on the front seat. "Stephi, before we all start smelling like breweries, turn around and head back for the Strand. I want to find a bookstore and maybe check into this."

Stephanie did so and in only a few minutes they had found their bookstore a few blocks from the Strand. And there, close to the check-out counter, Alex found her book, one among two or three others. She bought the one that looked the most complete and had the most pictures. Then, the group piled back into the car to head for the hotel.

On the way back, Alex thumbed through the book, looking at the photographs. The piles of smashed buildings and houses she felt like she had seen before. Also, in the distance were tall buildings and church spires she had seen before. She found a picture of an orphanage and read that it had been on the beach. *Could this be the source of that dream of dead children?* she thought.

"Hurry up, Steph. The beer's going to get hot," Josh piped up in the next seat.

Alex closed her book and looked up. "I think what we have here is going to be an important clue to what's going on," she said. "At least down here."

Paul turned back to his sister. "I remember another book, long ago, that gave us important clues."

"That's right, Pauli. I think this one's going to tell us something, too."

"What makes you say that?" Stephanie asked, her eyes straight ahead on the road.

"Well, for one thing, we have an orphanage here where most of the little inmates drowned."

"Oh, my God, Roomy. The little girl."

"I dare not put that two and two together yet, Stephi. We're in Galveston now so let's concentrate on Galveston first, shall we?"

They parked behind their hotel and ran to their rooms to change into their suits. Stephanie was now very curious about the book. But when she tried to ask Alex about it, she cut her off.

"Later," she said. "For now, let's enjoy the trip."

The girls changed quickly and sat in their room, drinking their beer and talking about what they had seen downtown. After a pause, Alex guessed at what Stephanie was thinking.

"I think we got a break now, thanks to Josh," she said. "Things might just start falling into place."

"You mean the book?"

"Yes, the book. Some of those pictures look very familiar.

I've seen some of that stuff in my dreams. I'm sure of it. I've been dreaming about this storm since April and now you seem to have started, too. The big question now is how does this tie in with what's been going on at the apartment."

"You mean the little girl and the other thing?"

"And the man."

"Could they be victims of this storm?"

"They most certainly could be."

"But they're in Houston. Shouldn't they be down here?"

"I don't know, Steph. But I think very soon, we're going to find out. They're the very core of the matter." Alex took a swig of beer and settled back on the bed. "And, as you know, at least one of them is dangerous."

At that moment, there was a loud rap at the door.

"Listen to that," Stephanie said, standing. "From the sound of that, they can't hold their liquor at all." She opened the door and in sauntered Josh and Paul, each holding beers.

"Look here, Alex. God and the Galveston cops can all see that these two yo-yos are drinking."

"Hold on a minute, Blondie. No one saw us come over here." Paul turned to Stephanie. "Besides, we're about ready for those other two."

"Oh, you think so, huh."

"Yep. Know so."

"Forget it. It's time to go swimming." Stephanie bent down and picked up her towel and turned to Alex. "Come on, Roomy. We'll continue this conversation later."

"Right. We might even include the guys in on it." Alex arched her eyebrows and looked at Paul and Josh in turn.

Paul gave his sister a sheepish grin. "What kind of conversation are we talking about, Sis?"

"What we had years ago, Pauli. This is Galveston; that is Houston. And we might be dealing with two different things or one great big monumental mess."

"As sensitive to these things as you are, Sis, I think you've got a point." Paul took a drink of beer and looked at Josh. "Big sister's got just enough ESP to attract all kinds of crap."

"Pauli, I told Stephanie that as long as these things confine themselves to dreams, I think we'll be all right."

"Okay, but those things at the apartment aren't dreams, Sis. And what about that monument affair this morning?"

"I know. But right now I'm not really sure if that was even real. Like the mirror in this room. And those things in Houston are up there, not down here. They haven't showed themselves here and I don't think they're going to." Alex rose and picked up her towel. "I guess we're just going to have to see."

"At least you got someone in the room with you. You're not by yourself."

"That's right, Pauli. There is, indeed, safety in numbers."

For the rest of that day, they forgot about the dark side of their trip and had a good time. And even at bedtime, Alex didn't worry about anything else happening. When Stephanie offered her a sleeping pill, she turned it down.

Both girls slept soundly until the next morning when they were awakened by a knock at the door.

Annoyed, Stephanie shouted from the bed. "You guys! You're up early! We're not up yet."

"We're going to get some breakfast. You want to go along?" The voice outside was Josh, who seemed cheerier than ever.

"No. We're not up yet, I tell you."

"Okay. When we get back, we'll go swimming. Oh Alex, the year was 1900."

"What?" Alex yelled in a sleepy voice.

"1900. The year of that storm was 1900. I remembered it last night before I went to sleep."

Alex was suddenly wide awake. *1900,* she thought. *Much of this town must still look the same.* She threw back the sheet and quickly jumped from bed. From the table she retrieved the new book and flipped it over. Sure enough, in the book preview on the back, she read the date, Sept. 8, 1900.

"What's up?" Stephanie asked, coming in from the bathroom.

"Monkey shines, Roomy." She put the book down and turned. "You and I both have been dreaming about the same disaster. Just as I thought. Josh clued me in on the date, as if I needed to be."

"Yeah. It's in the book, isn't it?"

"On the back even. You know, Stephi, one thing that really bugs me about this whole business is the hostility I felt that day in Mrs. Frank's attic. I mean if I hadn't turned around and left abruptly, I would have been attacked."

"But you were attacked. By the little girl."

"Oh, she just grabbed hold of my leg. I know she wanted to tell me something. Like I told you before, all of those things up there have problems and we've got to find out what they are."

They could hear Josh and Paul returning from breakfast and Stephanie opened the door for them. Paul stood in the doorway and eyed the bikini Stephanie was wearing, the first she had worn this trip.

"You're looking better all the time, Roommate," he said, smirking.

"Yeah? This is for any hunk who happens along down there." Stephanie put her hands on her hips and stared down into Paul's face.

"Hunks, my ass. We're the only hunks who are going to be down there this early." Paul turned to his sister. "Sis, are you ready to go?"

"Yes, Pauli. And I think I have a bit more insight into what's going on."

The four descended to ground level and walked across the street, Alex and Stephanie wearing cover-ups to be doffed when they reached the beach. As soon as they stepped off the seawall steps onto the sand, Paul and Josh started tossing a football to each other.

"I hope you don't plan to keep that on the whole time," Paul said, grinning at Stephanie.

"I should. What's underneath really isn't intended for little boys who grease up the potty." Stephanie hugged herself and smirked at Paul.

"Hey, Paul. I think you really made an impression on her," Josh said, loud enough for all to hear.

Alex heard but paid no attention. Instead, she walked away from the others, and continued a short way down the beach. Shortly, a strange feeling of fatigue came over her and she closed her eyes as she walked. When she opened them, the beach was strangely deserted.

Suddenly, she felt something grasp her ankle. She turned and looked downward, expecting to see a piece of seaweed or someone's trash.

It wasn't either. There, half buried in the sand, was the remains of what up to a few hours before had been a woman, its eyes paling in death and mouth filled with sand. One dead arm extended toward Alex's foot, its hand, claw-like, grasping her ankle.

Opening her mouth to scream, she looked around to discover what appeared to be bits and pieces of things scattered about. Then, she lifted her eyes upwards to a panorama that was breathtaking in its sheer horror.

All the way up the beach was wreckage and bodies. Near the top, an extended ten-to-fifteen foot pile stretched along the horizon. Beyond that could be seen the tops of buildings and steeples, many of them wrecked or damaged.

Alex felt like someone had kicked her hard in the stomach. She screamed, loud, then collapsed in a dead faint. The next thing she knew she was being shaken awake by Stephanie and Josh. Bleary with confusion, she shook her head to and fro. Paul stood over her, a look of wide-eyed worry on his face.

"Jesus Christ, Sis, what happened?" he exclaimed, kneeling by her side.

"Pauli…Pauli… Oh, Jesus. I don't know what happened to me…I…I…am I…"

"You're right here on the beach," Josh replied. "We didn't see you lie down. We just saw you walking away. Then we heard you scream and came running."

Alex put a hand on Stephanie and Josh and they helped her up. She was still breathing hard and still unsure where she was.

"My God, what's happening to me," Alex cried. She put her hands on her stomach and closed her eyes. She could see a number of people on the beach and she could see her companions were clearly worried. "I've got to get out of here," she said. "This crap is coming to a head."

"What, exactly, happened to you, Sis?" Paul asked, gently putting his hand on her shoulder.

"From what…" She swallowed hard. "From what I can tell, I was taken back to Galveston the morning after the storm. I was grabbed by a corpse, Pauli, a damned corpse. Then I saw this whole town destroyed." Tears rolled down her face and she choked on what she was trying to say next.

"And then?" her brother asked.

"And then…And then…When I awoke, you were there."

"Sis, something like that happened before."

"Yes, Pauli, I know. Stehle's door. But it couldn't be that. It was nowhere around. I would have seen it. You would have seen it. No, this was something different." Alex suddenly looked at each one of her companions in turn. "And I think that this is worse than Stehle's door. Stehle's door can be avoided. This can't. I think at this point whatever is going on is playing games with my mind to the point…to the point…"

"To the point of you're going crazy," Stephanie said, quietly.

"Exactly."

"We've got to get out of here, guys," Stephanie said, again in a quiet and reserved manner.

"I think you're right, Steph." Paul put his arm around his sister and hugged her to him. Then, Josh put his arm around Alex's shoulders and the four walked back to the hotel.

There, they packed up their things and checked out. Since they were scheduled to stay in Galveston one more night, they debated on what to do the final night. They decided to return to Houston, to the girls' apartment, and decide what to do there.

As she put her things in a suitcase, Alex thought about what might be waiting for them at the apartment. For now, however, she needed to get out of Galveston. Occurrences here were obviously escalating and they were even affecting Stephanie. Something told her she was visiting the very heart of the foul, evil developments she had been experiencing since Easter. And as for anything waiting for them in Houston, she knew there would be.

Chapter Eleven

"We can put you guys up downstairs for the night," Stephanie said as she drove down Broadway toward the high bridge out of Galveston. "Mrs. Frank is still gone, I'm sure. So, there's really no one around to question what's going on."

Just as soon as they crossed the bridge, they ran into a thunderstorm and had to slow down to a crawl.

"As usual, as always," Paul said, turning to the back seat.

Stephanie couldn't see the road so she turned on her lights and kept going even when other cars had pulled off . However, after fifteen minutes, they gave up and pulled into a service station and food store to buy something for lunch. There they waited until the rain subsided. When they left, the rain had stopped.

At the apartment an hour later, they found Mrs. Frank gone just as Stephanie had said. The whole area was drenched so it had rained there, too.

"I think Houston has developed its own monsoon season," Stephanie said, pulling her small suitcase from the backend. "Alex, why don't you stay with the guys and I'll go get the cats."

"Okay. I'll make us all some iced tea." Alex unlocked the screen and then the front door.

Inside, everyone put his stuff down except Alex who wanted to check the place out. She looked over the upstairs before she put her overnight bag and small suitcase down on her bed. A few moments later, she announced that nothing seemed out of the ordinary.

"It's as if nothing was ever here," she said, heading for the kitchen. "Nothing's happened at all." She made a face while taking out four tall tumblers and filling each with ice. "The inconsistency of this crap is enough to drive you crazy."

She filled each glass with instant tea and gave one each to Paul and Josh. "God, I'm glad to be back here," she said, settling on the couch. "Who knows what would have happened if we had stayed in Galveston."

"I'm thinking you got an honest-to-God glimpse of the past, Sis." Paul said, quietly. "through a dream."

"I know I did, Pauli. A dream that was so damned real I could feel things and smell things. Jesus, a dead woman had hold of my ankle. She looked like she'd been crushed."

"God," Josh muttered. He had said nothing, but had sat, wide-eyed, sipping his tea.

"Sis, I think you're right. You've got yourself some victims up here, but the question remains. Why up here?"

"That I don't know, Pauli. Yet." She paused to sip tea. "There's some connection between this house and Galveston. The Galveston of 1900. Mrs. Frank didn't mention anything along those lines the other night. I don't think she knows."

"Do you think she even knows her house is haunted?" Paul raised his eyebrows and looked over at Josh.

"No, Pauli, I don't. If 'haunted' is the word we want to use." Alex smiled suddenly. "In that case, I guess our apartment is haunted, too."

"Bingo." Paul smiled at his sister.

"That old house is certainly a good candidate," Josh said suddenly.

"Oh, you don't know the half of it." Alex turned to Josh. "You haven't encountered any of the things that haunt it."

"Sis, I want to see the attic."

Alex suddenly turned to her brother. "What?" She sat for a moment, speechless, then spoke in a slow, controlled voice. "You want to go up there?"

"Yes. You said there's something up there. I want to try to get a look at it."

"Pauli, that day I was up there, I have never been so frightened in all my life," she said in an even voice. "Even years ago, I don't think I've ever been so filled with fear as I was in that attic. Pauli, for all I know," her voice rose in excitement, "every bit of this shit emanates from that attic."

"Sis, I think we should go up there and maybe put your fear to rest."

Stephanie appeared at the door, a cat carrier in each hand. "Just ninety dollars for these two this trip," she said. She set the carriers down and opened each door. Each cat bounded out and quickly ran up the stairs.

Alex, who had risen and walked toward the front door, froze. "Now what?" she exclaimed.

"That's weird." Stephanie said.

The boys had moved up behind Alex so she turned to them. "The cats don't eat well at the vet's, so they always head straight for the food bowls when they get home." She turned back to Stephanie.

"They're scared?" Josh said behind her.

"That's exactly right, Josh. They are." Alex headed up the stairs, followed by her roommate. On the landing neither cat could be seen.

Alex found Sabrina in her room on her bed. Gathering the animal in her arms, she returned to the hall where she heard Stephanie in the office.

"Henrietta's under the computer desk where I can't get to her," she said. "She's scared to death."

"I know, Stephanie. Both of these cats are scared." Alex stood in the doorway and watched her roommate on the floor, trying to coax her cat out. "Something's close. Something's real close."

Stephanie straightened up and got to her feet. "What could it be," she asked, wide-eyed. "There's nothing here now."

"It seems like there's nothing here now." Alex turned, cat in arms, and walked toward the stairs. Stephanie, abandoning her cat for the time being, followed her down to the living room.

"Either something was here earlier and they sense it," she announced to the boys, "or there's something close by."

"Nothing is evident now," Paul said, taking a sip of tea.

"I know. That's what's so frustrating." Alex bent down and picked up her tea glass. "Like nothing's happened." She made a mock toast toward Josh.

"Oh yes it has," Stephanie remarked behind her. "There's still poor little Tom buried out there in the garden."

"Tom?" Paul turned a quizzical look toward his sister.

"A poor old tomcat we befriended and fed," Alex said, quietly. "Something tore him to pieces in the alley."

"Something, Roomy?" Stephanie's voice rose in emotion. "Something horrible. Something you saw."

A dark look descended on Paul. "You think something like that happened to him? You know tomcats get in fights all…"

"Not this time, Pauli," Alex interrupted. "What was left of him was scattered all over the alley. And what I felt in Mrs. Frank's attic that day is certainly capable of doing something like that."

The four sat for a few minutes, lost in thought, then Paul spoke.

"Speaking again of Mrs. Frank's attic, I think I should take a look now while I've got the chance."

Alex turned to her roommate who had a look of panic on her face. Then, she stood up. "I'm going with you, Pauli."

"Me, too," Josh said, and stood up.

Alex turned again toward Stephanie, who now looked like she was cornered.

"All right, you guys. I'll go with you." She tried to smile but her hands shook. "I've seen one of those damned things around here. Face to face with it. It was not pleasant." Her voice rose like a little girl's.

"Well, Stephanie, at least now if you run into something, you won't be alone." Paul smiled at her and turned back to his sister.

"I don't think Mrs. Frank is due back until tomorrow evening," Alex said. "So we'll have that whole house to ourselves."

"Oh, wonderful," Stephanie chuckled. "A whole goddamned haunted house to ourselves."

"Aw, Stephanie. Where's your spirit of adventure?" Josh chided.

"My spirit of adventure!" Stephanie's voice rose again but this time in indignation. "I pissed all over myself when I came face to face with that horrid thing in the backyard that day. Since then, I've been on pins and needles."

"Okay, Stephi, you can stay down here." Paul put his arm around Stephanie's shoulders.

"No…No, I want to go with you. Alex keeps saying there's safety in numbers. And I do want to find out what's going on. I have a part in it, too, you know."

"That settles it. We all go." Alex retrieved the key to Mrs. Frank's house from the kitchen and all four trooped across the driveway to the dark old house.

Inside the door, they assembled at the back stairs and formed a single file, Paul in front, the girls in the middle and Josh bringing up the rear. Slowly, they ascended the stairs to the second floor. There they stood at a narrow, steep staircase that seemed to lead to only darkness. Since it turned twice, they couldn't see the top of the stairs. Screwing up their courage, however, Paul mounted the stairs and the others followed.

At the top of these stairs, Paul opened a door that Alex didn't remember from the day she had been up there. The attic, however, she remembered very well. Just inside the door, they stopped.

The doors on either side of the attic hallway were open, just as Alex remembered they had been that day she was there. Windows in the rooms lit the hallway somewhat, but when Paul tried the hall light, it did not come on.

"That's very odd," Alex mumbled. "I've seen it on any number of times."

"Well, it's burned out now," Paul said, looking in all directions. "Probably the bulb."

"God, it's dusty in here," Josh said, clearing his throat. "Someone's been here, though."

"Yeah, my sister, a month ago." Paul turned to the others and motioned for them to follow him down the hall.

They crept down the hall to the crossing hall that was fully lit by stained-glass windows on either end. There, Alex noticed something unnerving.

"When I was up here before, that door was closed," she said, pointing to a single door in the opposite wall. "In fact, I was standing right there when that hideous sensation struck me. I went no further than that."

Paul walked over to the door in question and turned the knob. It turned almost three quarters of the way around.

"Well, it's open," he said. He pushed on the door but could

not budge it. “Josh, come here and give me a hand.”

Together, they threw their weight against the door, but still it stood firm.

“Boy, I can see why you didn’t get all district in football,” Paul remarked. He stepped back away from the door. “Come on. Let’s try once more.”

However, the next effort yielded no results.

“Maybe it’s really locked,” Josh said. He tried the knob himself and it turned almost completely clockwise.

“No, it’s not locked.” Paul stepped up and felt around the edge of the door. “It’s stuck for some reason.”

Again the boys threw themselves against the door, but this time it opened. A cloud of foul-smelling air wafted out of the room and enveloped Paul who was poised to enter the room.

“God, no one’s been in here for a long time.” He coughed and leaned against the door frame.

Alex didn’t say anything. She still saw the open door in her mind. Now it seemed the door hadn’t been open in many years. The boys entered the room while the girls followed them.

The room was a long one, taking up the entire front of the attic. At one end was an old fashioned four-post bed with a canopy torn and covered with dust. A vanity and a wardrobe, also dusty, stood at the opposite end of the room. In the wall five feet from the end of the bed was a fireplace covered by a tarnished brass screen. Stacked against the wall opposite the fireplace were two wooden crates. Dust and spider webs covered everything.

Paul coughed and tried to wave some of the dust away. “There’s been nothing in here for years,” he said, and coughed again.

“Well, I didn’t come in here, Pauli. I was too scared.” Alex put her hands on her hips and looked about the room.

“What was this room?” Stephanie asked, standing in the doorway.

“Well, it was obviously a bedroom.” Alex walked over to the bed and put her hand on the spread. A small whiff of dust rose as she took it away.

“Whose?” Paul asked. “One of Mrs. Frank’s sons?”

“Pauli, this was obviously the bedroom of a girl. Or a lady.

A boy wouldn't have a bed like this. And a vanity?"

"I guess you're right, Sis."

"Except for those crates, none of this stuff was stored up here," Alex continued. "This was obviously some girl's bedroom at one time. I don't think an older woman would want an attic room."

All four turned and filed out of the bedroom into the hall. Josh walked over to the hall light fixture and, after quickly dismantling the fixture, unscrewed the light bulb.

"This bulb's so long dead it belongs in a museum," he said, shaking the bulb by his ear.

"Well, some light's been coming on up here." Alex looked about the hall ceiling for another light. "If not that one, which one?"

"Maybe a light in one of the rooms."

"Pauli, that rear window at the end of the hall was ablaze with light. It would have to be the hall light; it couldn't be any other."

They glanced into the other rooms but found little but undisturbed dust. Then, one behind the other, they descended the stairs.

When they got to the first floor, Alex walked straight to Leo Frank's office off the parlor at the rear of the house. Standing in the doorway, she studied the tiny room.

Although recently cleaned, there was a thin veneer of dust all around. The lamp sat on the desk as it had the morning Alex had seen someone, or something, standing next to it. Nothing seemed to be disturbed.

"God, Roomy, without Mrs. Frank here, this house gives me the creeps." Stephanie had come up behind Alex while the boys waited in the parlor.

"It does me, too, Steph. There's something here. You couldn't' tell it by anything we've seen today, but there is something here, right now, in this house."

That night the four of them settled into the apartment. No one even thought about staying in Mrs. Frank's house even though their search of it had turned up nothing out of the ordinary. The boys would sleep on a couch bed downstairs, while the girls occupied their regular bedrooms upstairs. With this arrangement, Alex thought, if something did pop up downstairs in the middle of the night, it would not escape detecting.

After a supper at a nearby fast food restaurant, they sat about the apartment, talking softly with the TV on, and sipping ginger ale. Nothing seemed amiss. Even the cats had settled down and finally come downstairs to eat. At ten thirty, Alex made up the downstairs bed and she and Stephanie bid the boys goodnight.

Upstairs, preparing for bed, Alex wondered what kind of dream was in store for her this night. Would she endure a continuation of her experience that morning? That, she knew, would be too much.

She settled into her bed with Sabrina, turned out the light, and quickly fell asleep.

Although her sleep was undisturbed, she was awakened shortly after two AM by a violent thunderstorm. To Alex, this was an evil omen, as if the thunder and lightning would usher in some new horror, one she was not prepared for. She lay in bed, the cat plastered against her side, and hoped the storm would soon pass.

Moments later, she started to get up to go to the bathroom when Stephanie appeared at her door.

"For God's sake, Alex," she whispered. "If it isn't one thing, it's another. This town is going to float away."

"This should pass pretty soon." Alex turned in her direction. "Any trouble with dreams?" she asked, genuinely interested.

"Nothing, thank God." Stephanie stepped into the room toward the bed. "I'm still scared, though. I'm glad the guys are down there."

"They're probably sound asleep." Alex laughed and rose from the bed.

"They seem to have scared off everything but the damned rain."

"That's about right." Alex headed for the bathroom while Stephanie followed her and returned to her own bedroom.

When Alex returned to bed, the storm has lessened in intensity, and she was able to get back to sleep, and, with no disturbances, wake at seven o'clock refreshed. Putting on a housecoat, she headed downstairs to start a pot of coffee.

"Good morning, Sis," Paul greeted her in his shorts and socks at the base of the stairs. "I checked out Mrs. Frank's house during that storm last night from the front door. Nothing happening. Everything was dark."

Alex hadn't thought about that. She wondered why she hadn't. "Well, you must have had some misgivings during the storm, too."

"Yeah. Just enough of a noisy thunder-boomer to wake me up."

In the kitchen Alex prepared coffee while Paul and Josh put their clothes on. When Stephanie came down, they sat down in the living room, sipping coffee and eating the rolls Alex had heated up. Paul mentioned again the attic window.

"Black as pitch," he said, reiterating what he had told his sister earlier. "In fact, the whole house was dark."

"Well, that's one good thing, I guess." Alex rose and walked to the front door, which was open. Through the screen, the old house appeared particularly foreboding, even in the morning sun. *What makes me want to go over there*? she thought.

Later that morning, Josh left for Katy and Alex and Stephanie took Paul home after eating a light lunch at the apartment.

Shortly after three PM, Alex drove to the Rand building, a large, five-story business center which featured an art exhibit announced in her seminar. In the lobby, she found a guest book and featured pictures exhibited on easels. Quickly, she wrote titles and descriptions of two of these and then read a placard telling her that the older pictures were on the third floor.

Hurriedly climbing a nearby staircase, she found the pictures she was most interested in.

Oddly, this floor was deserted. She stood at the juncture of two long halls, both of which were empty. Shivering, to reassure her there was life on this floor, she glanced through the window of an office door to see five people working on computers.

Somewhat reassured, she found a large picture, mounted in

the middle of the hall, of the Civil War siege of Vicksburg. After examining this one, she advanced to the next one, a depiction of the same campaign, only this one done in a more primitive fashion. Here, she surmised, this painting might have been done by a soldier who had actually been there.

She started writing a description when she heard behind her, soft and near, a footfall. Turning, she saw no one. The halls were still empty and silent. Had someone been there and gone into one of the offices?

She began to feel cold and wondered if the building air conditioners had only just come on. With nothing around to disturb the silence, she returned to her description, but had written only a few words when she heard it again: the same footfall, this time a little louder.

"What the hell," she whispered. She turned, but again there was nothing. Closing her notebook, she moved down the hall toward a stairwell. At the juncture of two halls, she stopped. The footsteps were distinctly following her.

"Jesus, what is this?" She sniffed loudly and hurried to the stairway, terror rising in her. Almost tripping on the stairs, she descended to the second floor where she encountered a man with a briefcase coming out of an office.

He turned toward her and nodded and Alex smiled back, trying desperately to hide the tears that were beginning. When he passed her, he headed up the stairs to the third floor. Whatever was following her, he would surely pass. Or encounter.

In the meantime, Alex headed to the first floor, not stopping to see if her silent pursuer was still there. She knew that whatever was behind her had not manifested itself to the man she had encountered.

Breathing heavily and on the verge of panic, she arrived at the lobby. She had to go to the bathroom but she did not want to be cornered in the ladies' room by whatever was behind her. Fortunately, a smartly dressed woman entered a restroom just off the lobby. Alex wiped the tears from her face the best she could and then followed her into the restroom. Inside, the woman stood in front of a mirror and smiled at Alex who made her way into one of the stalls.

There she waited, hoping to God the woman would stay where she was as long as Alex needed the restroom. She was momentarily unnerved, though, when a second woman opened the door and entered the restroom. The new lady began a conversation with the other concerning a conference they had just been to. Alex, remembering another restroom incident weeks ago, thanked God for the chatting ladies nearby.

She finished and made her way to the sink, both ladies turned to her and smiled. Alex tried to act as natural as she could. She fixed her hair and put on a bit of lip gloss before leaving.

The lobby was crowded with people in suits, apparently just returning from the conference Alex had heard about in the restroom. If anything were still near her, she couldn't hear it with all the commotion in the lobby. Seemingly, though, everything was back to normal.

Still shaking, she decided to go home and return later to finish her project. She left the building and walked around to the back to the parking lot where she had parked in a space just off the street. She wanted to leave as soon as possible, so she unlocked her car but noted, in horror, she was alone again. Throwing her notebook and purse in the car, she caught something in her peripheral vision. Instantly, she turned, and, like she knew she would, she saw it.

Across the street, on the roof of a small house, was the menacing female figure she had seen at the apartment. It squatted, knees up in the air and filthy, brown water pouring from its mouth, and watched her. Instinctively, she knew that this was what had stalked her inside.

Numb with terror, Alex got into her car and fumbled in her purse for the keys. She found them, put them in the ignition and started the engine right up. But suddenly, a heavy force landed on the roof, shaking the vehicle violently to and fro. When the car quit shaking, all four windows began to roll down. A pale claw grabbed the edge of the driver's side window as it lowered, its knife-like nails scraping the glass.

Panicking, Alex hit the accelerator heavily and turned the car, tires squealing. She prayed she wouldn't hit another car as she exited the parking lot, the car bouncing heavily and banging a front bumper on the street.

She bolted through a stop sign and sped down an old residential street, all the time wary that the sharp claw, gone now, would suddenly come through the window. Ahead, at a red light, she hit her brake. The tires squealed again and the car turned slightly to the right. There, tears streaming down her face, she waited for what would come next. Hearing something outside her window, she turned.

A large, African-American Patrol Sergeant approached her and indicated with a hand gesture for her to stay put.

"Oh, my God, a cop." Alex said to herself, relieved.

"Miss, are you all right?" the Sergeant said in a stern but not unkindly voice.

"Yes…Yes, Sir," Alex answered, trying to smile but aware of her tears. "I'm…I'm just a bit upset, I'm afraid."

The policeman stood at her window and looked down at her. "I think you better pull up and park over there." He indicated a corner across the street.

She did as she was told and stopped the car in the indicated spot, the policeman following her on foot.

"May I see your driver's license, Ma'am," he said as he arrived at her window.

Alex dug out her license and handed it to him.

"I see a parking permit for Rice University. Are you a student?" he asked, examining her license.

"Yes, Sir. I'm a student at Rice University." It occurred to Alex she would like to have the policeman nearby all the way to the apartment.

"Miss Zunker, I would not advise you to drive when you're upset." He handed Alex's license back to her. "When you do, you do not have full control of your faculties and you endanger yourself and those around you. What you do is you wait and calm down before you drive."

"Yes, Sir. I…I think I'm all right now, though."

"Where are you going, now?"

"I'm…I'm going home. I don't live too far from here. I was at the Rand Building working on an assignment."

There's nothing in what I just said that would upset me, she thought. *And if I did tell him what happened, he would think*

I was crazy.

"And I was upset by what a friend told me there," she lied.

The policeman stared at her for a moment and then stepped back from the window. "Okay," he said. "You can go on, now. But drive safely."

Driving home as conscientiously as she could, Alex waited in horror for her attacker to return. She was glad to see traffic all around her now, though, and there were many people lined up at traffic lights.

When she reached the Heights, she prayed Stephanie would be home. She did not want to enter an empty apartment and, vulnerable as they both were, she needed the comfort and safety of her roommate.

At the apartment, she found not only Stephanie's car but Mrs. Frank's also. She pulled in front of the garage, got out and examined the top of her car.

There was nothing to indicate the presence of a body heavy enough to make the sound it did. The whole car had shook, yet there was no dent, no scratches, not even any disturbance of the thin veneer of dirt from the constant rain. She examined the rest of the car and shook when she looked over the windows. All four had lowered instantaneously, as if to allow four entranceways to get to her. The memory of a demon-like claw not one foot from her head made her reel with horror. When she finished her examination, she turned to see Stephanie crossing the patio and driveway to her.

"Well, how was the exhibit?" she asked, not noticing Alex's condition.

Ignoring the question, Alex answered her in an even tone. "I've just gone one round with my little friend."

"Who?" Stephanie's face clouded.

"My little friend with the claws." Alex's voice was now matter-of-fact. "She followed me around at the exhibit and then jumped me in the parking lot.

"Oh, Jesus, Alex. Wasn't there anyone around there?"

"Yes, thank God." Alex was feeling better now that her roommate was there to talk to. "That damned thing was invisible inside the building, Stephanie. I couldn't see it but I could hear it behind me. I ran into some people and for a time it vanished. But when I got to the parking lot, there it was, squatting on a roof just like it was when I saw it here."

A tear rolled down Stephanie's cheek and Alex wanted to hug her but she continued instead.

"I jumped into the car and started it up but it landed on the roof and somehow rolled down all four windows."

"Oh, my God, how?"

"I don't know," she cried, but the thing's claw was right next to my window. Oh, Stephanie, it's just like it was years ago. I was scared out of my wits. I floor-boarded the car out of the parking lot and down the street. The next thing I knew I had piled up to a stop light and there was a cop right there. Thank God."

"Did…Did you get a ticket?"

"No, but I wouldn't have given a damn if I had." Alex stopped, momentarily, and tried to regain control of herself. "That thing wasn't there, of course, while that cop was talking to me. After he let me go, I came straight home." Nervously, she glanced at the roof over the garage to make sure nothing was there.

Stephanie put her arm around her and they entered the apartment where Alex collapsed on the couch. Somehow she knew her adversary was through for the time being but this newest aspect, that of following and attacking her in an altogether strange locale, frightened her to the point of immobility. Now, she knew she was in danger anywhere as long as there was no one around. Literally this thing had transcended the secretiveness which Alex had always associated with these things. The only aspect of this that had remained was that when another human being had come on the scene, the thing was not around.

Stephanie, who had been to the store earlier, entered the room, a full wine glass in her outstretched hand.

"Here's a bit of St. Genevieve," she said. "I went to the Fiesta while you were gone."

Alex sat up and took the glass. She noticed the fear still plainly evident on her roommate's face. "Yes, there were just too many people about for it to do any real damage today."

Stephanie sat in a chair across the room. "Do you think that thing was trying to kill you?" she asked in a controlled tone.

"Maybe. When it landed on the roof, it sounded like it weighed a thousand pounds. Like with the other episode with the downstairs bathroom. It sounded like a truck had hit the door that day." Alex took a sip of wine and looked about the room. Then she looked back at Stephanie and smiled faintly. "I hate to keep using an old cliché, but there is safety in numbers," she said. "So far that thing hasn't come around when we were together. And when you came in with Tom that morning, it vanished. I know it wants to catch me alone and isolated."

"Then, I think we should stay together. What about at night when we are in separate rooms?"

"I don't know. So far the only thing we've had in that situation is these damned dreams." She sighed and took another sip of wine. "But, you know, Steph. You can't second guess these things because you never know what they'll do next. They are truly full of surprises."

The look of terror had never completely left Stephanie's face. She sat, wine glass in hand, straight up in her chair.

"What do we do if that thing comes back tonight, Alex?" she asked. "In the middle of the night when we're asleep."

"I don't think it will, Steph. I think it's through for the day. As things go now, I don't think it will come around again, not with both of us here." Alex stood up and set her glass on a nearby coaster. She hoped deep down that what she had just said was right. "In the meantime, I think we could brain-storm a few things to do if that thing catches me alone somewhere."

"Alex, if that thing comes near me, I don't know what I'll do. This is just absolutely weird," Stephanie whined.

Alex picked up her glass and walked to the kitchen. "As of now, it hasn't come near you," she said. "I need another one of these today." She refilled her glass and returned to the living room. "The only thing you've encountered is a few crazy dreams and the little girl who, aside from trying to scare the crap out of you, is trying to communicate with you." Alex smiled.

"Alex, I don't want any of these goddamned things around me." Stephanie thrust both feet up underneath her on the chair as another tear rolled down her cheek.

"Stephanie, you have to keep a cool head on your shoulders." Alex now was afraid of her roommate's panic. "That is vitally important. That's the first step in defeating them." And she felt sorry for her. Again Alex suddenly remembered how frightened she had been when she had first encountered these things. "Stephi, I think you and I can handle these things together. What we really need to do is get to the bottom of this. For instance, what is the reason for these things to be coming around these last few months? The little girl obviously wants to communicate with us. We thought she was trying to warn us against the other one. She very well could be. And the man I saw was gesturing something, too. Again, this was an attempt at communication."

Alex took a sip from her wine glass and settled back on the couch. "I'm pretty sure our conclusion about the 1900 storm is correct. These are victims of that storm. But why are they up here? Like I told Pauli, there's no Stehle's door, there's no trigger, there's nothing like that. So how the hell did they get here and why are they here?"

She paused and looked over at her roommate who now seemed to have gained full control. "In answer to your earlier question, Steph," she continued. "I think that thing was trying to kill me. Or possess me, one or the other. It is absolutely malevolent. That's why we absolutely need to stay together."

The two girls sat, quietly, for some minutes, sipping their wine and seemingly lost in thought. Finally, Alex spoke. "I'm going to call Dr. Vernon Blassingame. I think it's time we called on a professional for our problem. He came down here and helped us years ago and I think he'll be interested to hear what's going on now."

"I'm also going to call Pastor Gerlach. He was the youth pastor at St. John's when I was in high school and he also helped out years ago. He got a call a couple of years ago and he's in North Dakota or somewhere. Papa will know where he is. Anyway, he'll know what I'm talking about. I just hope to God I can find these two guys."

"And of course there's your little brother and Josh."

"Yes. They're a party to this, too."

"Your little bro is something else, Roomy. One moment he's greasing up my ass and the next moment he's leading the expedition to the attic. I was scared to death up there."

"I know, Stephi. We all were. And Pauli's a good hand to have around with these things. Like I said, he solved our problems years ago. He and the others."

Alex was glad to see that Stephanie had perked up a bit. She smiled at her across the room. "It was so good of you to get St. Genevieve to help us this evening. Legal or not, it hits the spot."

"Oh, speaking along those lines, the beer man called while you were gone."

"Howie?"

"The same. He's back from Beaumont and working part time at Shaeffer's Interiors. He said he came by when we were in Galveston. He saw some lights on so he rang the bell. Did we leave lights on when we were gone?"

"No, we didn't, Stephanie."

Suddenly, Stephanie's face clouded again.

"We had a visitor or two while we were gone. It doesn't surprise me." Alex suddenly looked about the living room. "We'll have to ask Howie if he heard anything."

"Jesus, Alex. You're so nonchalant about this."

"You have to be. Like I said, don't show them fear and show them an ordinary routine."

Alex put on her best face for this answer. The idea that the apartment had been occupied while they were gone unnerved her. There was an entry somewhere in the apartment and now she felt like she needed to find it. She remembered the window by her bed.

"Roomy, the properties of these things are still virtually unknown to me," she said, softly. "They might walk through walls or they might walk through doors. We never clarified that completely years ago. That thing that was after me this afternoon goes through walls. I know that because somehow it got to the downstairs bathroom door without going through the front door. And it got there fast. So that's part of the answer. But what else can they do?"

"From what you say, they seem extraordinarily strong."

"Yes. Even the little girl shows this. That night I encountered her, she nearly pinched my leg off."

"Alex, if they can walk through walls, they can come around

anytime."

"Yes, but please remember what I said earlier. When we're both here together I think we're relatively safe from that thing that attacked me. It stands to reason that if it catches you alone, it can do the most damage.

The two girls finished their wine in silence and then went out to eat, both of them wondering what might be in their apartment in their absence. Upon their return, however, they found nothing disturbed. They watched TV downstairs for some time and then made ready for bed.

While Alex was dressing, she thought about the day's events. She knew she would see her attacker again but when? She had to be ready for it. But how?

Feeling tired and knowing she would sleep soundly, she didn't even worry about possible dreams. If they came, they came. After all, they couldn't hurt her. Or could they?

She reached over and turned out the light, then petted her cat for a few minutes. When the animal moved to the foot of the bed, she turned over and prayed, giving thanks to God for the man on the second floor, the two women in the restroom and the patrol sergeant.

Chapter Twelve

The night passed without incident and so did the next day. Several days and nights passed without even the return of the disturbing dreams. June turned into July which brought a July fourth party at the home of a Zunker family friend where both Paul and Josh asked Alex if anything had happened since the fateful Galveston trip. Alex simply replied that she had experienced another run-in with her friend with the long nails.

"I'm awful worried about that," Paul replied.

To this Alex simply shrugged her shoulders and said that she had been watching out for her. She didn't want to get into a long discussion now, especially with a bunch of people around.

Alex never returned to the Rand Building. Instead she and Stephanie found a Texas Hill Country art exhibit at a local art gallery to fulfill their requirement. Alex worried there was something at the Rand building that had facilitated the monstrous attacker to stalk her. The most terrifying factor of the whole incident was the newest aspects of its appearance, one of which was invisibility. It had come on her totally unseen and she wondered if it could possibly attack her in the same guise. She wondered what other monstrous capabilities it may have, for it was indeed different from those she had experienced years before.

One morning shortly after the Fourth, she spotted something that if she had noticed it before she had not paid any attention to it. Sitting on the roof of Mrs. Frank's house next to the windows for the front room of the attic was a small, square turret. She couldn't remember any evidence of it the two times she had visited the attic, but she knew there had to be a door somewhere because it was obviously a room of some kind.

What could be in there? she thought.

Back in the apartment a few minutes later, Alex dialed her

parents' house, hoping her brother was there. Told by her mother he was at work, she dialed his cell phone, now hoping he would be able to talk a few minutes.

Paul answered the phone, thinking it was his parents.

"Can you talk for just a few minutes, Pauli?"

"Yeah, Sis. What's up?"

"Something I've never noticed before about Mrs. Frank's house. There seems to be a room in a small tower or garret on the roof. Have you seen it?"

"Oh, yes, I've seen it. I haven't paid much attention to it, though."

"Do you remember seeing a door or any other entranceway to it the other day when we were in the attic?"

"No. The only doors I remember were the two in the front. The two that led into that room you were so scared of."

"I don't remember anything up there, either, Pauli."

"What's the deal, Sis? What are you thinking?"

"I'm thinking there might be something in that room connected with what's going on."

"Don't go up there by yourself, Sis."

"I'm not. I'm going to wait for you. I guess I could get Stephanie to go with me but she'll hear a squirrel on the roof and pee in her pants. In a few days Mrs. Frank is going to Conroe. Can you come over and we'll have a look?"

"Yeah. I think I can manage it."

"Great. There's something else I want to run by you. I'm going to call Pastor Gerlach and tell him what's going on. And I'm going to try to get in touch with Dr. Blassingame, too."

"Pastor Gerlach? God, if it wasn't for Pastor G, I would have had my head split open like a watermelon. He's pastor of a church up in North Dakota now, isn't he?"

"Yes. I'm going to get his number from St. John's, unless Papa has it. I'm thinking since he saw those things years ago with you, he might be able to throw some light on what's happening now."

"That's a good idea. Blassingame, though. I remember he was connected with a college somewhere. Bonham… Brenham…Brendon…"

"Brendon…I think that's it. If I can find him, I'm sure he

can help out. I need you to look around home and see if you can find that phone number."

"Sure, Sis. I need to get back to work. Tell Pastor G hello for me."

"You bet. I'll talk to you again in a couple of days."

Brief as it was, Alex's talk with her brother excited her. She resolved to talk with her former youth pastor that very night, thinking the best time to catch him would be in the evening. Hurriedly she dialed St. John's Lutheran Church to get his current number, knowing she would have to wait until later to talk to her father.

Later that evening, Stephanie and Alex took Mrs. Frank out to eat. Alex wanted to ask the old lady about the garret on her roof, but something told her she wouldn't know anything about it. Her husband Leo probably sealed the door up with a wall or something. That would explain why no one had noticed a door when they were up there. But why would he do that? She would try to find a door before they broached the subject with Mrs. Frank.

Alex had better luck when she got home and dialed North Dakota. The young pastor was at home, watching television.

"Alex, how good it is to hear from you," he said with genuine enthusiasm.

"Great. How are you? How's the new church and how does it feel to be a senior pastor?"

"Tiring. I made a hospital visit tonight and visited a shut-in. Everything is going so good up here. And we're growing. We confirmed twenty-seven people last spring."

"That's great, Pastor. I remember there weren't many people there when you got there."

"Oh, yes. We've grown by leaps and bounds in the almost two years since I've been here. But how about you? You're going to Rice, I believe."

"Oh, yes. Tiring, too. I've kind of taken the summer off. Just one humanities seminar. But I wanted to talk with you about something that's going on here."

"Oh, sure. Go ahead." The young pastor's voice turned immediately serious.

"I remember you, Pauli, Papa and Dr. Blassingame dealt

with some things years ago successfully. But now they're back."

There was a lengthy pause on the other end. Obviously the young pastor was not ready for what he had just heard.

"Alex, the dead soldiers are back..."

"Not the dead soldiers, Pastor. Other things. One of these things is much worse than the soldiers." As briefly as she could, she told of the events beginning last spring with the little girl. When she got to the part about her encounter with the spirit with the claws, she heard a breathy, "Oh my God" on the other end. She went on to tell him of her experiences in Galveston and at the Rand Building. In conclusion, she told him about her theory that these beings were victims of the 1900 Galveston storm.

When she finished, there was another pause on the other end. Only when Alex thought the pastor may have put the phone down did he speak.

"This one manifestation, Alex, the one that is threatening you, what do you think it wants?"

"I don't know, Pastor. All I know now is that it frightens me to death. And it seems to be stalking me."

"Alex, this seems different than the things we encountered years ago. From the way you describe it, it seems demonic."

"A demon?"

"I think that's a very likely possibility."

Alex had thought about the possibility of demonic possession before. But this thing had not acted like she thought a demon would act. Furthermore, it had more than one opportunity to posses her and it hadn't.

"I don't know, Pastor. It doesn't strike me that way."

"You know our Lord encountered demons on a number of occasions and he cast them out. He encountered the Devil himself."

"I know that, Pastor."

"Demons do exist, Alex. And the Devil can do anything. I know that for a fact. Have you prayed about this problem?'

"Yes, Pastor, I have."

"Well, you know you can find support and help in your faith and your church."

"I know that, too, Pastor. That's one of the reasons I called you."

"I'm glad you did. I wish I was there to help you. What does your family think about all this?"

"They're concerned, of course. And I have Pauli full in my corner."

"A very good man to have."

"Very much so."

"You know, Alex. Demons can be kept away by faith and prayer."

"Yes, I know, Pastor." Alex sighed and momentarily closed her eyes. She knew that what she was up against was no demon. It was something different, something that once had been a human being but now was a monster.

She felt like she wanted to cry. She respected Pastor Gerlach for what he was, what he knew and how he had helped years ago. But now, she thought, he was pointing her in the wrong direction.

After a bit more small talk and further assurances from the young pastor, Alex hung up. Although she had really gained nothing, again, she did feel good knowing that some-one outside of her immediate circle knew about her problems.

She went to the couch and lay down, listening for any indication of Stephanie upstairs. Hearing her walk down the hall, she closed her eyes and thought back about Pastor Gerlach and her experiences with him at St. John's.

Without announcement, Stephanie appeared in the living room.

"I could use a beer or two tonight," she said. "We ought to call Howie."

"I just talked to my old youth pastor, Stephi. It seems he's missed the mark entirely."

"Oh, yeah."

"Yeah. He thinks I'm up against a demon."

"A demon?"

"He's wrong, you know." Alex sat up on the couch and looked straight to her front. "Had that thing been a demon it would have possessed me by now. And you know some-thing else? If that thing had wanted to kill me it would have done so by now."

"What…What do you mean?"

"Well, think about it. There's a couple of occasions that apply here. For example, that day in the downstairs bathroom, it apparently came in through the front door or the front wall or something. Why didn't it come through the bathroom door? If it had wanted to harm me, it would have done so. And the Rand Building? Same thing. I was very vulnerable on the third floor and it was very close. Invisible but close. And later in the parking lot it had a straight shot. It should have come right in through the window and it would have had me. All of those times there was no one around. For all I knew no one within screaming distance. No, Stephanie, it's up to something, something I don't know about. Something to do me harm. Somehow, some way." Alex took a deep breath and turned to her roommate who was still standing in the archway to the living room.

"What I'd like to know is how that thing is connected to the little girl. And the man you saw."

"That I don't know either. But I do think it's a safe guess that those two are trying to warn us against that thing. It couldn't be anything else."

"I'd like to know what they know about it."

"Well, who knows? Maybe they'll tell us."

"Alex, the less I have to do with them, the better. They're hideous."

"I know. You've told me that before."

"And that thing that's stalking you, I don't know what that thing is. Maybe your former pastor is right. Maybe it is a demon."

"It's not a demon, Stephanie. I'm telling you." Alex rose from the couch and went into the kitchen for a glass of iced tea. "No, Stephi, that thing is a spirit of some kind," she said as she mixed water and powdered tea. "It seems to have singled me out. What I need to find out is what, or who, it is. When I've done this, I think I can figure out what it's up to."

"How are we going to find this out?"

"Well, I think a good place to start is through reading. I have one book on the Galveston storm and I'm going to get others. I need to find out just exactly what went on there and about who was involved. A list of victims would be helpful." Alex returned to the living room, iced tea glass in hand. "I already know about the orphanage. The little girl might be one of them, especially in light of that dream I had. And you had."

"Yes."

Alex could tell by looking at her that Stephanie would just as soon forget about the whole thing. But she was involved whether she liked or not. "Stephi, both of us need to keep our eyes peeled around here. And make sure that neither of us is left alone for any length of time. Nothing has happened for a number of days now but that doesn't mean that these things are gone. I know from past experience that it is only a matter of time before something else happens.

The terror on Stephanie's face was evident. "Like what?"

"Steph, if I knew that I could take some steps to prepare for it. Or maybe prevent it."

Later that night in bed, Alex read as much of the book on the Galveston storm as she could. It told the story in some detail but there were other accounts that Alex wanted to read. Personal accounts would help. So would newspaper articles of the time. The book had a bibliography that Alex scrutinized just before she put out the light.

Later that night she was visited by a horrific dream in which she swirled around in water in a violent disturbance that combined wind, darkness and waves that kept her submerged. Struggling to keep her head above water, she felt things bump into her, things that were hard and others that were soft.

After a short time, she felt herself being pulled under and she struggled more to keep her head above water. Then, she was completely submerged.

Oh, Jesus, she thought. *I'm drowning. Oh please, God help me.*

She felt water filling her lungs and her legs became heavier and heavier. Trying desperately to grab hold to something with which to pull herself up, she flailed away in all directions in the water. When she felt herself strike bottom with her heel and her hip, she awoke.

She lay on the bed in the dark but she was out of breath. Her pajama top was soaked with sweat, likewise her face. She breathed deeply, filling her lungs with air, the horror of nightmare still with her.

"Jesus," she sobbed. Tears mixed with sweat as she sat up in bed, still trying to take full control of her faculties. Her soaked clothes clung to her body as if she had been submerged in water and she wondered if any of the nightmare had come back with her.

Suddenly she realized that in the dead silence of her bedroom something was missing. The low moan of her window unit air conditioner was. Also, her cat Sabrina, always at her side or at the foot of the bed, was not there. She turned about on the bed to restart the air conditioner and noticed that the window curtain near the foot of the bed was moving.

"What in God's name?" She moved down the bed to investigate and lifted the curtain. It had moved in a gentle incoming breeze, for the window behind it was full open.

Terror filled Alex again. She knew she had turned the air conditioner down before she got in bed like she always did. But now it was completely off and the window, the same window that had presented problems last spring, was open. Where was Sabrina? Had she gone out the window? Had the air conditioner broken down?

Suddenly feeling alone and very vulnerable in the dark, she reached over and switched on the light. Then she turned on the air conditioner. It hadn't broken down; it had been turned off. She looked about the room for her cat but couldn't find her. Peering out the open window into the darkness, she could see nothing.

"She's probably gone downstairs to eat," she said, trying desperately to console herself. "I hope to God that's where she is." The open window terrified her. Shivering, she closed and locked it and then listened for any sound that may indicate something in the apartment. There was none. She mustered enough courage to get out of bed and walk toward Stephanie's room, turning on all lights on the way, including the one on the landing just outside her roommate's room.

The light woke Stephanie.

"Alex, what's going on?" a sleepy voice within asked.

Alex stood in the doorway. She couldn't see Henrietta

either. Hopefully the two were downstairs together. "Stephanie, I've just had one hell of a nightmare," she replied. "And the window was open and the air conditioner was turned off. And both cats have disappeared."

Stephanie swung both legs over the side of the bed. "What time is it?"

"I don't know. I didn't look at the clock."

"What the hell? You're soaking wet."

"I think it's sweat, Stephanie. I hope to god it is and not sea water."

"What?"

"I had a dream that I was drowning, that I had drowned. God Stephi, I think I was going to die in that dream. And then when I woke up, I noticed that damned window was open and Sabrina gone."

"My God, Alex. There's something in the house." In wide-eyed desperation, she looked about her bed. "And Henry's not here."

"I know. They're both gone. Hopefully, they're downstairs eating. I didn't hear anything. But I want us both to go and see."

Stephanie turned toward her clock. "A quarter to five," she said.

"Stephanie, did you have any kind of a dream tonight?"

"No, not that I'm aware of."

Come on. We'll turn all the lights on as we go."

Slowly, the two girls made their way downstairs to the living room, turning on lights as they went. When they reached the kitchen, they found the two cats together by the back door. As expected, they had gone downstairs to eat.

"When do you suppose they came down?" Stephanie asked.

"I don't know. It doesn't look like anything scared them." Alex tried the back door and checked the kitchen windows. They were all locked. "If something had, I would have heard Sabrina."

"But that window upstairs."

"Well, it was wide open when I shut it. You would think something opening that window would wake me up but it didn't. I was right in the middle of one of the most hideous dreams I've ever had." Alex looked down at the two cats again. They did not seem alarmed as they had at other times. "Let's make some coffee," she continued. "We might as well stay up. I'm scared to go back to sleep at this point."

Stephanie walked to the kitchen door and then turned back to her roommate. "I guess you think your dream was connected with that window," she said, eyes wide with terror.

"It has to be. It's apparent that now there is nothing inside the apartment. But who, or what, opened that window? And when did they do it? There's not a trace that anything ever was there. There's no indication, no smell, no nothing. The cats don't seem disturbed and their coming down here in the middle of the night is nothing out of the ordinary.

"They would be shaken up if something had come into the apartment."

"I know that." She reached down and rubbed Sabrina's neck. "That dream is gone and so is whatever opened that window. The only thing I can think of was that window was opened after the cats went downstairs. Maybe just before I woke up and whatever was there was scared off when I turned on the light. But what about the air conditioner?

That had been on and I know for sure that I adjusted it just before I went to sleep."

"Alex, you know the cats don't go downstairs together unless they go with us. When they go downstairs in the night, it's usually by themselves. The other one is asleep."

Alex had not thought about that. Her terror over her dream and the open window along with her worry about Sabrina had not brought that idea to mind. "You're right, Stephi. And when we found them in the kitchen, they were together."

"They've been on pins and needles ever since this crap started in April. Remember what they did after I picked them up from the vet's."

"Yes, something was definitely scaring them. And, as usual, there was no trace of anything in the house."

Alex thought back over the bizarre behavior of the cats over the last three months. Often she had awakened in the middle of the night and Sabrina wasn't there but when she awoke in the morning, the large, orange tabby was always by her side. Tonight, however, the two of them were downstairs together, apparently going to stay there until daylight.

"There's something else we can do, Stephanie," she said, slowly looking at each cat in turn. "We can watch them closely. They're good indicators of anything around."

Alex and Stephanie took their coffee to the living room as they always did early in the morning. There they settled on the couch and Alex told her roommate the details about her dream, the most disturbing one yet.

"It sounds to me like you were dreaming about the storm again, Alex. You were right in the middle of it."

"I was reading about that storm before I went to sleep. But, obviously, that did not cause the dream because I dreamed about it long before I got that book." Alex took a sip of coffee and turned to her roommate. "You know, they say that if you die in a dream, you die in reality. I drowned in that dream, Stephanie: I was dead. But I woke up. Why did I wake up?"

"Perhaps something woke you up."

"That could be, but what? There was nothing to indicate anything had been there except the open window and the air conditioner. And if one of our weird visitors had been around, there would have been a smell, or something else."

"That is not so totally strange, Alex. You've had bad dreams before, recently."

"Not as bad as this one, though. It's like they're getting worse."

Alex tried to think about the dreams before. All of them, it seemed, had been connected in some way to the storm. Stephanie had even experienced one of the same dreams and Alex was worried if her experience tonight would be repeated with her.

There was a brief silence that Stephanie suddenly broke.

"Alex, do you think we ought to look around outside."

"Outside?" Alex had intended to look outside for her cat if she hadn't found Sabrina downstairs.

"It's still dark out but we can get the two flashlights and turn on the porch lights." The worry on Stephanie's face was evident.

In the pre-dawn darkness, they searched about the

apartment but found no trace of anything. Alex examined the second floor window with the flashlight beam but found nothing out of the ordinary. No trace of it having been tampered with from the outside.

It was just getting light when Alex walked to the front of Mrs. Frank's house to pick up the newspaper. Retrieving it from the driveway, she turned, but froze in her tracks. In the attic front window, there was a light on.

She stood still, hoping to see some trace of someone in the room. There was none.

"Could this have something to do with what has just happened in our apartment?' she asked herself. She walked toward the front of the house, her eyes still on the lighted room. *Could Mrs. Frank be up there?* she thought. *And if she is, what is she doing up there?*

She wanted to knock on the door but knew the old lady never got up before seven thirty on any morning. As quietly as she could, she walked up on the porch and tried to see into the house. Everything on the ground floor was dark. Mrs. Frank's bedroom on the second floor was dark, also, but this was usual since it was too early for her to be up. Looking around quickly for anybody who might be out and about, she ran around the house to the apartment, almost knocking down her roommate who was emerging from the back yard.

Alex started to say something when she noticed Stephanie was as white as a sheet.

"What the…"

"That little girl was in the backyard again. I just saw her."

"The little girl? What was she doing this time?"

"Just standing there by the birdbath. I went into the backyard with the flashlight to see if anything had been there and when I turned around, there she was, with her back to me."

"God, Stephi. What did you do?"

"I…I just stood there and watched her. Finally, as quietly as I could, I got out of there. There's no telling what that thing would do if she saw me."

"Probably nothing, Stephi." Alex opened the backyard gate and peered in. The yard was empty. "Well, she's gone now."

"Alex, I think she opened that window. I think she was in

the apartment, she scared the cats downstairs, and…"

"I don't think so, Stephi, but what if she did? She's the one we need to communicate with, remember. I'm sure she's definitely a key to what's going on around here."

Stephanie hugged herself and tried to hold back her tears. "Alex, that thing scares me out of my wits."

"You big baby." Alex wanted to hug her but something made her refrain. "There was a light on in the attic just now. In that room that scared the hell out of me."

"That's where…That's where the other thing is…"

"Something's up there. The whole house is dark. I thought about Mrs. Frank being up there for some reason but then remembered she never got up before seven thirty." Alex put her hands on her hips and looked again in the backyard. Then, sighing, she turned back to Stephanie. "Look at us, standing here in the daylight in our PJs. Come on, let's go inside before every dirty old man in the area gets an eye-full."

Later that day, Mrs. Frank knocked quietly on the apartment door and announced that she was cooking supper that night and would Alex and Stephanie like to join her. Usually they went out to eat together but occasionally the old lady cooked. She didn't like to eat alone.

Alex quickly accepted the invitation, thinking that supper would be a good time to ask Mrs. Frank about the light in the attic. Of course, she couldn't let on that she had been up there on two occasions. She'd asked about the attic before, but this time she could tell her that she had seen lights on in the attic again and was still curious about them.

After serving chicken and dumplings that night, Mrs. Frank made an announcement of her own.

"I saw that child the other evening," she said. "You know, the one you saw last spring."

Alex perked up and momentarily forgot about her question. "A little girl in an off white or tan dress?" she asked, glancing at her roommate who sat, wide-eyed, across from her.

"Yes. Did you ever find out who that child is?"

"No, Mrs. Frank, we didn't. But Stephanie saw her this morning."

"This morning?" The old lady raised her eyebrows in

concern.

"I went out to get the newspaper early this morning and Stephi apparently followed me and saw her in the backyard."

"So early in the morning." Mrs. Frank looked from Alex to Stephanie and then back to Alex. "The other day right before dusk, I went out on the back porch to get a can of peaches out of the pantry and there she was. In the backyard."

"Did she have her back to you, Mrs. Frank?" Stephanie asked, glancing across the table at Alex.

"No. I saw her from the side. It looked like she had something in her hand." Now the old lady's expression had become quizzical. "When I went out the back door to ask the little thing where she belonged, she was gone. In a flash, just like that. I don't know how she did it. Nobody could jump that fence except maybe a big ol' boy."

"I don't know how she does it either, Mrs. Frank." Alex looked again at Stephanie and then at her hostess. "We've tried to catch her but she's always gone."

"She must belong around here somewhere close. I can't think of anywhere she could come from." The old lady put her napkin in her lap and prepared to eat. "I swear parents are so irresponsible nowadays. It's incredible. That little thing wandering around at all hours. Why, anything could happen to that child."

The three of them ate quietly for five minutes and then Alex asked her question about the attic.

"Oh, that must have been the exterminator, Honey," Mrs. Frank replied. "He was up there the other evening."

"No, it was this morning, just before dawn."

"Oh, my goodness. You don't suppose he left that light on and it has been on all this time."

Alex wanted to offer to check it but something made her not to. She ate quickly, again casting glances at Stephanie.

"I'll have to go up there, I guess, after we finish eating and check that," the old lady said. "I just hate to climb those attic stairs. They're so steep."

"We can check that after it gets dark, Mrs. Frank," Stephanie piped up. "Just go outside and look up."

The old lady chuckled. "It's got to be still on," she said.

"The exterminator is the only one who's been up there since I don't know when."

Later, after dessert, it had gotten dark enough to tell if an attic light was on and the three of them went out the front door to the front lawn. However, there was no light on, either in the front windows or the garret Alex had been curious about. Since she knew from earlier experience the light would not be on, Alex asked about the garret.

"I think that's a room of some kind," the old lady replied. "My Leo never mentioned it and I was never curious about it. He was the only one who ever went up there since he used it for storage." Mrs. Frank put her finger on the side of her head in thought. "I understand, though, Leo's parents and the Diehls before them used the attic for bedrooms and guestroom. Raymond and James never had rooms in the attic. They always wanted rooms on the second floor."

Alex nodded her head in silence. "I think you were right the other day, Mrs. Frank. I think there is a short up there."

"Oh, we'll have to get that fixed, Honey. Those can be dangerous." The old lady started back for the front door. "Let's go back in and have some iced tea."

The three of them had settled in the dining room for tea when Mrs. Frank suddenly left the room, but before Alex and Stephanie could get a conversation going, she reappeared with an old picture album.

"Here are some pictures of people who lived in this house all the way back to when it was built," she announced. She positioned the book in front of Alex and then scooted her chair around beside her. Stephanie moved in on the other side.

"That's Mr. and Mrs. Diehls sometime in the 1890's," Mrs. Frank said, pointing to a faded cabinet card just past the front cover. "I believe they had that taken just after they moved into the house."

Something about the pair looked vaguely familiar to Alex, but she figured she had probably seen a picture of the pair sometime before.

"And this is a picture of their daughter." The old lady flipped the page.

Alex glanced down and almost dropped the full tea glass in

her lap. There, in a cabinet card much clearer than that of her parents, was the thing that was stalking her.

"Her name was Johanna. She died when she was seventeen."

Alex turned her face, flushed with horror, away. "How... How did she die?" she said, meekly, wiping a tear from her face.

"Oh, my, Dear. That was a terrible tragedy. I remember now. She died in that horrible storm in Galveston in 1900."

Alex was breathing heavily but the old lady apparently didn't notice. She went on.

"She had gone down there to visit a friend and was caught, along with the girl's family, when the storm hit. I understand the house was demolished, like most of the town was. And Johanna and some of the people in the house with her died. Anyway, my Leo heard from his father that Mr. Diehls went down there to look for her as soon as he could get down there but he never found her. They found some of the people that had been in the house, but I don't think Johanna was ever found."

Stephanie, alarmed at her roommate's disposition, reached over and turned the page. "Who is this, Mrs. Frank?" she asked.

"Oh, that's Walter and Helen Frank, Leo's parents, just after they were married."

"Excuse me for a minute," Alex said, still keeping her head turned away from Mrs. Frank. She stood and headed for the restroom just off the main hall.

There she dabbed cold water on her face. She had started crying but hoped Mrs. Frank hadn't noticed. After fixing her hair she had just about collected as much of her composure as she could when Stephanie came through the door.

"Good Lord, roomy, what's up?" she said, alarmed.

"Johanna Diehls is up." Alex looked her straight in the eye and her roommate's alarm deepened.

"What?" she asked, weakly.

"Johanna Diehls is what is stalking me. She's what scared the shit out of me at the Rand Building and what sat on the garage roof that day. Stephanie, she's the spirit that's in this house, as dangerous as she can be. I know that she hasn't even begun to torment us, particularly me, yet."

"Oh, my God, Alex. The girl in the picture that Mrs. Frank was talking about?"

"Yes, Stephanie. She's a victim of that storm just like I thought. That storm has haunted my dreams for over three months."

"Alex, Mrs. Frank is now in on it, too. She said she saw the little girl."

Alex turned to the side and placed her hands on her stomach. "I heard that, Stephanie."

"Well, should we tell her what we know about her?"

"Tell her what? She thinks she's somebody's kid. What could we tell her? That she's nobody's kid? That she's the spirit of a poor little thing that drowned in that goddamned storm and is now back here to tell us God knows what." Alex threw her hands up in bewilderment.

"All of us now are going to start seeing her."

Alex turned and put both hands on her roommate's shoulders. "Yes, Stephanie, all of us are going to be seeing her until we find out from her what the hell is going on."

A tear rolled down Stephanie's cheek. "I'm worried about Johanna."

"I'm worried about Johanna, too. At least now we know who she is, or who she was. She's hideous. If you saw her you would agree with Pastor Gerlach that she's a demon."

"Alex, I think what we originally thought is correct. I'm sure, too, the little girl is trying to warn us of Johanna."

Alex was now almost in control of herself again. The impromptu talk with Stephanie had helped her even though now she worried that her roommate was more shaken up than she had been. "I don't know, Stephanie," she said, slowly and deliberately. "There's a hell of a lot more here than meets the eye. One entity we now know belonged here. I'm pretty sure now that room in the attic was Johanna's bedroom. The sensation I felt that day up there alone told me that." She looked up at her roommate who was wiping another tear from her cheek. "You big baby. We've both been bawling and that's not going to help."

"God, I need a drink. I don't give a shit if some people believe it's a sign of alcoholism."

"I know. Let's go back in there and give Mrs. Frank a few more minutes. She's probably wondering what happened to us by now. Then we can go back to the apartment and find St. Genevieve."

"Thank God for her." Stephanie turned and, in single file, she and Alex returned to the dining room.

"My goodness, girls, is everything okay?" The old lady greeted the two with a worried look.

"Everything's fine, Mrs. Frank. We just had a little girl-to-girl discussion in the bathroom. Nothing to worry about." Alex smiled and sat back down in her place.

They looked at the rest of the pictures but there was nothing else in the album that concerned the goings-on at the Frank house.

Later, in the apartment, Alex and Stephanie, over glasses of wine, continued the conversation they had left off in the bathroom.

"Yes, Stephi, like we thought, disaster victims." Alex took a sip and settled back on the couch. "We've seen three and I think there's more of them."

"More? What makes you think so?"

"I don't know. I just think we're not finished seeing all of them yet. There's got to be some connection between them besides that damned storm" Alex focused her eyes on the ceiling in concentration. "Between six and eight thousand people died in that storm," she continued. "And we've only seen three of them"

"Could they be related? If they are, wouldn't there be a picture of the little girl?"

"Not necessarily. I'm thinking about what Mrs. Frank said this evening. Johanna was in a house where other people died. The little girl and the man I saw were in that house, maybe a lot more of them."

Across from Alex, Stephanie silently drank her wine. A bit too fast, Alex thought.

"For now, though," she continued, "we focus on Johanna and the little girl. I mentioned Dr. Blassingame before. He's a scholar and former parapsychologist who now teaches history. I'm going to give him the full story. I never met him but Pauli has. He says this guy really helped at that final confrontation years ago. I just hope he's still where he was."

"Don't parapsychologists have certain equipment and assistants who help them explore this kind of stuff?" Stephanie's face was flushed, partly from the wine and partly from her experience that evening.

"Yes, but like I said, this guy is no longer working as a parapsychologist. He was a history professor years ago, but he helped us out because he was interested in our case. I know he'll be just as interested in this one."

The two girls finished their wine and then retired for the night. Nothing disturbed their rest that night but Alex fell asleep deep in thought about the revelations from Mrs. Frank. Her problems now had a partial identity but there still were no motives; no motives for the little girl's attempts to communicate other than speculation; and certainly no motives for Johanna's malign attentions on Alex. And Alex knew, even without her slight bit of ESP, that this adversary certainly lay in wait for her.

Chapter Thirteen

The next day Alex called Brendon University but learned that Dr. Vernon Blassingame had retired two years before. Apparently, he had bought a small farm in Illinois and was currently busy writing textbooks for history and sociology. Alex wanted to ask about parapsychology but hesitated when she thought the secretary she was talking to may not be aware of Dr.Blassingame's prior experiences with the paranormal. She did receive a phone number, however, and was eager to dial it.

But there was no answer. Irritated, she dialed the number again to no avail.

"He's not there," she called up the stairs to Stephanie. "I hope he hasn't moved again."

Stephanie descended the stairs in her underwear, the rest of her clothes in her hand. "What, exactly, do you think this guy can do, again, Roomy?" she asked.

"Tell us how to contact these things on our own terms, I hope."

"Contact these things," Stephanie whined. "I thought you said we were going to get rid of these things." She stood there in her bra and panties and, under other circumstances, Alex thought the scene would be funny.

"Stephi, in order to get the things to stop, you have to find out what they're up to. I thought you understood that."

Pouting, Stephanie donned a pair of shorts and a light blouse. "If that hideous little thing shows up, I'm going to run the other way," she mumbled.

Alex crossed her arms across her chest and frowned. "Stephanie, did you sleep peacefully last night? No dreams?"

"No. Nothing."

"Good. After that doozie of mine the night before last, I figured you'd be in line for one."

"Well, I didn't have one. Thank God."

"Yes. I'm going to talk to Mrs. Frank today. I want her to tell me more about the Diehls family. I have to find out more about Johanna." Alex studied Stephanie's face to ascertain a reaction but there was none. She continued.

"She's obviously got it in for me. The sooner I get to the bottom of her, the better."

"Alex, I don't think Mrs. Frank knows any more about Johanna than what she told us last night."

Alex knew that her roommate was probably right, but since Mrs. Frank had lived in the house for many years and her husband and his family a lot longer, he may have unearthed information she had forgotten to mention the previous night.

Around noon, Alex found the old lady busy in her front flower bed, pulling weeds and replacing washed away dirt. She kneeled down beside her and smiled.

"Mrs. Frank, you aroused my curiosity last night, particularly about Johanna Diehls. Such a tragedy is intriguing. You mentioned last night that Mr. Diehls never found her. Her body was never found?"

"No, it never was. I think a lot of the victims were found and identified, though. There were so many of them, they finally had to burn them. I guess there was just too many of them to bury. But Caleb Diehls looked and looked and just couldn't find Johanna. They said that her body had probably just sunk to the bottom of the bay."

An image of brownish water flowing from Johanna's mouth and nose filled Alex's mind. "Good Lord, how horrible," she said.

"Oh, yes. They later had a plaque put in a cemetery honoring her." The old lady turned back to her flower bed and started troweling top soil around her plants. "Leo told me the mother never got over it. She died in 1911, just after the family moved."

"How terrible," Alex mumbled.

"That poor woman. I don't know if I wouldn't have been the same way if something had happened to my Raymond or James."

"When I saw that picture of Johanna the other night, it just struck me she looked like someone I've seen before."

"Oh?"

"Yes, Mrs. Frank. I've seen a girl that looks like that recently."

Of course, Alex wasn't lying. Johanna Diehls was a very real presence, too real as Alex had found out. But presently, there was no way she could speak of this to Mrs. Frank. And although she had seen the little girl, the old lady didn't realize what she was. Johanna was completely beyond her belief.

"It just surprised me last night when I saw her picture," she continued.

"Yes. I usually don't like to show those pictures because of the tragedy behind them, but since you had asked about the history of the house on more than one occasion, I felt obligated to show them."

"I'm glad you did, Mrs. Frank. Thank you."

Alex rose and returned to the apartment, the photograph still vivid in her mind. She wondered where Mrs. Frank kept it, although she didn't know what she would do with it if she had it.

When she entered the apartment, she encountered Sabrina sitting on the stairs about half way up.

"Well, hello, baby cat. What are you doing there?" She climbed to Sabrina and reached out for her.

In seconds, the cat leaped to its feet, arched its back and hissed at her.

"What is the..."

It lunged at Alex's left hand and bit it hard between the index finger and the thumb.

"Ow, shit, Sabrina. That hurt!"

The cat abruptly turned and raced up the stairs and down the hall.

"Sabrina, what the hell is the matter with you?" Alex cried. She followed the animal up the stairs and down the hall to her room. But, turning into her room, she stopped in the doorway.

On her bed was Sabrina with another cat, a large black and white cat with big ears flattened out almost in a straight line. It had its back to Alex at the door and Sabrina was licking its face, like she often did Henrietta.

Alex froze in horror. "Tom?" she asked in a breathless voice, backing up instinctively. She heard Stephanie on the stairs.

Then, she quietly turned and tiptoed to her roommate at the top of the stairs. "Stephanie, come here," she said, quietly. "There's something I want you to see." She grabbed her roommate's arm and pulled her back to the door of her bedroom.

The cats were still there, Sabrina still licking the larger one whose head was now turned to the right and appeared in profile.

"My God, that looks like Tom," Stephanie exclaimed.

"That is Tom, Stephanie."

"No…No…It…It…can't…" Stephanie pressed both hands to her stomach, bent over and stared at her roommate in horror. Then she turned around and headed for the stairs, Alex just behind her. In three steps she reached the bottom and out the front door to the garage where she grabbed a shovel.

"Stephanie, don't do this." Alex grabbed her arm but the girl shook away and headed for the backyard. She threw open the gate and made her way to the spot where they had buried the remains of the unfortunate cat.

Alex stood at the gate, tears in her eyes, holding her hand which now was bleeding.

Stephanie didn't have to dig far to encounter the animal's vermin-covered remains. Then she started sobbing, heavy rasping sobs.

At that moment, Alex didn't know what to do. She wanted to take her roommate in her arms but hesitated, not knowing how Stephanie would take it.

"This is just one more thing, Stephi," she said, in a gentle tone she hoped Stephanie would hear. She did.

Stephanie turned a tear-stained face to her roommate. "Alex…Alex, what is that thing up there?"

"It's Tom, Stephanie," she replied. "Something has brought him back, probably…" She hesitated a moment. Her hand had begun to hurt more and more. "Probably to harass me."

"But why?"

Another question she could not answer. The answer to this question she would like to know herself. "I don't know," she could only say.

Then Stephanie noticed Alex's injured hand. "Oh, God, what happened to you," she said, trying to regain her composure.

"Sabrina bit the crap out of me. Then she ran up the stairs. When I followed her, I found her in there with that other cat."

"You better put something on that. Animal bites can be bad news."

"I know. Are you okay?"

Stephanie walked up to her, spade in her hand. "I guess I'm okay now."

"Go put some dirt on what you dug up."

Stephanie turned back and reburied the pitiful remains. Then the two girls returned to the apartment, Alex apprehensive about what might be in her room.

Since Alex's wound seemed serious, they went to a neighborhood clinic where Alex received a tetanus shot and a query about Sabrina's vaccination for rabies. Of course, the animal had received its shots and Alex was annoyed when a nurse questioned her in depth and would not take her initial affirmation for an answer. However, with a bandaged hand, Alex and Stephanie returned to the apartment where they ran into the large, orange tabby at the foot of the stairs.

Alex made a face at the animal and headed up the stairs, her roommate just behind her.

"I want to see just what the hell is going on in my room, now," Alex said in a firm voice enhanced by aggravation at the day's events.

"And where the hell is Henrietta?" Stephanie stopped in her room and searched it for her cat which wasn't there.

In Alex's room there was nothing to indicate that anything had been there. Even her pajamas were still crumpled on the bed just as she had left them.

Alex put her hands on her hips and turned to face Stephanie who had reached her doorway. "Now, whether that was Tom or some other goddamned wraith is beside the point. What matters is that it was here and it or some other force made my lovable Sabrina bite the hell out of me." The pain in her hand throbbed and Alex pressed her other hand to it. "There's definitely a growing diabolical force in and around this apartment," she blurted. "And I know Johanna Diehls is a major part of it."

Henrietta appeared and began rubbing against Stephanie's leg.

"My God, Henry," she said. "I hope you're not afflicted with this."

"She isn't, Stephanie. I think this little episode is over."

Alex and Stephanie returned downstairs where they found Sabrina stretched out on the couch. When Alex sat down beside her, she leaped to her feet and immediately plopped down beside her, her body pressed against Alex's leg. Reluctantly, Alex reached out and petted her.

"They've always been as much a part of this crap as we have," she mumbled.

"Alex, you know they prowl at night. What's to prevent them from getting into some kind of trouble or even attacking us in the night?"

"Nothing. But they won't. For some reason I think they want us wide awake. Or at least aware of what's going on."

"Who's they, Alex?"

"Whatever forces are at work around here," she replied. "When you think about forces, you think about demons. But I'm sure they aren't demons. They're some kind of spirits bent on a mission, harmful or otherwise. Like I said before."

The two girls sat facing each other and thought silently for a minute. Alex broke the silence.

"I wonder if Mrs. Frank has any more pictures of the Diehls. Or even old letters or documents concerning them. I would like to go through these. They might tell us, even in part, what Johanna is up to."

"But how would you go about explaining that to Mrs. Frank? You've already asked her about them a number of times. And you know she doesn't even believe in this stuff that's going on. The little girl is someone's wayward kid, according to her."

"I know. It's going to take some kind of strategy."

That evening over salads and baked potatoes, Alex explained her next move to her roommate.

"I'm going to ask Mrs. Frank if she has any old pictures of

her house. I mean old pictures going back to the time of the Diehls. I'll tell her I need them for our humanities seminar, which isn't exactly a lie since Dr. Tomlin told us to locate real photographs of old architecture."

"That's right, Alex. She did."

"Chances are I'll be able to find out where she keeps that old stuff in her house. Then, later, we can go through it."

"Yeah. When she's gone."

"Also, I told Pauli I want to go back up to the attic. I'm pretty sure now that was Johanna's room that we were in up there. Another thing. I want to find access to that garret. I know there's a room in it, but I don't remember seeing any door to it when we were up there before."

"I don't either. God, that place gives me the creeps, Alex."

"Me, too. But it's obvious there's a key to our problems up there."

"You're likely to run into Johanna up there."

"I'm likely to run into Johanna down here, Stephi."

"Yes, that's true."

"Anyway, Pauli's going to come over this weekend when Mrs. Frank is gone and we're going to go back up there. You can come with us if you like, but I wouldn't blame you if you didn't want to."

"I don't know, Roomy."

An hour after supper, the girls were busy with a humanities project when the phone rang. Since Alex was upstairs in the office on the computer, she answered the phone on the desk. However, there was no response to her greeting.

"Stephanie," she hollered downstairs. "Check the caller ID and see who that was."

"Out of area," Stephanie answered back a few seconds later.

"Another crappy wrong number," Alex mumbled, going back to her computer listings for the Romantic Movement in music.

But a few minutes later, the phone rang again.

"Out of area again, Roomy," Stephanie called up the stairs.

Annoyed, Alex picked up the phone. "Hello, who is this?' she asked in a blunt voice.

A thirty-second pause was followed by a soft "Alexandra."

"What? Who is this?"

"Alexandra!" Much louder and somewhat garbled was the response this time.

Alex froze. The voice was unmistakably female. The latter enunciation obviously the same voice but much harsher.

"Who is this?" Alex asked, again in a forceful voice. "Tell me who you are!"

Suddenly the line went dead. Alex remembered the day in the shower when her name had appeared in the mist on the mirror.

She hung up the phone and sat, staring at it. Deep down, she knew who the caller was, but she hoped it was someone playing a joke, a friend, maybe under the influence of evening drinks, playfully calling acquaintances at random to chide and annoy. But Alex knew better.

"What was that, Alex? Did they say?" Stephanie had appeared silently in the door behind her.

"Johanna. This thing, it seems, has a voice."

"What?"

"My little friend spoke to me. It knows my name. Those damned things years ago didn't speak to me. This one did." Alex turned in the swivel chair to face her roommate." I guess I'm to assume she's getting closer." She suddenly smiled and stood up. "Maybe not."

"How can you be so nonchalant about this?" Stephanie asked, her eyes revealing both perplexity and alarm.

"Remember what I said the other day, Steph. It's a good way to keep them at bay," she sang.

"I know but it still scares the hell out of me."

"Yeah, me too."

"I heard on the news there's a bad thunderstorm coming. It's supposed to be here later tonight."

"So what else is new?"

"Yeah. I know." Stephanie turned toward her room next door. "I'm going to bed. I closed everything up downstairs."

"So am I." Alex looked down to see Henrietta reach the top of the stairs and head into Stephanie's room. "Your little bunkmate's here, I see." She smiled at her roommate then trotted downstairs to get a drink of water.

A few minutes later while Alex was dressing for bed, she thought about the phone call earlier. This was obviously some new manner of harassment designed by Johanna or something else to vex her. The idea of Johanna using a telephone seemed more ludicrous than horrible. But the fact that for the first time she had heard her speak unnerved her. Still there was the chance that it wasn't Johanna at all.

She finished dressing and then retired, thinking she might read for thirty or forty minutes, but she was tired and soon fell into a deep sleep only to be awakened at two-thirty by a loud clap of thunder. She sat up in bed and glanced about the room, now illuminated by lightning. Sabrina, it seemed, was doing what Alex had wanted to do, sleeping through the storm.

She settled back in bed and turned over on her side to return to sleep. Nervously, she waited for the next clap of thunder, hoping the storm would soon pass and she could return to sleep in peace.

For fifteen minutes, all she could hear was the pouring rain. It seemed to her that the storm was passing so she scooted down under the sheet to return to sleep when a loud, high pitched scream of a cat broke the silence left by the storm. In an instant, Alex knew the noise was louder than anything Sabrina or Henrietta could make.

She sat up and turned to see Sabrina awakened and perked up, her ears high to catch the next sound. After a minute of silence, there was a snarl, a low, menacing, metallic sound that resounded through the apartment.

Sabrina leaped off the bed and darted through the door.

"What the hell…" Alex started to get up when she was stopped by a voice, far off, downstairs.

"Alex…Alex, help me." It was clearly Stephanie.

Alex proceeded to get up but was stopped by the appearance at her door of a very large cat, its black and white fur illuminated by the lightning flashes of the dying storm. It lifted its head toward Alex, its eyes two lustrous dead white marbles.

"Get out of here, Tom," Alex said, slowly and deliberately, terror rising in her, water filling a bottle.

The animal didn't move, but stood, perfectly still, staring at her. Again, lightning illuminated it as it moved closer to the bed. Now Alex could smell the putrefaction she knew only too well.

Nausea and fear drove her to desperation. Instinctively, she picked up a pillow and hurled it at the spectral animal. She grabbed a second pillow and prepared to throw it when she noticed the first lying on the floor at the closet door. The apparition was gone, and so was the storm.

Alex sprang out of bed and headed for the hall, where she collided with Sabrina in the darkness. The cat let out a yell and darted down the stairs ahead of her.

Reaching the living room, she looked around for Stephanie but didn't immediately see her. Only when she heard a noise behind her did she turn to see her roommate backed against the wall just beside the entranceway.

The little girl, her left hand on Stephanie's hip and her right grasping her inside the thigh at the groin, was emitting a garbled noise, her head turned upwards towards Stephanie's face. She was attempting to speak but what came out was unintelligible.

"Alex," Stephanie cried, painfully. "Let me go, you little toad. Alex."

Alex wanted to approach the phantom child but couldn't. Something, another fear, kept her away.

"Little girl, what do you want?" she asked, loudly.

With that, the child released Stephanie and turned toward Alex. Stephanie moved her hands down to where she had been grasped and pressed them to it. Slowly she moved away from the child out into the entranceway.

After pausing a moment, its mangled face now partially illuminated by moonlight now streaming through the front windows, the child slowly moved her left arm and hand upward and pointed upwards, toward the front door.

Alex recognized the direction, the same one toward which the man upstairs had pointed when Alex had encountered him.

Then Alex pointed in the same direction. "What?" she asked.

The child made a garbled sound like a growl but it seemed to Alex an attempt to form a word. But with that she was gone.

"Are you all right, Stephanie?" she asked, in a high whisper.

"She…She hurt me, Alex."

"You're okay, Stephi. Just sore a little bit, like I was that time." Alex moved over and turned on a lamp. In the new light, she noticed her roommate's tear-stained face. "She was clearly trying to tell you something, Stephanie. She was trying to tell me something too, but she vanished." Stephanie looked so pitiful Alex felt sorry for her. "Stephanie, what were you doing down here?" she asked, trying to smile.

"The storm woke me and I headed for the bathroom. When I returned to my room, Henrietta was wide awake and sitting up on the bed. When she saw me in the door, she took off, running right by me and down the stairs. I followed her but when I got downstairs, I couldn't see her in the dark. I started to turn on a light when I collided with that thing in the dark. I backed up into the wall but she grabbed me, here. Oh, God, that smell. That smell was terrible. And that thing vomited water on me." Stephanie began to sob but continued. "She…She wouldn't let me go, Alex."

"Stephi. Stephi, whatever she's trying to say is important. Important to us. If she hurt you, it was because she wanted you to hear what she had to say. Only she couldn't say it. Not to you and not to me. I…I don't know what the matter is with that child, Stephanie. If that was that goddamned Johanna on the phone last night, why is she able to talk and the child can't." Alex threw up her hands and turned. She thought about sitting down a while but the clock on the mantle chimed three.

"Stephi, we've got to get back to bed. We're going to be dead tired tomorrow and we've got to go to class." Alex turned off the light, took Stephanie's hand and headed up the stairs. "I think those two cats went back up. I hope they did."

"Alex," a pitiful voice behind her said. "Alex, why is that horrible thing coming after me?"

"Because you were the first to confront her. Remember?"

"I thought…I thought she was a human child. I didn't know she was some kind of…of a ghost, or spirit, or…I didn't know she was going to come after me."

They paused on the landing outside Stephanie's door. Alex

could tell her roommate was still distraught and might not be able to return to sleep.

"Stephi," she said, as if talking to a child. "These things are gone for the night. Curl up with Henrietta and go back to sleep. The storm's gone; the little girl's gone. You're all by yourself in the comfort of your bed."

"I guess you're right. You've been right about this stuff before. I guess."

Stephanie turned and entered her room where her cat waited for her. Alex watched her settle into her bed before she returned to her own room.

Before Alex got into bed, she checked the window to see if it was secure. It was. It had occurred to her while she was talking to Stephanie it might be open. Also, she glanced at the attic window to check for a light. There was none. She wondered if Tom was still nearby, but everything seemed at peace.

Alex regretted she had not checked these things before she had gone downstairs. Of course there was a connection but Alex still didn't know specifically what it was. The puzzle was still grossly incomplete and it weighed on Alex's nerves. What was the little girl trying to communicate? Did she point toward Johanna tonight? Was Johanna nearby tonight? Alex had a feeling the attic just might have answered this last question. After all, it was in the direction the little girl pointed.

She climbed into bed and pulled the sheet up to her neck. As tired as she was, she knew she would return to sleep with no trouble, but she was worried about what was going to happen next.

And what about the man she had seen? Were there others she had not seen? And the large hideous cat?

In the silence, Alex could hear her roommate sobbing in her room. She wanted to go to her but she didn't know what she could do that she hadn't already done. Whatever was in the apartment had plans for Stephanie, too. The little girl had already singled her out as well as the dreams. Would other things come to her as well?

Finally, the crying stopped and Alex hoped she was asleep. In the moonlit room, she could see Sabrina sleeping peacefully at the foot of the bed. *How vulnerable we all are,* she thought. *If only I could find the key to all this.* But in the silence she realized she was not much closer to a key than she was when these things began last spring. And what was truly unnerving was that the occurrences were clearly intensifying.

Chapter Fourteen

"I don't know, Pauli. She just pointed like the man I saw did. She was trying to speak but she couldn't."

"You said her face was mangled. Do you suppose that could be the reason for her inability to speak?"

Alex switched the phone to the other ear and leaned against the wall under the stairs. Her brother had called her early the next morning and she had immediately launched into a description of the night's events.

"I don't think so," she replied. "The gaping wound is in the side of her face. It doesn't affect her mouth or throat as far as I can see."

"Can we be sure she's trying to warn you against the other one?" he asked.

"Yes. I'm pretty sure now. And speaking of the other one, I now have a name for her. It's Johanna Diehls. Mrs. Frank showed us some pictures the other night and she was in one of them. She died in the Galveston storm but her body was never found."

"How did Mrs. Frank come by a picture of a victim from Galveston?"

"She told us Johanna had gone to Galveston to visit friends for the weekend and got caught in the storm. Apparently she and just about all of her friends died. Also, Pauli, that's her bedroom we saw in the attic. It was her presence I felt when I was up there that day alone."

"God, Sis, that's something. How do you suppose the little girl relates? Could she be her sister?"

"I have no idea, Pauli. Mrs. Frank hasn't mentioned a little girl and she and Johanna do not seem to resemble each other as far as I can see. O course, under the circumstances, you can't really tell."

"Do you think the little girl could have come from the family she visited?"

"I think so. That's also something I need to ask Mrs. Frank about but she probably doesn't know anything about the friends unless there's letters or something about."

"Have you seen Johanna lately?"

"Not since the last time I talked to you. But there's something else, Pauli. Something really weird. Last night I received a phone call that registered "out of area" on the caller ID. Whoever it was called twice. The second time a voice, distinctly female, said my name. My guess is that caller was Johanna."

"So that one talks, huh. Your guesses are usually right."

"I'd bet money on it."

"Tell me, Sis. Why do you think she's picking on you? I mean, why hasn't she gone after Stephanie?"

"That's what so crazy about this, Pauli. Again, I don't know. I think it's only a matter of time before she goes after Stephanie. She's never even seen Johanna. Not yet, anyway."

"Didn't you tell me your roommate accosted the little girl first?"

"Yes, she did. And she scared the shit out of her. But, Pauli, as to the communication thing, what else could she possibly be trying to communicate except a warning?"

There was a pause during which Alex heard her brother sigh. After two minutes, Paul broke the silence.

"I talked to Josh last night. He's curious to know what's happening, too."

"Oh, yes. We haven't gotten together much lately. We've been so busy. In fact, I haven't seen him since we got back from Galveston."

"Yeah. And he has been out of town. But he was somewhat worried about you last night and said he was going to call you tonight."

"I'll be glad to hear from him." Alex paused a minute and thought. "Pauli, can you come over Friday night? I'm going to try to get Josh over, too. As you know, the more, the better. Mrs. Frank is going to Conroe for the weekend and I want to go back up to the attic. There's some things I want to check up there and I sure as hell don't want to go alone.

"I don't blame you. I think I can, but I have to work 'til six."

"Okay, if Josh comes, it'll take him a while to drive in from Katy."

"Right. Maybe we can stumble across something then."

"Maybe so. I hope so."

Alex hung up and returned to the paper she was writing. But since she had broached the subject on the phone, she couldn't take her mind off Mrs. Frank's attic. The sheer horror of the situation had blocked out any detail she might have noticed on her first visit up there and on the second, she hadn't noticed much of anything but the contents of the front bedroom. Since this had probably been Johanna's bedroom, why might it not be the center of the disturbances. Suddenly, Alex wanted to sneak up there before Friday but something told her not to.

Later that afternoon, Alex went jogging with Stephanie and as they rounded St. Andrews Episcopal Church to return to the apartment, Alex told her of the plans for Josh and Paul for Friday.

"Josh was out of town?"

"Yeah. But Pauli talked to him last night."

"So, you've already set it up. Good."

"Like I said, you don't have to come with us if you don't want to."

"I'm coming, Roomy. I don't want to be there by myself while all of you are in that attic."

"Alex turned to her in mid stride and smiled. "I'm glad."

At home, the girls prepared to shower, Stephanie first, and then Alex. While Stephanie was in the shower upstairs, Alex sat in the front room in her jogging clothes and sipped tea.

Her thoughts about Josh and why he hadn't called her as soon as he got home were interrupted by the telephone. Slowly, she got up and answered the phone by the stairs.

"Hello, Alex," a voice on the other end sang.

"Joshua Hamilton, you jerk. Why didn't you call me when you first got back?"

"How ya' doing, Babe? I talked to your brother last night. I would have called you but it was kind of late so I figured I'd just call you today. Anyway, Paul called me to ask me if I'd heard about the Cardinals' tryouts. And, of course, I had. While we were in New Orleans."

"New Orleans?"

"Yeah. Mom took us all to New Orleans so I'd miss that. Pretty devious, huh?"

"Yes, it is. Kind of funny, too. But Gretchen Hamilton's a pretty neat person, though."

"Yeah, Mom is. It's pretty obvious she doesn't like ball players."

"She wants her son to be a doctor. I don't blame her."

"Thanks, Partner." Josh's sarcastic reply was followed by a snort and a laugh.

"Anyway, Paul called again just now and told me something I thought was pretty interesting."

"Oh, yeah?"

"He said that thing that's after you is named Johanna Diehls. D-I-E-H-L-S." He spelled the name slow, like a child.

"Yes."

"I dated a girl with that name in high school. Anna Diehls. She was the only person with that name I'd ever known."

"Diehls, yeah." Alex thought once again about the family who built Mrs. Frank's huge, old house. "Josh, where did she live? Did she live in Katy?"

"Yeah. She lived with her mother and stepfather. Her real father died when she was in elementary school. He had congenital heart trouble or something. What was weird, though, or so I thought, was that she loved her stepfather. Apparently, they got along great. How many people do you know can get along with their stepfather? Or stepmother, for that matter?"

"Not many. Her dead father's name was Diehls?"

"Yeah. Her stepfather's name was Rex. Rex Hempstead. He was a great guy. I met him. I liked him right off. He was a welder. A cowboy."

"Josh, did she ever tell you anything about her father? Her family?"

"No. Not her father. She did tell me about her great grandfather, though. He died in World War I. Went down with a ship somewhere."

A picture of the Lusitania, long absent from Alex's mind, suddenly flashed into it.

"Did she mention what ship it was, Josh? Like maybe the Lusitania?"

"No. No, she didn't. She had his stuff, though. She showed it to me one night when I was over there."

"Does she still live in Katy?"

"No. She goes to school in Lubbock. Texas Tech."

"That's very interesting, Josh. I'm curious. What did she look like?"

"Oh, medium height. Blond. Real light blond hair. It was natural, too. I don't remember seeing any dark roots. She had these jeans with both knees out. She loved to wear them. She even wore them to school until she got sent home to change."

Alex built a picture of the girl in her mind. Then, she compared it with Johanna. "Josh, I'm thinking your girl friend is a great niece of this thing that's stalking me. From what you say, their appearances are similar. The other day, Mrs. Frank said something about two sons, brothers to Johanna Diehls. One was younger. One son was your girl's great grandfather. It would seem at this point both siblings found a watery grave."

"It looks that way. Anyway, Paul told me he was coming over Friday night. I'll be there, too."

"Good. Mrs. Frank is going to Conroe again. We're going back up to the attic to check some things. This time it'll be at night."

"Great. Maybe we'll see something."

"I hope to God we don't. But there are some things I want to find out. I think we'll also look for more pictures, letters and things. I think a good place to start looking for that stuff is that office."

"I'll be looking forward to it. I like that old house."

After saying goodbye, Alex plopped down on the couch and thought about what she had just learned. She remembered Josh had brought a blonde girl to the Reformation Sunday picnic at St. John's two years before but she couldn't remember much of what she looked like. At the time, Alex had not been interested.

Stephanie came halfway down the stairs in her underwear

to announce she was out of the shower.

"Steph, Josh is going to join us Friday night. And get this. One of his old girl friends is like a great niece of Johanna Diehls. I'd bet my life it's the same family. That name is not common at all."

"Wow. Living, breathing descendants. They must have come from one of the brothers Mrs. Frank told you about."

"Very likely. This guy drowned during the First World War, according to Josh."

"Jesus, Roomy. You don't suppose he's around here, too."

"I don't think so. I think we're dealing exclusively with storm victims here."

Stephanie ran back upstairs to her room and Alex followed her to take her shower.

In the shower, Alex tried again to picture the girl Josh had been with at that picnic, but she was just a haze. She couldn't see a face at all except when she tried to fit her with Johanna's countenance.

Later, as Alex lay in bed trying to read, she thought again about the strange girl. This time a pale, white-blonde girl in ragged jeans emerged. But this picture, too, faded out. All Alex had was a name. Anna Diehls.

At eleven PM, Alex rose and checked on Stephanie and noticed that Henrietta was not in the usual place beside her sleeping mistress.

"Not again," she muttered to herself. Annoyed, but feeling also somewhat apprehensive, she made her way downstairs, turning on lights at the foot of the stairs and the living room.

She found Henrietta eating quietly in the kitchen, but she had the feeling that she was not alone; that something or someone was near.

Quickly, she looked around the apartment and then outside. There, she checked the attic window. It was dark.

Ah, so we're not at home, she thought. *Where could we possibly be?* When she turned back to the door, it started to rain.

"At least it's not messing up the day this time," she said to herself, locking both locks on the front door.

Alex returned to bed, the feeling still with her. *There's nothing around that's apparent,* she thought as she lay in the darkness. She cupped her hands behind her head to lie awake awhile but the fatigue of a long day put her to sleep quickly.

Soon after, she began dreaming. She walked down a city street amid people in old fashioned clothes who were solemn and silent. Fearfully, she looked about the buildings close by and recognized two of them immediately. She had seen them both on her last trip.

“Oh, Jesus, Galveston,” she sobbed. She started running down the street and turned into another to find still more people. For some reason she dare not look these people in the face, but she kept running along this street, thinking she might get away from them.

At the corner, she ran out of the business district and stood on the edge of a residential neighborhood. In the distance, at the end of this long street, were breaking waves splashing into the air at least twenty feet.

Terror rising in her, Alex turned around and started running back toward the downtown area. Only this time something stopped her in front of a small bookstore sandwiched between two large buildings. Unable to go on, she entered to find only one person there.

A girl with light blonde hair and ragged jeans stood with her back to the door before a table full of books. Silently, Alex walked up to her, immediately recognizing that something about the girl besides her hair and jeans was very familiar. When she was almost to her, the girl turned.

Alex looked into a smiling face she knew she had seen before. Instead of saying anything, the girl giggled, staring into Alex’s eye. Then, she became serious.

“My great aunt is going to kill you,” she said, and then giggled again.

An icy hand grabbed Alex’s heart and started to squeeze it. Then she awoke.

On the verge of a scream, she sat up in bed and looked around quickly in the darkness. Sweat dripped down her body and stuck her pajamas to her. She swallowed hard and bent forward, her arms crossed over her stomach.

Nothing was in the room with her except her cat, now perked up at the foot of the bed. The humming of the air conditioner provided the only sound and Alex wondered why she still sweated while the room temperature was so cool. She listened closely in the dark for any sound from any part of the apartment.

"Oh, God help me," she whispered and stifled a sob.

It occurred to her to check the attic window again, but something told her she would find nothing. The dream was still vivid in her memory; it would not fade. Alex wondered if it would return if she returned to sleep even though dreams in the past had not.

Clearly a warning, this nightmare had been a combination of other dreams and a newly discovered presence in her psyche. She wondered where Josh's old girl friend was. Was she really at Texas Tech? Was she even alive? This nightmare had picked up a newly discovered connection to the past and frightened her out of her wits with it.

She was still tired and sleep beckoned but Alex had no desire to return to the hideous streets of Galveston.

Who am I kidding, she thought. *I'll be asleep in a pinch.* She lay back down, her eyes wide open, studying the ceiling and line of windows by her bed. *I wonder if that window is still locked,* she thought. Slowly, she rose and scooted to the end of the bed to reach over and test the lock on the window.

Locked. As she knew it would be. She glanced at the clock. 2:30 AM, three and a half hours before she usually got up.

Sliding back under the sheet, eyes still wide open, again she wondered if sleep would bring the nightmare back.

"God help me," she muttered, and closed her eyes.

Nothing else disturbed her sleep, however, and she awoke when Stephanie shook her at a few minutes before seven.

"You and I are due at seminar at eight thirty, Roomy," she said, breezily, and trotted back down the hall to get dressed.

Alex arose and rubbed the sleep out of her eyes. Although she had slept soundly after she fell asleep the second time, she was still tired. She knew she wouldn't be able to get the hideous dream out of her mind. Out of the silence, usually notable in these nightmares, a voice had warned her of what she had known all along. Johanna was after her.

Stephanie padded back down the hall, pulling a pair of

jeans cutoffs up to her waist.

"Go on downstairs and make the coffee," Alex said. "I'll be down in a minute." She got up and followed her roommate as far as the bathroom. There she thought about the day she had found her name in the mirror. *That was probably a warning, too, but I didn't know it at the time,* she thought.

In her room, she slowly put some clothes on and went downstairs to get some coffee.

"Another bad one last night, Steph," she said, pouring a cup from the carafe.

"Not another one. I'll probably have the same damned dream," Stephanie whined, standing in the kitchen door, coffee cup in hand.

"Not this one," Alex replied. She took her coffee and sat down at the dining room table. "This little tidbit belongs to me."

"God, Alex. How can you stand this crap? If I were in your shoes, I don't know what I'd do." Stephanie moved to the table and took a seat across from her.

"After you went to bed last night, I felt something was in the apartment." Alex set her coffee cup down and stared at it momentarily. "I looked all around the apartment and outside and there was nothing. Nothing tangible, Stephanie. Nothing human." She looked over in Stephanie's face. "I feel this presence right now. It's very close."

"Johanna?"

"Probably. But I'm not sure. And the damndest thing about it is I'm pretty sure what it's up to. It's responsible for these dreams along with these other things." She took a sip of coffee and looked about the room. "Yes, it's up to something, and I got a feeling I'm going to find out what it is. Pretty quick."

Stephanie's eyes were wide, pale-blue expressions of fear. "What do we do now?"

"I hate to keep sounding like a broken record but we wait. What can we do? Just wait and see." Alex smiled and drained her cup. "I'm going upstairs and fix my hair. It looks like it's been through the washing machine."

That morning, after seminar, they stopped in a place for lunch. Later, after a visit to a bookstore, Alex drove home, not unmindful of the fact that something may lie in wait for them.

Of course the apartment was empty. After a superficial look about the downstairs, Stephanie took a nap upstairs while Alex got interested in a movie on TV. She still had the feeling, however, that something, or someone, was nearby.

This feeling had not been with her while she had been at seminar, or any other place she had gone that day. She remembered, with a shudder, that Johanna had followed her to the Rand Building, but then she had not been conscious of her presence until she had heard her on the third floor. And the remembrance of Johanna's invisibility made her even more terrified of the sensation she had now.

Thankfully, the movie she was now watching was an action picture, full of noise and shouting, that somewhat took her mind off her situation. Still, when the movie ended, Alex looked about the apartment again, upstairs and down, and then woke Stephanie. She needed to get out.

"We need to go to the store, Steph. Remember, we need cat food and laundry detergent." Alex looked down at her roommate, groggy with sleep, and thanked God she was there.

"Oh…I'd almost forgotten." She rubbed the sleep out of her eyes.

"Almost forgotten? I'm almost out of clothes."

Stephanie sat up and threw both legs off the bed. "I don't worry about running out of clothes." She grinned. "I can always go naked through the world."

"I'd get a kick out of that. I don't think Mrs. Frank would, though."

"My God, Roomy. Can you just see me and my bare ass jogging down the driveway and then all the way over to St. Andrews?"

Alex laughed. "The guys would love it. You'd have at least twenty of them following you home." Then, she became serious. "Stephanie, you…you didn't dream, did you?"

"No. No, I didn't. Why?"

"I just wondered if a piece of last night's nightmare spread to you."

"Not now, Alex. I did dream night before last about Tom. I wonder if that has any bearing on our problem."

"Stephi, a cat an awful lot like Tom has appeared in this

apartment."

"I know."

"So, it does have a bearing on it."

"You think so?"

"Stephanie, like I said, if this shit stays in dreams, we're okay. It's when it comes out of dreams, we've got problems. Let's go on to the store so we can get back pretty quick."

Stephanie quickly put on her sandals. "Let's check the fridge. We might need a few other things. Also, I feel a St. Genevieve night coming on. I think tonight could be that night, before tomorrow night with the guys.

Alex grinned. "You bet. We don't need those two high-school-harrys getting soused on us."

"You're right about that." Stephanie turned suddenly to Alex and chuckled. "If we drink a lot of it, we'll both pee all night. That may solve the dream problem"

"God, Stephi. I haven't thought about that. But you're probably right."

The two girls laughed out loud and descended the stairs. At the store, Alex was conscious that the feeling was not there. Whatever it was had apparently stayed at the apartment *Curious,* she though. *But why can't I put my finger on it at home?*

They did just what they said they would that evening. Sipping wine and chatting in front of TV, they did not retire until after twelve.

Alex fell asleep immediately and slept soundly, not waking until six thirty the following morning. Did the wine help?

Making her way to the bathroom, she noticed her roommate still asleep and wondered if she had experienced any troublesome dreams. "As much wine as we drank last night, I'm surprised we even made it up to bed," she said to herself.

Back in her room, she collapsed on her bed and remembered there was no seminar to go to that morning. Instead, later in the day, she and Stephanie would travel down the Gulf Freeway to NASA to visit exhibits which offered art and models. The visit was Alex's idea based on a discussion at seminar in which she had described a trip years before when she had been impressed by the artwork featuring outer space and aircraft. Although she looked forward to the visit, she remembered where the Gulf Freeway led. The very thought of Galveston made her shudder.

She decided to get up, wake her roommate, and fix breakfast. After dressing, she hollered at Stephanie and headed to the kitchen to start the morning meal.

There she noticed the curious feeling she had experienced for two days was missing. Although she was relieved, she still wondered why. She was still worried. After all, Johanna had come to her at the Rand building completely unheralded.

"What time are we going to NASA?" a sleepy voice asked from the staircase.

"Good morning, Steph."

"Good morning," on the end of a yawn.

"We'll probably leave around ten. It's pretty far out there and we need to get back to get ready for the guys." Alex put two slices of bread in the toaster and then flipped four breakfast sausages. "We can eat lunch out there somewhere."

Stephanie returned upstairs while Alex put two more pieces in the toaster. She was munching on a piece of toast when Sabrina appeared at the door.

"Hello, baby cat. Are you hungry?" Alex glanced at the cat bowls on the counter in front of the kitchen window. They were empty. "Of course you are."

She poured a bit of dry food into both bowls and, while Sabrina jumped on the counter to eat, retrieved the soft food from the refrigerator.

"Here you go, Baby." Can and spoon in hand, she glanced up at Sabrina, sitting straight up behind her bowl.

Suddenly the cat leaped to all fours and hissed violently, at something behind Alex. Then the animal leaped back into the kitchen window, striking it so hard it should have broken.

Alex didn't have time to make a full turn when it was on her. The pale, long dead corpse of Johanna Diehls, its knife-like claws extended toward Alex, its mouth regurgitating filthy, warm liquid, knocked her violently against the kitchen counter.

Fortunately, Alex caught both wrists before any of the pointed, ragged nails could enter her.

Although the body was light, the strength of the thing was

like iron, slowly driving the nails toward Alex's body. The face, hideously animated, moved closer and closer to Alex's. When Alex screamed from the bottom of her throat, it belched filthy liquid again all over her. The pair collapsed to the floor.

There, with one nail digging into her hand, Alex screamed again. And again, this time with Stephanie's name. The smell was becoming unbearable and she knew she couldn't hold on much longer. One sharp set of nails had reached her chest.

But Stephanie appeared at the kitchen door.

"Alex! Alex! Holy Jesus! God!"

Suddenly the crushing presence loosened its hold and evaporated, leaving Alex, sobbing, huddled in the corner, and the stifling smell, temporarily.

Stephanie stood, wide-eyed in terror, tears streaming down her face, frozen in the doorway.

Slowly, Alex rose to her knees, her head facing a kitchen cabinet, and lost all that was in her stomach. Sobbing and retching, she tried to rise to her feet. Finally, her plight brought her roommate to her.

Putting her hands on Alex's shoulders, Stephanie, herself sobbing, pressed her body to Alex's back.

"Alex. Alex. My God, Alex."

In a moment, Alex turned and took her roommate in her arms, blood from the wound in her hand getting on Stephanie's shirt.

The two girls stood, embracing, leaning against the kitchen counter, for several minutes. Finally, Alex spoke.

"You scared that damned thing off, Stephanie," she said, in a tiny, faraway voice.

"What?"

"It was Johanna. You scared her off." Alex put her hands on Stephanie's shoulders. "It caught me off guard. Alone. All I could do was scream my lungs out and hold it away from me."

Stephanie's tear-streaked face turned to Alex's. "That... That thing was just a corpse, like the little girl."

"Yes, Steph. Like the little girl. But much more dangerous." Alex examined the wound in her hand. "One of her nails got me. It looked...It looked to me like she was trying to plunge all ten of them into me."

"God, Alex. The smell. I smelled it the other night with the little girl."

"The smell. The smell of a corpse dead a very long time. It goes with these things."

The girls dropped their hands and stepped away from each other.

"I'm sure that thing could push those nails into my body," Alex continued. "And probably inflict serious wounds. Was I ever lucky you were here."

"When someone else shows up, they vanish? The little girl didn't."

"She does. The same thing happened years ago. It's like… It's like they can't be seen by more than one human at any one time." Alex tried to smile even though a tear streamed down her face and her hand had begun to throb. "There's really something to that safety in numbers thing."

"The little girl left pretty quickly after you appeared the other night."

"Exactly." Alex turned to Stephanie and put her hands on her shoulders. "Thanks for saving my neck."

"Don't mention it. You better put something on that hand."

"Yes. I don't think it's bad enough to require stitches. It's just superficial." Again, Alex examined the wound. Then she took a paper tower and wiped it clean. "I knew in the back of my mind that she was waiting, just waiting until she had a chance to attack me. I've felt her presence for a couple of days now. She's been close by, just waiting for a chance."

"Alex, I remember you mentioned that to me."

"I wasn't really sure what it was all about, Stephanie." She ran some water over the wound and then pressed a clean paper tower to it. "For all I knew, it could have been the little girl or someone else close by. I wasn't really sure it was Johanna because in the past Johanna has always turned up all of a sudden." She turned and walked into the living room.

"Stephanie, come with me upstairs. I want to clean this wound and put something on it and I really don't want to be by myself. I want to get something for my stomach, too. We'll clean up down here afterwards."

Upstairs, Alex cleaned and bandaged her hand while

Stephanie stood in the bathroom door. Only afterwards did she notice the dampness and smell of her shirt.

"That damned thing threw up water all over me," she said, coming out of her shirt.

"Water?"

"Yeah. It's sea water." Alex headed into her room to change all of her clothes. "When you drown, you're full of it."

"That crap comes out of the little girl, too."

"I know."

In her bedroom, Alex changed her clothes, even her underwear. "The way I figure it, I was really lucky this morning," she said. She passed Stephanie, dirty clothes in hand. "I ought to burn these. They're full of filth and they stink."

"They should come clean, though, in the washer."

"I don't know, Steph. With this stuff, you can't ever tell." Alex breathed deeply and walked swiftly toward the stairs. "I'm going to try to wash them, I guess. Stay with me, Steph," she said over her shoulder. "I don't feel anything now, but that thing might still be somewhere close by."

Stephanie didn't say a word but trotted along after Alex to the garage and the clothes washer.

"Are we still going to have the guys over this evening?" she asked, while Alex loaded the washer.

"Yes. As a matter of fact, I'm going to call both of them." Alex slammed the lid down and spun the dial. It sprang to life. "I know I can get Josh so I'll call him first. Pauli might be at work."

"Why are you going to call them? Don't they know…"

"I'm going to ask each of them to bring something over; something I'm going to need, starting this evening."

Without another word, Alex went to the entrance hall phone and dialed Josh Hamilton in Katy. As she had expected, he answered.

"I want you to bring your most recent high school yearbook with Anna Diehls in it," she said into the phone while looking her roommate straight in the eye.

There was a pause while Alex listened and licked her lips.

"I want to see what she looks like," she continued. "I had a dream about her and I want to see how much she matches the girl in my dream. I'm curious about her resemblance to this thing around here."

Josh agreed and after a few more words, Alex hung up the phone.

"You didn't tell him about this morning?" Stephanie asked.

"No. I'll do that tonight." Alex picked up the phone again and dialed her home number.

Elizabeth Zunker answered the phone but Paul was there. He had taken the day off to run some errands.

"I had some overtime," Paul said when he got to the phone. "So I figured I'd make a long weekend and get some chores done.

"I'm glad you did, Pauli. Still on for tonight?"

"Yeah. Josh, too."

"I know. I just called him." Alex shifted the phone to her other ear. "Pauli, do you remember that baseball bat you bought at the flea market a few years ago? The big one? Bring it when you come over tonight."

"God, Sis. What's up? That's a big league bat."

"I know. It'll do just nicely."

"Do for what?"

"I need it as a weapon. I'll tell you why when you come over tonight."

"A weapon?" Paul's voice rose in alarm.

"Yes, Pauli, a weapon. I'll tell you more when you get here. Just remember to bring it."

Alex calmed her brother with a few more soothing words and then hung up the phone. Then, she turned to her roommate, standing nearby, eyes like saucers.

"My first defense against that thing close up is that bat," she said. "It's heavy and can probably do a lot of damage to it."

"Alex, a baseball bat? What about a gun?"

"Stephi, a gun is no good against something like that. You could put six bullets through it and it wouldn't faze it. We're dealing with a damned corpse, remember?"

"Yeah, but a bat?"

"It's the best thing. You don't even see these things until they're right on top of you unless they want you to see them." Alex found herself doubting now if the baseball bat would work. Johanna would have to be very close for it to be effective. The idea of that rotted corpse anywhere near her almost unsettled her.

"I think the best defense is to run."

"You're right, Steph. I've run from that thing before. But when we grapple, like this morning, I've got to have something to use."

The two girls didn't leave the apartment all that day. All plans were cancelled. Nor did they let each other out of their sight. Both were vigilant for the rest of the day. If there was a shred of Johanna left there, Alex wanted to know about it.

Any feeling she had of her presence was gone now, completely. She hoped this signified that this malicious spirit was presently very far away. But she now knew that Johanna could turn up anywhere and anytime.

Chapter Fifteen

That night Paul and Josh arrived at the apartment within two minutes of each other. As each arrived, he was settled into the living room with iced tea. Stephanie played hostess while Alex rounded up flashlights for the evening's activities. Carrying two of them, she descended the stairs five minutes after the boys arrived.

"I have only two flashlights," she said. "But I'd like everyone going up there to have one, so you're going to have to get those in your trucks."

"Hi, Sis." Paul jumped up and faced his sister.

"Hello, Pauli. Josh."

Josh was slower to get up, but as he did, he produced the school annual requested.

"Good, you brought it." Alex glanced momentarily at the book and then back at him. "Find me the best picture of Anna Diehls. It'll probably be her class picture. Pauli, did you bring your toy?"

"It's out in the truck, Sis."

"Run and get it right quick, would you?"

"Here's a picture of Anna." Josh brought the open annual over and put it in front of Alex. "It's her senior picture. The best one."

Alex glanced at the picture and was somewhat relieved to find a girl who bore little resemblance to the one in her dream. In fact, the only similarity was the light blonde hair. In a moment, Alex concluded that her "dream girl" had been influenced by the brief, frenzied glances she had had of Johanna.

"Nope. Never seen her," she said. "Thank God."

Paul brought the bat in, slamming the screen door behind him.

"Here, Sis. All ready for you."

"Good. Let me see it."

He handed the heavy bat to his sister. "That's what they use at Minutemaid Park and Yankee Stadium."

"I'm going to use it right here." She put both hands on the bat and brought it back, a batter at the plate.

"Have you seen that thing again?" Paul asked, a note of seriousness in his voice.

"Yes, Pauli. As a matter of fact I have." In an even tone, she related the story of what happened that morning to Paul and Josh, leaving out no detail. The boys stood, quietly listening, their eyes growing wider. When she was finished, Alex put her hands on her hips and turned to her roommate.

"I firmly believe," she said, "that if Stephanie hadn't shown up, I would have been cut to pieces. Fighting that thing was like fighting a machine, a filthy, stinking, damp killing machine."

"And it cut your hand, Sis?"

"Yes. That thing cut my hand."

"And it just vanished?" Josh seemed dumbfounded. "Like that?"

"Just like that." Alex snapped her fingers.

"I saw that thing." Stephanie suddenly stepped in front of the boys. "It was the most hideous thing I've ever seen. Even much worse than the little girl. I don't know what I'd done if that thing had come at me."

"I do, Steph," Alex interjected. "Probably die." Then she became even more serious. "Just like years ago, Pauli. These things mean us harm. But now they're much worse. This thing this morning was like a demon."

"You think you can fend it off with a baseball bat?"

"I think so. If it gets real close, I think it will be vulnerable to a blow. They have to become vulnerable to do you physical harm."

"And they vanish when someone else comes along?"

"Yes, Josh."

"And this thing, Sis, is particularly sinister. It can do anything."

"Yes it can, Pauli. And the baseball bat is my only chance

against it. From what I can tell, this thing has a grip like steel. It can come and go as it pleases, through doors, even walls. It can fly through the air and even pounce on me. Also, it can move about in an invisible state, not to mention the long, sharp nails." She raised her bandaged hand and showed it to the boys.

"Does that hurt?" Josh asked, his eyes growing wider.

"Yes, Josh, it does. But it's bandaged and it will heal. I don't even need a tetanus shot because I got that when my goddamned cat bit me!"

"Sis, we've got to find Stehle's Door."

"Find Stehle's Door? I don't even know how to begin doing that." Alex threw up her hands in frustration. "God knows I've thought and I've thought about it. That's one of the things I want to look for tonight."

The four stood silent for about a minute. Then Paul spoke up.

"You think the best place to start looking is Mrs. Frank's attic?"

"I don't know what to think, Pauli." She crossed her arms over her chest and looked from Paul to Josh in turn. "Years ago, it seemed so simple. Now, it's become so damned complicated." She looked down at her feet, then up again. "I want to look for a door to that garret room. There's got to be one somewhere. I want to see in that room even if we have to climb out on the roof in daylight and go in the window. Given the fact that Johanna's room is right next door to it, I think there might be a key in that room. The trick is getting in there."

Paul sighed and slapped his flashlight into the palm of his hand. "Well, let's go see, gang." With that, Alex and Stephanie took a flashlight apiece and Paul and Josh retrieved flashlights out of their trucks. When they returned, Alex threw her bat over her shoulder and turned toward the kitchen to get the key.

"Don't you think Josh could swing that better?" Stephanie asked. "After all, he is a baseball player."

"Josh doesn't know what we're looking for, Stephanie. And if he saw that thing, there's a good chance he'd freeze up." The image of ten, long sharp nails flashed through her mind, but was cancelled by the realization there would be four of them going up to the attic. "I'm pretty sure that thing is not going to appear to all four of us." Quickly, she walked to the kitchen to get the key to Mrs. Frank's house. "Come on," she said, leading the way. "It's going to be dark pretty quick."

When they got to the foot of the back stairs, Paul took the lead. Since the staircase light was very dim and the fading day provided little light through the windows, they all tried their flashlights before proceeding up.

At the second floor landing, Paul opened the hall door.

"Any need to look in here?" he asked.

"Not really. Mrs. Frank sleeps just down that hall." Alex shined her light up the stairs toward the attic but saw little past the first landing.

Paul first, then Alex, Stephanie and Josh bringing up the rear, trooped up the last flight of stairs. At the attic landing they were met by a surprise.

The door to the attic had been boarded up. Four large two-by-sixes had been nailed across the door from the top to about a foot from the floor. The size of the nails used made one wonder why they hadn't split the boards.

"Good God! When did this happen?" Paul gaped at the boards crossing the door.

"I have no idea, Pauli." Alex was more calm. She put her hands on her hips and studied the door.

"I guess Mrs. Frank doesn't want us to come up here anymore," Stephanie said.

"Stephi, Mrs. Frank doesn't know we've ever been up here. We've never told her." Alex moved closer to the door. "Besides, Mrs. Frank didn't do this. Look at the size of those nails."

"This looks like something done by a giant." Josh stepped up by Alex and ran his hands over the boards.

"Maybe she hired someone to do this."

"Stephanie, does this look like a hired job to you?" Paul turned from Stephanie back to the door. "It doesn't to me. Look how haphazard it is."

"And when was this done?" Alex asked. "It has to be recently. We were up here just a few weeks ago."

"When this was done, you would have heard it."

"Josh, we haven't heard anything." Alex put her hand on

one board and tried pulling it.

"It was probably done while you were gone. Probably at your seminar or something." Paul stepped back from the door and shined his light down the stairs and then back at the door. "Someone, or something, doesn't want us in the attic anymore."

Alex was about to reply to this when she heard something, a faint scuffling sound, on the other side of the door.

"Quiet! Shhh!" She put her ear to the door between two boards.

"What the hell?" Paul stepped to the door beside his sister and tried to listen.

"Something's moving on the other side of the door," Alex whispered, and turned to the other three.

Stephanie seemed frozen in horror so Paul moved over beside her. Josh moved up to the door and put his ear to it.

"There is something in there," he said. "I can hear it. It sounds like someone walking across that hall."

"Yes. Pauli, come listen to this." Alex took Paul's place beside Stephanie, but when he got up to the door, the noise stopped.

"Whatever it was has stopped now."

"There's someone in there, Pauli."

"Sis, do you know of any other entrance to the attic? A trapdoor or something?"

"Not that I know of." Alex crossed her arms over her chest, her flashlight shining on the floor. "As far as I can tell, if anyone is in there, they either climbed in a roof window or…" She paused deliberately "Or they went through this door."

"Shit! Johanna."

"We don't know that, Stephi," Alex replied quietly.

"Well, there's nothing left to do but go downstairs." Josh shined his light on the stairs. "We're not doing any good here."

"Good idea." Alex turned for the stairs but before she had descended three steps. there was a terrific crash against the other side of the door, a force so strong that it knocked one board outward, a good inch and a half of its nail visible between it and the door.

"Jesus Christ!" Stephanie exclaimed. The group bunched up on the stairs, each with his or her arm around the other.

"We've got to get out of here!" Stephanie cried. She turned and started bounding down the stairs, followed by Alex and the boys.

When they reached the second floor, they stopped. They stood, in silence, listening for any sound from above. There was none.

"God knows what that was," Paul said in a breathless tone which surprised Alex.

"Johanna," Stephanie replied, hugging herself. A tear rolled down her cheek.

"Maybe…Maybe," Alex said, her voice barely above a whisper.

"Isn't that what she did to you that day you were in the bathroom?" Stephanie stepped over in front of her roommate.

"Yes, but since then I've learned that if Johanna wanted to come through that door, she would have. But now we're too many for her to tackle at one time. She wants to catch one of us alone, preferably me." Alex turned to the door to the second floor hallway. "Pauli, didn't you open this on the way up?"

"I opened it, slightly, Sis, but I left it closed. I know I did."

Alex stepped into the darkened hallway, followed by the other three.

"I don't want to go in there." Stephanie, in the rear, suddenly turned to the right. "I'm going to turn on a light," she said, feeling the wall for a switch. When she found one, she flipped it. "Shit, it doesn't work."

"That looks like a lamp over there." Josh walked carefully over to a lamp on a small stand by a door. "This doesn't work either."

"People, I know good and well these lights work." Alex's voice rose in fear. "They're on all the time. Mrs. Frank keeps them on because she doesn't want to go up to bed in the dark."

They shined their lights around in the hall but nothing seemed amiss. Through Mrs. Frank's bedroom door at the end of the hall, they could see her neatly made bed with the nightstand next to it. They tried the light in her room but it also wouldn't work.

"It's like someone cut the lights at the box." Paul tried other switches in the hall and in another bedroom. "Or the breakers are out."

"Where would the breakers be for this house?" Josh asked, shining his light through a stained glass window at the end of the hall.

The four walked over to the main stairwell and shined their lights down to the bottom of the stairs.

"The breakers are on the back porch," Alex said. "They're in a cabinet on the wall. I've seen them."

"We're going to have to check them." Paul turned and stepped away from the railing on the main landing. "Otherwise, someone has been messing with the switches."

"It's chilly in here." Stephanie, behind the others, hugged herself again.

"Chilly? Wait a minute." Alex ran back to Mrs. Frank's room. Before she got there, she turned. "Mrs. Frank always keeps two air conditioners on to keep the second floor cool for when she goes to bed." She then turned and proceeded into the bedroom, followed by the others.

There she found the window unit by the nightstand. It made no sound, so Alex squatted down and tried the switch.

"It's off," she exclaimed. "And it won't come on. Neither will the other one."

"If it's been off," Paul tried the switch himself. "Why isn't it hotter than hell in here?"

"Heat rises quickly in this weather." Stephanie, her arms still crossed around her body, bent over to look over the silent window unit. "And the humidity and heat outside are god-awful all the time."

"That's just weird." Alex straightened up and turned. "The electricity is off and it's still cool."

"The electricity in my house went off during the last storm and it was hotter than hell in no time." Josh flashed his light over the room, looking for other things electrical. Suddenly he stopped and stared. "The digital clock is on."

All four of them turned and stared at Mrs. Frank's bedside clock on her nightstand. In bright numerals appeared nine-twenty, the correct time.

"That's probably on a battery," Stephanie said.

"Hell, no, that's not on a battery," Paul exclaimed. "Look

at the cord."

"Jesus, why isn't that off?" Stephanie moved in closer to the others.

The four of them were still standing, staring at the clock, when they heard the first footfalls above them. The steps of one person, then two, then three, could be discerned.

"My god, who is that?" Stephanie, on the brink of tears, hugged herself again.

"I don't know," Alex whispered.

Several sets of footsteps could now be heard. The four gaped at the ceiling.

"Is it Johanna?' Paul turned to his sister.

"Not unless she's a goddamned caterpillar, Pauli."

"Let's get out of here." Stephanie, a tear now rolling down her cheek, turned to each of the others in turn. "It's freezing in here."

"Yes, it is." Paul suddenly breathed out forcefully. "Look. I can see my breath."

"I can, too." Josh, eyes like saucers, turned to Paul, then Alex.

"Come on. Follow me." Quickly, Paul, shining his light all around, led the others toward the backstairs. The door to the stairwell, however, which Paul had opened and closed earlier when they came in, was locked.

Paul turned immediately. "To the main stairwell. Come on."

Flashing their lights around the hall and then into Mrs. Frank's bedroom again, the four headed in single file to the main stairs. However, when they rounded the corner to the stairwell, they stopped so suddenly, Stephanie ran into Josh's back.

There, at the head of the stairs, stood two figures, a man and a woman. Both wore ragged, light clothes that appeared to be drenched. The figures were light enough to be seen in the dark. When the two turned toward the four in the archway, the woman regurgitated liquid down the front of her clothes. Neither figure had eyes, only two dark holes in their faces.

"Jesus Christ!" Paul exclaimed, holding out both arms to stop those behind him.

"There's two of them, Pauli," Alex said. Almost instantly she noted that the man was not the same she had seen in the apartment. And the woman was a completely new apparition. "I've never seen either one of them before," she whispered.

"My God, are they what I think they are?" Josh spoke like he was out of breath.

"That's right. They're ghosts." Slowly, Alex moved up next to her brother, followed by Josh, who put his left hand on her shoulder. Stephanie, in the rear, put both hands on Josh's shoulders and tried to stay hidden behind him.

"Jesus. A real haunted house."

"No, Josh, it isn't. There won't be a trace of these two or any others around the next time Mrs. Frank comes up here to go to bed." Alex stared at the two figures which now were motionless.

Then, the man slowly raised his right arm and pointed toward the front of the house. His gesture was followed by the woman, who, slowly and hesitatingly, performed the same movement.

"What in the name of Holy God does that mean?" Paul, still in front, reached out for his sister's hand.

"I'm still not sure, Pauli. I think it has something to do with Johanna."

"Johanna?"

"Yes. I told you, it's a warning of some type." Alex turned to her left. "Stephanie?"

"What?" a weak voice replied behind Josh.

"You see them pointing? Just like the little girl."

"Yes." She sounded like she wanted to cry.

"This is really weird." Josh started forward but Alex put her hand out to stop him.

"Don't get too close, Josh" she said. "There's no telling what they'll do. And they're capable of doing a lot of things."

"Alex," Paul said, staring at the two figures who, in the meantime, had dropped their hands. "They're not down from the attic. The main stairs don't go to the attic."

"I'd say they were up from the first floor, Pauli."

Suddenly, the two figures disappeared. Just as quickly, a light in the hall that one of the four had tried and not flipped off, came on.

"Well, that's all the show for the night," Alex said.

The coolness was gone, and they could hear the soft whirring of Mrs. Frank's room air conditioner.

"Everything's back to normal, it seems." Paul stepped back into the hall and looked around. "It's hot in here."

"I have to go to the bathroom." Stephanie, still visibly shaken, walked up to Alex.

"There's one right over there." Alex pointed to a darkened room down the hall toward the rear door.

"Alex, would you please come with me. I don't want to be in there alone and I want to close the door. I really don't need a male audience when I sit."

"We won't look, Stephi," Paul said, softly.

"She knows that, Pauli. Come on Stephanie."

The two girls went into the bathroom, turned on the light and closed the door. While Stephanie did her business, Alex talked.

"Those two on the stairwell, I've never seen before," she said. "They're brand new. And all those footsteps in the attic. Stephi, this house is full of people. Spirits. And their pointing. God, that pointing is just plain weird. Just like the little girl and the man in our apartment."

Alex turned to Stephanie, but she remained silent. So she continued.

"I used to think the little girl pointing was a warning against Johanna but now I don't know. The two on the stairwell pointed to the front of the house. The only thing I can think of is they're pointing at Johanna's bedroom. But, it wasn't Johanna's room. It was Mrs. Frank's room or somewhere very near it. If we had been in the attic, it would have been Johanna's room."

"Alex, are all these things capable of hurting us?"

The question took Alex by surprise. Then she realized she had been going on about their actions but what about their capability of harm.

"I…I don't know, Steph. I think the two we just saw are harmless enough." Alex paused and thought a moment. "I think the greatest fear of these things is fear of the unknown. The one with the only clear malice is Johanna."

"The little girl hurt me." Stephanie straightened her clothes, crossed her arms over her chest and confronted her roommate.

"Stephi, let's not go over that again. You know what was going on that night."

"She still hurt me. She can hurt me. These things scare the shit out of me!" Stephanie's voice rose in agitation.

Alex put her hands on her shoulders. "No one knows that more than I do," she said, gently. "I was knocked down and damn near torn to shreds this morning until you showed up. You saw what happened. That should tell you that together we can defend ourselves against these things." Then, she turned and led Stephanie out into the hall to meet the boys.

"Anything else happen?' Alex asked her brother, who stood in the hall light and played with his flashlight.

"Nothing. Except your man Josh here can't wait to go back to Katy and tell everybody he's seen a ghost."

"No one will believe him, Pauli." Alex turned to Josh and smiled. "All those cowboys he runs around with out there will call him a liar before he says three words."

Paul turned to Stephanie. "You okay, Good-looking?"

"I'm a bit better off, I guess. Thanks."

"And thank you for saving my sister's ass this morning."

Alex could tell Paul was trying to cheer Stephanie up and put to rest as much of her remaining fear as he could. "As long as she's got you nearby," he continued, "I think she'll be okay."

"And I guess the same goes for her."

"You bet." Paul switched his flashlight on. "Let's douse this light and go back to the apartment," he said. "I'd like to talk about what we saw over a little bit of wine, if you got it. Oh, and Sis. I don't expect Papa and Mama to be home tonight when I get there. I'll go straight to bed."

"Fine, Pauli. Just don't get too loaded to drive."

"Better still, why don't you stay over," Stephanie piped up.

"Because I don't have my excruciatingly sexy PJs with me." Paul grinned. "One glass won't hurt me, though. Besides, tonight's got to be an early night. Got to go to work tomorrow. I need the extra time."

Later, after they locked up Mrs. Frank's house, the four

settled in the apartment with glasses of St. Genevieve. Although rain had been predicted for that evening, it had not arrived yet. Alex wondered if it was going to arrive at all. She hoped it wouldn't.

"Something tells me, folks, that I've got some allies over there against Johanna." Alex took a sip of wine and tucked her feet underneath her on the couch. "When those two things we saw tonight plus whatever was in the attic are around, I don't think she's going to be anywhere near."

"What tonight tells me, Sis, is that Stehle's Door's got to be someplace in that attic. Or at least somewhere in that house."

"That could very well be, Pauli. I won't deny it. But I've never seen any sign of it. It's like those things came from somewhere else."

"You haven't forgotten what happened years ago, have you? Everything that came around had a source."

"I know. But now everything is vastly different from what I can see." Alex took another sip and glanced over at her roommate who still seemed shaken up. "Poor Stephanie is completely unnerved by all of this."

"I'm better than I was," Stephanie said quietly. "But this morning I nearly lost it. I wanted to turn and run like hell but I knew you were in trouble. Thank God that hideous thing vanished."

"Once again, thank you for intervening, Steph. God only knows what would have happened if you hadn't."

Stephanie perked up a little at the compliment, but she still seemed nervous. "Something else that bothers me is this constant waiting around for whatever is going to happen next."

"I know, Steph. But what else can we do?"

"There's nothing we can do." Stephanie's mouth turned down in a pout.

"Well, I guess later we can take another shot at Mrs. Frank's house." Paul drained his glass and set it on a nearby coaster. "Something tells me that attic is not going to stay boarded up."

"I think you're right, Pauli."

They finished their wine while talking about Mrs. Frank's house as well as other things and then, at ten thirty, the boys left for home. As both had something to do early the next morning, the early evening seemed appropriate.

Even before they left, Alex caught herself wondering what the night had in store for her. *Probably another crazy dream,* she thought.

Later that night, Alex was turning down her bed when she looked up to see Stephanie standing in the door, sleeping bag and sheets in hand.

"I don't want to be alone tonight," she said, apologetically. "I remember what you said about being caught alone."

"That's okay, Steph. That's a good idea." She smiled at her roommate and motioned toward the closet. "Go ahead and put out your stuff over there. I won't be needing the closet tonight." Alex was as glad to see her as she was to be there.

Stephanie spread her sleeping bag on the floor and then sandwiched herself between her sheets. "To us old-time campers, this is very comfortable," she said, grinning at Alex, who lay in her bed on her side.

"That's great, Stephi. Now all we need is a wiener roast and ghost stories."

Stephanie grinned and reached over to pet Henrietta, who had settled on the pallet behind her mistress' back. "Roomy, as far as I'm concerned, the wieners are in the fridge, uncooked, and I've had enough ghost stories around here to last a lifetime."

With that Alex chuckled and cut the light by her bed. She lay in the dark and thought about the new developments of that evening. The number of manifestations was growing. Two new ones this evening plus what seemed like a host of others in the attic.

She was puzzled, however. Wasn't Mrs. Frank's attic Johanna's territory? Was Johanna among those walking around in the attic? The incident of the attic door certainly seemed to testify to this. Also, Alex wondered if any of the other manifestations were as malicious and dangerous as Johanna was. Dwelling on these thoughts, however unnerving they might be, put her to sleep.

She was awakened a few hours later by something pulling on her bedding. Thinking it was her cat, she jerked on the sheet and turned over. Then, she felt freezing cold. She rose up and looked around to see small, shadowy figures surrounding her bed. Beyond those at the foot of her bed she could see the window, wide open and the curtains blowing inward. Terrified, she tried to move to the wall side of her bed but there were figures there, too.

The figures were only shadows. She couldn't make out any details. Then, she felt a small hand on her leg just above the knee.

"These are children, for God's sake," she whispered. She wanted to scream but remembered Stephanie was in the room.

Another icy hand made its way up under her pajama top and pressed against her stomach.

The figures were making a low murmuring sound as if communicating with one another. Some of them pointed toward Mrs. Frank's house; all seemed focused on Alex in bed.

She turned on her side suddenly, so the hand dropped away. She saw her roommate across the room, sound asleep, with two small figures bending over her.

"Thank God she's asleep," she said to herself.

Alex turned back over and scooted toward the head of the bed and sat up.

"What do you want?' she whispered heavily to the figure closest to her.

There was no answer. Instead, those nearest her moved closer to her. Now, Alex could see their faces, pale, dead and empty. Also, she could see that some of the figures had ragged clothes on but some were naked.

What appeared to be a little boy and girl moved very close and put their hands on Alex's body. Their icy touch froze her and made her sick at her stomach.

"What are you doing?" she asked in a stage whisper. "Are you warning me?" She looked over the closest figures, the boy and girl in turn. The smell, which she had not noticed until now, made her nauseous.

The boy and then the girl began making a distinctive grunting sound which sounded to Alex like they were attempting to form her name. Each time they made the sound, their heads moved closer to her.

"What are you trying to say?" she asked. "Is it a warning? Is it Johanna? Nod your head for yes and shake it for no. Is it Johanna?"

The two figures, the boy and then the girl, slowly shook their heads.

My God, Alex thought. *They know what I said. They answered me. They did what I told them to.*

Suddenly, Alex's room filled with light. A car had driven up in Mrs. Frank's driveway. It seemed the old lady had returned late from Conroe.

The figures vanished with the light. Not even the smell was left.

Alex got up and shut the window at the foot of her bed. Then, she tried others to make sure they were locked.

A shuffling sound nearby told her that her roommate had been awakened by the light.

"What's going on?" a sleepy voice asked.

Would you really like to know? Alex thought. "Mrs. Frank just got back from Conroe," she answered. "She wasn't supposed to be back until tomorrow but something must be up tomorrow." Alex saw no reason to mention their immediate visitors at that moment. She would at a later time when her roommate might be more receptive.

"What time is it?"

"Almost one o'clock." Alex settled back in her bed while Stephanie got up and headed for the bathroom.

Momentarily alone now, Alex thought about the phantom children who had surrounded her bed only a few moments before. They were obviously the same children who had been digging on a beach in one of her previous dreams. They had been burying a corpse. Or had they been digging one up?

And then there was the fact that they had listened to her and answered her question. They had acknowledged no warning against Johanna. If they were not warning her against Johanna, what were they up to? And what were the others doing pointing toward the front of Mrs. Frank's house?

Alex knew she needed help now more than ever. She needed help beyond her brother and anyone else privy to what was going on. Things were accelerating and some were getting worse.

She would make another attempt to contact Dr. Vernon Blassingame. It was time, once again, for a true professional to be called in.

Chapter Sixteen

The next morning, Alex was determined to find Dr. Blassingame even though the day was Saturday. She told her roommate she had decided on this course after the events of the previous evening, and Stephanie concurred immediately.

"Didn't you say he was here to help with the trouble years ago?' Stephanie asked.

"Yes, he was. I never met him. I was in the hospital in Memphis, Tennessee, but Pauli and Papa met him and he helped with solving the problems at home.

"Do you think he could do this again?'

"Maybe so. Or at least give us some idea of what we're up against and how to deal with it. The stuff years ago was as new to him as it was to us so he learned a few things, too."

Later that day, Alex called the number of Dr. Vernon Blassingame she had been given earlier; however, again there was no answer. This time, Alex left a message on the answering machine. She placed the number by the hall phone, determined to call it again very soon, and left for the grocery store with Stephanie. When the two returned, however, around noon, there was a message flashing on the answering machine. Excited, she pressed the "play" button.

"I heard your message on my answering machine," a deep voice said, slowly. "It took me a few minutes but I recognized the name. I've been engaged since retirement in doing some historical research for projects at Brendon and the University of Illinois. None of this research has to do with parapsychology or the paranormal but I'm beginning to have a yearning to get back to it. So, Miss Zunker, I've called you back and I can be reached at the same number all day today."

Stephanie couldn't contain her excitement. "Now we can start getting this stuff under control," she gushed to her roommate, also excited.

"We don't need a ghost hunter, Steph," Alex cautioned. "These damned things are very easily found. We just need help finding out what is going on and figuring out how to deal with it.

After they ate sandwiches, they sat down with tea in the living room, and Alex dialed the number of Dr. Blassingame on the cordless phone.

"Alexandra Zunker, I must be getting senile not to have recognized your name right off, but since I deal with so many people on the phone, I just thought you were one of my contacts."

"Getting a bit slow in your old age." Alex chuckled. She recognized the voice immediately. It hadn't changed in four years. "I heard you had retired, Dr. Blassingame, and moved to Illinois."

"Retired from teaching, yes. But I'm afraid I'm going to be one of those people who work more after retirement than they did before it."

"One of those you can't keep down, huh."

"Yes. History has always been my first love. Civil War era Illinois I have found fascinating. Right now, I have three projects going simultaneously, one of them due to the publisher in about three weeks." There was a brief pause while Alex changed hands on the phone. "Well, Alexandra, what have you been up to lately that you have rattled my cage again?"

"Well, Dr. Blassingame, first I could use some advice. Carefully, Alex told him everything that she could remember concerning what had gone on since the previous spring. When she reached the part about the time lapse on the beach at Galveston, Dr. Blassingame muttered. "Sounds familiar."

"I'm not really sure that was Stehle's Door that time, Dr. Blassingame," Alex replied. "In fact, I'm not sure of a hell of a lot of things except that I'm practically insane and my roommate is scared to death."

Alex finished her narration by mentioning the ghostly children from the previous night. Fortunately, she noticed, Stephanie had gone into the kitchen. When she finished, there was another pause.

"Once again, you have me completely baffled, Alexandra." Dr. Blassingame breathed into the phone. "Tell me, is your brother in on this?"

"Yes, but he doesn't live with us. He's still across town at home. I will talk with him about what I learn from you, though."

"About what you learn from me, huh."

"Yes. You were such a great help years ago."

"That clearly was the most fantastic case I've ever encountered. You remember my telling you about the pictures I took."

"Oh, yes." Alex recalled how Dr. Blassingame's pictures had not come out, that they were pictures of an empty room, void of the characters they were to depict. "That was very spooky, Dr. Blassingame. That those things cannot be photographed unless they want to be. I guess they're like vampires in that respect."

"Yes, Alexandra. This thing you call Johanna sounds very dangerous. Can you think of any reason for her malice?"

"No, sir, I can't." Alex paused and breathed deeply. Stephanie had returned to the living room and gotten as close to Alex as possible on the couch. "Yesterday morning, when she came out of nowhere and attacked me, my roommate showed up and apparently drove her off. Like I said earlier, Johanna seems to want to catch me alone. But I have no idea what her motives are."

"And the pointing is curious, too. I agree with you that it's a kind of warning. These are obviously benign spirits that are trying to communicate something to you."

"I'm fairly sure of that. But the only conclusion I've come to about that is that they're warning me of Johanna."

Dr. Blassingame paused a minute, apparently in thought. "That may be. But wouldn't it seem to you that if this were true, they would turn up before she appeared? Particularly before an attack like the one yesterday."

Alex remembered she hadn't told him about her communication with the two spectral children. She had just mentioned them.

"Furthermore, if they were trying to protect you from her,

wouldn't they do more than just point?"

"I really haven't thought of that, Dr. Blassingame."

"I would say these manifestations are concerned with something a bit bigger than the malicious intentions of one of their number."

"But what could it be? I've tried to think of other things, particularly after last night."

"How about another storm?"

"What?"

"Another storm. You told me you concluded that all of these manifestations with the exception of the cat are storm victims. That's how they died; wouldn't that be what they're concerned with?"

Alex paused to let what Dr. Blassingame said sink in. It seemed logical. Alex had not paid much attention to the weather except to check a local forecast to see whether or not it was going to rain.

"That sounds reasonable," she said. "I…I haven't thought of that."

"Quite often, manifestations of the paranormal have served to warn the living of impending dangers. For instance, there was a woman who had a voice whisper in her ear that she had cancer. She went to a doctor and sure enough, she had ovarian cancer. In West Virginia, there is an apparition that warns motorists of a treacherous mountain road."

"I guess that's right, then, Dr. Blassingame. It is logical. Storm victims warning of an approaching storm."

"That would be my guess at this point, Alexandra. But I don't know what to make of Johanna, I'm sorry to say. And I think the cat is some type of harassment."

"I think you're right there. I'm pretty sure Johanna had something to do with that. I know it was she who tore the poor thing to pieces in the alley behind our apartment. I'm sure she's responsible for the animal coming back."

"Alexandra, it seems like you have your hands full. I wish I could be more help, particularly with that one."

"Well, sir, I don't think she'll try anything when I'm with someone. My roommate and I are together constantly. Now we don't let each other out of our sight."

"That's good. You can help each other."

Dr. Blassingame went on to ask about Paul and Thomas and everyone else who was a party to the problems four years before. The conversation ended with some small talk and a promise to keep in touch.

Alex hung up and started walking toward the kitchen when the phone rang again. Stephanie started upstairs, so Alex picked up the phone first.

"Alex, something weird, weird, has happened!" Josh's excited, breathless voice surprised her. "I tried earlier but your line was busy."

"What, Josh? I was talking to Dr. Vernon Blassingame. I finally found him. I mentioned him last…"

"Alex, I just got a call from Anna Diehls. Out of the blue, just like that. She said…She said, 'tell Alexandra that my great aunt is going to kill her.'"

Alex nearly dropped the phone in horror. Her hand started shaking and she leaned against the staircase to control herself.

"Tell me that again, Josh." In her mind she could see the picture of the girl Josh had shown her in the yearbook the previous evening. She looked nothing like the girl who had told her the same thing in her dream.

Josh repeated the fearful statement, this time slower.

Alex regained control of herself somewhat. "Where was she calling from? There in Katy?"

"No. The caller ID said out of area. She was probably calling from Lubbock. Texas Tech. That's where she is."

"Josh, did you ever mention me to her?"

"No. I swear to God I didn't. I only knew you back then. That's what is so weird. She and I quit going out a year and a half ago. Long before you and I started dating."

"Josh, I remember you took her to the Reformation picnic at church. Did you by chance mention…"

"I didn't even know you were there, Alex. What's this all about? You told us about Johanna but how did Anna learn about it?"

"That I don't know. Somebody or something has somehow contacted you're old girl friend and given her that tidbit of information to harass me or frighten me. I don't know." Alex remembered she had not told Josh about her dream where the same statement played a major role. She told him now.

"My God, Alex. That is weird," he said, after a pause.

"Yes. I was really relieved when you showed me the picture of Anna and the only resemblance between her and Johanna was the blonde hair. But now, something has prompted her to make that call."

"This was the first I've spoken to her since we quit dating."

"Josh, you said the caller ID said out of area. Of course there is no number so you could call her back and ask her why she made that statement."

"No number, Alex."

"Probably a damned cell phone," Alex whispered to herself.

"I can call her mother and step dad to get her number at Tech," Josh continued. "I can tell them I want to ask her about the University or something."

In a way Alex didn't want him to do that. Why bring someone new into the situation. On the other hand, Johanna had obviously communicated with the girl. How and why had she done this?

"Josh, hold off for a while," she said. "I want to think about things. But if she calls you again, call me immediately."

"God, Alex. This is so weird. She doesn't even know you."

"She has a long dead family member that does, though. And it's obvious they are in touch."

Josh ended the conversation by telling her he'd see her Friday night as planned and the two hung up.

Alex turned to Stephanie there by her. "Josh got a call out of the blue from his old girl friend. She said her great aunt, Johanna, is going to kill me. So what else is new, right?"

"Alex, is that the girl in the yearbook?"

"The same. But not the girl in the dream I told you about."

"Yes, but isn't the sentiment the same?"

"That is what's so weird. Johanna has obviously gotten in touch with her grand niece and God only knows what else she's doing to her."

"Can't Josh call her and find out what's going on?"

"I told him not to."

"Why?"

"Because she's probably just an innocent bystander and doesn't need to be dragged into this. She's probably had some kind of mind control worked on her and she's probably unaware even of what she said. Or, God forbid, she was possessed. Now, if Josh asks her anything, she won't know anything."

"Still, it is a threat."

"I know. But not one I haven't heard before."

The rest of that day was spent in cleaning house and doing laundry. Alex waited for another call from Josh but it never came. Apparently, there would be only one message from his old girl friend and that was a load off Alex's mind.

Later, Alex and Stephanie went over to see about Mrs. Frank and found her entertaining company. They were introduced and sat for refreshments but soon Alex stated she had to get back to the apartment to get some work done for her seminar. After excusing themselves, she and Stephanie made their way through the dining room and kitchen to the back porch.

There, Alex stopped abruptly and turned to her roommate. "While Mrs. Frank is tied up in there, I'm going to sneak up to the attic and see if it's still boarded up. I've got a feeling it isn't."

"Alex, there were heavy boards and huge nails in that door. How could it be any different, now?"

"Funny business, Roomy. It couldn't be anything else."

Alex could see the blood flow out of Stephanie's face as she anticipated what was to be said next.

"Stephi, I want you to come up with me. You don't have to go all the way; you can come to the base of the stairs on the second floor."

"Alex, it's dark up there." Stephanie wanted to cry. "Can't we turn on some lights?"

"Of course, we can turn on lights. No one's going to see lights in the back of the house. They're all in the living room."

"Okay…Okay. I guess we need to stay together."

"Good. Come on." Alex flipped the switch by the back door that lit up the staircase to the second floor.

"What if Mrs. Frank comes back here?" Stephanie asked,

following Alex up the stairs.

"She won't. She's busy with her friends in the front room."

They reached the second floor where Alex turned on another switch that lit the attic stairs only halfway.

"I'll go on up there, Steph. There's a switch on that landing there. Stay at the bottom of the stairs and keep me in sight. And when I go out of sight, listen for me."

Very cautiously, Alex reached the attic landing. Even in the darkness she could see the boards were gone from the door. She flipped the light switch by the attic door.

"Just as I thought," she said. "Stephanie, you can come up here. There's nothing here."

Stephanie joined her quickly. "Oh, my God," she said. "What's happened?"

"The boards are gone. If you look a bit closer, you'll see there's even no nail holes."

"Alex, those nails were huge. And those boards."

"Gone. All gone."

"I don't suppose you have any idea what's happened."

"I don't, Steph. Our friends are screwing with us. These things play mind games with you. I remember Dr. Blassingame talking about that years ago."

Alex wanted to open the attic door and go in to look around but something told her not to. Instead, the two girls descended the stairs and returned to the apartment.

Nothing occurred the rest of that day, or the next day, or for a week after. Alex and Stephanie were busy winding up their seminar with a flourish of activities. There were two plays they had to see as well as a showing of Orson Welle's *Citizen Kane* which they found at a video rental. There was also an optional concert in Galveston on the list of activities which Alex declined.

The whirlwind of activities kept the girls so busy Alex wondered that maybe their constant activity kept their unwelcome visitors at bay. She was very familiar, though, with the lapses of time between visitations. The next Saturday found them working on final reports and critiques in front of TV on which Stephanie had put a movie they had rented along with *Citizen Kane.*

"Did Josh mention anything about his old girl friend last night?" Stephanie asked out of the blue.

Lost in a difficult choice of descriptive adjectives for a performance of "As You Like It," Alex looked up.

"Not about her; I had to ask later." Alex smiled. The previous night she and Josh had gone out to dinner and a movie. "He did pester me about anything else happening since he and Pauli had been here, though. When I told him nothing had really occurred, he seemed disappointed."

"I think he believes this is some kind of a game or unique experience that he can't wait to take part in."

"I think you're right about that. It's clear he has the wrong idea. If he gets a load of Johanna, he's likely to fill his pants up."

"That's for sure. Those things in Mrs. Frank's house the other night were nothing compared to that thing, what I saw of it." Stephanie glanced momentarily at the TV. "I think he thinks we're ghost busters, or something."

"Something like that."

"What'd he say about the former girlfriend? Anything?"

"Not much. He went ahead and tried to contact her parents but learned they had moved to Odessa."

"Oh, wow. Then she really was out of the area."

"Yeah. He wanted to call up to Texas Tech and try to find her but he decided not to. It's just as well. She hasn't called again and I don't look for her to." Again, Alex tried to picture the girl in the yearbook in her mind. The more she tried to depict her, the more the girl began to resemble her deadly great aunt. Finally, Alex put her out of her mind and went back to her work.

Time passed. August arrived with the end of seminar. Alex and Stephanie turned in reports and evaluations for which they would receive a grade.

Three weeks had passed since the cryptic phone call from Josh Hamilton. Since there were no others, he had apparently relegated it to the back of his mind.

Alex hadn't, however. Three weeks without a manifestation of any kind bothered her. This was the longest gap of time between occurrences since the problem had started last spring. She knew from past experience anything could happen at any time.

Stephanie had perked up and she and Alex had begun jogging daily. Alex knew her roommate wanted to ask her about the absence of paranormal activity but something kept her from it. *Perhaps she thinks if she doesn't bring it up it'll stay away,* she thought.

One day when Mrs. Frank had a lunch date with friends, Alex made her way back to the attic. She knew she was taking a chance alone, but something told her she would be safe. As before, there were no nail marks, or boards, but this time, the door was ajar. Momentarily startled, she turned and retreated down the stairs.

Later, she told Stephanie what she had done.

"That's still very strange, Roomy," she said, chewing on a piece of apple. "It's like nothing ever happened up there. And the door was open?"

"Yep. I don't think there was anything around, though."

"Do you think Mrs. Frank went up there?"

"No." Alex thought for a minute. "It's like the whole thing was a dream, isn't it." She crossed her arms over her chest and leaned back in her chair. "There's no indication anything ever went on up there. Even the lights have remained off over the last three weeks. And as for the open door, anything could have done that, even the wind. It's very drafty up there."

"Alex, you don't suppose this crap's gone for good." Stephanie finally got around to mentioning it.

"Don't jinx it, Steph. Or you'll invite it back." Alex smiled at her and stood up. "We don't want to let our guard down, do we?" She knew it was only a matter of time before the occurrences resumed. They had to be driven away forcefully.

Later that day, Alex called home, hoping to talk to her brother but learned he was working until late. "I'll try again tomorrow," she told Elizabeth. Alex wanted to ask him if he remembered what the longest time of peace was between disturbances years ago. She had a feeling that three weeks was something new.

"Maybe these things are gone after all," Stephanie said, picking up her purse in preparation to go to the store.

"I know better," Alex replied, door keys in hand. "They'll be back. All we have to do is wait" She regretted what she said because her roommate's perky mood gave way to a look of horror. "Stephi," Alex began in a gentle voice. "Like I've told you all along, we have to get rid of these things ourselves. And we will. Believe me."

Alex followed her to the door and when they were out she turned to lock up. As she started to pull the door to, she caught just a glimpse of a black and white cat's tail disappearing down the upstairs hall. She froze momentarily. "Well, it's back. What now?" she whispered to herself.

She did not mention what she saw to Stephanie but upon their return from the store, she explored upstairs while her roommate unloaded sacks in the kitchen. Of course, she found nothing, but she did notice both cats, Henrietta and Sabrina, were missing. After a thorough search of the upstairs, she was descending the stairs when she heard Stephanie yell from the kitchen.

"Alex, our cats are outside!"

"What?" Alex speeded up, taking two steps at a time. "How did they get outside?"

She asked from the kitchen door while Stephanie let the two back in.

"I don't know. I don't think we left the front door open, did we?"

"No, Steph. We never do." In her mind Alex again saw the tail she'd seen just before they'd left. "I'll check the windows. One of those might be open."

"Like that one in your room?"

"Yes." Alex ran back upstairs but the window in question, like all the others, was locked tight. Another curious thing was that the air conditioners, which Alex had left on low cool, had turned off. These she turned back on and continued checking the upstairs for any way the cats might have gotten out.

"This is certainly weird." Stephanie met her at the bottom of the stairs. "Everything down here is locked up tight."

"How long have they been out, I wonder." Alex looked around, hands on her hips. "The only thing I can figure is that they went out while one of us had the door open. That's the only logical explanation. They might have been out all day." Alex knew the real truth, though. She had seen the phantom Tom and knew that was the real answer. They had left the apartment with him, for what purpose she shuddered to think. The trouble had returned, just like she knew it would.

"Well, we better be more careful, Roomy," Stephanie said.

"Yes." Alex walked over and lay down on a living room couch. "I think there's enough spaghetti left for both of us tonight. In a few minutes, I'll get up and warm it."

A moment later she was asleep.

She didn't see Stephanie come downstairs in her running clothes, nor did she hear her invite her to join her on a run. Stephanie just stood, momentarily, and stared down at her sleeping roommate, and then, thinking everything was all right, left.

At eight PM, Alex stirred. Instantly, she knew she was no longer in the living room of the apartment. There was no time even to recognize her surroundings for they immediately collapsed around her, depositing her into a raging torrent of darkness, water, wind, rain and confusion. Stunned by the transportation, Alex momentarily thought she was in another dream, but the horrid reality that she was not hit her quickly.

Thrashing frantically about in the swirling waters, she tried to keep her head up but collided in the dark with wreckage. Close by she could hear screams and calls for help combined with the howl of the wind. Like in the dream she had earlier of the same situation, she knew her life was in jeopardy, but now waking up would not save her.

She hit a large floating object with her head. Although momentarily stunned, she grasped it with both hands and pulled her body as close to it as she could. She realized the object was a piece of wreckage, probably a piece of a wall, and she lifted herself up on top of it. Struggling and scuffing her knees, she flattened herself against the soggy boards, still hoping she was in a dream.

When she caught her breath, she moved slowly toward the center of the small, ragged platform, staying as low as possible as the platform was bobbing in the water like a fishing cork. An unexpected collision with something soft surprised her and she rose up on her side.

A body not one foot from her came alive and rose to a sitting position. A lightning flash told her she had encountered another struggling human being.

A blonde girl, surprised by the encounter, lost her balance and tumbled into the swirling water while Alex regained her flattened position on the makeshift raft.

A horrible thought went through her head but was instantly interrupted by a piece of flying wreckage striking her on the hip, and when she moved her hand down to the stricken area, another struck her head a glancing blow, knocking her temporarily unconscious.

She awoke immediately, finding herself sore, soaking wet and stinking on her living room floor.

"This was not a damned dream," she choked. She rolled over on her back and felt her aching head. Had she rolled off the couch on her hip and hit her head on the coffee table? Her smelly, saturated clothes told her she hadn't.

"Dear God, where is that damned door?" she said, huskily. She remembered her brother's insistence on the presence of Stehle's Door and knew, for sure now, he was right. Only this door into another dimension could be responsible for what just happened to her. Now she was sure that she and the others had to find this door.

Slowly, she rose to her feet, her clothes clinging, freezing, to her body.

"Stephanie!" she yelled.

There was no answer.

Alex could smell the rank residue of sea water all over her. Now that she was apparently safe in the apartment, she had to get upstairs to the shower, change, then find her roommate.

"She's probably out running," she said to herself. *She couldn't find me and just went out for a run,* she thought. *She probably thought I was with Mrs. Frank.*

Still sore in two places, Alex started for the staircase. Rounding the bottom of the stairs, though, she met, face to face, her roommate standing in the door to the bathroom.

"Stephanie, why didn't…" Like another blow on the head, it hit her.

Her roommate stood, completely still, her hands down to her side. Her running shorts were down almost to her thighs; her top was up almost to her breasts, and her hair was badly mussed. Her face was a complete blank, mouth open.

"Oh, my God, Stephi?"

It didn't seem like Stephanie was breathing, but she started advancing across the base of the stairs toward Alex.

She knew now that one of the worst things that could happen had occurred. Alex backed up into the living room, the thing that was her roommate following. The face had not changed; the staring eyes focused in the same upward direction.

Alex stumbled over an end table but regained her standing position. She thought about charging her roommate and shaking her but before she could move toward the thing, she froze in her tracks.

"You saw how you killed me," a husky, lifeless voice emanated from the open mouth. The thing kept coming.

Now it was clear. "You goddamned monster, get out of her!" Feeling behind her for any obstruction, Alex backed up across the living room toward the fireplace.

"You killed me." The thing inside Stephanie had not manifested its appearance on her but Alex knew who it was. "You killed me. I'm going to kill you." Now the voice had risen a few octaves to an alto on the verge of a scream.

Alex backed into the fireplace tools and thought about the poker. But she knew that if she struck the thing, she could kill Stephanie. The spirit within her could not be stopped in that way.

But it kept coming. Slowly.

"Go to hell!" Alex screamed again at the thing, now closer than ever. "Go to hell where you belong!" Mustering as much strength as she could, she sprinted toward the kitchen and the back door.

There, she made for the door, almost stumbling against it. It was locked. Frantically, she twisted the button on the knob but the door still wouldn't open. Apparently, it was jammed, but it had never jammed before. While she tried with both hands to pull the door open, the thing appeared in the kitchen door.

Slowly, it moved toward her again, its hands now reaching

up under Stephanie's bra and fondling her breasts.

"Oh, God," Alex sobbed. She wondered what the thing would do when it reached her. Not daring to think anymore, she reached into a drawer and grabbed a long butcher knife. Tears rolled down to her chest and mixed with the salt brine in her clothes. She pressed herself against the door, the knife out in front of her.

The thing was five feet away, now, and Alex knew she would have to do something. Four more feet and she would have to shove the knife through her roommate's midsection. She could easily do that to Johanna, but the thought of having to do that to Stephanie made her gag, forcing up what little she had in her stomach.

When the thing was three feet away, the doorbell rang. The monstrosity stopped and Alex moved instantly, sprinting around the thing toward the living room. Whoever was at the door was literally a lifesaver, an ally she had not counted on. She still had the knife in her hand when she reached the front door, but, remembering the back door, she dropped it and put both hands on the knob. It opened easily.

Behind the door screen, a grin over his face, stood Howie.

"Jesus, girl, what happened to you?" he said.

"Howie. Oh, my God, Howie!" She opened the door. "Come in. Come in, now!" She turned and ran back toward the kitchen.

On the floor, close to the kitchen door, lay her roommate.

"Oh no, Stephi. My God, Stephanie." Now Alex burst into tears. She ran to her and knelt beside her.

Alex could see that she was breathing. She picked her up and turned her over. The color was very much back in Stephanie's face. Slowly, she opened her eyes.

"Alex…Alex, what hap…" she said in a weak voice.

"Oh God, thank you," she choked. "Thank you. Thank you." She pulled the girl tightly against her and embraced her, rocking to and fro gently. She felt a hand on her shoulder.

"Alex. Alex, what's going on here? Can I help?"

"Howie, something horrible just happened here. And yes, you can help. You've already helped immensely, more than you know." She felt Stephanie move in her arms.

"Alex, is she all right?" Howie bent over to look at Stephanie in her arms.

Stephanie pulled herself out of Alex's arms and rose to her knees. Her hand still lay on Alex's knee.

"When I came in from running, I saw you on the floor," she said, weakly. "But when I started forward, something hit me from behind."

"You were possessed, Stephanie. Johanna possessed you." Alex thought carefully about what she was going to say next. "You came at me and cornered me in the kitchen, but the doorbell rang and I got away. Then, I guess she came out of you."

"Possessed?" Stephanie's eyes grew large.

"Yes, Stephanie, possessed. She tried to get at me through you."

"What's this about *possessed,* Alex?"

The voice behind her was gentle, but curious. Alex knew she would have to explain now that Howie was in on their problems.

The three of them rose and made their way into the living room where they sat and Alex quickly explained what had been going on.

Howie listened quietly, sometimes a quizzical look coming over his face.

When she finished, she glanced over at her roommate who sat silently, staring at the floor.

"It's gotten more serious now, Howie," she continued. "This thing has threatened me and now it has possessed Stephanie." She thought about the butcher knife she had almost used on her roommate. "It is extremely dangerous. I don't know what I would have done if you hadn't rang the doorbell."

"You're saying that this thing, Johanna, is scared off by the appearance of other people?"

"It would seem so. Stephanie drove it off when it was attacking me." Alex sighed. She had forgotten about her wet, smelly clothes. "Now that everyone's calmed down, I'm going to run upstairs, take a quick shower and change clothes.

"I've got some beer for you out in the car." Howie rose. "You remember you asked me to bring you some this weekend.

I'll go get it."

Stephanie came alive. "I'll go with you." She had straightened her clothes but she still hadn't done anything with her hair.

"That's good," Alex said, running up the stairs. "I think we could all use one about now."

Later, all three sat in the living room while Alex explained in detail what had happened earlier. She left out the part about the butcher knife because she didn't want to upset Stephanie any more than she already was. So far she had taken her experience better than Alex thought she would.

And Howie refused to believe the part about time travel. He was convinced Alex had been dreaming. "I'm too much of a pragmatist to believe in going back in time," he said. "I'm going to draw the line there."

Alex said nothing but went ahead and finished her story. She knew she'd hit Howie with too much already. She turned to her roommate and asked her how she felt.

"I'm okay now." Stephanie turned the beer can in her hand around and around. "This evening was something else," she said. "It was like I was knocked out, or something. I don't remember a thing after seeing Alex on the floor.

"I've always been scared of the possession thing," Alex said, turning from her roommate to Howie. "Years ago we feared that, too. But it never happened. Now that it has, I'm glad to see there's no harm done. At least not yet. It's something else we're going to have to be on our guard against."

"Alex, I must say this is the damndest thing I've ever heard." Howie moved about in his chair somewhat impatiently. He was just what he said he was, a pragmatist who didn't trust anything he couldn't see or understand. "I'm tempted to think you two are putting me on."

"We're not, Howie. You can ask my brother; you can ask Josh Hamilton. You can even ask my parents, who were in on that mess years ago." Alex thought a minute and then continued. "I wouldn't kid you about any of this, Howie. I wouldn't kid anyone about it."

"Alex, do you think I'll be possessed again?" a weak voice suddenly asked from across the room.

"I don't know, Steph. I'm thinking now that it's like all the other things involving Johanna. If someone besides you is around, it's not going to happen."

Alex hoped her reply would cheer her roommate somewhat, but by the looks of things, it didn't.

The three sat and talked quietly until after midnight when Howie excused himself and the two girls went up to bed. While Alex was putting on her night clothes, Stephanie appeared at the door again with sleeping bag in hand. After Alex turned off the light, the two talked a few minutes in the dark until both drifted off in sleep.

One thing Alex hadn't mentioned to Howie, or even Stephanie, and she might have even forgotten it herself. It would have been more likely, though, that she had put it conveniently in the back of her mind. The fact is as time goes on, the manifestations, no matter how much time passes between them, always intensify.

Chapter Seventeen

The next day was uneventful. In fact, the girls slept in and almost missed church. They did make it to eleven o'clock service, however, in company with an irritated Mrs. Frank, upset because she had missed Bible class.

On the way to St. John's, Alex sat in the back seat and pondered the events of the previous evening. Stephanie had almost been killed and so had she. Although she could not convince Howie she had gone back in time, she knew perfectly well she had. And her clothes, couldn't he smell them?

The previous evening had produced two more reasons for her to find the deadly Stehle's Door. It had sent her back to Galveston in 1900 and brought forth Johanna to attack and possess Stephanie. Alex shuddered when she thought how close she had come to killing her roommate. She knew the whole scenario had been planned, obviously with the help of Stehle's Door. In horror she realized her adversary was manipulating the Door. *After I killed Stephanie with a knife,* she thought. *Johanna would have been out of her and on me.*

It boggled her mind how devious and complete this hideous dead thing had been. Alex was made to believe she was responsible for Johanna's death. Was she now to be punished over a century later? Apparently she was.

After church, Alex cornered her brother in the parking lot alone.

"What do you suppose Johanna had in store for you?" he asked after Alex had explained the situation.

"My death, Little Brother. I suspect she was trying to use Stephanie to get to me and if Stephanie was killed in the process it was all right with her. Needless to say, I didn't tell Stephi I almost shoved a knife through her belly."

"Thank God for Howie."

"Yes."

"Alex, we've got to find that door. You know as well as I do Stehle's Door was nearby last night when all that was going on."

"Yes I do, Pauli. But years ago we saw it. Now I can't. It's like it doesn't exist and something else is bringing this crap around."

"Sis, you remember years ago it was around our house for months on end before I finally saw it that last night. Ever since then I've come to believe the only reason it appeared was that I had the letters and was hell bent to destroy them."

"That's another thing, Pauli. There's no trigger."

"There's got to be a trigger, Sis. You just have to find it." Paul paused a moment, collecting his thoughts. "I'm thinking from what we saw the other night, that the door is inside Mrs. Frank's house. And I'm thinking a good place to start looking would be that turret room in the attic."

"The one with no door."

"Yes. The only way we can get in is from the roof through a window."

"That's a good idea, Pauli."

"If we can get into that room that way, we'll probably see where the original door was. We'll probably see a lot more than that, too."

"I think Leo Frank walled that door up for some reason. I'm also thinking that Mrs. Frank knows a lot more than she lets on about that room. The attic was boarded up the other night, obviously to keep us out of there. Mrs. Frank has to have some knowledge of what is going on in there. I mean we were right outside her bedroom when we saw those two on the stairs the other night."

"And their pointing at the front of that old house. You don't suppose they're pointing at Stehle's Door. You know they also came through it."

"That may very well be. That turret room is at the very front of the house."

"A distinctly good possibility," Paul replied. "When is Mrs. Frank going to be gone again?"

"Next Wednesday and Thursday. She's going down to

Alvin to look after some land matters down there. I believe she has a niece down there to stay with."

"Good. Wednesday, then. We'll have to go up during the day right after she leaves.

We'll need the light."

"Sounds good to me. I'm worried about Stephi, though. After what she's been through."

"Get Josh and even Howie over since he now knows about everything. The more the merrier. I think with all these people around, she'll be okay. Besides, we'll probably need Josh to pry open that window."

"Good point."

"Sis, do you know of anything in Mrs. Frank's house that might have belonged to Johanna?"

"No, Pauli. You're thinking about a possible trigger, right? I don't know of anything. There's just that room in the attic we've been in and the furniture in it. But we really don't know if the furniture was originally Johanna's."

"That's right. It could just as easily belonged to someone else." Paul paused. "What we need is something with her name on it."

"I know. Something personalized. A perfect trigger for Stehle's Door."

"Something like that could let in the whole casualty list from the Galveston storm."

"As many of them as are still around."

"That's what we need to look for up in the attic. And you might ask Mrs. Frank if she happens to have anything that may have belonged to Johanna."

"I doubt that, Pauli. All she has is those pictures. I doubt if there's anything left in that house that belonged to any of the Diehls."

"Still, it's worth a try."

Alex knew that a personal belonging was a long shot. She looked at the ground and sighed.

"I'll ask her off hand if there's anything around there that might have belonged to Johanna or any of the Diehls family. Maybe she'll at least know about the furniture."

"Good. I'm thinking if we poke around up there in those

attic rooms real well, we'll come across something."

"Yeah. Something besides Johanna herself. I'm worried, Pauli. Her visitations are picking up. And they're clearly getting more dangerous."

"Just keep a look out and you'll be okay."

"That's what we're doing. Poor Stephanie slept in my bedroom again last night in her sleeping bag."

"If that's what it takes."

"Safety in numbers. Pauli, can you come over Wednesday about three. She should be gone by then. From what I can tell, those turret windows are a good five feet from the roof, so we're going to need a combined effort to pry them open. If Josh can't come, I guess I'll have to do it."

"What if someone sees us on the roof and asks Mrs. Frank later what was going on? Or worse still, what if someone thinks we're breaking in?"

"I don't think anyone's going to notice, Pauli. That part of the roof is pretty well covered from the street by those oak trees in Mrs. Frank's front yard. And as far as anyone down the street seeing us, I don't think anyone will pay any attention. And if they do notice, we'll just tell Mrs. Frank one of our cats got out and we chased it up on her roof, trying to catch it."

"I guess that'll work. We're going to need crow bars. I have one and I'm sure Josh can get one." Paul paused a minute and put his hand to the side of his head. "You know, once we get in there, we'll have to come back out the same way."

"I know. But once we get in there, we'll know where that walled up door is, though."

"We can't tear a big hole in the wall, Sis. What if Mrs. Frank goes up there and finds it."

"I know that, little Brother." Alex wondered if the turret room had once been part of the front bedroom they had associated with Johanna. If it hadn't been opened in years, this would mean there could possibly be personal possessions of hers in there. And knowledge of Stehle's Door and personal possessions were what Alex and Stephanie needed at this point. Since Paul apparently had nothing to say, Alex continued.

"Pauli, if we find a trigger and destroy it, that's all she wrote."

"I know." Paul put his hand to his mouth in thought.

Alex continued. "I'm thinking there's got to be something in the wall-up room. The very idea of its being walled up in the first place tells me something was wrong there, whether it was Leo Frank who closed it up or someone else ." Alex looked across the parking lot and noticed her parents approaching. "I've got to run, now," she said. "Call me later about Wednesday."

That night after a calm Sunday afternoon and evening, Alex and Stephanie lay in bed in Alex's room and talked about what Alex had settled with her brother.

"Alex, if we get in that room and find something, then what?"

"Then, we'll know what to do with it, Steph. Destroy it and hope that our problems will be gone."

"Johanna will be gone. But what about the others? Like the little girl."

"Stephi, I'm not worried about the little girl."

"The little girl hurt me," Stephanie pouted.

"If the others are still around, we can find out what they want to communicate besides another storm and maybe handle them, too."

There was a silence that lasted so long Alex almost drifted off to sleep. Finally, however, Stephanie broke it.

"I think all of us ought to go into that room, even though I'm sure it's really small."

"We will, Steph. But we're going to have to climb out on the roof, first."

"That's okay by me. I'm not staying anywhere alone."

Alex and Stephanie spent the next two days wary of anything that might suddenly occur in the apartment or out of it.

Since they had finished their seminar work and registration for the Fall semester was done by computer, they went to a movie Monday afternoon and all-day Tuesday was spent at the Galleria, a large shopping mall. But Wednesday, they awakened to a hard rain that began before dawn and lasted until almost noon.

"We can't do anything if this keeps up," Alex remarked as she spread butter on a piece of toast. "Mrs. Frank won't even be gone. She's not going to drive down to Alvin in this." She viciously took a bite of the toast she had just buttered.

"Maybe it'll stop before noon." Stephanie, on another diet, just ate an apple for breakfast.

"Maybe. You know how this crap is, though. It could go on for days."

"Well, we know the guys will be here. Maybe we could figure something else out."

"Stephi, I don't want Mrs. Frank in on this. At least not yet."

Stephanie took another bite of her apple, chewed it slowly and then swallowed. "Alex, I've been wondering. Why don't we let Mrs. Frank in on what's going on. She might be able to shed some light on some things. After all, she knows who Johanna was and what happened to her. And her husband was probably the one who walled up that room we're going to try to get into."

"Stephanie, when it's time to tell her things, I'll tell her." In her mind, Alex could hear Mrs. Frank pooh-poohing everything she had to tell her. "Now is not the time. I want to keep her in the dark until we're absolutely sure what's going on and know how to deal with it."

"Well, Roomy, she probably does suspect something. She's seen the little girl and she might even have heard or seen things in her house."

"That may be, but I don't want to have to do any more explaining about what's going on than I have to at the moment. Especially not now, that we may have a way to end all of this." Alex rose from the table, turned, and put her hands on her hips. "That is, if this damned rain will just stop."

Noon came and the rain slackened off. Alex, late in picking up the morning paper, was overjoyed to see the old lady come out her back door with a small suitcase in her hand.

"I slept in this morning, Honey," she said, smiling. "Why, I didn't get to sleep last night until almost one o'clock. All those noises in the house kept me awake more than usual. And now this rain."

Alex, caught off guard, thought a moment, then caught herself. She thought about Stephanie's earlier reference to Mrs. Frank's "hearing things." "You look refreshed now, Mrs.

Frank." She smiled at the old lady and opened her car door for her.

"Thank you, Hon. I'll be back in a day or two. Look after everything, will you? And when I get back, we'll go out to eat, if you and Stephanie don't have something else to do."

Alex was dying to ask her what kind of noises kept her awake, but she figured now was not the time or the place. "We'll keep a look out, Mrs. Frank. Drive safely." She waved as the old lady's big Mercury pulled out of the driveway.

Stephanie met her at the apartment door.

"Well, that takes care of that," Alex told her, pulling open the screen door. "The rain's finally stopped. We're all set."

"Good. The guys should be here about three, right?"

"Right." Alex chuckled softly. "Mrs. Frank said she was kept awake last night by noises in her house."

"Duh! Her goddamned house is haunted, remember?"

"Well, if that's the case, Stephi, our apartment is haunted as well." Alex turned to her roommate in a confrontational position. "The worst shit that has happened has occurred right here in our apartment."

At three o'clock, Josh Hamilton, Paul Zunker and the girls sat in the apartment, sipping iced tea and discussing strategy. All four were eager to climb the back staircase to Mrs. Frank's attic but all didn't have the same motive. Josh, who really didn't understand what was going on, wanted to see another ghost, while Stephanie was desperate to end the occurrences she didn't understand.

"We're probably going to have to pry open every window we go through," Paul said. "They probably haven't been opened since before Leo Frank died."

"The garret/turret window for sure, Pauli." Alex leaned forward and set her glass on the coffee table. "I'm pretty sure now that Leo Frank is the one who walled up that room up there. I don't really know why, but I've got a pretty good idea. And I'm thinking we might even have to break a lock to get through one of those windows."

"How can you wall up a ghost, Babe?" Josh turned to her and grinned. "Can't they go through walls."

"Yes and no. The one I'm thinking of has. And she's done

about everything else, too. Apparently, Leo Frank knew there was something disturbing coming out of that room, and with his limited knowledge about such things, he figured walling it up would solve the problem. And apparently it did, for a time. If it hadn't, he probably would have boarded up the whole attic, but he didn't. It's still open. We can get up there."

"One time it wasn't."

"I know, Stephi. But we went back up there later and it was open again. Pauli and I are thinking there's probably something in that turret room connected to Johanna. Something that belonged to her. Something with her name on it would be an excellent trigger. And when we find that, whatever it is, we're going to destroy it, and maybe bring a lot of this stuff, if not all of it, to a halt. That's how you handle Stehle's Door. Destroy the trigger, the trouble disappears."

"I'm thinking about what you said about Mrs. Frank, Sis. What we've mentioned before. She knows more than she's letting on. For starters, you know damned well she can tell you why Leo walled up that room."

"That may very well be, Pauli. But what if he closed it up before she came along? This was his house, remember. His family lived there a long time before she did."

"And Leo clearly used the attic for storage. Would he do that if he hadn't thought he had solved whatever problems there were up there. And didn't Mrs. Frank say something about her kids playing up there when they were little?"

"Yes, she did." Alex replied.

"Well, that's simple enough, Sis. That's the place to start looking for the cure."

"Okay, then, let's get started. I'll get the key and a flashlight." Alex rose and headed for the kitchen. When she returned, Paul stopped her at the door.

"You know, that roof is bound to be slippery after the rain," he said.

"So, when we get up there, we'll take our shoes off."

"What if something happens and we have to get out of there in a hurry?"

Alex put her hands on her hips and breathed deeply. "We'll take them off here, and just go barefooted over there." She looked around at the other two for further questions but instead found abject terror on Stephanie's face and (surprise) a look of fear on Josh's.

She knew in a moment something had to be done. If something were nearby, it didn't need to have fear to feed on. Without another thought, she knew what to do.

"We'll go over there in single file," she said, smiling. "And since he's so hot for Stephanie, we'll let her go after him."

Quickly, Paul picked up on what she was doing. "Great idea, Sis. I have wonderful memories of her in a 'kini.' I think of that often."

"Yeah, very often." Josh laughed out loud. "Especially at night in your bed, right, Paul?"

At that all laughed.

"Now that we mention it, I think what Pauli needs to really hope for," Alex paused and giggled, "is that Stephi has a thing for little boys."

"Yeah," Stephanie chimed in. "Ten-to-twelve-year-olds."

Laughing, the four, barefooted and in single file, exited the apartment and hurried over to Mrs. Frank's back porch.

Alex unlocked the door and all went inside but Paul stopped. The banter had cleared the air somewhat, but once they entered Mrs. Frank's house, the apprehension returned.

"What if the attic's boarded up again?"

"It won't be, Pauli. Trust me." Alex made a motion for him to start up the back stairs. "I don't think it would be closed up like that in the daylight hours."

In silence, the four made their way up to the attic where they opened the attic door easily enough. Light flooded the central hallway from a large stained glass window by the door as well as windows in the open rooms. But the dust and smell seemed thicker than usual.

"You would think nobody had been up here in fifty years," Josh said, bringing up the rear.

Paul turned to him. "When no one's around to keep it clean, it gets dirty fast."

"There might be a few more elements than just cleanliness involved here, Pauli."

"Are you talking about decay, Sis?"

“Among other things, yes.”

“Jesus Christ!” Stephanie piped up. “That’s all we need. To find a dead body in that room.”

“I don’t think we’re going to find anything like that, Blondie. And in regards to the smell, part of it might be jock man back there.” Paul laughed.

“Or your upper lip, Soccer man.”

Stephanie laughed while Alex put her hand up.

“Okay, you guys, cool it,” she said “Let’s get on with what we’ve got to do.”

They reached the large bedroom at the end of the hall where they examined each window, unlocking all and trying to lift them. All were stuck.

“Let’s pry the one nearest the turret open,” Paul said.

They moved boxes over to hold back the heavy, dusty curtains while Josh applied his crow bar to the base of the window. With very little trouble, he was able to loosen the window and, with Paul’s help, raise the window to the top. The screen opened easily and they figured they didn’t need anything to prop it open.

“If it becomes a problem,” Alex said, “we can take it off.” She pointed at the hinges at the top.

Slowly and carefully, all four of them climbed out on the roof, Paul first and Josh bringing up the rear.

“We’ve got to be careful to stay away from the edge,” Paul remarked. “We’ve probably got a roof here that’s over a hundred years old and it’s going to be fragile. Stay close to the windows and the turret.”

Josh passed the others up and made his way around the turret to the front windows. “There’s no window screen here,” he said to Paul, following close behind him.

“The window’s probably locked on the inside.” Paul pressed himself against the turret and tried to see a lock at the top of the dark window.

Josh put his face close to the glass at the bottom of the same window. Then he did the same to the second window. “Paul, I can see part of the lock. I think this window’s open.”

“You mean Leo didn’t bother to lock the windows before he walled the room up,” Alex rejoined from behind Stephanie.

"It looks that way." Reaching upwards, Josh put his crow bar into the base of the window and started working it up and down, taking care not to break the glass. The window frame had apparently been painted more than once and the paint proved a tough adhesive for the window itself. It seemed stuck fast.

Josh pulled a lock blade knife from his pocket. "I'm going to have to cut some of this crap away and maybe we can loosen it then."

Carefully, he worked the knife blade along the base of the window, cutting away as much of the old paint as he could reach. Finally, he tried his crowbar again at the base of the window. This time, the window moved and paint flicked off the top onto the sill.

"I thought so," he exclaimed. "This window's open. How lucky can we get?"

Very slowly, he pried the window up about one inch. Then, he inserted his hands and, pushing upwards, began pushing the window upwards. "Paul, help me with this."

Since Paul was several inches shorter than Josh, there was a limit to what he could do but, together, they opened the window halfway.

Josh moved over in front of the open window. "I think it's open now to where I can handle it. Standing on tiptoes, he pushed the window up another five inches. "We ought to be able to get through this," he said.

"Okay, guys, climb in and help us up." Alex gently pressed Stephanie forward toward the window.

With one hop, Josh propelled himself over the window sill into the turret room.

"What do you see in there?" Paul asked immediately.

"God, I can hardly breathe in here," he answered. "It stinks. And it's darker than I thought it would be. There are some things in here, though. I can see them."

"Here's the flashlight." Alex pulled the small flashlight from a pocket in her shorts and, reaching around Stephanie, handed it to Paul who passed it on to Josh.

Paul put out his hand. "Joshua, give me a hand. I'm coming over."

Josh grabbed Paul's left hand and immediately pulled him

upwards, but his foothold on the side of the turret slipped and his knee crashed into the rough masonry.

"Fuck!" Paul winced in pain.

"In your dreams," Stephanie quipped, standing right by him.

Josh guffawed. "Boy, Paul. Does she ever have your number!" He hung his head out the window and laughed again. "You're not even going to get out of the batter's box, much less to first base."

"Damn it, Mr. Touchdown. Shut up and give me your hand."

This time, Paul made sure of his footing and, giving himself a bit of a jump with Josh's help, made his way over the windowsill into the room.

Then, both boys helped the girls, first Stephanie, then Alex, into the room.

The turret room was an octagonal affair larger than it appeared from the outside. Dust was caked on everything and the air was heavy with the odor of decay and dankness. Apparently, the roof had been leaking for years. Water had run down one wall, creating a curious design over half of it.

They immediately found two doorways, one leading to the adjacent bedroom; the other to the hall. Both were in alcoves which housed a minute staircase of three steps downward. Paul tried both doors, but they were locked tight, apparently with a key. Around the room were three small pieces of furniture: an end table, a lamp stand, and what appeared to be a small bookcase. About the floor lay several articles, seemingly discarded.

"Let's look around at this stuff and see what we can find," Paul said. "Josh, shine the light on that bookcase over there."

In the light, the case appeared empty. However, there were three or four books on the floor near it.

In the meantime, Alex had picked up what appeared to be a purse and was examining it. "This might have belonged to Johanna," she said. "It certainly seems old enough."

"You can't be sure unless there's a name on it, Sis."

"I know that, Pauli. But we need to check out everything that's in the room."

"You know, if someone asked me what a haunted room looked like, this is what I would describe to them." Stephanie stood by the open window in the light.

"Me, too, Blondie." Paul picked up a cloth item that turned out to be a shirt. "This might have belonged to one of Mrs. Frank's boys, or maybe Leo."

"Maybe so. I couldn't see Johanna in a man's shirt." Alex glanced over at her roommate. "Stephi, don't you want to join us in the dust and the grime?"

Carefully, Stephanie kneeled down and picked up what appeared to be a perfume bottle. "This obviously belonged to a woman," she said.

"I don't know about that," Josh remarked. "You ought to see Paul's collection of those." Again, he laughed out loud.

Paul turned to the girls and smiled. "I think it's so grand that Josh is so full of shit that he keeps us in stitches most all of the time."

"Pauli, those books over there." Alex pointed to the scattered books near the bookcase. "Let's check those out."

Josh held the light while Paul, Alex and Stephanie each picked up a book.

Alex thumbed through the pages of a book the cover of which had once been ornate. "This is a volume of Milton's poems, but there doesn't seem to be anything in it."

"Bingo!" Paul exclaimed in a high whisper. He turned the book around and showed his sister the title page.

Below the title and author was an inscription, still very distinct. *To Johanna, with love in friendship, Katie. Christmas, 1899.*

"Oh, sweet Jesus, Pauli." Alex began breathing heavily in excitement. "Everybody, check out the rest of this stuff. Make sure we get everything with Johanna's name on it."

Nothing else was found, only the one inscribed volume of Elizabeth Barrett Browning's *Sonnets From the Portuguese.*

"Okay, everyone out," Paul said. "We need to shut this place back up. Alex, does your fireplace work?"

"Yes, but I'd rather burn that thing in the alley, in a trash can."

"Good idea. We don't know what's going to happen."

"Why do we need to burn it, again?" Josh asked.

"Because when you burn it, you destroy it completely," Alex explained "It automatically closes Stehle's Door to the entity that's been using the object to come through it. In this case, Johanna."

Again, Josh came out first and helped the others. Then, he and Paul lowered the window back into its original position.

Quickly all four of them climbed through the bedroom window and replaced it, all the time Alex worrying about something appearing. She knew Johanna could do anything and she shuddered to think that she might try to intervene.

"Pauli," she said from the rear of the file scurrying through the attic toward the back staircase. "I mentioned the alley so we can all keep a close watch around us. Remember what happened to Holly Peterson."

"Yeah. Good idea."

"Holly who?"

"Josh, Holly Peterson was a friend of ours in Arkansas who had the same problem we do. She was burning some stuff behind her house when this thing appeared out of Stehle's Door and tried to burn her alive."

"Burn her alive?"

"That's right. All her clothes were burned off and she had second degree burns."

When they reached Mrs. Frank's back door, Paul turned to his sister. "Alex, we're going to need some newspapers to make a fire with." Paul carried the book in his right hand but changed it to his left to open the back door. "We're going to need some kindling wood, too."

"I'm sure any wood out here is soaked from this morning's rain."

"You're right, Josh. Let's try to find something inside the apartment or in the garage."

"Paul, there's a couple of old crates in the garage." Stephanie pointed to the garage and carport. "They're real fragile. We can break them up easily."

"Great. That's just what we need."

"Pauli, I'll get some matches. All of you need to get that stuff together for the fire." Alex hurried to the apartment while the others went about gathering materials for the fire.

"I don't think we ought to have a long lasting fire. I'm sure there's an ordinance or something against it."

"No, Josh. All we need is enough fire to destroy the book."

Stephanie and Josh brought two crates from the garage to an empty trash can in the alley, where Josh shattered them with his crow bar. Alex brought matches and newspapers from three days. Paul arranged the newspapers and kindling wood at the bottom of the trash can.

"Everybody, let's keep a look out." Alex looked at each of the other three in turn. "Although there are four of us, something could appear."

"Okay, here goes." Paul touched a match to the papers beneath the kindling. Quickly, both paper and wood caught. "Okay, folks, now's the time." Paul grabbed several pages in the book, ripped them out and fed them into the fire. Then he tore more pages and the back cover off.

"Make sure you burn Johanna's name, Pauli."

"Definitely." He tore pages from the front out and then handed what remained of the book to Josh. Together they fed the remains of the book into the fire which was now built up enough to burn it quickly. All four stood by the trash can and watched the last of the book disintegrate in the flames.

"As soon as we're sure the book's gone," Paul said, "we'll get the hose and douse the fire. Well, nothing's happened." Stephanie turned and looked around the yard behind her. Then, Alex took a few steps and looked up and down the alley.

"Thank God for that. Pauli, you and Josh better put that fire out pretty quick. It's making a lot of smoke."

"That it is, Sis. This should be the end of your problems."

"It should be. But I wonder."

"Wonder? Why?"

"Well, for one thing, why was that room so easy to get into?" Alex put one hand on her hip and glanced down at the flames. "I mean, if Leo Frank took care to lock those doors he boarded up, why didn't he bother to make sure both windows were locked?'

"Why didn't he board up the windows, too?" Josh asked.

"Because it would look like hell from the street, Josh."

Alex glanced again at the fire, now dying down. "Maybe he did lock that window. Maybe something else unlocked it."

"Sister, dear. Why would Johanna open the way to a trigger that was going to put her away for keeps?"

"I know it doesn't make sense, Pauli. But I feel like that thing is up to something. I realize that what we are doing will put it away but I can't help feeling unsure."

"Maybe if we had an experience like Holly had, you wouldn't doubt so much."

"You're right about that. But this has been too easy."

"Alex, for God's sake, let's hope for the best." Stephanie walked over to her roommate and took her hand. "After all, it's all we have."

"I know. Let's hope so."

"I think we ought to get something to drink, don't you?" Josh smiled at the two girls and then turned to Paul.

"I'm with you, Jock man." Paul trotted over to the garden. "Let me douse this fire and we'll go inside."

Paul squirted water on the fire which was now nothing but a pile of ashes. "Well, that book's history and, hopefully, everything connected with it."

"It seems like a shame to burn up such a beautiful old book." Stephanie looked from Paul to Josh. "But I do understand it's for a very worthy cause." She looked about the yard and then at Paul, who was still shooting water at the fire.

"There," he said. "I think it's completely dead now." He moved the hose outside the garbage can. Little whiffs of smoke still rose from the soggy ashes. "I don't think that trigger is going to cause any more problems. Let's go inside."

"There's some St. Genevieve in the fridge," Stephanie chirped. "And I think there's some more in the pantry."

"All right. I feel a celebration coming on." Paul hurried over to the garden and cut off the water. Then he piled the hose neatly by the faucet.

"Not so much that you can't drive home, Pauli." Alex still glanced about the yard for anything out of the ordinary.

Although she did feel somewhat relieved, there still was that nagging fear that their efforts that afternoon had gone for naught. She and her brother knew only too well that the destruction of a trigger would send a manifestation back through Stehle's Door for good. But there was still that doubt. She didn't have the feeling of closure she would have liked to have. And if Johanna was gone, there were still the others. Was there another malicious type among them? Alex wasn't even sure what they were up to. Her business seemed far from over.

Chapter Eighteen

Later, after replacing the garbage can and making sure Mrs. Frank's back door was locked, Alex and the boys settled in the living room while Stephanie poured wine glasses in the kitchen.

"I remember wanting something to drink after we got rid of that bunch four years ago," Paul said in a comfortable, assured voice. He had seen the trigger destruction work first hand.

"What about those other things in Mrs. Frank's house, Paul?"

"Yes," Stephanie said, bringing two full glasses through the kitchen door. "That little girl is horrid and Mrs. Frank's house is full of those things."

"Well, why don't we call Ghostbusters for the rest of them." Paul laughed, joined by Josh and Stephanie.

"Pauli, I really don't find that very funny. It's obvious those things are around for a purpose, and has it occurred to you that we still need to find out what that purpose is?"

"I know that, Sis. But the real baddie is gone."

"We hope." Alex settled back and took a sip of wine "We need to find out pretty quick what's gone and what's still around. And there is still the matter of Stehle's Door."

"Stehle's Door should be closed, Sis."

"On just Johanna. But I'm thinking about the other things. They have to have a way to get in, too, don't they?" Alex breathed deeply and glanced over at Stephanie, who, a few minutes after bringing in the other wine glasses, was ready to refill hers in the kitchen. "There's something going on here that's bigger than Johanna," Alex continued. "Although Johanna was pure malice, there are other things that could be harmful involved here. What I'm saying is those things were not warning us against Johanna as we originally thought."

"What could that possibly be?" Josh asked. He didn't like wine and set his half empty glass away from him on the coffee table. "Those things the other night were pointing at something. What else could there be?"

"When I called him the other day, Dr. Blassingame mentioned another storm."

"Another storm?" Paul's eyebrows went up. "You mean another hurricane. God, Sis which one? There's at least five or six hurricanes every year. Most of them hit Florida or the Gulf coast around the Mobile or Biloxi area. They're usually little things that just rain like hell everywhere. Bad ones like Katrina and Ike are kind of rare."

"A dangerous storm, Pauli. Like those you mentioned. And like the one that hit Galveston in 1900. Coming at us again."

"Coming at Galveston?"

"Exactly."

Stephanie, whose eyes were getting bigger and bigger, finally rose to get her second glass of wine. "In Kansas," she said, "we have tornadoes. Those blow down tool sheds and garages and pick up trailer homes and throw them."

"And tear up a bunch of other things, too. Hurricanes are a might different, Roomy. Those tear up and flood whole cities, as you know."

"And Galveston has a seawall that will knock the stuffings out of any hurricane coming straight at it."

"And a large storm surge would go right over it and flood the city, Pauli."

"There was just a hurricane last week," Josh chimed in. "It went up the coast of Florida and petered out. I think all it did was blow over a few signs and rain a lot. Just like Paul said."

"There are hurricanes every year. A few are bad but most aren't any real problem."

"Yeah. But what kind of a storm would bring ghosts around."

"I'm not sure, Josh. Most likely a storm like the one they died in."

"I read somewhere that the Galveston hurricane of 1900 was classified as a four." Paul rose to get another glass of wine. "That's almost the worst there is."

"It did enough damage to be that and more." Alex leaned back in her chair and sighed. Then she turned to her roommate. "We need that little girl, Stephi. She seems to be the one most eager to communicate with us."

"If you say so. But you're going to have to deal with her. I don't want her anywhere near me."

"What'd she do to you, Stephanie?' Josh asked.

"She grabbed me. And it hurt. That little monster has an iron grip."

"Iron grip or no iron grip. We need her input." Alex set her glass down and rose. "I need to visit the little girl's room."

"So do I," Stephanie chirped and rose also.

"I'll go upstairs, Stephi. You go down here."

"Let me know if you need any help, Stephi." Paul cackled behind the girls.

"Yeah, right."

Alex laughed and took off up the stairs while her roommate entered the downstairs bathroom and slammed the door.

At the top of the staircase, Alex was halted abruptly by the same dreadful feeling she had experienced months before during her first time in Mrs. Frank's attic. A feeling of consummate overpowering evil was followed by a coldness she knew only too well. Not knowing whether to run or find out what this was, she walked to the bathroom door to find nothing there. But when she turned to the large mirror over the sink, she was struck as if someone had slugged her in the stomach.

Scrawled across the mirror in what looked like red lipstick were the words: *Die, Alexandra, Die, like I did. In the dark. In the water.*

She knew immediately what was responsible. She turned and faced the mirror, frightened, but somewhat annoyed at the same time. She was supposed to be gone.

While she stood, staring into the mirror, an image began forming behind the letters; an image, hazy at first, but quickly forming the face of a young girl. As the image became clearer, Alex recognized it as a face she had seen in a lightning flash not too long before.

The upper body appeared and the face grew larger. Wide blue eyes, blonde, almost white, hair, pinned back by a large beige bow. The face bore no expression but it grew larger to natural size. The face from Mrs. Frank's cabinet card had fleshed out. Then, when it began moving forward, it became animated and the mouth curved up in a hideous, toothy grin.

Alex, overcome with terror, moved backward impulsively. She put out her hands and started to cry out but no sound came from her mouth. Her stomach churned while she lost all control and saturated her clothes. She didn't feel urine running down her leg as she fell, sideways toward the bathroom door in a dead faint.

The next thing she knew, her brother was kneeling over her, gently slapping her cheek, while Stephanie moved in beside him with a cold rag she placed on her forehead.

"Alex! Alex! What happened?" Paul exclaimed, alarm all over his face.

"My God, Paul. She's peed all over herself." Stephanie quickly re-dampened the rag and dabbed at Alex's cheeks with it.

"The mirror," Alex croaked. "The mirror. there's…there's writing on the mirror."

In the corner of her eye, she saw Josh lean in and look at the mirror. "There's nothing there," she heard him say.

"Let's get her to her room on the bed," Paul said, and the three lifted her, head and shoulders first, but Alex, regaining her faculties, pushed herself to her feet. With their help she made her way into her bedroom and onto her bed.

As she lay on her back, Stephanie dabbed her again with the cold rag.

"Well…Well, my little friend is still around," she said with a sob.

"Johanna?"

"Yes, Stephanie. She appeared in the mirror, the way she was when she died."

"What about the writing, Sis?"

"It said, "'die Alexandra, die, like I did, in the water, in the dark.'"

"Jesus!"

Alex sat up on the bed easily but was still breathing deeply. "God only knows what would have happened if I hadn't passed out," she said. "I think if she had come out of the mirror she would have taken her other form, claws and all."

"We heard something up there go 'thump,'" Paul said. "And we wondered what it was. And when you didn't come down immediately, we all came up and found you lying on the bathroom floor."

"As you can plainly see, I was scared out of my wits. I wanted to scream but I couldn't. I wanted to run but I only fainted." Sluggishly, Alex turned and moved her legs off the bed. "I've got to change clothes," she said. "I think now she's coming back the same way all the rest of them are. She may have been around for a long time through that book we destroyed, but now I feel she'll be here as long as the others are." She got off the bed, retrieved a fresh clothes change from the dresser and headed for the bathroom.

"Do you want me to go in there with you," Stephanie asked, a worried look on her face.

"No, Stephi. My playmate is gone. At least for now." She entered the bathroom and closed the door.

While she undressed, Alex glanced at the mirror. Only the image of herself appeared where before there had been an image evoking sheer terror. There was no sign that anything had happened in that small room in the last hour. The mirror was perfectly clean and the counter top neat and orderly.

Thinking of the scrawled message, she opened a top drawer in the counter. Although she never used red lipstick, she had a tube that had been part of a gift. This item, however, had obviously never been used.

What did she write with, then? she thought. *Blood?* The answer to this question made her shudder. She checked her other lipsticks for a color similar to red that might have been used but found nothing.

She finished dressing and then sat down on the side of the bathtub. "In the water. In the dark. How so?" she whispered to herself. "In a hurricane? How could I drown in a hurricane up here? It would have to be the mother of all storms and even then it would peter out before it got to downtown."

"Alex, are you okay?" Stephanie's worried voice was following by a knock.

"Yes, just a minute, Steph." She rose and looked around for her dirty clothes. "When you piss on yourself, you have to wash." Retrieving her soggy clothes, she deposited them in the empty laundry hamper for the time being and opened the door.

"We were worried, Sis." Paul stood at the door alongside Stephanie, two somber faces in a row.

"Worried? That that thing was still here?" Alex sighed. "She's through."

The four of them returned to the living room, Alex leading the way, where they sat and finished their wine. Soon the boys were gone and Alex and Stephanie went out to a fried chicken place for an inexpensive supper.

As they ate their plates in silence, Alex thought about the day's events, coming to the conclusion that at this point she really didn't know what to do next. All anyone could do was wait. But they had been waiting ever since all these things had started. Alex made one plan, though. She'd make one last effort to find out everything Mrs. Frank knew about her old house, even if she had to tell her everything that had occurred.

As usual, an uneventful night followed a frightening day. Alex and Stephanie rose early and made plans to attend Astroworld. Since Mrs. Frank wouldn't be back until the next day, and Alex had a gate pass she had won in a raffle at church, they planned to spend the whole day at the popular Houston amusement park.

Neither of them wanted to stay around the apartment. After the previous day's events, Alex honestly didn't know what to expect. She didn't figure anything would happen so soon after yesterday, but at this point, she wasn't so sure. Johanna had proven herself capable of anything, apparently even in defiance of Stehle's Door.

The girls planned to leave before ten but a phone call from Rice University concerning a scholarship led to an errand at the school's finance office which took up an hour. After they had finished, they stopped for a quick lunch at a small restaurant near the school, and only arrived at Astroworld at noon.

The vast amusement park and all it had allowed them to forget their cares and become so preoccupied they didn't leave until after dark. On the way home, Alex wondered again, what, if anything, awaited them. Stephanie, driving, chatted away about the day's visit and only when they turned into Harvard Street did she stop. At Mrs. Frank's driveway, both girls froze.

From what they could immediately tell, there was not a single light in Mrs. Frank's house that was not on.

"Alex, look. Mrs. Frank is home a day early."

"Stephanie, if Mrs. Frank is at home, where is her car?" With a flip of her hand, she indicated that only one car, Alex's, stood in the carport.

"Oh, my God, Alex. What's going on?"

"I don't know, Steph, but our apartment is dark."

Stephanie pulled in front of the garage and parked. "You don't suppose something's waiting for us in there, do you?"

"Well, I'm going to find out pretty quick. Come on."

They bailed out of the car and hurried to the door of the apartment, Alex hastily checking the roof of the garage for anything in wait. The brilliant lights from the large house lit up the entire area so there wasn't the problem of seeing they usually had when they came home after dark.

Entering quickly and flipping on the light, Alex hurried to the hall phone.

"Alex, what are you doing?"

"Calling the police."

"The police?"

"Yes. When you come home and find lights on you didn't turn on, you call the police. You obviously have a break-in." She dialed 9-1-1 and didn't have to wait long for a dispatcher to answer. "Yes, Ma'am. I want to report a break-in at 815 Harvard Street.

I think it's a burglary in progress as lights are still on."

Stephanie, wide-eyed, stood by Alex, her hands clasped over her chest.

Alex hung up the phone. "Okay, Steph. Let's go outside and wait for them."

Sooner than they expected, a police cruiser pulled up in the driveway while another stopped at the curb in front of the house.

"Alex, there's two of them."

"Good. The more cops, the better." Alex stood, motionless,

with no emotion, and waited for the first policeman to come to her.

A middle aged officer emerged from the first unit and he, along with a younger officer moved gingerly about the side and front of the house, looking for signs of movement or intrusion inside. When they got to the back, the older man approached Alex.

"Ma'am," he said. "Are you the one who called about a break-in?"

"Yes, Sir. We just got home." Alex indicated Stephanie's car standing nearby. "When we pulled in the driveway, all of the lights were on. The lady who lives here, Mrs. Lila Frank, is gone for a couple of days and we know she didn't leave any of those lights on."

By now, the second officer approached the driveway, shining his flashlight into the garden and back yard by the house. The first officer turned and looked over the back of the house and then turned back to Alex.

"Do you happen to have a key to this house?" he asked her.

"Yes. I'll go get it."

Meanwhile, the other officer examined the garden, the back of the house and the other side. "No sign of a break in anywhere here," he said.

The man with Alex and Stephanie took the key and hurried up the back steps to the door. Cautiously, he unlocked the door and, weapon in hand, entered, followed by the other officer.

The two girls waited in front of their apartment.

"Stephanie, you and I both know, there's nothing in there. Nothing human."

"I know. What do you suppose they'll make of that horrid smell and that God-awful cold?"

"I don't think they're going to experience it, Stephanie. After all, tonight's show wasn't intended for them."

"I wonder what we would have found if we had gone in there without them."

"It's hard to say. There are possibilities, both positive and negative. I'm pretty sure the spirits from the storm wouldn't have turned those lights on unless, unless this was a ply to get us to communicate with them." Alex sighed. "Well, we didn't know. And there's the possibility that there's harmful things afoot."

Not long after, the officers returned through the back door.

"Ma'am, we went all through the house and we couldn't find any sign of a break-in." The officer walked up to Alex and Stephanie while the other stood behind him. "Do you know if the lady who lives here might have somebody with a key who might have come in while she was gone?"

"Well…" Alex started, but Stephanie cut her off.

"That cousin in Conroe has a key. She's been here before. Right after we started living here, she came to the house and went in while Mrs. Frank was gone."

"That's right," Alex said. "That cousin in Conroe. Mrs. Frank went to Alvin." She knew there was a cousin in Conroe with a key, but she also knew this cousin had not been there that night.

The officer handed Alex back her key, and then took the girls names and other information along with a statement. Then, the first officer turned to leave.

"You can go ahead and turn off the lights and lock up now," he said.

"Yes. Could you please help us with this? You see, we're a little nervous. We won't take long."

"Sure."

With the older officer following, Alex and Stephanie made their way through the house, cutting off lights. When they got to the attic, Alex noticed the door was wide open.

Odd, she thought. *I hope the cops left this open.*

When they had finished, Alex closed the back door and made sure it was locked. After thanking the officers for their help, she mentioned the only plausible conclusion concerning the lights was that the cousin from Conroe had visited while the girls were at Astroworld and left the lights on. Alex felt relieved when the officers seemed to accept the story. They told the girls to keep an eye out for anything suspicious and left.

In the apartment, Alex turned to her roommate behind her. "I think it's downright rude of our friends not to perform for those cops," she said with a light tone.

"Alex, I know you said we have to be upbeat." Stephanie

folded her arms over her chest, a worried frown on her face. "But what really bothers me is when you are so nonchalant about things that scare the hell out of me."

"Stephi, the only real way to get a handle on these things is to keep them at bay. I think I've mentioned this before." Alex sighed again. "The only way to keep these things away is to ignore them, which we can't really do, or to treat them in a whimsical off-hand manner, which we can do. Then, when they make a move, we deal with it."

"Yeah. Then they make a move that damn near kills us."

"That's Johanna, Roomy. And hopefully, we're going to get to the bottom of her pretty quick."

"Get to the bottom of her? What do you mean?"

Quickly, Alex walked to the kitchen for a glass of ice water and returned. Then, she settled in a comfortable chair and turned to her roommate, who still stood across the room.

"Well, Steph, from what I can surmise," she began. "Johanna has been around for a pretty long time. Longer than the others. I think she was here, basically, through the existence of the book we destroyed. That was the initial trigger that brought her back. For all we know, she could have been around practically since the day she died."

She sipped her ice water while Stephanie slipped into a chair across from her.

"Leo Frank had some idea of her presence, of that I'm sure. He may even have seen her a time or two but, from what I can tell, he never mentioned it to his wife. If he had, she probably would have told me something about it when I talked to her about the attic earlier. Anyway, since he knew absolutely nothing about Stehle's Door, he just figured the disturbances were occurring most often in the attic." Alex looked off toward the front door, in thought. "Somehow, he figured that turret room was responsible for the manifestations and he walled it up. Then, apparently, the things ceased."

"But Johanna was still around."

"That, I don't know. That's one reason I want to pin down Mrs. Frank. I want to find out just what Leo told her about that room. He's got to have told her something, especially since their kids played in the attic."

"Kids." Stephanie's face lit up. "Alex, you don't suppose Raymond and James knew something about this."

"They could. They could have even seen Johanna." Alex scratched her head in thought. "That could be the main reason Leo walled that room up. To keep the kids out of there."

"Or to keep her from coming out of it."

"That, too." Alex clucked her tongue and her roommate smiled. "Yep, Roomy, at one time that room was the sole filthy heart of that house. Leo figured that out, but, of course, he didn't know why."

"And all these other things. They have no…"

"Triggers?" Alex took another long drink of ice water and set her glass on the coffee table. "But they do have a way in. I have no idea what that way is, but I do know that Stehle's Door is still here somewhere. It has to be."

"And we need to find it."

"Bingo. And when we do, I feel we'll be able to put an end to all of this once and for all. We close that door like we closed the one in the turret."

"Alex, we were talking earlier about another storm. How, exactly does that figure in?"

"All I can think of is that they're warning us against it, if there's going to be another storm. This is the main reason we need to communicate with them. Starting with the little girl."

"The little girl again."

"Yes. Since she seems so eager to communicate with us, we need to find out what she has to say."

"She hasn't appeared in a while."

"I know." Alex screwed up her face in a puzzled look. "And I don't know any way to conjure her up."

"Maybe Johanna scared her off."

"I doubt that, Stephanie. I have a feeling, though, if we want her to come to us, she'll come."

"As long as you deal with her."

Alex bent over, took her glass and drank. "I hate to break this to you, Roomy, but you might be the one who'll have to talk to her. She seems to come to you more than me."

"Oh, great. Talking to a dead person." Stephanie breathed in and out deeply. Alex thought, momentarily, she was going to break out crying. Instead, she tossed her head and crossed her legs abruptly. “Alex, how many times do I have to tell you, I’m scared to death of these things. When I see them, all I want to do is turn and run.” Her face fell, then turned into a pout. “I’m not afraid of anything of this world,” she continued. “An intruder, an attacker, I can handle them. I have two years of martial arts training. But dead people? God in Heaven.”

“I know, Steph. It’s...It’s something that shouldn’t be happening in the first place.” Alex’s voice lowered almost to a whisper. Her heart went out to her roommate when she remembered how frightened she had been years before in her bedroom when she had first come in contact with thc paranormal. “Stephi, you know I’ll be here. And as much as anyone can handle these things, I think I can.”

“Alex, I’m sorry, but...but I guess I’m just a damned coward.”

“Stephanie, you don’t have to be sorry about anything. I’ve been where you are.”

“I guess I should feel privileged,” Stephanie said, after a pause. “After all, how many people have seen a ghost?”

“Some privilege.” Alex stood up to take her glass back to the kitchen. “Mrs. Frank comes home tomorrow. I think tomorrow night would be a good night for a dinner in, don’t you. We can go get some pork chops or something and cook them before she gets home. And she’ll probably make a dessert. You know how much she loves to do that.”

“And then over dinner we talk to her about what’s been going on.”

“Right. But not all at once.” Alex took her glass to the kitchen and returned. “I want to talk about that room up there first. Then, one thing will lead to another and we’ll mention the little girl and the other things we’ve seen in the house.”

“She’ll be surprised. She’s seen the little girl.”

“I know.”

“How do you suppose she’ll take the idea that we’ve been in her house when she was away?”

Alex thought a minute. “I’ll just tell her there were some things we needed to borrow and we went to get them. Like her industrial size vacuum that she keeps in the attic.”

"Oh, yeah. She did say if we wanted to borrow anything, we could."

"Exactly." Alex sat back down and crossed her legs. "That's a dandy excuse for being in her house, much less the attic."

"Are you going to mention tonight."

"Of course. Someone around the neighborhood is bound to have seen those cops. We'll tell it just like it is, except that when I get to it, I will have already told her about the paranormal manifestations in and around her house."

"God, Alex. I don't know how she's going to take this."

"I don't know either, but it's time to tell her."

Stephanie glanced at her watch. "It's past midnight. I guess I better hit the sack."

"Me, too."

Both girls rose at the same time and headed for the staircase.

"I may or may not mention Johanna," Alex said as an afterthought. "She might know all about that one."

"If that thing showed up, she'd recognize it, too, with the pictures she has."

"That's hitting very close to home."

Quickly, they settled into Alex's room and Stephanie cut the light. Alex, however, did not try to sleep. Still keyed up over the events of the evening, she went over and over what she planned to say to Mrs. Frank.

She knew the old lady, with her church background, didn't believe in ghosts or anything like that, so she would have to approach the paranormal judiciously. But how? There seemed to be no way, except not to mention occurrences at all. Of course, Alex would talk in detail about the turret room and get Mrs. Frank to tell her about that. From then on, one thing would lead to another.

Although she was late in getting to sleep, Alex woke before dawn, at a little after five. Wide awake and unable to go back to sleep, she crept downstairs, taking care not to awaken her sleeping roommate.

She could sleep through a bomb blast, she thought as she crept past Stephanie's pallet. *Thank God.* She remembered the night the ghostly children had surrounded her bed and Stephanie's.

In the kitchen, she made coffee, more so than usual, since she would need a few extra cups since she had gotten up first. Then, she ate a Jell-O cup and two tangerines for breakfast.

Settling on the couch, hot coffee cup in hand, she tried to hear any noise in the house out of the ordinary. There was none.

She heard the paper hit Mrs. Frank's drive way and rose to retrieve it. Outside, the cool predawn air stopped her just beyond the door and she paused to breathe in deeply.

What happened to the rain? she thought. *The weatherman predicted it for today and the sky is crystal clear. Oh well, we'll probably have a storm come up later this morning or this afternoon.*

Hurrying down the driveway in bare feet, she spotted the paper near the sidewalk. She picked up her paper and then turned, facing the corner of Mrs. Frank's dark, old house. Momentarily, she studied the empty windows of the turret and the attic. There was nothing there, as there had been nothing in her apartment.

"Not a creature was stirring, not even a mouse," she said to herself. *Maybe those cops frightened them off,* she thought. *What irony. The fearful presences of the dead have been frightened away by two Houston cops. God, if only they had.*

Slowly, she walked back up the driveway toward the apartment, paying no attention to a passing car, even though clad only in flimsy pajamas. Her coffee was empty and she craved another cup. And she felt she did have to check on her roommate.

Stephanie still slept, soundly, a quiet snore telling Alex she was sound asleep. *I wish I could sleep like that. On the other hand, wouldn't that make me more vulnerable?*

Quietly, she crept downstairs to the kitchen and poured her second cup. Afterwards, she lay down on the couch across from the TV.

The weather channel spoke of rain later in the day, but there seemed to be no other disturbances, around Houston or anywhere else.

Alex sighed and switched to the movie channels she had. A

thought came to her to write down what she was going to ask Mrs. Frank that evening, but since she was still unsettled in the details, she decided not to.

Sabrina suddenly appeared and cuddled next to her on the couch.

“Have you seen your not-of-this-world friend lately?” she asked gently, remembering with a slight shudder the large black and white tom that was supposed to be dead. “There’s nothing around or you’d know it, right?”

Henrietta appeared at the kitchen door, promptly to head upstairs to settle on her mistress’ pallet. Everything indicated it was going to be a day without events, a restful respite from the last two.

The disturbing factor in this peaceful prognostication, though, was that Mrs. Frank was not yet home. And something told Alex that their meeting that evening would not be what she expected.

Chapter Nineteen

When she found nothing on TV, she thought about checking on her roommate again, but, having heard nothing, she decided not to. After all, if something had happened up there, Stephanie would have let her know about it.

A chance thought prompted by the weather channel led her to the office computer to read up on hurricanes. Although she had lived in South Houston most of her life and had weathered Katrina and Ike recently, she really didn't know much about these terrific storms. Up until recently they were simply something she read about in the newspaper or heard about on TV. She had never studied them in school and, until her discovery of the Galveston disaster of 1900 this summer, she had never given them a second thought. They were simply something to run from if they came around and ignore if they didn't.

The first website she reached gave her a definition, a description, some important details about major hurricanes, including Galveston's, and the factor that hurricane "season" ran mainly from the last of July to the last of November.

Oh great, we're right in it, she thought. She knew from somewhere that hurricanes were classified one to five depending chiefly on the wind velocity involved but learned that a category five, labeled "catastrophic," was rare. Two examples, Hurricanes Andrew and Katrina, had been fives sometime in their careers.

"I remember them," she whispered to herself. "They caused more damage than any of the others, or something like that. Especially Katrina."

A graphic she found outlined hurricane tracks, a few of which led to the Texas coast. It seemed to her that the whole coast of the Southern United States was a target. Even hurricanes in the Pacific, called typhoons, could be tracked by satellite. She shuddered when she came across a satellite picture of a storm which took up most of the Gulf of Mexico.

A note on another page chilled her even more. Most of the deaths in hurricanes are the result of drowning. Drowning. Apparently, Johanna had drowned. And she wanted Alex to die the same way. *How can that be?* she wondered. *Unless I'm right in the middle of one of these storms.*

Footsteps in the hall meant that Stephanie was up on her way to the bathroom. Alex closed the computer and headed for her room.

"Morning, Stephi, did you sleep okay?"

"Like a log," a sleepy voice responded. "How long have you been up?"

"Since about five. Come on down and I'll fix you some breakfast."

Alex cooked some eggs and bacon while her roommate sat in the dining room, still yawning.

"I looked at hurricanes on line," Alex said, handing her roommate her plate. "Did you know we're in hurricane season right now?"

"Now? A hurricane season?" Stephanie took the plate and looked up. "Back home, we had tornadoes usually in the spring. But I thought hurricanes came around all year long."

"July to November, the note said." Alex sat down across from her. "And most deaths from hurricanes are caused by drowning."

"So that's how they died."

"It would seem so."

"How about the mutilations? Like the little girl's face."

"Probably done by wreckage, before or after death."

"Jesus." Stephanie took a bite of eggs and gazed off in the distance. Then she turned back to Alex. "Apparently, Johanna wants you to die like she did, drowning in a hurricane. How's she going to swing it?"

"I have no earthly idea."

"You know, 'in the water, in the dark,' that could be you in a swimming pool after hours with a load on."

"It could; however, I wouldn't be anywhere near a

swimming pool after hours and I would have to guzzle more hooch than either Pauli or Josh to have a load on. That just cannot be, Roomy."

Both girls laughed. An hour after the breakfast dishes were done, they went jogging. When they returned, they found a strange car in Mrs. Frank's driveway.

"Oh God, here we go again," Alex mumbled, panting as she walked quickly up the driveway toward the apartment.

When they reached the back, they were greeted from the back steps by Raymond Frank and his wife, Betsy. Both girls knew Raymond and Betsy from last Christmas when they had formally met them. Raymond was head of security of some corporation in Detroit and his wife taught in a community college. Noises from the back yard told them the Frank children were there, too."

"Hi, girls," Raymond called out, loud and amiable. "Alexandra and Stephanie, isn't it? We've tried both front and back doors and I don't seem to raise Mom. Is she gone? I don't see her car."

Alex greeted both Raymond and his wife cordially. "She went to Alvin a couple of days ago," she said. "She's supposed to be back today, though."

"Today? Great." Raymond scanned the backyard, garage and carport. "I called and told her I would be in today, but I guess she forgot. I've been transferred to New Orleans and we're taking a short vacation to San Antonio. I told Mom we would stay overnight here in Houston.

"That's great, Raymond." Alex looked around at her roommate who stood smiling behind her. "Let me go get the key and let you in. She should be back some time this afternoon." Alex turned and headed for the apartment, Stephanie just behind her.

In the apartment, Alex went straight for the kitchen and the key. When she emerged from the kitchen, she smiled broadly at her roommate.

"What do you say we query Mr. Raymond Frank tonight," she said. "I've got some real suspicions about him."

"Suspicions, Alex? What are you talking about?" Stephanie's voice was an urgent whisper.

"I think he saw Johanna," Alex answered in a matter-of-fact voice. "When he was a kid." With that she headed out the front door.

Alex trotted past the Franks and took the back stairs two at a time. "Do you have a place to stay?" she asked over her shoulder.

"Oh, yes. Right here. I wanted to stay at the Best Western and go swimming, but Mom wouldn't hear of it." Raymond and his wife laughed.

"She's very old fashioned that way," Betsy said. "She expects relatives to stay with relatives. That's what they did back before motels were invented. My parents are the same way."

Raymond chuckled. "There's no arguing with them."

"Oh, I know that." Alex unlocked the door and turned.

"How's school, Alexandra? Did you go this summer?" Raymond stopped just behind her.

"Just one seminar. I didn't want to load up like I did last summer."

"That's all right. You need some time off." He smiled and let his family into the house while Alex returned to the apartment.

Later, Alex and Stephanie went to the grocery store and on the way Alex told her roommate her plan for the evening.

"After dinner I'm going to get him started talking about the house and then I'll mention the attic. I want him away from his mother, though."

"I'll offer to help Mrs. Frank with the dishes. Maybe Betsy will, too." Stephanie was excited. "Or maybe Betsy will help Mrs. Frank and I'll watch the kids."

"Good idea, Steph. But if Betsy's there with her husband, it'll be okay." Alex went on to explain what she wanted from Raymond.

When they returned, Mrs. Frank was home from Alvin. Alex went to work cooking pork chops for dinner while Stephanie phoned Mrs. Frank and told her what they were going to bring.

"This is really fortunate for us," Alex said, carefully wrapping foil around the cooked meat. "I know I can get more from Raymond than I can from his mother."

"I just hope you get a chance to talk to him." Stephanie stood in the kitchen door, a serious look on her face.

"I think I will after supper, if we can decoy Mrs. Frank away."

At supper, the general mood was jovial due mainly to Raymond's good nature. He was the type of person one would often refer to as "the life of the party," for he never let the conversation cease or the spirit drop.

After supper, Stephanie offered to help Mrs. Frank with the dishes, but Betsy offered the same thing and asked Stephanie if she would mind watching the kids for a while. Stephanie, overjoyed with her prediction, agreed, and the field soon cleared for Alex.

"Well, Alexandra…Alex…tell me about school," Raymond said in a contented voice after a slow sip on his coffee.

"There's really not much to tell. Chemistry and advanced calculus last spring, along with history and an English course."

"Wow," Raymond chuckled. "That sounds like quite a load. But it is Rice University."

"Right. And a humanities seminar this summer."

"Humanities. Let's see. That's art and music, isn't it?"

"Right. And a whole bunch of other things. I particularly enjoyed the architecture part." Alex smiled, knowing what she was going to do next. "Stephanie and I got to use this house as an example of late Victorian architecture."

"That so? I grew up in this house and it has always fascinated me. When I went away to college, I missed it almost as much as I did my mother."

"Really? This is a fascinating house. And your mother has told us so much about it."

"I like old places like this. They might be dark and drafty but they have a personality all their own. New Orleans is full of them."

"They sure do. This is the kind of place people call haunted." Alex smiled again and sipped the last of her iced tea.

Raymond laughed. "That's right. A lot of people are scared of a place like this."

"Yes, they are." Alex leaned forward and propped her head up with her left hand on the arm of the chair. "When you were growing up, did you ever see a ghost in this house?" Behind her teasing voice, she was dead serious.

"You know, I was thinking about that just the other day." Raymond leaned back in his chair and stared at the ceiling. "We had just finished moving into our new house in New Orleans and we were driving around the Garden District, looking for a place to eat. The old houses there reminded me of this one. Anyway, I was reminded of a time when my brother Jimmy and I were playing in the attic here. Oh…we must have been about eight and nine. Or nine and ten." Raymond stopped and scratched his head in thought. Then he continued. "We were playing on the floor in the hall like we had many times before when, all of a sudden, a girl appeared."

Alex couldn't help her eyes growing larger and larger. She was getting just what she wanted.

"This girl was white. I mean real pale," Raymond continued. "And she had blonde hair…"

"Almost white," Alex interrupted.

"Yes," Raymond's eyebrows rose in puzzlement.

"And she wore a bow, yellow or beige, in her hair."

"That's right. How do you know this? This was at least thirty-five years ago."

"Raymond, she is still around here. Her name is Johanna Diehls. I've seen her a number of times."

"Still around? Jimmy and I were scared when we realized what she was. We told Dad about it but, of course, he accused us of making it up. He told us to forget about it. We never saw her again and, in time, we forgot about it."

"I'm pretty sure your father saw her too, Raymond."

"Dad? If he did, he never mentioned anything about it to us. He was the perfect realist. No one on God's earth was going to accuse Leo Frank of foolishness."

"Yes, Raymond, he saw her. And he connected her to that turret room in the attic." Alex's voice rose in excitement. "That's why he walled it up."

"Oh? He told us something about drafts and coldness in the wintertime. We were real disappointed when he did that because

Jimmy and I loved to play in that room."

"After your Dad walled that room up, that was probably the end of the sightings until recently." Alex wanted to tell Raymond about Stehle's Door but she was suddenly joined by Betsy and Stephanie.

"What are you two talking about in all seriousness?" Betsy asked, giggling.

Stephanie, who knew what was going on, changed the subject. "Betsy, your two boys are trying to grow up too fast. They've already inquired about my love life, my general outlook on sex, and whether or not I'm available to be their girlfriend."

"Oh, those two." Betsy suddenly became serious and turned to her husband. "God, little boys!" She rolled her eyes. "They're going to need a talking-to tonight."

"I will speak to them about gentlemanly propriety." Raymond regained his joviality somewhat but Alex still noticed the remnant of his worried frown.

Stephanie looked at her roommate and laughed. "Sometimes little boys don't really know what they're talking about."

"Still, they need to respect their elders." Betsy turned to Stephanie and crossed her arms over her chest.

Alex could see that Betsy was a conscientious mother who reared her kids by the book. "Oh, Stephanie can handle them," she said. "She's good with kids."

Just then, Mrs. Frank appeared at the dining room door. "Alex, I am so glad you and Stephanie joined us tonight. Those pork chops were delicious."

"We expected to be here, Mrs. Frank. But Raymond and Betsy were an added treat."

"Isn't that the truth." The old lady was ecstatic. "I wish they could stay longer."

"We'll drop by here on our way home," Raymond said. "We'll only be in San Antonio four days. We can spend a couple here."

"But, Mom Frank, Ray just has to have a swimming pool." Betsy laughed and turned to Alex. "He's just like the kids."

"Oh, I know it." Mrs. Frank beamed at her son. "He always

was one to go off in his own direction. Anyway, I'm so glad you all moved somewhere where I can see more of you."

The party broke up when Alex mentioned that she and Stephanie had to get to bed as they had to go out to Rice and buy textbooks early the following morning. This wasn't a lie as they actually did have to run this errand, but Alex did have a report to make to Stephanie.

Later, the girls prepared for bed in Alex's room. Alex told her roommate what Raymond had said earlier in the evening.

"So he did see her," Stephanie said, eyes like saucers, sitting on her pallet in a very skimpy pajama outfit.

"Yes, I knew he had." Alex buttoned her top slowly, sitting on the bed. "And so did father Leo. Raymond was surprised at that, though. Apparently Leo Frank never condoned monkey business."

"And when he saw that thing, he walled the turret up." Stephanie paused a moment in thought. "I wish I could have been with you when you talked to him."

"Well, you had your hands full with the kids."

"Yes, those little boys are something else."

"Something else?" Alex giggled. "Two little perverts."

"Well, let me just say I feel sorry for their little sister."

"That bad, huh."

"Yes. They were all over me." Stephanie made a face. "I practically had to pry them off."

"They recognize the mother figure in you, Stephanie."

"Right. Bullshit. But tell me, what did Raymond say about Johanna?"

"He described her to a tee. She appeared before him and his brother James while they played in the attic. He was very surprised when I told him she was still around."

"How many times did they see her?"

"Apparently, just once. He said they told Leo but of course he didn't believe them. But, like I said, he's got to have seen her too because Leo Frank wasn't the type of man who would wall up a room just because a couple of kids told him they'd seen a ghost."

"He had to see it to believe it."

"Right. Apparently, no one ever saw her again until just

recently."

"Alex, do you think Mrs. Frank has seen Johanna? I mean, here recently."

"No. But I'm going to talk to her again tomorrow."

The next morning Alex and Stephanie missed the departure of Raymond and his family as the girls left early to accomplish their errand. They stayed away all morning, looking about for supplementary readings and other things that would help them in the coming semester. At just past noon, they returned to the apartment.

Since Alex knew the old lady was probably taking her nap, she did not bring up the possibility of an interview that afternoon. However, when they entered the apartment, an invitation to go swimming waited on their message machine.

Although Alex wasn't sure about going, Stephanie insisted and two o'clock found the girls gone again, this time for the rest of the day. However, when they returned, the day was not over, for the ringing phone greeted them as they walked through the door.

Out of area appeared on the caller ID but Alex picked it up anyway.

"Hello, Alex," a male voice said instantly.

"Who…Who is this?" The voice sounded a bit familiar but she couldn't immediately place it.

"This is Raymond Frank."

"Raymond?"

"Yes. Betsy and the kids are up in the room and I'm down in the bar. I tried to call you earlier while they were swimming but no one was there."

"So, you're in San Antonio."

"Yes. At the Hyatt."

"Where'd you get our number?"

"From Mom. I told her I needed to tell you something about your school, Rice, so she gave me your number. I hope you don't mind."

"No. Not at all, Raymond. But what's up?"

Raymond took a deep breath and began. "I got up early this morning before anyone else. I went downstairs to make coffee and couldn't get the light switch to work. When I went into the dining room to turn on the light, I ran into what seemed to me to be a bank of freezing cold.

"My first thought was that a window unit had been left on full blast all night. I looked around for one and found one in the window, but it wasn't even on. I was messing with the controls when I heard a voice behind me.

"It called my name and I turned immediately. There in front of me in that dark room was the girl we talked about last night, the girl Johanna. She seemed to be lit up like she was phosphorescent or something. She said *tell Alexandra her time is short.* Then, she moved slowly backwards from the dining room into the living room. She wasn't using her legs; she was floating on air. As she moved away from me, she turned into this awful looking corpse. Finally, in the living room she vanished.

"Alex, I was a cop for many years in Detroit and there's not a hell of a lot I've seen that scared me. But this thing almost frightened me out of my wits. The way it talked; it didn't move its mouth. When it vanished, the cold disappeared. I just stood and hoped the thing was gone for good."

"Raymond, that thing has threatened to kill me. I'm not sure how, but she wants my death. She has stalked me and she's appeared a number of times before me."

"Oh, my God, Alex. That thing's in the house with my mother."

"Relax, Raymond. She's not after your mother; she's after me."

"Why?"

"It's a long story. I'll tell you later when you come back through."

"Jesus, Alex, do you know what to do against that thing?"

"Pretty much so. I handled things like her when I was younger."

"You're kidding."

"No."

"Anyway, I didn't mention this to Betsy because I didn't want to spoil the trip. God, but this is hideous."

"Yes. All of this began last spring. I'm going to talk to your mother about it, probably tomorrow."

"About that ghost?"

"Maybe. Definitely about the other things we've seen."

"Other things?"

"Yes, Raymond. There are other things that have appeared."

There was a pause for Raymond to collect his thoughts. "Alex, what other things?"

"A number of people, in your mother's house and our apartment. I am convinced that all of them died in the Galveston storm of 1900. I know Johanna did. It stands to reason the rest of them would come from the same place. One of them, a little girl, has been trying to communicate with us but we haven't seen her lately. Your mother's even seen her. She doesn't know what she is, of course; she thinks she's a child that wandered off."

Suddenly there was talking on Raymond's end of the line.

"Alex, I've got to go now. Betsy and the kids are here and we're getting ready to go eat. In a few days we'll be back in Houston. We'll talk about this then."

A few minutes after hanging up the phone, Alex sat down in the living room and took off her shoes.

"Who was that on the phone?" Stephanie asked from the stairs.

"Raymond."

"Raymond?"

"Yeah, Raymond."

"Calling here? Where is he?"

"In San Antonio. At the Hyatt Hotel."

Stephanie walked slowly in and sat down, her face deeply puzzled.

"He saw Johanna this morning before he left," Alex continued. "He called me to tell me that. To warn me."

"To warn you?" Stephanie's eyes grew almost too big for her face.

"Yes. Johanna said to him *Tell Alexandra her time is short.*"

"Jesus Christ, Alex." Stephanie seemed on the verge of tears. "How did Raymond react to that?"

"Well, I guess I don't have to tell you it scared the crap out of him. He hadn't seen that thing since he was a kid. And there it was."

"My God, Alex. What now?"

Alex perked up and smiled. "We just continue what we're doing, one day at a time." She could tell Stephanie was annoyed by her change of mood. Alex knew that her roommate wasn't going to buy into the lightheartedness thing this time. Presently, she wasn't sure if she should either, because she could tell things were rapidly coming to a peak.

Chapter Twenty

Since church was the next day, Alex did not deem it fit to broach the subject of ghosts and hauntings on the way to St. John's. However, she did find out on the way that Mrs. Frank was having a few friends in that evening for supper; therefore, she would have to put off their discussion until Monday. In the meantime Stephanie was still upset about Raymond's call.

"From what I can tell Alex, there is no limit to what that thing can do." She sat back on the couch in her church clothes, her feet propped up on the coffee table.

"It would seem so, Steph. But she does have her limitations."

"Like what?"

"Stehle's Door, for one. If we find it, she's gone. I am convinced now she has only one entrance left into our world that she shares with all the rest of them. We destroyed the entrance trigger she'd been using since God-knows-when. Although you might not believe it, that door is closed. Slammed shut."

Stephanie's face fell into a pout. Suddenly, she reached down between her legs and scratched herself.

"Excuse me, but I itch."

"That's okay, Steph. But I wouldn't do that in front of Pauli if I were you."

"Your little brother? Hah! Not on your life." Stephanie laughed out loud.

"It would probably give him the biggest thrill he ever had." Alex joined in the laughter.

"Exactly so. And Raymond's two little creeps would get a big holler out of that also."

Stephanie laughed again out loud. "Can you imagine…"

She was cut off by a heavy thump from above by

something obviously hitting the floor.

"What the hell?" Alex jumped up and hurried to the staircase, Stephanie just behind her.

The two climbed the stairs quickly and turned to enter Stephanie's room from which the sound seemed to have come. At the door they stopped.

There was a muffled sound of voices that faded very quickly. The distinct smell was very prevalent all over the second floor.

"Boy, there's no question about something being here." Alex turned to her roommate. "Come on, let's check everywhere."

Very quickly, they looked in all the upstairs rooms. There was nothing and the smell was quickly fading. Alex hurried back to Stephanie's room and opened her blinds.

There was nothing on the carport or the backyard, and nothing seemed amiss in Mrs. Frank's house.

"Why do they always pick on us?" Stephanie asked, breathlessly. "Why don't they ever bother Mrs. Frank?"

"I'm not so sure they're coming at us, exclusively." Alex turned back toward the bedroom door. "Come on," she said, motioning with her hand.

They raced down the stairs and out the front door to the side of the apartment. There, Alex looked all around the backyard, the alley and the driveway.

"What…what are you looking for?" Stephanie, her face puzzled, tapped Alex on the shoulder.

"Stehle's Door. I think we just heard them go through it." Suddenly, she remembered a day of horror years before when she had been trapped in an old courthouse by the deadly door and a hideous thing had come through it. Shivering, she put her fist to her mouth and headed out of the alley. "That's got to be where it is," she mumbled to herself, looking over the back of the apartment. "It couldn't be anywhere else." She walked quickly toward Mrs. Frank's house, all the time looking over all windows and upstairs porches of the huge old house. *Could it be there, too?* she thought.

Stephanie followed, trying to keep up. "How would you know if you saw this thing?" she asked.

Alex promptly stopped and crossed her arms over her chest. “It has a very distinct appearance. You couldn’t miss it.”

“A distinct appearance.”

“Yes. Swirls. Like a great wind that has been channeled to blow in a circle in a very small, confined place. It can appear and vanish in an instant. It’s very frightening.”

“Frightening? Everything about this crap is frightening, Alex.”

“Well, Steph. I hope you never see it. But, on the other hand, what if it takes another form? It’s obviously the source of these things, including Johanna. It has to be huge, too, but I don’t see anything around here.”

“Alex what about the trigger thing? We destroyed one, doesn’t there need to be another?

“Usually there has to be. But in this case, I’m not so sure. The storm thing is the only thing I can think of, now. But it’s only a theory. That’s why we needed to communicate. That’s why I wanted to find something upstairs in your room just now.” She sighed and turned back to the old house. “There’s nothing here,” she said.

Slowly, they walked back to the apartment, Alex lost in thought. Could these things be leaving? Is that what they’d just heard? And if so, why? “You know something, Roomy,” she said suddenly at the front door. “I’ve got a distinct feeling that we’re going to find out a whole lot about what’s going on in a day or two.”

Stephanie swallowed hard, the fear still stamped on her face. “What are we going to find out?” she asked in a stage whisper.

“Why all of them are here, of course. All of them except Johanna. I pretty much know what that thing’s up to.”

“Of course. After what she’s done.”

“Yeah. And what she’s capable of doing.” She opened the door and went in. “Anyway, Mrs. Frank bright and early tomorrow morning.”

The rest of the day was uneventful. Alex and Stephanie debated going to a movie, but found one on TV instead. Little was said over supper except a few words about the upcoming semester at Rice, a brief conversation carried mostly by Alex for Stephanie seemed to be preoccupied. At nightfall, she found out what was bothering her roommate.

"I'm always nervous at night," Stephanie said. She stood at Alex's bedroom window and looked out on Mrs. Frank's house. A late evening rain earlier had cooled things off and the girls had turned their air conditioners to low cool.

"I know, Steph. You've been in here on the floor for a while, now."

"I mean, even in here I get nervous as hell."

"Somehow, I don't think anything is going to bother us tonight." Alex stood up from her bed and retrieved a hair brush from the top of her dresser. She decided earlier not to tell her roommate that tonight may be the calm before the storm. "I wish something would show up." She ran the brush through her hair. "We'd have a chance to talk to it. Where is the little girl when you need her?"

Stephanie sat on her pallet and hugged her knees. "I wish that horrid little thing would show up, too. So you could talk to it."

"I would." Alex, furiously brushing for one minute, stopped and leaned forward. "I'd ask her exactly what's going on, why she's here, what does she and the others want and how could we help to send them on."

"Send them on?"

"To Heaven or to hell. Whichever."

"God, Alex. I didn't know…"

"What'd you think? That everyone who dies is floating around down here stirring up mischief for us mortals?" Alex grinned down at her roommate, then she looked up at her door and frowned. "No. There are only a select few; a few who died violently or prematurely. Who were not ready for death and seem to be struggling against it. And Stehle's Door helps them. It helps them into this world."

"The dead in that storm, Alex. There were thousands."

"Of the thousands who died, there are a select few who have a mission to perform. An errand…"

"Even Johanna?'

"Johanna. She's a classical example of hatred beyond the grave. A bundle of hate-generated psychic energy who'd like nothing better than for me to join her on the other side. Even trying to make me think I caused her death."

"Then, her mission is to kill you."

"Apparently so, if she can." Alex rose and replaced the brush on her dresser. "We're just lucky there's just one to look out for."

Sabrina had settled on the bed already and had to be moved. Alex lay back and spread the sheet over her while Stephanie turned off the nightstand lamp.

"They're gone now but they're not too far away," Alex said in the darkness. "Even though it's still just a theory, I'm pretty sure now their presence has to do with some coming storm. When this materializes or shortly thereafter, they'll be gone."

"And what about Johanna?"

"Johanna will be gone, too." Alex rolled on her side facing her roommate's pallet. "We talked about that earlier, Roomy."

"Oh, yes, I know. I'm just so damned worried." Stephanie sniffed loudly in the darkness and then rolled on her side. "What if that book we burned wasn't the only trigger up there?"

Alex thought a minute about the copy of *Sonnets from the Portuguese* they had destroyed. Then she thought of other things: a purse, another book. Could these bring Johanna back, too? *We can burn that stuff also,* she thought.

Henrietta had curled up with her mistress on the pallet, but Stephanie was still wide awake. "If Johanna's time is short, like the others, she could be worse than ever," she said.

"Maybe so," Alex said quietly. "Her comings and goings are still a question mark, a big, dangerous question mark. And like the others, she's close by, too. You can count on it."

The two girls drifted off to sleep to be awakened by a thunderstorm the next morning at 5:15 AM. Stephanie rolled over and tried to go back to sleep but Alex got up and groped her way toward the bathroom. She knew she couldn't go back to sleep so she headed downstairs, the previous night's conversation vivid in her mind. She wondered if the rain in the last months had any bearing on her problem. *These thunderstorms are bad in themselves,* she thought as she plugged in the coffeemaker.

She drank her first cup and was preparing breakfast when her roommate appeared at the kitchen door.

"Good morning, Glory."

"I heard that crap coming on in the middle of the night," Stephanie said, just before a yawn. "I had to get up and go to the John and I heard thunder."

"Well, it lasted until almost dawn." Alex shoveled the omelet onto a plate. "This one turned out real good. Do you want it?"

"Yeah." Stephanie picked up the plate and a fork and headed for the dining room.

Alex followed. "Today's the day I talk to Mrs. Frank," she said. "I'm going to catch her this afternoon after she wakes up from her nap. I'm not going to use any pretext or anything: I'm just going to tell her about all the things we've seen, in her house and ours."

"She'll think you're crazy."

"I don't think she will. I've said all along she knows a lot more about things than she lets on. Yes, I've got a real feeling she's going to fill in some gaps."

"Gaps? What do you mean by gaps?"

"Well, for starters, hubby Leo and that room. What did he tell her about it? We've got Raymond's story about it; now I want hers."

"Yeah. Why he walled up the room."

"That's right, among other things." Alex took a sip of coffee and smiled. "I talked to Josh last night while you were in the tub."

Stephanie perked up. "Well, how is our footloose baseball player doing?"

"Fine, of course. He had to end our conversation with 'seen anymore ghosts?'" For the last three words, Alex lowered her voice to a masculine growl.

"God, how clueless! What did you say to that?"

"Oh, I told him, sure we have. All the time."

"He thinks all this is some kind of bullshit high school game. I wonder how he'd like to get a load of Johanna."

"He'd fill his pants up, like I said before. Anyway, Roomy, I thought I'd just mention that to show just where he stands on this. Pauli can be full of shit but he's dead serious when it comes to this stuff. He knows better."

"I know." Stephanie finished the last bit of omelet and set her fork down. "Anyway, as you were saying, you're going to catch Mrs. Frank after lunch?"

"Yes, I am. We'll know by tonight what she knows about all this."

"Don't you think it's odd, Alex, that she hasn't mentioned anything before now? I mean, we've dropped a whole bunch of hints."

"No, it's not odd. We're all supposed to be Christians, aren't we? And Christians aren't supposed to believe in ghosts. If she does know something, that's probably the reason she hasn't brought it up."

Later, Alex and Stephanie were washing Stephanie's car when they noticed Mrs. Frank unloading a package from her car. Alex saw her chance.

"Stephanie, go ahead and finish the inside. I'm going to talk to Mrs. Frank right now. Give me twenty minutes and then come over and join us."

"Right. Twenty minutes."

Alex had picked the most advantageous moment because the old lady had two other packages to carry in. Alex grabbed the two and then followed her inside. "I guess I came along at the right time," she said, propping the door open with her foot.

"Oh, yes. I would have had to make two more trips." Mrs. Frank indicated to Alex to set the two parcels on the kitchen table. "I had Betty Langeford order these for me because she has an account with Strongware and I don't." The old lady chuckled. "I should have picked them up last week but as you know, I've been out of socket for a couple of days."

"Yes. Have you heard anything from Raymond?" It had occurred to Alex that Raymond might have called his mother to warn her of Johanna.

"Oh, no. With so many things to do in San Antonio, they have probably little time to even sleep or eat."

Alex laughed. "That's certainly true, Mrs. Frank." It was now or never. "Mrs. Frank, when your son was here, he told me about an incident that occurred here when he was a child."

The old lady stopped unwrapping a package and looked up. "Oh," she said, her brows raised in curiosity.

"He and his brother James were playing in the attic, it seems, when they encountered the ghost of a young girl." Alex swallowed hard and gritted her teeth.

Mrs. Frank's expression did not change, nor did she say anything, so Alex continued. "They told their father about it but he, of course, didn't believe them."

"That's understandable," Mrs. Frank replied. "My Leo was a very practical man."

"Yes, I know. I bring this up, Mrs. Frank, because Stephanie and I have seen things around here, too."

"Things? People?"

"Yes, people. We've seen people, in your house and in our apartment. I've gone over to borrow a few things while you were gone and seen people in your house." Alex's fib wasn't far from the truth as she had borrowed some kitchen things from Mrs. Frank in her absence.

"You've also seen them, then." The old lady picked up a package and moved it aside. Then, she sat.

"Them?" Alex's face darkened.

"The people of the storm, Dear. They're here in this house."

Alex grew faint and she had to sit down. "You've seen them, too, then," she whispered huskily.

"Yes, I've seen them. They are the things that often keep me awake."

"How…How long have you been seeing them?" She began to breathe heavily, still not believing what Mrs. Frank was saying.

"Not too long. About a month, I guess."

"Mrs. Frank, why didn't you tell us about them?"

"Oh, I didn't want to scare you, Dear."

Alex swallowed hard to stifle a guffaw. "Mrs. Frank, we've been seeing these things since last spring. The first one was the little girl we asked you about."

"I remember that," the old lady said, matter-of-factly. "The little girl was named Mary Henderson."

"Who…How did…"

"Oh, Honey, when I had seen a number of things a couple of times, I thought I recognized one or two of them from old pictures. I checked those old albums and, sure enough, one of them was Max Henderson. He died in the Galveston storm along with Johanna Diehls and his little daughter, Mary. One reason I went to Cousin Ida's in Alvin was to find a picture of the Henderson family and, sure enough, when I did, there was little Mary. I recognized her easily. "I've seen that poor little thing face to face."

Alex was dumbfounded. "Mrs. Frank…Mrs. Frank, another of those things is Johanna Diehls."

"Johanna?"

"Yes, Ma'am. Johanna Diehls."

"Oh, I haven't seen Johanna."

"I have, Mrs. Frank. Several times. She's been stalking me and she's tried to harm me on three different occasions. She wants to kill me."

"What?"

"Yes. She wants my death."

"Your death? Why?" The old lady's mouth dropped open in astonishment.

Alex leaned forward and propped her head on her hands, elbows on the table. Mrs. Frank did the same. She then told the old lady of her experiences with Stehle's Door and other things connected with it, even mentioning that her parents knew all about it. When she was finished, she wondered what happened to her roommate. More than twenty minutes had elapsed.

"That is amazing, Honey." The old lady tried to smile. "Only a short time ago, I wouldn't have believed a word of it. But so much has happened in the last weeks. My Leo never told me about the ghost in the attic. He was sure I wouldn't believe him and the last thing he ever wanted was to play the fool. I know now that you tell me that they probably did see a vision up there."

"Yes, Mrs. Frank. They saw Johanna Diehls. Raymond verified it."

"Oh, my stars. That Johanna. Honey, these things don't impress me as wanting to do any harm. In fact, I think they're trying to help."

"That's what we think, too. A friend of mine who used to work with parapsychology said they are probably here as a warning. He mentioned they're possibly here to warn us of another storm and I'm inclined to believe him."

"Another storm? You mean another hurricane, like Katrina."

"Yes, like that one. And the one that hit Galveston. I think my book said that one was probably a type four. And I think Katrina was a four when it hit. Maybe Ike was, too."

"The one in Galveston destroyed the whole city, I understand."

"Almost. I have a whole bunch of pictures of the aftermath. It was pure carnage."

"Honey, this Stehle's Door you talk about. You said it might be around here?"

"I'm sure it is, Mrs. Frank. In fact, we're looking for it now." In the back of her mind, Alex knew there was something wrong. Stephanie had never failed to show up when she was supposed to. Now it had been forty minutes and she was not there. "Mrs. Frank, I wonder if you would excuse me. Stephanie was supposed to come over earlier and now it seems she has been detained. I better go over and see what she's up to."

"Oh, yes, go ahead. I want to talk to you some more about this, though. It's fascinating."

"Certainly. Maybe we can go out to eat later. Excuse me, please." With that, Alex rose and hurriedly left the house. At this point, she knew something was dreadfully wrong.

The front door of the apartment was locked and Alex remembered she'd left it unlocked. She didn't have her key so she rang the doorbell. When there was no answer, she rang it again, knocked, and called Stephanie's name. Still no answer.

Terror mounting in her, she raced to Mrs. Frank's kitchen to get the spare apartment key. The old lady met her at the door.

"Mrs. Frank," she said, in a halting voice. "Something is terribly wrong. I need the spare key."

"Oh my. Do you want me to call the police?"

"No. Maybe later. Just wait a moment now while I find Stephanie."

Alex grabbed the key, ran to her front door and quickly

unlocked it. Inside, she was met by a blast of ice cold air, colder than any air conditioner could make any room. In a moment she knew what was happening. She turned toward the living room and walked to the entrance way where she stood motionless.

Across the room in the dining area sat her roommate in a dining table chair. Above her, its claws on her shoulders and neck, stood the hideous apparition that had dogged Alex for months now.

The face was what it had been at death; the claws were those of a long dead corpse. The nails dug into Stephanie's shoulders but the thing stood motionless. Suddenly, it opened its mouth, as if to speak, and filthy brown liquid streamed from it.

"Al…Alex," Stephanie cried. Alex could tell her roommate dared not move.

"Let her go," Alex said, in a level tone with as much authority as she could muster in her horror.

The presence opened its mouth further. The stream of liquid stopped.

"Alexandra," it said. "It's here." The lips did not move. Only the words, deathly even, emanated from the aperture in the face.

"Let her go, you goddamned monster!" Alex yelled. She started forward but the specter began to grow. As it did, its nails became small daggers that dug into Stephanie's flesh.

Alex backed off. "Please," she said. "Let…Let her go." A tear rolled down her cheek.

The presence continued to grow. Now its head, almost the size of a medicine ball, had reached the ceiling. Still, it kept its hands on Stephanie.

Alex was terrified of what it would do if she made a sudden move. The monster kept growing.

Suddenly, it leaned forward and opened its mouth again, its regurgitation falling on Stephanie.

"Alexandra!" it shrieked. "It's time!" It opened its mouth fully wide and a terrific, foul smelling wind caught Alex like a giant hand, knocking her backward through the living room entrance into the hallway. She fell backwards on her rear end at the base of the stairs.

She recovered and started to rise but was quickly pinned to

the floor by the monster, now back to its regular size. Its nails dug into Alex sides, its face moved closer to hers.

The smell gagged her and the face, now just inches from her own, had become that of a drowned corpse. The mouth open, foul liquid fell on Alex's face.

She jerked her body to the side to try to dislodge herself from the hideous thing, but it was pressing against her to pin her to the floor. Feeling more and more helpless, she then tried to grasp the claws and pry them away from her body, but they seemed like steel, welded to her.

Panic rose within her. Now she could not move and the dead face was almost on hers. *Oh, dear God,* she thought. *I'm going to be possessed.*

Suddenly there was an explosion nearby. The body on top of her shook, then began to withdraw. When it did, Alex could see a ragged hole just under its right breast.

About two feet from her, it quickly vanished with a scream, leaving only the stench and Alex, bedraggled, on the floor.

"Jesus Christ, Alex. Are you okay?" a weak voice nearby asked.

Alex sat up and looked about. Five feet away stood Stephanie, Josh's old Colt military .38 in her hands. She'd forgotten he'd brought it over earlier.

"God, Alex, I had to do something. I got so close to that thing that I couldn't miss her or hit you."

Alex's eyes widened. "You hit her all right. You almost hit me."

"I shot her in the middle of her back at an angle."

"The bullet came out of her lower chest." Alex lowered her head and said a brief prayer. Then she looked up and tried to smile. "I'm sure glad you're a good shot. Anyone else would have shot me."

"It drove her off."

"Yes." Alex breathed deeply and slowly got to her feet. "If she'd been mortal, she'd be dead, but, unfortunately, you cannot kill something that's already dead."

On her feet, Alex noticed the wounds to Stephanie's shoulders and neck. "Let's go upstairs and put something on those."

The two girls mounted the stairs, Stephanie with the old pistol still in her hand. It had been placed in an end table drawer after Josh brought it over and forgotten until just now.

"I'm going to put this in your room," Stephanie said, "where I can get to it if I need it at night."

"Okay. Put it in the night stand." Alex turned into the bathroom while Stephanie stowed the gun. Then, Alex, still the worse for wear, sat her roommate down in the bathroom.

She treated Stephanie's wounds and one she had in her side. None of them were really bad, fortunately. In her mind Alex could see them both sitting in a local clinic having to explain where their strange stab wounds came from.

Afterwards, the girls heard Mrs. Frank at their front door. Quickly, Alex descended and opened the door.

"Alex, Honey," the old lady said in a worried voice. "What happened? I thought I heard a shot."

Alex couldn't think of anything but the truth. "We're alright, now, Mrs. Frank. It was a shot. Stephanie shot Johanna."

"What?"

"Yes. That thing was on top of me and Stephanie shot her. She drove her off." She looked down into the old lady's perplexed face. "I told you she was a threat to me. Now it seems, she's gone. At least for now."

Where did you get a gun? I didn't know you had a gun." The old lady's eyes widened in fear.

"Josh brought it over one night when he was worried about me. Apparently he doesn't realize you can't kill something that's already dead." Alex thought back to when Josh had brought his grandfather's old military .38 over a few nights after Paul had brought the baseball bat.

"My God, Honey. Is Stephanie all right?"

"She's better off now than I am, Mrs. Frank."

Alex invited her in for some iced tea and the three of them sat down in the living room where Stephanie began her story.

"That thing was waiting for me when I came in from the garage," she said. "She grabbed me from behind and threw me down in a chair. In a few minutes you were there," she said to Alex. "That thing is so god-awful strong. I could see her crushing you there on the floor before I fired at her."

"Crushing me, Steph? I don't think she wants me crushed. I think she wants me drowned." Alex leaned back in the chair and looked down at her hands in her lap. "This time, though, I think she was trying to possess me."

"Possess you?"

Mrs. Frank looked back and forth from Alex to Stephanie, her eyes widening.

"Yes. Possess me. Did she say anything to you before I came in?"

"No. Nothing. She was so overpowering."

"I'm wondering why she didn't possess you like she did the other time."

"God, Alex, I didn't think of that. I don't know."

"Unless she wanted to deal with me directly." Alex glanced over at the old lady, then over at the stairs.

"I'm glad I got to her before she could do that."

"I'm glad you did, too." Alex could see that Stephanie was proud of her rescue of her roommate. Up until now, she had been powerless around these things. "Apparently, Johanna didn't think you'd do anything. I need a refill. Anybody want another glass.?"

"Yes, thank you."

Silent until now, Mrs. Frank spoke up. "Oh, Lord, girls, I didn't think these things meant any harm. None of them ever tried to hurt me. They just seemed to want to talk to me."

"What?"

Alex returned with two glasses in her hands. "I forgot to tell you, Steph. Mrs. Frank has seen these things in her house."

Stephanie turned to the old lady. "You have?"

"Yes, she has. She's even put a name to some of them."

"How did you do that, Mrs. Frank?"

"From some old pictures I have. I matched some of them up." She looked up at Alex. "I found more old Henderson pictures in Alvin and there they were. The little girl we've seen is named Mary Henderson and her father is around here, too. I've seen him."

"I think he's the one I saw upstairs that time," Alex interjected.

"Mary Henderson," Stephanie whispered to herself.

"Mary, the father Max, and Johanna Diehls died in the storm in Galveston," Mrs. Frank said. "The mother, Katherine, and the oldest daughter, Phoebe, survived. They were fortunate to recover the bodies of Mary and Max. They buried them in the city cemetery off Broadway Street."

"But Johanna was never found."

"No. Johanna Diehls was never found."

"Well, Johanna Diehls was here today, Mrs. Frank." Alex sat down across from her roommate. "And from what Stephanie and I can tell, she came back almost immediately after her death. We both know she's been in this world a long time."

"It seems like she's been waiting for you." Stephanie lifted her legs and crossed them underneath her.

"Waiting for me. And probably waiting for some other things, too."

"Like a storm."

"Like a storm. Katrina wasn't aimed at Galveston so it wasn't that storm. Ike hit West Galveston so it wasn't that one. And earlier storms that did hit Galveston, I wasn't here." Alex shifted her position in the chair, took a sip of tea and continued. "The others want to warn us, Mrs. Frank. And that's probably what they're trying to do with you. But Johanna wants to kill me. In a certain way. At a certain time. She could easily have taken care of me today." In her mind, Alex could see the words: *Die Alexandra, Like I did, In the water* scrawled on her bathroom mirror.

The old lady lifted herself to her feet. "I better get back over there. I'm expecting a call from Raymond. Now he calls me every day from San Antonio and tells me what they did the day before."

"That's good, Mrs. Frank. With a son like that, you can't go wrong."

They let Mrs. Frank out of the apartment and then sat down to a light lunch. Following a brief discussion about what to do, they left the apartment for the afternoon. That evening they went out without Mrs. Frank.

Neither of them had spoken of the day's events at all, but nightfall brought gloom and a heavy wariness on both of them.

As they prepared for bed, Stephanie winced as the pajama rubbed against the wounds in her shoulders, bringing the events of that morning back in vivid detail to Alex. She didn't believe that Johanna would be back anytime soon but she had trouble convincing her roommate of that.

"What if that thing comes around when we are asleep?" Stephanie complained.

"Has she ever done that, that we know of?" Alex lay in bed and stared at the ceiling. She chewed on a piece of gum from earlier that evening. "No, our friend likes her victims to be fully aware of her. It's more fun for her that way." Alex turned to her roommate and grinned.

"Roomy, those shitty, little happy jokes don't fit my mood right now."

"Stephi, how many times do I have…"

"I know. I know. Be upbeat. Be happy. Put on a happy face. Shit. That thing cut me up this morning and would have done a lot worse if you hadn't come along."

"I know. She was on top of me, too."

"And I seem to remember a scratch or two to go along with mine."

"Yeah. And she'd probably done a lot worse to me, too, if Calamity Jane hadn't put a bullet through her." Alex giggled. "You know, if Leo comes back, he's going to be pissed that you shot a hole in his beautiful parquet floor."

"God, Roomy, you're impossible." Stephanie plopped back on her pallet and gathered Henrietta in her arms.

Alex read until Stephanie fell asleep and then she turned out the light.

In the dark, the same questions came back. When would Johanna strike next? What would she do? What about the storm the others were seemingly warning them of? When would it come? Where would it come from? And were the others still here, or was it just Johanna now? And still there were the old questions about Stehle's Door. Where, when, how, and so on. So much had not been answered.

But then so much had been revealed. They had narrowed things down considerably and they now had a good ally in Mrs. Frank who knew about everything. Alex felt a pang of concern thinking about the old lady across the driveway alone in her huge, old house. *Johanna wouldn't bother her,* she thought. *She wants me.*

She turned in her bed to sleep. "There is so much still to be found out," she whispered to herself, and then fell asleep.

At the moment, she had no way of knowing that the answers she sought were just days away.

Chapter Twenty-One

Two days later, the girls began getting things squared away to return to school for the fall term. Since the last few days had been quiet, Alex and Stephanie felt a lot better. Stephanie even thought about going back to her bedroom. Alex, however, was still wary. After all, she knew better.

In the meantime, she had talked to Mrs. Frank again about her ghostly visitors and learned that she had seen quite a number of people in her house. Alex remembered the footsteps she had heard in the attic that night she, Paul, Stephanie and Josh had been in the house. The fact that Mrs. Frank had not seen Johanna disturbed her, however. It made her feel like she was Johanna's "special project."

Wednesday morning, Alex was cleaning the dashboard of her car when Mrs. Frank came out the back door.

"Honey, I just got off the phone with Raymond," the old lady said. "They're coming in this evening, one day earlier than planned. Would you and Stephanie like to join us for dinner?"

Alex looked up and thought a minute. Raymond was coming back prematurely. "We'd love to, Mrs. Frank. Can we bring anything?"

"Yes, if you don't mind. Bring some of that good potato salad you make."

"Sure. I have the stuff. I'll make some." Alex put her cleaning rag down and got out of the car. "Mrs. Frank, did Raymond say why he was coming back from vacation one day early?"

"No, he didn't. It seems kind of odd, though. With those kids, they could have used another day in San Antonio, what with all there is to do there."

"Oh, yeah. That's why I was thinking it was kind of strange, too."

In her mind, Alex could see herself and Raymond comparing notes about Johanna that evening. His odd, shortened vacation could be the result of anything but she was still curious about it.

The arrival of Raymond and family was announced at four o'clock that afternoon by screaming kids in the backyard that woke Alex from a long nap. She was getting up when Stephanie appeared at the bedroom door.

"Hear that, Roomy?" she asked, a smirk on her face. "This time you get those two little twerps while I visit with Raymond and Betsy."

Alex looked up and grinned. "This time, I'm going to do the smart thing and let Betsy take care of her own little hooligans. Besides, I need to talk to Raymond about his encounter with our little friend."

"Oh, yes. I forgot about that."

"Yes. He makes three of us that have seen that damned thing." She reached down and grabbed a shoe to put on, then looked over at Stephanie and grinned again. "I think those two little knuckleheads have you pegged for their girlfriend."

"Oh, wonderful." Stephanie feigned indignation. "Just what I needed. I think I'd rather encounter Johanna again than baby-sit those two little perverts."

"Watch what you say. You might get your wish. There's a lot worse things around here than a second grader grabbing your butt."

"You want to bet?"

Toward evening, the girls had started across the driveway when they encountered Raymond at the top of the back steps.

"Well, hello," he said, cheerily. "I need to corral three little hoodlums and I'll be in in a minute."

They both greeted Raymond and entered Mrs. Frank's kitchen where they found Betsy unpacking some dishes she had bought for her mother-in-law in San Antonio.

"Hi," she said. "Is that that delicious potato salad I've heard so much about? Set that right over there." She pointed at a side table. "I bought these for Mother in San Antonio. They have such great prices in those antique stores there."

"Those are very pretty, Betsy." Alex smiled and set down

her bowl. “Did you have a good time?”

Before she could answer, three children trooped into the kitchen, followed by Raymond. The two boys greeted Stephanie while Alex turned away to stifle a laugh.

“I told that crew to head for the living room and stay there,” Raymond said. “And not to touch a single thing.” He looked up and grinned at each girl in turn. “We brought you each a souvenir from San Antonio. I hope you like them.”

“Thank you, Raymond,” Stephanie said, “That was very sweet of you.”

“They came from Sea World.” From a paper bag on the counter, Raymond produced a stuffed killer whale for Alex and a rubber shark for Stephanie. ‘We didn’t have time to go to Fiesta Texas and do all the other stuff we wanted to do,” he continued. He glanced at his wife. “Yesterday, Betsy saw a weather report on TV that announced a new tropical depression in the South Atlantic and anything resembling a hurricane anywhere near our New Orleans home drives her to distraction, even though it’s thousands of miles away. It’s only natural, I guess, after what Katrina did to New Orleans.”

Alex shuddered. *A tropical depression,* she thought. The announcement had a truly sinister ring to it. There had been some hurricanes in the Atlantic in July, but this new one and memories of Katrina and Ike made her shiver. She smiled at Raymond and then turned to Mrs. Frank. “Mrs. Frank, do you have some eggs I can borrow for omelets tomorrow morning? I just remembered I don’t have any.”

“Oh, yes, Honey. They’re in the refrigerator here in the kitchen.”

“Thanks. Steph and I will run these home and we’ll be back at six-thirty for supper.” She helped herself to the eggs and then left, followed by her roommate.

“Outside, Stephanie jabbed Alex in the back with her finger. “I think you’re wrong about those two little turds, Roomy. I’m surprised one of them didn’t pinch me in the ass as he went through the kitchen.”

“Stephanie, I’m going to put these in the kitchen,” Alex said in a serious tone. “While I’m doing that, I want you to turn on the weather channel.”

"The weather channel?"

"Yes. The weather channel. I want to take a look at that tropical depression Raymond mentioned."

"Okay. But didn't he say that thing was in the South Atlantic. That's a long..."

"Yes. But that's where most of them come from."

"Most of what?"

"Hurricanes."

A cloud came over Stephanie. "Hurricanes," she whispered. Apparently she had not connected "tropical depression" with "hurricane." Without another word, she went straight to the TV.

They had to wait through the local forecast and then two other features to get to the tropical depression in the South Atlantic just below the Equator. As this was its third day of existence, it had begun to move northwestward and its wind velocity had increased beyond thirty-nine mph. Therefore, it had been christened a tropical storm and given the name "Billy."

"Weren't there similar storms earlier this summer?" Stephanie asked, standing behind the sofa on which Alex now sat.

"Yes, one just a few weeks ago. It just went up the East Coast and petered out somewhere around Virginia." Alex leaned forward toward the TV. "It was just a small one. I think it was only a category one."

"What do you think this one is?"

"Just a tropical storm, now, Steph." Alex stared at the satellite picture of the storm system. It seemed very large. Of course, she didn't know many of the details about it. The announcer said its winds had just reached sixty-five mph, and it was moving west, northwest.

She wondered if this storm would blow itself out near the East Coast, like the earlier one. Something told her it wouldn't. And its size bothered her. She tried to think about what she had read about the Galveston storm, but she couldn't remember anything about its origins. Apparently, no one really knew much about the storm then because meteorology was still a lot of guesswork in 1900. After all, hurricanes then were usually spotted and reported by ships at sea. Now, satellites picked up their images at their very inception. For instance, everyone knew what Katrina and Ike looked like before they even stirred up the Gulf.

What Alex felt about Billy was more than a gut feeling. This could well be the very storm their ghostly visitors had come to warn them against. She felt a hollowness in the bottom of her stomach and her heart beat faster and faster.

"Alex, they're saying this one will probably head up the east coast but because of its size will probably hit northern Florida or Georgia." Stephanie scooted around the end of the couch and sat down.

"No one can really tell where it's going to go, Steph."

"They're saying it's not really that big, yet." Stephanie seemed excited. "Maybe it'll never be a full blown hurricane."

Alex said nothing. Instead she sat and stared at the mass in the South Atlantic.

The commentary ended with the meteorologist's promise that they would keep a close eye on Billy and keep the audience informed as to its movements.

Alex jumped up and headed upstairs. In just a few minutes she was on line researching hurricanes. On a map she found almost immediately, she discovered, to her horror, that dangerous storms had originated in the same vicinity Billy was in now. Some had skirted Cuba or the southern tip of Florida and struck the Gulf coast. One, Andrew, had originated in the general area of Billy, had hit the Bahamas, the southern tip of Florida, and then gone on across the Gulf to strike the coast of Louisiana. Katrina had hit South Florida as a category three, and then come across the Gulf and plowed into Louisiana, Mississippi, and Alabama. A note near the map called Katrina the most destructive hurricane, property wise, in US history.

Alex's blood ran cold. A note on the site stated that the Galveston hurricane had originated somewhere in the South Atlantic or Caribbean as well. In her mind she saw the dead children on the beach and the weird, empty streets of her dreams.

Stephanie appeared behind her. "God, Roomy, look at that damned thing." She said in a stage whisper.

"Yes," Alex croaked. "That's Andrew, one of the worst

hurricanes ever to hit the United States. It caused millions of dollars worth of damage but little loss of life."

"Little loss of life?"

"Yeah, probably because everybody ran like hell. We weren't so lucky with Katrina." Alex clicked away at her mouse, skimming through some technical data about hurricanes. "I used to think that hurricanes that hit the Gulf coast originated in the Gulf. That they just caused a lot of rain and a big blow. Then, Katrina came along. I learned different. After reading up on the Galveston hurricane along with our experiences with its victims, I know enough to realize that we are in jeopardy."

"That we're in jeopardy? But it's so far away from us."

"Stephi, Billy's not a hurricane; it's the hurricane. I'm pretty sure it's the one they wanted to warn us against. And now it's the one that's going to come at us."

"You're joking. We're seventy miles inland."

"Stephanie, some of these things are so huge they wreak destruction for hundreds of miles inland. Floods, wind damage, power outages; they're regular monsters and they're unstoppable."

"God, Roomy." Stephanie leaned over and stared over Alex's shoulder at the computer screen on which there were some pictures of the destruction wrought by hurricane Katrina.

"Look, Stephi. This damned thing tore up property in Jackson, Mississippi." She tapped the screen and then spun around in her chair and stared up at her roommate. "You take your Kansas tornado and multiply him by a thousand and you have your bad hurricane. You have Katrina. You have Ike. And you have Billy."

"Alex, Billy's still in the middle of the Atlantic. They don't even know…"

"Stephanie, I know he's the one, damn it. I know what he's going to do." She turned back around to the computer and clicked back to the page on Katrina. "Billy's going to be just like her." She said, tapping the screen on which appeared hurricane destruction in New Orleans. "Maybe even a lot meaner."

That evening over supper, neither Alex nor Stephanie mentioned the impending storm. There would be too much to explain. In fact, Alex didn't speak to Raymond about Johanna as she felt there were too many others around who might be upset by that revelation. Raymond had said he was keeping it from his family. However, at bedtime, Alex did tell Stephanie that she would talk to her brother about developments the next day. Everything was falling into place and all that remained now was what to do about it.

The next morning Alex told Paul to meet her and Stephanie for lunch at La Paloma Blanca Mexican restaurant off Loop 610 close to downtown. She told him about the hurricane development and mentioned what they had previously said about the possibility of a storm and its relevance to what had been going on at the apartment. When she got off the phone, she told Stephanie about what she was going to do.

"We're at a point now where we need Pauli's input again," she said, plopping herself down on the couch. "There's still the problem of Stehle's Door and I have a few ideas I want to run by him. And on top of that, with this storm, there's a distinct possibility of an end to all this."

"That would be absolutely great." Stephanie, coffee cup in hand, sat down across from her. "I had another bad dream about that storm last night."

"Oh?" Alex sat up, raised her eyebrows and thought momentarily. She had forgotten about dreams as they had not affected her for some time now. The main problem had been out in the open, away from the safety of sleep.

"We were trapped here in the apartment in twenty feet of water," Stephanie said. "We couldn't get out and we couldn't go upstairs. Both of us were drowning."

"It sounds like some of the stuff I dreamed last spring," Alex remarked. "Not much reality working there, though. Like you said yesterday, we're a full seventy or eighty miles away from the coast. The worst that could happen to us is wind damage, or a hurricane spawned tornado.

"A tornado? Shit."

"Yes. These things spawn tornadoes when they come inland. They cause damage just like other tornadoes do. Hurricanes blunted by Galveston's sea wall have spawned tornadoes in the city itself."

"So what we have is one great big destructive monstrosity."

"Something like that. I wouldn't worry too much about the tornado bit, though. They're kind of rare." Alex looked up and smiled. "And don't worry about drowning unless you're thinking about driving off the road into a bayou during a rainstorm."

"God, I'll be glad when this stuff is over."

"Me too. It won't be long now."

At La Paloma around noon, Alex and Stephanie settled into a table where they could see the door. Just after they received their menus and gave drink orders, Paul arrived.

"I took the afternoon off," he said, pulling out the chair across from Alex. "Told them I had some things to do about college. Hello, Pretty Bod," he grinned at Stephanie.

"Pauli, a lot of the stuff I wanted to talk about I mentioned to you earlier this morning."

"Yeah. That storm. God, Sis, just before I left work there was a guy on TV talking about how it was going to run up the East Coast like the one a few weeks ago. Katrina and Ike, I guess, were enough for him."

"He's full of shit," Alex announced. "This is the one we've been waiting for, Pauli. I know it. I can feel it."

"Sis, isn't this a bit early to make such a judgment? I mean, even if it does go past Florida, or even hits it, it'll probably go north and land at the Florida panhandle."

"Or here. Pauli, that storm is coming here. It will follow a path similar to that of the Galveston storm."

"The Galveston storm?"

"Yes, Katrina was the most destructive hurricane in US history, but the Galveston storm laid the groundwork for this one."

In silence, Stephanie munched on tortilla chips and castigated Paul with her eyes.

"Katrina wasn't too long ago," Alex continued. "And Ike tore up west Galveston. So people ought to remember them. Especially those in Billy's path."

"Let's face it, Sis. Nobody knows where that storm is going to hit. Not now. Even your little bit of ESP couldn't make that prediction. If it could, don't you think more people would know where these big storms were going?"

"Little Brother, you know perfectly well about my hunches." Alex was getting impatient. "This one is as accurate as it can be. Billy is coming here. Whether or not it hits Florida or hits Cuba, it will enter the Gulf and come straight at Galveston. Stephanie and I have had more than enough warning from beyond the grave about this storm."

The conversation was interrupted by a server who took orders. Paul was last to order, after which he leaned over to Stephanie.

"Stephi, what do you think of all this?"

"It scares me to death, Paul, because I know she's right." Stephanie took a sip of tea and then reached for another tortilla chip. "I've been through a tornado," she said. "But from what I've seen of Katrina and Ike, a hurricane is ten times worse."

"The positive side of all this, Pauli, is that after Billy does his worst, the manifestations around our apartment will be gone, including Johanna." Alex glanced over at her roommate. "What bothers me is what Johanna and possibly others have cooked up for us in the meantime."

"Just spook you, I guess."

"Spook me?" Alex voice rose. "Johanna wants to kill me, you knucklehead. She has said as much. She has done as much."

"She would have crushed her the other day if I hadn't run her off with a gunshot." Stephanie became animated and scooted back in her chair.

"All right. Okay." Paul put his hands up as if holding back an onslaught. "If Billy comes here, it'll be here within the next eight to twelve days. I've heard hurricanes move at different speeds. How can I help you in the meantime?"

"First, I need you to wrack your brain. You've seen Stehle's Door more often than I have. You've even dealt with it." Alex, calm again, put a hand to her mouth and again glanced at her roommate. "Most of what's happened at the apartment you know about. And you were there when we saw those things in Mrs. Frank's house. I'm going to tell you in detail what happened a few days ago. Stephanie has already mentioned it as I have previously."

"Sis, one thing along those lines I did think of. That day when Josh and I were over there and you went upstairs, you said Johanna appeared to you in a mirror."

"Yes, Pauli, I did." Alex perked up and so did Stephanie.

"Have you seen Johanna or any of those other things associated with mirrors other than that one time?"

Alex thought a minute. The man she had seen outside her bedroom had stood in front of a mirror. Also, there were mirrors in every room of the apartment except for the kitchen.

"I see what you're getting at, Pauli," she said. "Stehle's Door could be a mirror."

"Or it could be all of them. Can you think of a better passageway from another world into this one?"

Stephanie quit munching, a dark shadow covering her face.

"That's right. That time I saw Johanna, she was in the mirror and coming out of it." Alex paused to think. "The Rand Building. In the lady's room, mirrors covered one wall. Johanna would surely have been in there had not two women been in there with me. She would not even have had to come through the door."

"And she can take her pick of what mirror to come through."

"Mrs. Frank's house is full of mirrors," Stephanie croaked.

"That's right. With a great big, tall mirror in Johanna's old room."

"Pauli, now that we've come up with this possibility, what do we do about it?"

"That, Sis, is a good question. We can't smash all the mirrors. And even if we did, we both know that Stehle's Door moves around. It would just go somewhere else."

"What if they're using just one mirror in particular?' Stephanie asked. "What if Johanna is just using one mirror? The bathroom mirror." Her terror had given away to urgency.

"If that's true, that is her entranceway. I've caught her in it. But she's also written on the mirror in the downstairs bathroom."

Paul put his elbows on the table and balanced his head on his hands. "We must assume then that all mirrors are doorways."

"Again I ask, what do we do about it?"

Paul sat a moment and thought. "Why don't we turn them to the wall?" he finally said. "Those doorways would then be closed, wouldn't they?"

"Supposedly."

"Alex, I can't get dressed without a mirror."

"I can't either, Stephi." Alex sighed. "Pauli, this doesn't seem to me to be the right idea, but at this point I'll try anything."

"Right. And when you get dressed, you can turn one around temporarily. It would stay facing the wall when you weren't around."

"This whole thing is just crazy as hell." Stephanie put her napkin down. "I'm going to the rest room." After she rose, she turned to Paul. "After all I've seen these things do, it doesn't seem to me to be much of a problem for them to get around a mirror turned to the wall."

"She has a point, Pauli." Alex rose to join her roommate.

"Yes, but like you said, shouldn't we try everything?"

Later, Paul followed the girls back to the apartment, determined to turn all mirrors to the wall, until Billy blew through or petered out. It would only be for a few days and to buy a few days of peace, Alex and Stephanie would do anything.

The mirrors were easy except for those in the bathrooms. Paul unscrewed the fasteners in the one in the downstairs bathroom and turned it to the wall, but the mirror in the upstairs bathroom was fastened securely.

Alex recommended covering that mirror with a blanket and then knew immediately that it would not do any good. Finally, though, Paul unfastened the heavy mirror and turned it flush to the wall.

"What are we going to dress by in the morning?" Stephanie asked when they were finished.

"You turn around the one in your room and I'll use the one in the hall." Alex could see herself turning the hall mirror around in order to fix her hair and put on make-up. But couldn't something come through that mirror just at that moment? Deep down, she felt the futility of what they had just done.

They had just settled in the living room when the doorbell rang. Stephanie ran to the front door to let in Howie, a twelve-pack of beer under his arm.

"Just got in from Beaumont yesterday," he announced, smiling. "And I've got a couple of questions about late registration." He thrust the beer at Alex. "Put these in the fridge and open one for everybody."

"God, Howie, you're the last person I expected to see," Stephanie said, laughing. "I thought you were off working."

"Yeah, I was. But we have to go back to school pretty quick." He took a beer from Alex. "I was up near Kilgore, kinda far away. So I shut everything down and came home."

Alex gave a beer to her roommate and then chided Paul about driving home.

"Tom Satterwhite, my boss up there, got me a visit to an off-shore rig for future work purposes," Howie continued. "That's all going to be shut down, though, because of Billy."

"Billy?" Alex's ears perked up.

"Yeah, Billy. The off-shore drillers are scared to death of him. Katrina tore up rigs and drove them toward land. So did Ike. They've already started shutting down off Mississippi and Alabama."

"Howie, Billy's still in the middle of the Atlantic." Alex's mouth hung open in amazement.

"Isn't it supposed to go up the Atlantic coast like the last one," Paul chimed in.

"No, Billy's going to be a biggie. Like Katrina, he's coming into the Gulf." Howie took a sip of beer and then parked himself by Stephanie on the couch. "If a hurricane's near, the drillers shut down and clear out, the sooner the better. They take as much valuable equipment with them as they can carry because who knows, when they come back, there might not be a rig left."

"Howie, do you think Billy's going to be that big?' Alex walked over and sat down on the arm of the couch by Howie. Alex knew what Billy would be but she wanted affirmation.

"Yeah. Take a look at the weather report. He's already got his basic shape and he's heading for the Bahamas."

"How…How big is he?" Stephanie's mouth dropped open.

"A three at least. I haven't heard that yet but what I can see, he's definitely a growing boy."

"Shit, here we go again," Stephanie muttered.

Alex froze in horror. Almost at the Bahamas. In her mind she could see these islands lined up on the way to Florida. She tried to think of whether Katrina had hit the Bahamas but she couldn't remember.

"Howie, I think Billy's going to come straight at us," she said, quietly. "He's going to hit Florida, like Katrina, or Cuba, and then go straight into the Gulf."

"Well, I'm thinking you're right about that, Big Gal." Howie took a swig of beer and then chuckled. "You know, hurricanes can be funny. They never do exactly what you think they're going to do. I remember my folks were afraid Andrew was going to come ashore right near Beaumont. Even though we were inland, we ran all the way up to Tyler."

"He hit Louisiana instead."

"Right. And he was somewhat petered out when he did." Howie turned toward Paul. "How about a suds, Little Brother?"

"Howie," Alex whined.

"That's all right. He's a big boy now. If I'm going to contribute to the delinquency of two minors, it might as well be three." Howie chuckled again. "One shouldn't hurt him and I bet he's got a roll of breath mints on him for the folks."

Paul took a beer and stuck out his tongue at his sister.

"Well, how about your problems here? Anymore?" Howie turned to Alex.

"A few, but we've got them on the run." Alex lied because she really didn't want to get involved with a long conversation about that subject with Howie.

"That's good. For a while there I know you were worried." Howie looked about at Stephanie and then Paul.

Alex answered Howie's questions about late registration but wanted to return to the subject of hurricanes; however, her guest announced he had to leave.

The three of them walked with Howie to his truck where they stood and talked awhile. Then, with Howie backing out of the driveway, they returned to the apartment.

They had just reentered when they heard a loud slam

upstairs, followed by a similar noise as each mirror in turn was forcefully turned back around.

"Oh Jesus…God," Stephanie cried.

Alex stood and stared in horror while Paul put his hand on her shoulder.

When the noises stopped, there was silence. They had not seen the mirror near the front door turn around, but when Alex quietly stepped forward and checked, it was right side out again.

Then, all three stood, motionless, and listened for any sound. There was none.

"Whatever was here is gone," Paul whispered.

"Don't count on it," Alex muttered. She reached over and took her roommate's trembling hand. "Are you okay, Steph?"

"I'm still not used to this crap." A tear rolled down her cheek.

"I'm not either, Stephi." Alex turned to her brother. "I think now we're right about Stehle's Door. It is the mirrors. They've got to have their entranceway wide open." She walked forward cautiously.

Before she got to the living room entranceway, all three of them heard the TV come on by itself. Quickly, they entered the living room and stared at the satellite picture of Billy while an announcer commented on its wind velocity building.

"It's Johanna. Her, at least." Alex whispered heavily. She reached for the TV control and turned it off. Then she looked around the room for anything besides the mirror that had changed. There was nothing. The coldness and smell that usually accompanied these manifestations was not present.

That is odd, she thought. *If she were here, or any of the others, there would be a residue. There's nothing. It's like nothing was here at all.* The three stopped and listened. There was no sound, only a lawn mower in the distance.

"You're right, Sis." Paul said, breaking the silence. "The mirrors are Stehle's Door. They need the right side out in order to go through at their leisure."

"And we can't do anything about it." Alex crossed her arms over her chest and turned again to the large mirror in the entrance hall. "If we move them out, they'll come back in again. And if we smash them…"

"They'll probably find some way to repair them." Stephanie finished Alex's statement in a whisper.

"Right." Alex turned and walked into the living room where she sat down heavily on the sofa. She switched on the TV and found that the hurricane report was still on. Billy would hit San Salvador in a few hours time if he maintained his present course. His wind velocity was up to 110 miles per hour.

In the meantime, Stephanie retrieved beers from the kitchen and offered one to her roommate, then asked Paul.

"No thanks, I've got to drive home and I really need to be going anyway. I think your friends are gone for the time being but if anything happens, you know what to do. Call my cell phone."

"Right, Pauli. We'll keep in touch."

That evening, Billy pounded the ancient landing place of Columbus with torrential rain, 110 mile an hour winds and a twelve-foot storm surge. Then he passed over it like it had never existed, leaving severe damage, massive flooding and death.

Chapter Twenty-Two

"Billy hit San Salvador last night," Paul said into the phone first thing the following morning.

"I know, Pauli. I saw that on the weather channel right after I got up." Alex, still groggy from sleep, had seen pictures of smashed beach homes and badly flooded streets. Billy's first victim had suffered the worst damage ever.

"He's headed for the Bahamas next."

"He's already there. He passed over Cat Island and he's headed toward Nassau now."

Alex paused a minute to remember all she had seen in the latest TV report. "There were hurricane warnings issued in Florida a few days ago."

"From the looks of things, Billy's already created more of a mess than the storms earlier this summer."

"It looks that way, Pauli."

"Did everything go all right last night? Did anything else happen?"

"Nothing at all. I didn't think anything would. You know I can sometimes feel these things coming on. But nothing last night. I slept like a baby and so did Stephanie. She's still in the sack."

"That's great, Sis. Oh, by the way, Mama wants a picture of you on your first day of class."

"Again?"

"Again. Tradition, remember?"

"Okay. I'll have Stephanie shoot one for her."

"Good, Sis. Don't worry. She's going to want one of me, too."

"Honestly, Pauli. You'd think this would have ended after high school."

"Well, you know how Mama is about traditions. Think of it

as our just deserts for not going away to school."

"Absolutely."

Alex hung up the phone in a pleasant frame of mind. She had two morning classes to meet today while Stephanie had three, one in the afternoon. They had decided to take separate cars to school. In the meantime, after Alex got out of class she was to come home, take a nap, and then prepare chicken and dumplings for the evening meal.

Quickly, she grabbed her notebooks and shot out the door to her car.

On the way to school, she thought again about Billy. Apparently he was heading straight for Florida as Katrina had. She compared the two of them and remembered that Katrina intensified on the way across the Gulf. She had been only a two when she hit Florida, but she had reached level five in the Gulf. Silently, she said a prayer that Billy would not do the same.

After meeting her classes, Alex picked up a bite of lunch and headed for the apartment. Later, she and Stephanie would work out a schedule where they would take only one car, but for now both girls were on their own until late afternoon. Alex stopped on the way home to pick up the supper ingredients and rent a movie to pass the time until her roommate came home.

Just before she reached the apartment, an old apprehension returned. She would be in the apartment alone. How vulnerable would she be?

She thought momentarily about going to a mall or to a movie but she had chicken that needed to go into the refrigerator. And then there was Mrs. Frank. If need be, she could keep her company.

When she turned into the driveway, she thanked God that the old lady's car was there. After she had stowed the food, she would simply knock on the back door and get some pointers on how to prepare chicken and dumplings.

In the apartment, however, she could neither feel nor sense anything. She was really there alone. Then she wondered if the old lady was taking a nap. If that were the case, she didn't need to disturb her unless she just had to later.

Lying on the couch in front of the TV, she promptly dozed off but was awakened quickly by something moving through the apartment upstairs.

*Stephanie? S*he thought. *Home early?* It sounded like her.

"Stephi!" she called out.

"Hi, Roomy. I just got home."

"My God, what time is it?" Alex called out again. "I must have slept longer than I thought," she whispered to herself.

When there was no answer from upstairs, Alex checked her watch. Two fifteen. Only thirty minutes after she herself had gotten home.

She jumped to her feet and headed for the staircase. "Hey, what happened to your afternoon class?" Alex called from the base of the stairs.

"It got cancelled," came the reply from inside Stephanie's room.

"Why, Stephi? You needed that class." She hurried up the stairs to Stephanie's room. "Now, you're going to have…" She stopped abruptly in her roommate's bedroom. There was no one there.

"Stephi," she said, bewildered. "Honestly, what kind of bullshit is this?" She turned and opened the closet. Nothing.

Suddenly, she remembered her roommate's habit of putting her books on the table in the entrance hall. She didn't remember seeing books on that table before she came up, but before she could think any more about it, the figure had come out of the full length mirror and was on her.

Alex screamed as loud as she could as the skeletal figure of Johanna grasped her in both of its hands. Feeling sharp nails digging into her chest and shoulders, she backed as hard as she could into the closet door. The face of the thing moved up as close to Alex as it could and regurgitated filthy liquid all over her front.

"It's time, Alexandra," the hideous manifestation said, in a slow, deliberate voice, its facial features frozen. "It's time."

Summoning as much strength as she could, she shoved the thing away from her and bolted through the bedroom door for the stairs. Reaching the top of the stairs, she glanced back into the room she had just left but could not see Johanna.

Halfway down the stairs, she remembered the heavy baseball bat she had left in an umbrella stand in the entrance hall. As quickly as she could, she retrieved it and ran for the front door, intending to reach Mrs. Frank's back steps.

However, just outside the front door, she felt a pressure on her back and two bony arms reached around her to her chest and stomach. She spun in the thing's grip in an effort to break free but before she could, the head fell on her left shoulder and sank long dead teeth into her bare flesh.

Alex screamed again as loud as she could and caught Mrs. Frank, in her peripheral vision, coming down her back steps.

Her left shoulder bleeding heavily down the front of her blouse, Alex again pushed out of the grasp of the hideous entity and backed away about eight feet. Both hands now on the bat, she raised it to strike.

Mrs. Frank had come close to Alex and, with wide eyes, was regarding the macabre figure.

"O my God, Johanna," the old lady sobbed.

"Mrs. Frank, go in the house!" Alex barked, her eyes riveted to the dead figure still threatening her.

"Alexandra, what in the world?" Mrs. Frank turned to Alex, who still carefully watched the figure, her bat raised to strike in an instant. "Alex, Baby, you're hurt."

"Mrs. Frank, please. Go in the house!" A tear rolled down Alex's face. Now the pain in her shoulder hit her, blood still rolling down her blouse.

Seeing that Mrs. Frank did not move, she carefully moved over toward her to get between her and the monstrous apparition that still stood motionless, its blank, dead stare mechanically following her every move.

Finally, Alex reached Mrs. Frank and stood just in front of her, facing her adversary, which had moved around with her.

"Come on, you goddamned monster," Alex said through clenched teeth. "Come and get me now. I'll send you straight to hell."

She felt a hand laid gently on her back. "Mrs. Frank," she sobbed. "Don't move from behind me, please."

While she watched, the apparition vanished, leaving no trace that it had ever been there. Convinced that the thing was truly gone, she turned and the old lady took her in her arms.

"That damned thing bit me, Mrs. Frank," she cried,

hugging her, blood running over both of them.

"It's gone now, Honey. Come on and let me fix that wound."

Their arms around each other, the ladies made their way up the back steps and through the back porch to the kitchen.

Alex sat at the kitchen table while Mrs. Frank retrieved bandages, alcohol and antiseptic cream from her downstairs bathroom. Slowly and deliberately, she dressed Alex's wound, saying it wasn't deep enough to require stitches after all. After that, she dressed wounds in her right shoulder and chest made by fingernails.

In the meantime, Alex told Mrs. Frank all that Johanna had done to her up to that point. She even mentioned the curious "dream" in which she had accidentally knocked Johanna off the floating wreckage. Knowing that all she had told her was probably enough, Alex did not mention her suspicion that that particular dream might have been a trip back in time via Stehle's Door. She figured she had stretched believability enough.

Later, Stephanie arrived home to find Mrs. Frank and Alex on the back steps. Alex caught her roommate's alarm at her bandaged shoulder.

"She bit me," she said.

"Oh, my God, Alex. That thing? When did this happen?"

"About an hour and a half ago. She came out of the mirror in your room to tell me 'it's time.'" She tried to mimic the dead thing's voice. "Which means Billy is everything I thought it would be all along. Probably worse than either Katrina or Ike."

Stephanie took a close look at Alex's shoulder and then gave Mrs. Frank a half-hearted smile. "Billy's almost on top of Nassau heading toward Miami. I heard it on the radio just before I drove up." She looked from Alex to Mrs. Frank in turn.

Alex turned to her roommate. "Thousands of people are leaving South Florida. They remember Katrina." She sighed. "So much for Billy going up the East Coast."

"God, those people had better get out of there."

"That's right. By now I bet that storm is a four."

"I didn't hear that."

Alex reached down and flicked a leaf off of her shoe. "It's

been building strength since it left San Salvador. I'm sure it's a category four by now."

"Which means South Florida is in trouble."

"Good lord, girls." Mrs. Frank put her arm gently on Alex's back. "You remember how scared we were when Ike came through. We were afraid of Andrew, too. That was just before my Leo died. I remember him thinking about boarding up the windows but it turned out we didn't need to."

"Yes, it came ashore in Louisiana, like Katrina did." Alex turned and looked at the large bandage on her left shoulder. The smaller wounds in her upper chest and right shoulder hurt more than her left shoulder did at this point. "Mrs. Frank, you did a very good job of patching me up. I don't know what I would have done without you."

"Don't think anything about that, Honey." The old lady answered. "I just wish I had paid attention to what you told me earlier."

"I didn't even know you had been experiencing such things until just recently. We've been seeing the people of the storm as you call them for months." Alex breathed deeply and then looked up again at her roommate. "But I don't know how much more of Johanna I'm going to be able to take. And I know damn well she's not finished."

"Soon this storm will be over, Alex. And she'll be gone."

"Oh, God, Roomy, I hope you're right." Alex smiled faintly and then looked over at Mrs. Frank, then back at her roommate. "One good thing is that now all three of us are in it together. And the more of us the better."

"Maybe we can get the guys over here."

"That reminds me. I need to call Josh. We haven't talked in so long I bet he thinks I've fallen off the edge of the world."

"Oh, he's probably off playing baseball somewhere."

"Pissing off his mother." Alex and Stephanie laughed.

"You know, Alexandra, that boy looks like a baseball player." Mrs. Frank beamed.

"Don't tell his mama that."

At that all three of them laughed and Alex and Mrs. Frank got to their feet. They walked slowly over to the apartment and entered, Alex walking ahead.

"I'll make us some iced tea," she said. She could really use something stronger but Mrs. Frank was with them and Alex wasn't sure how the old lady would take her drinking beer or wine.

Alex made the tea and the three of them settled in the living room.

"I remember when my Leo remodeled this place," Mrs. Frank said. "This was the room he started with."

"He sure did a good job," Stephanie remarked.

Alex started to say something but she was cut off by the sound of footsteps upstairs. Instantly, she jumped up and retrieved the bat from the hall.

"Come on down here, you monster!" she screamed up the stairs. "I've had more than enough of your shit!" Her chest heaved as her eyes scanned the top of the stairs and the landing.

"Come down, I said!" she screamed again.

The apartment, in its entirety, began to shake, very little at first, but increasing steadily until the whole building and its insides shook as if in an earthquake. The floor moved, forcing Alex to grab the balustrade.

In the living room, Mrs. Frank and Stephanie had set down their tea glasses and now held on tightly to the arms of their chairs.

"Stop it!" Alex screamed, hugging the balustrade. Now tears rolled down her face.

The apartment continued to move. First one picture, then another, dropped from the wall.

"Alex, what's going on?" Stephanie cried from the living room.

"Poltergeist crap. From Johanna," Alex spat. Desperately, she wanted that thing up close to her, close enough for her to swing the heavy bat and shatter its skull like a dried gourd all over the ground.

Still the building shook.

Alex still stared up the stairs, hoping for an appearance by the monstrous apparition. She knew, however, that the cause of this disturbance was not going to appear.

"Alex, when's this going to stop?" There was now a desperation in Stephanie's voice, an alarm and urgency combined with a fear of the unknown.

Abruptly, the movement stopped. Bat in hand, Alex ran to the living room.

"Mrs. Frank, are you all right?" she asked, with obvious fear in her own voice.

"Yes, Honey. Just a little bewildered." She still gripped the chair arms tightly. "That's certainly nothing I've ever experienced."

With all of the movement, the tea glasses had not toppled, or even spilled, and Alex picked hers up and took a sip.

"That thing's upstairs," she said. "I can feel her up there."

"It probably came out of my damned mirror," Stephanie said forcefully. She glanced over at Mrs. Frank, ashamed of what she'd blurted out, but the old lady just sat and stared, her hands till on the chair arms.

"There's all kinds of ways she can get in here, Stephanie," Alex said in a slow and deliberate voice. "Not just your mirror."

The air began turning cold, slight at first, but steadily intensifying, the same way as the building movement.

"Now, what in hell is this?" Alex whispered, heavily enough to be heard. Knowing that this type of cold precipitated a paranormal experience, Alex grabbed the bat and held it close to her. "Get ready. She might be coming." She barked at the other two.

The room, however, just grew colder. The mirrors filmed over and all three ladies could see their breath. Alex wondered how cold it would get.

"Alex, what's happening now?" a painful voice from nearby asked.

"Alex, I don't know how long I can stand this." Mrs. Frank rose from her chair, hugging herself.

Alex moved closer to the others. When she put out her hand to touch Stephanie's shoulder, the room suddenly became dark. In the darkness, Alex thought about turned off electricity but remembered that at this time of day, they did not use the lights. The apartment was usually bright enough without them.

Now, however, it was pitch black; pitch black and freezing. They could see the bright mid-afternoon light through the windows, but inside was darkness where they couldn't see their hands in front of their faces.

The three frightened women clasped each other, standing in the middle of the room.

"Jesus Christ, Alex. What's going on?" Stephanie sobbed.

"I…I told you, Stephi. This is poltergeist stuff, brought on by Johanna, I'm sure." Her right arm clutched her terrified roommate to her chest; her left encircled Mrs. Frank, who was now clearly shaking.

Alex thought that the three of them, moving quickly together, could get to the front door. The back door was closer but it was rarely used, double locked and shut tight. Somehow, though, she felt if they did get to the front door, it wouldn't come open. She would try it anyway.

"Mrs. Frank? Stephanie? I want us to start scooting toward the front door. If we can get to it, we can get out of here."

"Alexandra, this is horrible."

"I know, Mrs. Frank. We're going to try to get out of it."

Both arms clasped tightly around the others, Alex began moving the three of them toward the front door. They collided with an end table that turned over, spilling objects into the darkness. Alex could see the faint outline of the front door coming closer.

They reached the entrance hall and turned to the right. Only twelve feet to go.

"We're almost there, girls. Hang on!" Moving a bit faster, Alex herded the other two ladies toward freedom.

Six feet from the door, however, they met a huge blast of wind that blew open the front door and toppled the three women on top of one another.

"Shit," Stephanie squeaked, underneath Alex.

"My…My God," Mrs. Frank choked, next to Alex. She coughed roughly.

Her hands still on the other two ladies, Alex sat up. She realized that the wind hadn't come from outside, but from upstairs. Turning toward the staircase, she started to get up but a second blast sent her backwards on her bottom.

Meanwhile Stephanie and Mrs. Frank hugged the floor.

The second blast ended abruptly as the first had so Alex sat up and turned to her roommate. She beheld a look of pure horror on Stephanie's face, aimed at the ceiling. She followed her gaze upwards.

Twenty feet above them in the entrance hall, Johanna hovered, her face and body that of a dead young woman, but her outstretched arms and hands those of a long dead corpse. Her luminance emitted no light, for Alex could see her plainly but nothing else in the room, except the freedom beyond the front door. Mechanically, Johanna opened her mouth and showered the three of them with filthy, vile-smelling water.

"Oh, Lord God. Johanna, let us alone, please." Mrs. Frank, on her back, had taken it full in the face.

Alex, dripping wet, tried to remember where in the living room the baseball bat was. For her to attempt to get it, however, would be futile.

She turned over abruptly on her back and, in the process, mashed her injured shoulder against the floor. Crying out, she squared herself, staring up at the floating apparition above them.

But now, Johanna began to descend, growing larger all the time.

Alex, in a panic, did the only thing she could think of to do. In an instant, she sprang to her feet and darted toward the front door, blasting through the screen and colliding with a heavy obstruction just outside. Josh Hamilton went tumbling backwards onto the driveway.

"Josh, for God's sake, help us!" Alex screamed in her horror.

Quickly the two of them recovered themselves and raced back into the apartment. They found Stephanie and Mrs. Frank still on the floor and Johanna gone. The light had returned but a terrible stench hung in the air; a stench Alex knew only too well.

"What in hell is that smell?" Josh gasped, just inside of the door.

"A filthy, dead body, Josh. A rotting, stinking, goddamned, filthy dead body," Alex said through clenched teeth. She helped Stephanie get Mrs. Frank to her feet.

"She…She vanished just as you went through the door." Stephanie sniffed. Slowly the apartment reached full illumination. "I can't believe this shit. Natural light, too."

"Mrs. Frank, are you okay?' Alex asked in a gentle voice.

"I've…I've never seen anything so horrible in my entire life," the old lady answered, breathing heavily. "I'm okay, Dear. Just a little shaken up."

"Alex, what's going…"

"Johanna's going on, Josh. You scared her away this time." Alex looked at him and then back at Mrs. Frank. "It seems that thing can't take a lot of us at one time. Just like all the rest of them. They don't like crowds. When it gets too crowded for their comfort, they hook it."

"Alex, what are you talking about?"

"I'm talking about paranormal manifestations that become very, very physical, Josh. She bit the hell out of me earlier." She pointed to her bandaged shoulder.

"I wanted to get that gun," Stephanie said from behind Mrs. Frank.

"That wouldn't do any good, Stephi."

"I'd have shot her to ribbons."

"Yeah. And blown a bunch of holes in the ceiling."

"Is that the pistol I brought over?" Josh put his hand to his mouth.

"Yes, Stephanie shot Johanna with it and ran her off the other day."

"I shot her right through the body. You can still see the hole in her front."

"Well, it sure didn't stop her from coming today, did it." Alex had recovered, but Mrs. Frank and Stephanie still appeared a bit shaken.

She stood, Josh's arm around her waist, and wondered what to do next. Johanna was gone for now but Alex knew she'd be back. Indeed, her assaults, both on her sanity and her physical body, would intensify even more until Billy blew through. She thought about leaving the apartment. She could take Stephanie with her, but what about Mrs. Frank. The old lady was now as vulnerable as she and Stephanie were. They couldn't seek refuge in Mrs. Frank's house because it was as open as the apartment was at this point. Indeed that was where she had first seen Johanna. And if the three of them left, what if Johanna followed them as she had Alex to the Rand building.

And what about the cats?

Alex would have to face it. She and Stephanie and probably now Mrs. Frank were potential victims, played with like a cat does a mouse, by a vindictive supernatural force clearly as monstrous as the hurricane keeping her alive.

Chapter Twenty-Three

That same afternoon, a WP-3D Orion Hurricane Hunter from MacDill AFB, attempting to fly directly into Billy, encountered such heavy turbulence that serious damage to the aircraft resulted. It turned back, its mission aborted.

Early the next morning, Billy made landfall just south of Miami's center. What little people were left there and in South Florida braced for one-hundred fifty mile-an-hour winds and a twenty-foot storm surge. Miami, as a result of lessons learned from Katrina and others, was now virtually a ghost town, as was almost all of South Florida and the Everglades.

The satellite picture, presenting a monstrous Billy enveloping all of the Miami area as well as South Florida, presented a sickening spectacle to all who were watching. The storm, now clearly the largest ever, was moving fast, crossing South Florida and entering the Gulf. Massive numbers of rescue and recovery units stood poised to enter the afflicted areas as soon as Billy's outer rings cleared the west coast of Florida..

Since Miami and most of South Florida were clearly above sea level, all thought helicopter units wouldn't be needed for long to rescue survivors trapped on house tops since the water was expected to recede quickly. All concerned expected to find extensive wind damage and almost complete displacement from the monster's storm surge.

And indeed, the damage was worse than expected.

At seven o'clock that morning, Alex, alone downstairs and uneasy, sipped coffee and watched the reports from Miami. An occasional satellite picture of Billy depicted what she had known all along. He was headed straight into the Gulf.

She said a prayer for the people of Miami as well as one for herself, Stephanie, and Mrs. Frank, knowing that the day would probably bring another appearance of the demon-like

Johanna.

The previous night Stephanie had asked her again if Johanna would be gone after Billy had run its course. And again Alex reassured her that she would. But now she had doubts herself. Was there another trigger somewhere? After all, this had been Johanna's home.

The nagging doubt and the fear of her surroundings made Alex wake Stephanie, something she needed to do anyway since they had class that day. One good thing was that the girls would be at school most of that day. Alex already had an assignment and she decided to start it that afternoon in the library.

They breakfasted and then prepared for school. Alex called Mrs. Frank and told her what they were going to do that day. The old lady's telling her she was going to a church function relieved Alex somewhat but she still worried about what would be waiting when all of them came home later.

The evening before Josh had stayed late and Alex told him she was going to call her brother between classes to tell him what had happened the previous day and make plans to come together during the time Billy was in the Gulf and if possible, afterwards. The five of them together would definitely create a measure of safety. After all, they could weather poltergeist phenomena together, but even the thought of her and Johanna one-on-one was terrifying.

At nine o'clock, Alex decided to go ahead and dial her brother at home, remembering that he had to attend class himself later that morning.

"Pauli, there's a matter of some urgency here."

"Yeah. Josh called last night. He told me he walked in on something yesterday afternoon."

"Did he ever. Johanna, trying to turn the apartment on end. Even Mrs. Frank was in on this one."

"He told me about that. He said you got hurt yesterday."

"Yes, earlier. Johanna bit me. Pauli, that goddamned thing stayed around all afternoon. We're going to stay away all today."

"What about tonight?"

"I think we're going to spend the evening and the night with Mrs. Frank. Although the three of us together apparently didn't help yesterday, I still think we have a better chance of fighting her off together. We'll probably go out to eat and then come back and watch TV or something at her house. I've rethought Mrs. Frank's house. I think we're safer over there than we are in the apartment. There's a lot more room to move around in. We'll sleep over together, with Stephanie and me in the same room, of course. We're going to stay over there until Billy blows through."

There was a pause, seemingly for Paul to collect his thoughts.

"Sis, do you still think that thing's going bye-bye after Billy? I mean the rest of them seem to be gone, but she's still around. And in a big way."

There was the doubt again. "I…I think so, Pauli. We got rid of the trigger she'd been using for years. And what could there be besides that storm?"

"I don't know, Sis." Paul paused again to think. "I seem to remember some other things in that turret room."

"I do, too. But we got the one with her name on it, remember?"

Seemingly convinced, Paul changed the subject. "Billy hit Miami early this morning."

Alex paused and shut her eyes. "I know. I have it on TV now."

"There's no way they could have gotten all of those people out of there in time."

"I know, Pauli. Most of them got out, though. There's still so much to remember about Katrina." Alex paused and collected her thoughts. "I think about what's been going on around here. Those people, that little girl, what they were here for. It's so obvious they were here to warn us against Billy." A tear rolled down Alex's cheek. "And we did nothing."

"What could we do, Sis? The weather service isn't going to believe that we got an advance warning from a bunch of ghosts. And it took us awhile to figure out what they were pointing at, remember? Hell, we believed for the longest time they were pointing at Johanna."

"Yes, I know," Alex croaked. She sighed, heavily, and switched the phone to the other ear. "Pauli, I've got to go now.

Stephanie and I have got to get out of here."

"Okay, Sis. Let me know if anything happens later."

By ten o'clock, Alex and Stephanie were on their way to Rice University. Mrs. Frank had left before they had and they knew she wouldn't be home until late afternoon. There-fore the apartment and the huge, dark old house would be empty for the day. Or would they? Even parking in a student parking lot, Alex could feel Johanna very close.

The girls attended their classes, ate lunch, and then settled in the library to work on assignments and read. Although there was a question at this point that Rice would close with the rest of Houston's schools, the library and campus were crowded as usual.

Later that afternoon, they paused at a TV monitor to get a glimpse of Billy. Its eye had now cleared the west Florida coast and was headed across the Gulf. Its mass covered South Florida and most of the Eastern Gulf. The announcer said that mandatory evacuation had started all along the Gulf Coast as far as South Texas at Brownsville. There were pictures of lines of vehicles trekking up from Pensicola, Biloxi, Mobile and points in between, all ravaged years before by Katrina. Thousands of cars were now making their way up Highway Forty-Five out of Galveston and areas around South Houston and Highway thirty-seven out of Corpus Christi toward San Antonio. Even farm and ranch roads were used for evacuation throughout the South. New Orleans, once again remembering Katrina and still trapped between two major bodies of water, had begun its own evacuation north toward Baton Rouge and Shreveport. Hundreds of thousands of people were on the move. But Billy had not yet chosen his target.

Alexandra Zunker knew what it was. The usual one. At five that afternoon, the girls left the library and Alex called Mrs. Frank. She found the old lady settled on her couch, watching the hurricane account on her TV.

"Honey, you should have seen them on Forty-Five and Ten heading out of here," she said. "Lines of them, just like when Ike was threatening." Mrs. Frank paused a minute. "You know, they don't even know where that thing's going to hit yet."

"I know, Mrs. Frank. We saw it at school." Alex glanced

over at Stephanie, who was driving. "If that thing's coming here, it shouldn't be here for another couple of days. We're coming right home. Do you want us to stop for anything? I think the three of us ought to stick together until this is over."

"Oh, no, Honey. Let's go out tonight."

"Good idea. Mexican food okay?" Alex waited for an answer and then said goodbye and closed her cell phone. She turned to her roommate and smiled. "We're going to La Paloma tonight and then we'll join Mrs. Frank for movies at her place."

"Sounds great. I really don't want to hear any more about that storm."

Stephanie put on a brave front, but Alex could tell she was a bit scared. Even though she had weathered Katrina and Ike, her Midwestern upbringing had not accustomed her to these gigantic storms.

"Nope. Billy's on the back burner. At least for tonight."

"And so, I hope, is that thing."

"I hope so, too, Steph."

They returned home and, though wary, dropped their books in the apartment and hurriedly got their night clothes and necessities together so they wouldn't have to return later that night. Even in the hot, humid afternoon, the whole area seemed dark and threatening. Although the brightness of the apartment would seem cheery at any other time, now there was a burdensome sense of foreboding that the girls just wanted to escape. Johanna could appear at any time.

"We ought to get Josh and your brother over here tonight," Stephanie said, standing behind Alex at Mrs. Frank's back door.

"I thought about that, Steph. But it wouldn't work. Pauli has an eight o'clock at U of H and Josh has to drive to Huntsville in the morning. And we don't know if schools are going to be called off or not. And that mob on the highways."

"I was just thinking of what you always say about the more of us the safer we are."

"I know. We're just going to have to go it on our own. Somehow, I don't think we're as vulnerable in Mrs. Frank's house as we would be in our apartment."

Stephanie perked up and put her hand on Alex's shoulder. "Alex, you don't suppose any of the other spooks are still around here, do you? I mean, Billy's still pretty far off."

"That's what I was thinking, too, Stephanie. I kinda feel there are. And if they are, they'll be in Mrs. Frank's house. And, if you'll remember…"

Just then, Mrs. Frank opened the back door. "Hello, Dears," she greeted them, cheerily. "Just take your stuff up to your room just across the hall from mine."

"Thanks, Mrs. Frank. By the way, our treat tonight at the restaurant."

"Oh, no, Honey. I love to take you out. I don't have that much to spend money on any more except bills."

Alex smiled at the old lady and she and her roommate hurriedly stowed their stuff in the large bedroom across the hall from Mrs. Franks'.

Since the room was large, Stephanie had ample room for her pallet. Alex thought about the cats and, with Mrs. Frank's permission, she and Stephanie brought Sabrina and Henrietta over to the large house for the duration. They set up the litter box in the second floor bathroom at the back of the house and let the two felines go exploring. When they came downstairs, Alex felt much better and believed they truly had a good, safe haven for the night.

Later, on the way to La Paloma Blanca, they saw scores of people nailing up sheets of plywood to protect picture windows. Others were taping windows and putting vehicles into the shelter of buildings. Many buildings had large, mesh screens over their windows already but many front doors had been boarded up. Alex thought the whole scene was one of unsettling chaos and surreal urgency.

Mrs. Frank figured her house and the apartment were relatively safe since Leo had put up heavy screen windows as a security device years before. The only windows that were not so covered were the small windows in the turret and the attic. Still, she said, she feared damage from an uprooted tree or flying debris.

While many people prepared for Billy, those running from him clogged the freeways. The major highways and thoroughfares were choked with evacuees from the South and the East. Alex avoided them by choosing a route through minor thoroughfares and residential neighborhoods. She noticed a hotel just off Highway Ten was filling up with people who thought they had gone far enough. *What about those windows?* She thought, noting the large windows in each hotel unit.

La Paloma Blanca, a popular restaurant, was a large, stucco building with recessed windows of thick glass so Alex thought there wouldn't be any hurricane preparation here. And since businesses hadn't started closing down yet, this restaurant was noisy and crowded as it usually was on Thursday night. The girls and Mrs. Frank settled in the middle of a large room and studied menus.

Just after a server brought chips and took drink orders, the girls eavesdropped on a family at the next table, apparently from New Orleans. Alex thought about Raymond and his family. Were they in Houston? Surely they would have called. Vivid in her mind was the horrible flooding in New Orleans after Hurricane Katrina.

They heard the father at the next table say that if New Orleans took a direct hit this time, it would never recover. Such a revelation made Alex wonder how safe Houston was, sixty miles inland. Also, what about Clear Lake, and her parents' house? She thought that maybe they should call Thomas and Elizabeth and ask them to come up to Houston to wait out the storm. However, with the roads in the situation they were in, that would be next to impossible now.

But, they had their own worries. After their meals came, Alex discussed the plans for the night with Stephanie and Mrs. Frank.

"We'll all be very close," she said. "So if something happens, we can help each other. If you see anything, scream."

"Don't worry," Stephanie mumbled.

"I think we'll be all right together," Mrs. Frank remarked. "I'd feel better if you had that baseball bat, though."

"Don't worry, Mrs. Frank. I brought that over this afternoon and it's right by the bed." She glanced over at her roommate and smiled. "I told Steph to leave the gun in the apartment, though. She doesn't need to be shooting one of us."

"Ha! As if I would." At last, Stephanie smiled and looked over at the old lady.

"I have some bourbon at home," Mrs. Frank said in a soft voice. "When we get home, I think a nightcap or two might be in order. I don't think I'll be prosecuted for corrupting the youth under the present circumstances."

Stephanie laughed. "Mrs. Frank, I think many nightcaps are going to be drunk tonight all over this town."

After supper, Alex let Stephanie drive so she could call her parents on her cell phone and find out if they still planned to stay in their house. She learned that Thomas had put plywood over the windows of the house and had decided not to evacuate as many of their neighbors had done. He maintained that since they were thirty miles inland the worst that could possibly happen would be the flooding from the ship channel he had gotten from Rita. Now, he wanted to be on hand to prevent as much damage as possible.

Alex, with some reservations, agreed with him and promised to keep in touch as the three ladies made their way home through neighborhoods still preparing for Billy after dark.

Safe in Mrs. Frank's house, they watched as Billy made its way into the central Gulf, veering west by northwest. Scenes of Miami flashed on the screen after the current report about Billy. The city, badly flooded with beach areas smashed, was still in the thralls of massive rescue as legions of coast guard and navy boats covered the inundated landscape, looking for those still living.

Oh Jesus Christ, those poor people. Alex thought.

She also learned that a WC-130 that afternoon finally got a wind speed on Billy. Two hundred miles per hour. Clearly a category five.

"What if it kept going straight?" Stephanie asked.

"It would hit Mexico," Alex answered, settling back in an easy chair and sipping on a drink. "Or it would hit the Rio Grande Valley. I heard on TV earlier the people down there are having a hell of a time with their evacuation."

"I heard that, too." Mrs. Frank had entered the room unnoticed with a large pitcher of bourbon and coke. "There seems to be no adequate roads down there going north."

"Well, there's all kinds of problems here, too." Alex glanced over at her roommate and noticed she had drained her glass and was ready for another. “I’ve never seen so many people in my life. Even more than when Rita and Ike blew through.”

“My God, poor souls.” Mrs. Frank refilled Stephanie’s glass and Alex handed her hers. “They don’t know if there’ll be a home to go back to or not.”

“When you look around at all this, it’s no wonder that we’ve been warned about Billy from the great beyond all summer.” Alex looked about the parlor and noticed a distinct quiet in the house. “You know something. I think we’re alone here. At least for tonight.”

“Jesus, I hope so.” Stephanie settled back in her chair with a full glass. “Why didn’t those things come around when the other hurricanes hit?”

“Because Rita missed us, Steph. It hit far East Texas and Louisiana And Ike…”

“I guess that means this one is coming right at us.”

Mrs. Frank chuckled slightly. “God, I remember Carla. I was so young, then.” The old lady trailed off, shaking her head.

That night, they watched two movies, comedies, to take their minds off their own situation as well as the approaching storm. Alex felt warmed by the drinks and she noticed that her roommate was slightly drunk but said nothing. Given the circumstances, she wished she was drunk as well.

It was eleven thirty when the three decided to go up to bed. Stephanie had made up her pallet earlier so all she had to do was fall into it. They found both cats lying on the pallet when they entered the room.

“Well, those two certainly aren’t stirred up,” Alex observed, remembering feline reactions on certain occasions in the past.

“If something were around, wouldn’t they react to it? They did in the past.” Stephanie, a bit unsteady, was taking off her clothes and throwing them in a corner of the room. “I don’t think I’ll wear pajamas tonight,” she said. “It’s awfully muggy.”

“I’d have something on,” Alex commented. “In case we need to evacuate the house.” She winked at her roommate.

Stephanie giggled. “Wouldn’t that be something? Joining the trek to the north in the buff.”

"All I can say is that my brother would be sorry he missed it."

Stephanie giggled again and Alex noticed her putting on her pajamas. Alex grabbed her PJs and headed for the bathroom after saying goodnight to Mrs. Frank.

Settling in, the girls switched off the light and then talked a while, until Stephanie drifted off into a heavy sleep. Alex lay awake, though, and tried to hear anything that might be happening in the house. Usually, she could hear something going on in the apartment, but Mrs. Frank's huge house was something else. It had creaks and groans that Alex wasn't used to. Finally satisfied that all was well for the time being, she turned over and went to sleep.

She had not been troubled with nightmares for some weeks, but tonight they returned. In her dream she was walking toward downtown Houston along a street she didn't recognize. In front of her, tall, glass skyscrapers loomed skyward, but their tops were obscured by heavy, black lightning-filled clouds. A sense of gloom and foreboding lay everywhere. There were people but they paid no attention to her but went on about their business. "You must evacuate," Alex heard herself say. She had trouble breathing in the stuffy air.

Suddenly, she was alone, at the end of a street across from a large park she thought she recognized. Then, she noticed, something was behind her; something evil, biding its time, in no hurry to come up behind. She dared not turn around.

Quickly, she walked over the cross street and headed into the park, moving faster and faster. She came to a playground, deserted, but all the swings and merry-go-rounds were moving, as if children were on them. Looking up toward the skyline, she observed that the dark clouds had descended, enveloping the buildings.

Suddenly, an immense wall of water rose up behind the buildings, growing taller and taller as it came on.

When it broke over the Houston skyline, Alex heard from behind her.

"Die, Alexandra. In the water. Die," a gravelly voice said.

She didn't look behind her but stared straight ahead at an onrushing mountain of water that had covered the skyline before her and was now bearing down on her. She tried to cry out but couldn't hear herself for the roar of the water swiftly closing on her.

Without thinking, she turned to run, only to confront the girl that Josh had known, her arms outstretched with long claws waiting. She put her hands up to knock away the awful claws but at that moment awoke in terror.

Breathing heavily in a panic, she looked around the dark room. Nothing moved.

"As usual," she muttered. "If I've only got a dream to worry about, I'm okay."

She turned toward her roommate, who lay sound asleep, one leg sticking out of her pallet.

Alex smiled slightly. *She's dead to the world,* she thought. *Next time I go to bed, I'm going to be as drunk as she was.*

She listened again for any noise in the house, but all was quiet. A slight sound nearby directed her attention back to Stephanie. Henrietta was repositioning herself up against her sleeping mistress. Alex looked around for Sabrina and found her cuddled up against a pillow next to her.

The old house was silent as a tomb. Mrs. Frank had seemingly been right. It was a safe haven. Alex wondered why. She had first seen Johanna down in the parlor office and not too long ago it had been occupied by a number of unfortunate storm victims whose spirits were supposedly there to warn the living against Billy. Now, it seemed, only three vulnerable souls slept in the great house and there was apparently nothing around to torment them.

Alex glanced at her nearby travel clock, hoping it was morning, but was annoyed to find that it was only two o'clock.

"Four more damned hours," she whispered to herself. "What do I do now? Back to sleep and another dream?" Although she knew that her nightmares had never come in pairs, she still didn't trust the circumstances. She wanted to get up, go downstairs, and watch TV but realized quickly she would be alone down there. Frustrated, she lay back in the bed and closed her eyes.

In two days Billy will be gone, she thought. *And then things can get back to normal. But here and in the apartment, what can normal be? God, from what I can tell, Johanna has been around here for generations.*

"Poor Stephi," she whispered, and turned on her side toward her roommate. Before Stephanie had one too many the previous evening, she phoned home to Kansas to tell her family she would be all right. Of course, they had been worried and had been following Billy faithfully on TV. Earlier, they had tried to call Stephanie at the apartment to no avail.

"First, Katrina then Rita, then Ike," Alex whispered in the dark. "And it's still new to her. As strange and as unwelcome as the bad dream I just had."

She closed her eyes and said a prayer, for her roommate, and Mrs. Frank, her parents and brother, all those who had been displaced by this disastrous storm and especially those in Miami who had already suffered from Billy's wrath.

She felt better and turned over to go back to sleep. "All will be well soon," she said to herself.

Quickly asleep again, she had no way of knowing that Billy had turned even more toward Galveston.

Chapter Twenty-Four

"I knew it. We knew it all along." Alex, coffee cup in hand, confronted a sleepy Stephanie at the base of the stairs. "Billy's coming straight at us. They don't know if it's going to weaken like the others or not."

"Andrew was a three when it made landfall in Louisiana, I believe." Stephanie yawned and stretched on the bottom step.

"Ike was supposed to be a two, but it wasn't."

"Maybe Billy won't be as bad as Ike was."

The old lady was up but had not yet come down, so Alex was in the process of making breakfast. The TV was on in the parlor and Alex would step in from time to time to check the weather channel.

Mrs. Frank shortly followed Stephanie down and the three of them settled with coffee in the parlor in front of TV. Since today was Friday, Alex would ordinarily be going to class, but the TV announced earlier that Rice was closed. It seemed everything was closing down for Billy as it had for other bad storms.

After breakfast, Alex tried calling home but got no answer. "I wonder where they went in this mess," she said to Stephanie, who stood behind her, coffee cup in hand.

"Maybe they evacuated after all. You know they did during Rita and Ike."

"No. They said they were going to ride this one out, and one thing my family does is stick to their word. Besides, they barely even got flooded during Rita." Alex, a frown of concern on her face, dialed her father's cell phone. There, she got his voice mail. "He probably hasn't turned it on," she announced. "He always does that."

The weather channel stated that Billy was expected to make landfall the next evening somewhere along the eastern coast of Texas or Western Louisiana. If it did hit Galveston as a four, Alex wondered what would happen to West Galveston this time. With the murderous storm nearby and the sudden absence of Johanna, she was tense to the point of tears. Exacerbating this, of course, was the strange absence of her parents.

Mrs. Frank made more coffee and then returned to her post in front of TV. It wasn't long before Alex and Stephanie noticed a stark contrast between the noisy, high-pitched weather accounts and the total silence of Mrs. Frank's large, old house. Alex wondered if her apartment was just as silent.

After she tried to call her parents again, to no avail, she phoned Josh and got his mother. He was home in the backyard and puzzled over Alex's strange request to call her parents on his cell phone. Josh did as he was requested and returned to the regular home phone.

"There must be something wrong with that line," he told Alex after he reported he had gotten Paul who told him everything at home was fine. "He said he'd call you in a couple of minutes."

"I don't know what the hell's going on, Josh." Alex, relieved to hear everything at home was okay, was still annoyed, however. "It's just damned spooky. I feel like we're cut off, here. In the middle of limbo."

"Maybe that's a good thing, considering what's just off shore. Except for that big line of traffic headed down Ten everything here in Katy is fairly normal."

A few minutes later, Paul called as he had promised and Alex lost no time in picking up the phone.

"Bad-ass Billy's still a category five, Sis," he announced. "And Miami's flattened."

"I heard that earlier. What's going on there? I tried to call earlier twice, and got no one."

"That's weird, Sis. I've been here all morning," he replied. "And I was up at the crack of dawn. Mama and Papa have gone to the grocery store to get a few things. Apparently, they're still open."

"Well, this phone thing has me bugged, Pauli."

"Maybe there's something wrong with Mrs. Frank's line."

"The cell phones, too?"

"Now Papa probably didn't turn his on. You know how he is."

"That may be so. But all I get from the regular phone is rings. I've been trying to call over there since we got in from the restaurant last night."

"That is strange, Sis. We were all here last night. We sat around drinking iced tea, playing cards and watching the weather. Later we got sick of that and turned on a movie."

"Well, I don't know what the hell's going on."

"Listen, Sis. These big storms cause all kinds of weird things to happen. And the closer they get, the more things are screwed up."

"That's a possibility, I guess."

"Everything else all right over there?"

"Not a peep from anything. It has been quiet as a churchyard around here. All we hear is the wind."

"That's good. Hey, put your sexy roomy on. I want to cheer the little girl from Kansas up."

Alex gave Stephanie the phone and stood nearby, one hand across her chest while the other held her coffee cup.

"I made some more bacon and toast." Mrs. Frank appeared at the kitchen door.

"Good, Mrs. Frank. We're talking to Pauli."

"Oh, that's good. You finally got through."

"He got through to us."

Stephanie, laughing, handed the phone back to Alex. "He said after this is over, he wants to take me to Sylvan Beach. He said that beach would be least affected by the storm."

"Just under ten feet of water, Steph." She took the phone and covered the mouthpiece. "He just wants to ogle your primarily nude body." Then, she placed the phone to her ear. "Pauli, Pauli, at it again."

"Worth a try anyway, Sis. And besides, she might just go. She said she'd think about it."

"Pauli, call us later this evening. Keep in touch. And tell Mama or Papa to do the same. We're on pins and needles around here. I wish you all would evacuate."

"I do, too. But you know how Papa is. We're not going anywhere."

"Talk to you later. Give my love and concern to Mama and Papa."

She hung up the phone in better spirits. "One thing about him, he knows how to cheer someone up," she said to Stephanie.

They sat in the kitchen and munched breakfast. As they ate in silence, all they could hear was the TV from the parlor. Alex wondered if this would be a good time to share her dream but decided not to. Everyone had enough on her mind at the moment.

She was about to return to the parlor when they heard it: a loud feline roar snapping the silence, a combination of loud growl and snarl followed by a long, metallic whine.

"Jesus Christ, what's that!" Stephanie shot up from her chair.

"That's not Henrietta or Sabrina. I know good and well it isn't."

"Where…Where is it?" Mrs. Frank retained her seat but a sharp look of alarm had spread across her face.

"Somewhere in this house." Alex carefully tried to hear something else, but the house had returned to silence.

"Alex, I don't hear anything moving."

"I know." She looked down at the old lady who was about to rise herself. "Mrs. Frank, I know what made that sound. What's left of him is buried in your backyard flower bed."

"Oh, my God. Tom," Stephanie whispered.

"That's the one."

"You mean that's a dead cat?" The old lady's eyes were wide with horror.

"Yes. Johanna tore him apart in the alley. He's been back before."

"Alex, our cats are upstairs."

"I know."

"Do you think they're okay?"

"Let's go see. Mrs. Frank, would you come with us, please."

The three headed up the main staircase to the second floor. In the bathroom, they found one cat while the other lounged on Alex's bed. They did not seem disturbed. Alex picked up

Sabrina while Stephanie put Henrietta on her shoulder and they headed for the stairs to return to the kitchen.

But the loud feline voice broke the silence again. This time it seemed louder, closer, more like a scream than before.

Seemingly it came from the back of the house. The three of them headed down the hall toward the back and its three-story staircase.

Of course there was nothing there.

"Look, the dust hasn't even been disturbed," Alex said, pointing at the floor.

"I don't ever come back here." Mrs. Frank put her hands on her hips and shuffled onto the second floor landing. "I need to get Martha back here to clean."

Alex followed Mrs. Frank and headed around the banister to the attic stairs. Climbing to the last landing, Alex found the door to the attic wide open.

"Don't go in there, Alex," Stephanie said from behind her.

"I'm not. But I don't think anything of this earth opened that door." She returned to Mrs. Frank at the bottom. "Have you been up in the attic lately?" she asked.

"Honey, I haven't been up there in years. Like I said, I seldom come back here and those stairs are the only entrance to the attic."

"That's what I thought." Alex glanced again up the dark stairs. "Whatever that thing was, whether it was Tom or something else, is gone now. I can feel it. But I wonder what its purpose was." Alex turned toward the others, a frown on her face. "Other than to scare the hell out of us."

"Let's go downstairs and feed these cats." Stephanie headed for the door to the hall.

Downstairs, Alex still puzzled over the strange cat, if it had been a cat at all. Tom had appeared before her before, so he was the obvious source of the frightful noise. But, still, she wasn't sure.

At noon, the three ladies sat down to sandwiches and milk.

Alex ate her ham and cheese and then munched on Fritos. "I wonder if I should try to call Papa and Mama now," she said.

"I guess you can, Honey." Mrs. Frank was pulling more chips out of the pantry and putting them in bowls. "They should be home now."

"On second thought, I think I'll wait." She rose and headed for the parlor and the TV. "I really don't feel up to another unanswered phone call at this point."

Soon after, the ladies settled into the living room. The bright sunlight streaming through the windows seemed out of place, considering what was going on outside, all over town.

Alex was hot. She wondered if she could get to a swimming pool, but decided it would be too much of a hassle. Rising slowly from the sofa, she turned to Mrs. Frank.

"Can I put the air down a bit?" she asked the old lady, who was dozing in a chair across the room. "It's a bit stuffy in here."

"Go ahead, Hon. I usually keep it cooler when I have company."

Alex walked to the window unit and pulled the little lever down. The coldness of her apartment during Johanna's last visit flashed into her mind. The thought to leave the air alone occurred to her, but she wanted to take a nap and she couldn't in the present stuffiness of the living room.

Now she re-settled herself on the sofa and closed her eyes. *I wonder if I could have a nightmare with two other awake people in the same room,* she thought. *Or would they have to be asleep, too?* She fell asleep on this thought but awakened soon after to the jangling of Mrs. Frank's downstairs phones.

The old lady answered the nearest phone in the kitchen. Alex figured it was one of her friends so she settled back on the sofa and closed her eyes again. But then Mrs. Frank appeared at the living room entrance.

"Alex, this is Pastor Gerlach for you," she said.

"Pastor Gerlach?" Alex's eyes widened in wonder. She had called the young pastor months before about their present problems, but she had not expected to hear from him now.

She picked up the phone and clutched it in both hands. "Hello…Hello, Pastor, how are you?"

"I'm fine, Alex. How are you, considering that storm coming in?"

"Oh, we're waiting it out here."

"Alex, I tried your apartment earlier but there was no answer. So I tried your folks' house and luckily I got them.

They're packing up to leave."

"Thank God," Alex whispered into the phone. "They've finally decided to evacuate, Pastor. I wanted them to."

"Yes. And they told me you were at Lila Frank's house and they gave me that number."

"Yes. Like I said, we're waiting here for the storm to blow through. This house is like a fortress."

"I know. I've been there." The Pastor paused a moment to collect his thoughts. "Well, with all of this news of the storm, I was reminded of something that happened a few months back, shortly after you called. Alex, I certainly don't want this to upset you, but I got to thinking about it, and I prayed about it, and, with possible high water coming, and I not knowing where you were in all of this, I wanted it to serve as a kind of warning."

"What is it, Pastor?"

"I had a dream. I dreamed that you were drowning. You were in some kind of stormy water and you were drowning."

"Drowning, Pastor?" A wave of terror struck Alex and almost caused her to drop the phone.

"Yes. Like I said, I don't want this to disturb you and I probably wouldn't have even brought it up except for the hurricane down there now. Now, that I know you are safe, I feel a lot better. It was only a dream and it probably means nothing at all."

"I've had dreams about that, too, Pastor. I don't think they mean anything except maybe as reflections of our innermost fears."

"You're right about that, Alex. In psychology, we take pains to analyze dreams, but very rarely do they mean anything important."

"My feelings exactly." Alex knew what they meant, and for her, they were only too real.

"So, I guess this all means you better stay in Lila Frank's big old fortress." The young pastor chuckled.

"You bet." After a bit more small talk and reminiscing, Alex hung up the phone and turned to her roommate, now sitting at the kitchen table. "Pastor Gerlach had a dream of me drowning in a storm."

"Oh, lord, Alex. How do you suppose that happened?"

"I don't know, but I have my suspicions. You and I both know that's how Johanna wants me dead."

"Alex, I can see that dried-up creepy thing causing that dream, but I can't see her actually drowning you. I mean, look where you are."

"I don't know, Steph. She's been awfully good at other things."

"You better keep that baseball bat with you."

"I plan to."

Mrs. Frank entered the kitchen, bringing a large bag of chips from the pantry. "This is the last bag, girls. But I think there's some popcorn out there, too."

"Popcorn is great, Mrs. Frank." Stephanie turned to the old lady and smiled. "We ought to go search the movie channels for a good flick to watch with it."

Alex, sitting at the table with her head propped up on her fists, was still worried. Was Stephanie right? Had Johanna caused one of her favorite friends to dream what he had? Or was it coincidence? Knowing what she was up against, she knew it wasn't.

Momentarily, she tried to put it aside. "Let's see what's on those channels," she said, trying to affect a cheery voice. She didn't want to upset Mrs. Frank with Pastor's message.

They returned to the living room and the large TV. Alex, on the way, whispered to her roommate not to tell Mrs. Frank about the curious phone message.

But as soon as they were settled, Mrs. Frank asked about it anyway. "He was such a nice young man," she said, smiling at each girl in turn. "When I was in the hospital that last time, he visited me twice."

"He was my youth pastor, Mrs. Frank. We were catching up on the latest news." Alex smiled, slightly. "He's worried about us and Billy."

"As he would be." The old lady picked up the TV control and turned to the movie channels.

They found a movie to pass the time until evening. Since Alex had learned that her parents were apparently leaving, she would be expecting them later that evening. But the roads were still jammed with evacuees.

When Mrs. Frank left to make more popcorn, Alex whispered to Stephanie. “Something is wrong, Steph. I can feel it.”

“You and your little dab of ESP. What’s it about? That call?”

“That, and my parents. How are they going to get through all that mob on the highway now?”

“All they have to do is get across town.”

“But that might take hours. And my father has no patience for traffic jams.”

“They’ll be here.” Stephanie reassured her and seemed assured herself.

Later, at eight o’clock, with her parents not there, Alex again thought about trying to call. *Surely one of them will have a cell phone on, now,* she thought.

When the movie ended at eight thirty, she dialed her brother’s cell phone and reached him. She learned that they had tried to evacuate but had run into more and more streams of people the closer they got to town. Finally, stuck in traffic for over two hours, they made their way back home.

In a way, Alex was glad they were home, but she still wished they were there with her. “They’ll be all right where they are,” she told the two other ladies after she hung up. “When Rita came through, they just got a little wet. If you’ll remember.”

With the coming of night, Alex was still uneasy after the day’s events. Stephanie announced she wanted to watch a late movie and Alex acquiesced. Mrs. Frank offered to fix a punch with vodka in it, but added that she was going to bed.

Shortly thereafter, after sandwiches, the girls cooked more popcorn and settled in the parlor in chairs more comfortable than those in the living room. One thing adding to Alex’s uneasiness was two windows in the parlor looking out on the apartment, but she figured after a few drinks of the loaded punch, it wouldn’t make any difference. Stephanie closed the curtains anyway.

“We don’t want to see any of their funny business over there, now, do we?” she said, a tall juice glass filled to the top in her hand.

For the first time that day, Alex lightened up. "I think two of those are going to take care of you, Steph," she said. She giggled and took a drink from her own glass.

The night passed quickly until it was time for bed. Although Alex felt better, there still was that nagging fear that she knew wouldn't be completely gone until Billy passed into the record books. She and Stephanie cut the lights and went up to bed around one AM.

In bed, Alex, though comfortable, hoped her uneasiness wouldn't keep her awake. Her roommate, warmed by the vodka punch, was soon snoring nearby. Alex, who thought she'd had as much to drink as Stephanie, was still awake, however, to hear Mrs. Frank's massive old grandfather clock downstairs chime two. She tossed herself again on her side facing the wall and closed her eyes. *What am I worried about?* she thought. *There's nothing here now and Billy's history this time day after tomorrow. It's just about over.* She whispered this last thought over and over and was soon in a fast sleep.

Just about dawn, though, she was awakened by a pressure centered on her chest. The sensation momentarily surprised her because she didn't remember going to sleep on her back.

She opened her eyes and stared into the dead face of a cat, the black and white tom whose pitiful remains they had buried in the garden. The phantom animal moved its face closer to Alex's and opened its mouth, its long sharp teeth standing out in the dark.

Alex quickly realized the horror of the situation for she could almost feel the animal's foul jaws close on her face. "Jesus…God…" she sputtered, turning her head away from the filthy smelling creature on top of her.

She brought her hands up to try to reach the animal to throw it off, but couldn't grasp it.

"What is this shit, now?" she choked. She knew these things could be touched when they were close by. But not now.

After a futile effort to turn her body to the side, she screamed. The animal then vanished, leaving only a foul smell as residue.

Stephanie stirred and then sat up. "What in God's name.

What…Alex?"

"Tom, Stephanie. Or what's left of him." Alex threw her legs over the edge of the bed and sat up. Breathing heavily, she continued. "That goddamned thing was right on top of me. Oh, Jesus, Stephanie," she cried, tears running down both cheeks. "I thought it was…it was going to bite me."

Stephanie rose and sat on the bed beside her roommate, putting her arm around her shoulders. "Alex, this crap can't end soon enough."

"It will." Alex sniffed loudly and wiped tears away from her eyes with her hands. "But in the meantime, we're going to have to be ready for round two today."

And the monster storm, still a five, came on.

Chapter Twenty-Five

At breakfast, Alex and Stephanie ate in silence, not wanting Mrs. Frank to know about the incident with the cat. When the old lady asked Alex how she slept, she answered "Like a log." Stephanie stared at her across the table, her mouth quietly munching Cheerios.

"This is the last day, Mrs. Frank," Alex suddenly said. "When big, bad Billy blows through tonight, it will all be over. Everything will all be gone."

"What about that awful cat noise yesterday?"

"That, too. All of it." Alex rose from the table and headed for the parlor where she parked herself in front of the TV. On the screen two forecasters were predicting Billy's landfall, somewhere on the east coast of Texas, probably close to Galveston.

In her mind, Alex could see Galveston hit directly by a hurricane, a wall of water pouring over the seawall and flooding the areas behind it all the way to Broadway Street. In 1900 there had been no seawall. Now, there was one that wouldn't do much good against Billy's storm surge. And Billy was clearly bigger than either Katrina or Ike.

"They're saying it will come in around ten o'clock tonight," Stephanie remarked, seating herself across the room from Alex. "Maybe even much sooner. It's moving pretty fast."

"When it gets here, we'll certainly know it." Alex thought again about her parents, and then gazed back at the TV screen. Billy was dead on a collision course with Galveston. *Just like I knew it would be,* she thought.

Later that morning at ten o'clock, it began to rain, a steady, blowing rain that obviously indicated that something worse was coming.

Alex was lying on the couch in the living room, reading, when it began. Of course, her roommate had to ask her about it.

"It means Billy's coming, Stephi. You know that," she answered. "You always get rain, whether the storm is coming at you or not."

Stephanie plopped down in a soft chair nearby and threw her legs over the arm. "How long does it last?"

"It lasts until Billy has moved through. That should be sometime early tomorrow morning."

"I guess we're good and safe here."

Alex could tell she was scared. She felt apprehensive herself. Not of the storm. That would be normal. But of something else. Her sixth sense told her something was not quite right. The specter feline earlier had brought this feeling on, like it all had been planned. And the empty, quiet old house was not normal either. It reminded her of a tomb, a tomb from which something could easily emerge.

She put her book aside and sat up. "I imagine most of the streets are clear now." She looked over at her roommate and smiled. "It would be a good time to jog if you don't mind running in the rain."

"I'd drown. You sure seem to have perked up despite all this."

"It's like everything else these past few months, Stephi. You put it out of your mind, as much as possible." She gazed off across the room at the main staircase and wondered if the noisy, little monster from earlier was somewhere upstairs. "Like our little friend from this morning is gone now. So you try to forget it."

They both heard the phones ring, suddenly, in the kitchen and parlor. Mrs. Frank picked up the one in the kitchen.

"Alex, it's your brother." She appeared at the entrance to the living room.

"Okay, Mrs. Frank, I'll take it." She lifted herself from the couch. "I wonder what he wants so soon."

Alex found out from Paul that he and Thomas were going over to a friend's house to help him secure items from a possible flood, but that Elizabeth would be home.

"Thanks for telling me that, Pauli."

"You did say to keep in touch."

"Yes, I did." She hadn't tried to call home since the last

time she talked to her brother. It occurred to her to hang up and try to call back but she was afraid of what the result might be. Instead, she told Paul about the phantom cat.

"You've seen that thing before, haven't you?"

"Yes, Pauli, in the apartment. But that was quite a while ago. And when it showed up this morning, I was not ready for it. But if that's the only thing that comes around, we've got nothing to worry about."

She went back to the couch after she hung up and lay down. "Papa and Pauli are going out in this crap to help a friend. How's that for Christian love?"

"That's just what I'd expect from them, Roomy."

"I guess you're right."

That afternoon, the weather channel announced that Billy's winds had gone down to one hundred eighty-five miles per hour, still catastrophic. Landfall was expected for some time that night.

As she watched Billy's satellite picture, Alex thanked God that her family was thirty-five miles inland and not right at the coast. But those on the coast had been evacuated.

She rose from the chair she was in and stretched out on the couch, where she promptly fell asleep, something she hadn't really wanted to do since her frightful experience that morning was still vivid in her mind. But while Stephanie and Mrs. Frank kept their eyes on the weather reports, she slept for an hour and a half. When she awoke, the rain had intensified.

"Mother of God, it must be coming in sooner than expected," she whispered to herself, hearing the rain beating down on the window awnings outside. She looked at her watch. Three- thirty, not even the middle of the afternoon.

Stephanie, who had been helping Mrs. Frank in the kitchen, appeared and suggested a game of cards, to which Alex agreed. They prepared to play on the kitchen table so they could keep an eye on the TV in the parlor. After three hands of Hearts, though, Alex was getting bored. Mrs. Frank was dealing a fourth hand when the phone rang.

"It's your house, Alex," Stephanie sang out from the parlor. "The number's on the caller ID."

Alex picked up the kitchen phone but there was no

immediate answer.

"Hello," she said again, a little louder. *It must be Pauli preoccupied,* she thought.

"Alex," a faint voice said on the other end.

"What…Mama?"

"Alex…Alex, I'm…I'm…" Now the voice was louder and clearly something was terribly wrong.

"Mama! Mama! What's the matter?" Her voice, now alarmed, rose.

"Alex, I can't find your father. He…He and Paul went over to Otto Krause's house to help him…to help him…"

"Mama, Mama, what's happened?"

Again, there was a pause. The voice, fainter now, continued. "I was getting some things down from the cabinet…the cabinet over the stove and…and I fell. I think I dislocated my shoulder."

"Oh, my God, Mama!" A tear rolled down Alex's face. "Stephanie!" Alex turned to the kitchen table in alarm. "Get your cell phone and try to get Pauli, would you? You know the number." She switched the phone to the other ear. "Mama… Mama, I'm going to try to get Pauli and Papa. Just stay on the line, please."

Alex put the kitchen phone down, and she and Stephanie dialed Paul's and Thomas' numbers on their cell phones, but one phone reached voice mail and the other was busy. "Papa forgot to turn his on, as usual, and Pauli's probably talking to some goddamned chick," Alex said in exasperation. She returned to the phone with her mother.

"Mama, we can't get them."

"Alex, Honey, I think…I think I'm going to faint. I think I'm going to pass out."

"Mama, for God's sake, sit down! I'm…I'm going to come out there." For a moment, Alex hadn't realized what she had just said. She would be driving in pouring down rain over partially flooded streets. It was the only thing she could think of to do, however. "I'll be there as soon as I can get there."

She hung up the phone and turned to her roommate and Mrs. Frank, both of whose faces showed alarm.

"I've got to get out there," she said. "Mama has fallen and hurt herself badly and the guys are nowhere around."

"Alex, call 9-1-1 and get them over there!" Stephanie's voice was a shout.

Quickly, Alex dialed the three numbers. Another busy signal.

"Damn it," she exclaimed. She picked up her cell phone and dialed and so did Stephanie. Again busy signals.

"My God," Mrs. Frank said, obviously feeling helpless. "With the storm coming in, there's probably a whole bunch of problems." Her worried look reflected a feeling that there was something afoot worse than the coming storm.

"I've got to get to her." Alex, now on the verge of tears, wrung her hands. "What a fine time for something like this to happen. I'll…I'll just stay down there with them until this thing passes through. Probably early tomorrow."

"Alex, how are you going to drive in all this rain?" Stephanie asked in a panicky voice.

"I don't think it's rained enough to cause many problems with the elevated roads yet. Hopefully, I can get down there before it does.

Alex left with the rain beating heavily down on the roof of her car. Although it had been raining for some time, now, she had been right. The streets to Highway Ten, the cross-town freeway, were still passable. Once on this elevated highway, she would be all right until she got to Forty-Five South, the Gulf Freeway.

As she had expected she made fairly good time to Forty-Five and beyond. On this southbound highway, she encountered a few cars, all going in the opposite direction. Last minute evacuees? She thought of her parents again.

With the usual traffic absent, she had no trouble making her way through the downtown area and southward. Now it was only a question of time before she reached NASA 1, her turnoff. She wondered how much water she would encounter there.

Suddenly, she felt an intense gloom come over her, a depression the source of which she couldn't pinpoint but one which made her wonder why she was driving through the pouring rain to her parent's house from an obviously safe haven, far from Billy's immediate wrath. And the wound in her shoulder had begun to hurt again. But her mother was obviously in trouble so she tried to put the odd feeling out of her mind.

Coming up on her before she could clearly see it was a barricade in the middle of the highway, announcing that Forty-Five South was closed to everyone except emergency vehicles. She sped on past the barricade and hoped there was no one around.

The closer she got to her turnoff, the blacker the sky in front of her. Her lights were on but they did no good, so she took great care to read the signs as she approached them in the heavy rain.

Her heart lifted when she saw it, NASA 1. She flipped her turning signal and started to turn onto her exit. Slowing almost to a crawl, she noticed water covering the entrance way. She prepared to negotiate the exit ramp slowly, but found that she couldn't turn the wheel any more to make the cut off.

Instantly she was overpowered by a presence which pressed hard against the whole right side of her body and grasped her thigh firmly in skinny, sharp fingers. The car speeded up immediately and passed the cut off, barreling into the rain and darkness straight ahead.

Alex screamed and tried to regain control of the car but it had swerved over to the left toward a lane with very shallow water and was picking up speed.

She knew who was there with her long fingernails ripping painfully through the denim of her capris into her thigh. The other claw was apparently on the wheel to try to steer the car, but Alex, fearing a wreck to which immediate aid would be almost impossible still struggled to regain the steering. But now she felt Johanna's foot on top of hers, pressing the accelerator, making the car go even faster. The presence, however, was not yet visible.

Alex's immediate fear was that the monster would bite her again on her right shoulder and she couldn't see her coming. As much as she could, she scooted her body to the left, screaming again as loud as she could, while trying to retain some control of the car. Tears in her eyes and sick with horror, she emptied her stomach on the side of the door and her left leg. Trying desperately to gain some control of herself, she felt weaker and weaker. A new sensation suddenly came over her.

"Goddamn you, don't you try to possess me," she screamed again, fighting the wheel as hard as she could. Her body, in her seatbelt, had limited movement and she could feel Johanna pressing more and more against her. In the meantime, the car moved back toward the center of the road.

She did not see the barricade through the heavy rain and her concentration on the thing beside her now clawing her wounded left shoulder. When she hit it, she sent pieces of it flying to either side of the road. A moment later she became aware of a police car, siren and lights on, behind her. She put her left foot toward the brake to stop the car if she could, but found it was blocked by the presence of Johanna, whose body was now visible between her and the wheel.

The hideous head had appeared just below hers, its mouth open belching the usual filthy water with dead eyes aimed upwards. And the stench, slight at first, was now overpowering.

In vain, Alex screamed again. "God, she's trying to possess me!" Again summoning as much strength as she could she tried to turn the car to the left to strike the guard rail, but found this to be a futile gesture as now the thing had control of most of her body. Suddenly, the car swerved back across the left side of the road, still picking up speed.

She could hear the police car behind her using its loud speaker but she couldn't make out what was said through the noise of the rain and her own frantic struggles.

The thing now buried its claw into Alex's right side and thrust down on the accelerator to make the car go even faster. Alex threw her body forward in a vain effort to push the corpse on top of her off and onto the side of the seat. This effort achieved some success as the foot left the accelerator. Now she put her own foot next to the accelerator pedal to check any movement of Johanna's toward it.

But the thing's dead face appeared again immediately before hers as it clasped Alex's neck in its claw. Gritting her teeth, she let go of the wheel and threw her body against Johanna and succeeded in pushing the thing off to the side this time.

Oh, Jesus. What's she up to now? Alex thought. She knew Johanna had enough strength to crush both her and the car but obviously she was taking her somewhere. And she knew very well where they were going. To Galveston. To her death.

The speeding car began making its way through the water toward the right side of the road once again. Alex grabbed the wheel, conscious of the thing's claws still on her, digging into her. She could feel blood running down her right side. Since the car was moving to the right, she turned the wheel to the right to run off the road but something restricted her from doing this. Only gradually did the car move toward the right.

Out of nowhere, something appeared ahead. Alex, her eyes on the road ahead as well as the presence by her, did not notice it immediately for it was not in the road but off beside it. A circular apparition moved through the rain slowly toward the road. It was not until she was just about to it that she recognized the deadly swirls of Stehle's door.

Terror enveloped her now completely for she knew immediately what was going to happen. She screamed again and again and jerked the wheel sharply to the left. The car's wheels turned to the left almost at a ninety-degree angle to the car as it collided solidly with another road barrier that Alex had not seen.

The heavy wooden crossbar, hurled into the air by the impact, shattered Alex's windshield and speared the place in the seat where Johanna's presence had been. In the meantime, the car spun to the side of the road and finally stopped.

Alex was struck by flying glass and her head hit the steering wheel when the car jerked to a stop. Semi-conscious and bleeding from a number of wounds, she heard policemen approaching her car and opening its doors. Before she could move, she slipped to the seat in a dead faint.

She awakened, she knew not how long after she had passed out, in an ambulance, its siren easily recognizable in the still pouring rain. Slowly, she looked around in the dark. She made out two figures, one of them just next to her and the other sitting close by. Groaning, she moved her hand up to her stomach.

"Miss Alexandra Zunker?"

"Yes...Yes...?"

"I'm Deputy Fillmore of the Harris County Sheriff's Office. I must say you gave us quite a time back there." He informed Alex that she was under arrest for running through barricades and evading arrest. He then informed her of her Miranda rights.

"Did you understand your rights?" he asked her.

"Yes…Yes Sir."

"What was that all about?" he asked.

"I…I…My mother. My mother was hurt and I was on my way to her house. Somehow…Somehow…I missed…"

"Is this your mother on your identification?"

"Yes, Sir." Alex could hear the wind picking up but the rain seemed to have slackened a bit. She wondered about Billy and how far it was off shore. And she wondered about Johanna. Was she somewhere nearby? Am I…Am I badly hurt?" She tried to raise up.

"We don't know that yet," the other figure just by her said. He gently put a hand on her arm. "We're on our way to the emergency room at St. John's now. We should be there soon.

"I need to call my family…"

"We have a call in to them, Miss Zunker. They're going to meet us at the hospital."

"You contacted…contacted them?"

"Yes, Ma'am. Right after we put you in the ambulance."

Alex lay quiet for a moment and wondered what was going to happen to her. With these two men in the ambulance with her, Johanna, of course, wouldn't be around. But she wondered where she was and what she was going to do next.

She turned her head slowly to the left. "Did I…Did I cause much damage?"

"Well, you tore up a couple of barricades and led us on a merry chase." The officer nearby changed his position. "Did you not hear the sirens behind you, Miss Zunker?"

"I couldn't hear much of anything but the rain, Sir."

"Did you see the lights behind you?"

"No…No, Sir. I was trying to concentrate on the road ahead." Alex realized the lie she told and wondered if the officer would buy it. "I…I missed my turnoff and I was looking for a place to turn around."

"While picking up speed?"

"Yes…Yes, Sir. I was trying to get to the next exit as fast

as I could. The weather was getting worse and I had to get to my parent's home." Alex could see very little of the deputy in the shadows and she wondered what he was thinking about..

"The man next to her suddenly put a cold pack on her head. "Here," he said. "This should make that bump on the head feel a little better.

"Thanks."

"Miss Zunker, where do your parents live?"

"443 Peachtree Avenue. Close to the Kima Highway."

"And how do you get there from Highway Forty-Five?"

Alex wondered what the officer was up to. "I get off at NASA 1 and go down…down to Highway 145, then turn south for two miles and Peachtree Avenue is…"

"Yes, I know where Peachtree Avenue is." The officer was writing something with the aid of a penlight. Alex wondered what kind of a ticket she would get. Or if she would be taken to jail.

Nothing else was said until they arrived at the St. John's Hospital emergency room, sooner than Alex had expected. Attendants brought her in and then wheeled her into one of the rooms. Surprisingly there were not that many people there.

When the attendant turned the gurney sideways from the door, Alex saw her parents and brother enter the room. She suddenly shook with horror. "Mama. Mama, are you all right?"

"Yes, Honey. How about you?" Elizabeth walked over and put her hand on Alex's head.

"I…I…had a wreck on the Gulf Freeway, trying to get to the house." Slowly she looked around the room. Temporarily, she was alone with her family. "I got a call. I got a call from you, saying that you were lying on the floor helpless, helpless and…and hurt. You sounded horrible."

"What, Alex? What about this call?" Elizabeth's face turned dark.

"I see it…I see it now, Mama." Now Alex realized what had been done. "That call came from Johanna, Mama. She was in the car with me. She was trying to kill me, Papa?"

Thomas and Paul had advanced to her side, both with worried expressions on their faces.

"Papa. Papa, I know you know about Johanna. Pauli, this

was it. This was what she's been leading up to. All summer, Pauli. That was where she wanted me to be, in that storm, drowning."

"What are you saying, Sis? That Johanna was in the car with you?"

"Yes, Pauli. In the car with me. Speeding down that highway toward Galveston. She would not let me get off the road or even crash the car into the side-rail. The police were behind me but they couldn't do anything."

"Alexandra, you say this thing lured you into your car and down here with a phone call?"

"Yes, Papa. I had been having trouble recently getting through to you. I had to call Josh one time and then I got through after I talked with Pastor Gerlach. After that Everything seemed okay. So when that call came through from Mama, I really thought she was in trouble."

"Alexandra, how could that thing manipulate the phone lines?"

"I don't know, Papa. But she did. She sounded just like Mama over the phone. She even knew Otto Krause's name and that you and Pauli had gone over there. Oh, Jesus, I panicked and…and…"

Just then a doctor entered the room followed by a nurse pushing a cart carrying supplies for bandaging wounds. "Could I trouble you to step outside for a few minutes?" the doctor said.

The doctor examined Alex's head as well as other parts of her body and then said she was basically all right. The nurse dressed Alex's wounds, picking glass out of two of them. The doctor told her she had no concussion and she could take a sedative. As for now, the nurse continued with what seemed a never-ending job. He re-dressed Alex's shoulder wound, asking where she had gotten it. Thinking fast, she replied that her dog had bitten her while playing and hoped he wouldn't ask any more questions about it. At last, she received some pain medications and a sedative.

A few minutes later, she was taken to an empty room on the third floor, leaving all of the rooms in emergency open for possible storm victims. The new room, on the north side of the hospital, had a window through which Alex could see, in what light there was, the first signs of Billy's wrath as it moved ashore almost forty miles to the east. Trees close by the hospital indicated the strong wind and most had lost limbs. Already, the street in front of the hospital was filled with debris, much of which was carried down the street by the flooding rains.

This is as good a place as any to ride this damned thing out, she thought. She still hadn't recovered from the shock of earlier events and she wondered if Johanna could find her in that hospital room.

The sedative had begun its work and now she felt sleepy. Despite her apprehension, she soon fell asleep, with her family close by in the room.

Once again, she began to dream. She stood in Mrs. Frank's house at the front door at the head of the entrance hall. It was dark, inside and out, and she could hear rain and wind outside the house.

She tried the light switches beside the door but they would not turn on. Although all was pitch black she could see somewhat from a modicum of light, the source of which she could not identify.

They must be in bed, she thought, but then two flashlight beams appeared at the end of the hall. These began to come toward her through the darkness. The light that was there illuminated Stephanie in front, but although she flashed her beam directly at Alex, she did not acknowledge her roommate's presence. She was saying something over her shoulder to Mrs. Frank that Alex could not hear.

The two ladies advanced, heading apparently for the front door, but when Stephanie reached the large hall mirror, she stopped. She appeared startled, and turned her head to the right.

Suddenly a large entity poured out of the mirror and slammed Stephanie's body against the staircase. Then it formed up in front of the mirror and right away Alex knew who it was.

She watched, helplessly, as Johanna, newly returned home from her trip down the Gulf Freeway, lifted Stephanie easily in her arms and slammed her body to the hall floor. Becoming invisible, she continued her assault upon the fallen girl, apparently kicking her in the stomach and abdomen, and then picking her up to throw her down again.

Alex tried to intervene, but she couldn't feel anything; her physical presence wasn't there. She tried to put her body in front of Stephanie's, but the maneuver made no difference. It was hopeless. With tremendous force, the invisible presence of Johanna continued to pummel Stephanie mercilessly.

Then, Alex was startled by a high screaming voice out of the darkness nearby. Mrs. Frank, who had been behind Stephanie in the hall, now realizing what was going on, was trying to intervene. Alex tried to yell at her but her voice could not be heard.

"Goddamn you, you monster, you leave that girl alone!" Mrs. Frank moved forcefully toward Stephanie, who had fallen again to the floor against the staircase. "You filthy, vicious bastard, get away from her!" Her voice rose to a screech.

Mrs. Frank succeeded in covering Stephanie with her body. "Goddamn you to hell, you monster. Now you can go to work on me!" Mrs. Frank put both arms around Stephanie, but her head was turned sharply to the left and she was still screaming. "You want to beat an old lady to death! Go on, you filthy shit! I'm ready. Go on!"

Alex could feel the tears streaming down her face as she watched helplessly.

The monstrous presence, however, did not attack Mrs. Frank, but left, quickly, by what means Alex couldn't tell. Almost as quickly, she awoke.

She rose up in bed and looked around. All three of her family members were asleep in chairs nearby.

The sedative weighed heavily on her and she lay back again. She wanted to call Mrs. Frank's house but before she could reach the phone, she was asleep again. This time she didn't awake until well into the next morning.

She awoke to see sunlight streaming through. "We thought we would let you sleep," her mother said by her side. Billy went through last night between ten and eleven."

"It must have just gone through when I woke up," Alex muttered.

Thomas appeared beside Elizabeth and informed Alex that she had been released on a PR bond pending a hearing at a later date, so she was free to go home with her parents that day.

"We can't get hold of Stephanie or Mrs. Frank," Paul said, coming through the door with his cell phone in his hand. "There has been no answer and I've called three times now."

Oh, my God, Alex thought.

"They brought you some breakfast a little while ago." Elizabeth stepped aside and moved a tall portable table up to the bedside. "We figured you'd be hungry since you apparently haven't eaten anything since early yesterday."

"Oh, lord, Mama. I saw something horrible last night."

"What? You had a dream?"

"I hope to God it was, Mama." Pulling the table with the food close to her, Alex quickly related her dream about the savage attack on Stephanie to her family at her bedside.

"That was a dream, Honey. You weren't really there."

"I'm not so sure, Mama. That thing's pulled all kinds of stunts since it first came around. I'm afraid this is another one of them."

"Then we need to find Stephanie and Mrs. Frank pretty quick," Paul said. "I'll try to call again."

"Try the apartment, Pauli. They might be there since Billy's long gone." Alex began to eat breakfast, slowly and deliberately. While she ate, she continued. "That thing is gone now, along with Billy."

"God has been good to you, Baby," Thomas said, gently. "You could have easily been killed yesterday."

"I know, Papa. How well I know."

"As soon as they release you, we need to go home. There's apparently been massive flooding and wind damage with this hurricane."

"I'm sure of that, Papa. If it's just…"

Just then Paul came back through the door. "I got Mrs. Frank," he said, holding his cell phone up. "She just got home."

Alex took the phone. "Mrs. Frank? This is Alex. My God, we've been trying to get you. What's been going on?"

"Alexandra? Precious Jesus, Honey, how are you? I tried to call you last night, but I couldn't get you. I tried your parent's house as well as your cell phone."

"We've all been at the hospital, Mrs. Frank. I had an accident and got banged up pretty bad. I'm…I'm all right now, though. We're going home pretty soon."

"Oh, dear God, Honey. Stephanie's in Memorial Northwest in Intensive Care. I stayed with her all last night and I just got home."

Alex nearly dropped the phone and fell back in the bed. Waves of nausea rose up in her and she had trouble catching her breath. "Oh, Jesus, Mrs. Frank," she sobbed.

"Yes, Honey. Last night, well after dark, the lights went out in the storm. We had trouble finding flashlights but when we did, we decided to go upstairs to bed. We were both so worried about you."

Alex, tears streaming down her face, listened, both hands on the small phone.

"We were on our way down the hall to the staircase when Stephanie was suddenly attacked by that thing. That Johanna thing. It came out of nowhere and started beating that poor girl to a pulp."

"I know, Mrs. Frank, I know." Alex sobbed. "I saw it. I saw it in a dream, probably as it was happening. I was there but I couldn't do anything."

"I managed to cover Stephanie with my body and that thing left." Now Mrs. Frank sounded tired. "My God, I've never seen anything like that in all my life. If I live to be a hundred, I'll never see anything more horrible."

"Mrs. Frank. Yesterday evening, Johanna attacked me in my car on the Gulf Freeway. Apparently, she was trying to lead me to Galveston, or into the heart of the storm and somehow drown me the way she had said. That's how I got hurt. She caused me to wreck my car when it hit a barricade."

"Oh, dear God." Mrs. Frank replied in a solemn, quiet voice. "I know it was that Johanna. Stephanie screamed her name. And I screamed her name. She was pounding that poor girl. I tried to stop her but I couldn't even see her."

"I know. I know." From what Alex could tell, after Johanna had left her in her wrecked car, she had come back to Mrs. Frank's house and vented her fury on Stephanie after she had caused the lights to go out. She realized now that both encounters had been attempts to kill both girls. She had nearly succeeded.

Mrs. Frank went on to say that Stephanie would probably be in the hospital for quite a while since she had serious injuries. She had told the attendants that Stephanie had fallen from the second floor landing while changing a light bulb. Apparently, they had bought the story as she had not been asked again.

"I'm going over to that hospital this afternoon if I can get there."

"Good, Honey. If they let you see her, I'm sure she'll be glad to see you. We've both been so worried about you. I'm all worn out. I barely could drive home." Mrs. Frank paused a moment. "I've got to get to bed, but call me after you see her."

"I will, Mrs. Frank. Thank you ever so much for everything you've done."

Alex closed the phone slowly and related what had happened to Stephanie to her parents. When she had finished, they stood speechless.

"As soon as we get home and find out about our house, I'm going over there, Papa."

"I'm going with you," Paul said.

With that resolve, Alex, shaken to where she couldn't finish her breakfast, lay back in the bed to await her dismissal from the hospital. She didn't know how badly Stephanie was hurt, but she knew all too well what Johanna was capable of. With that in mind, she closed her eyes and feared the worst.

Epilogue

Alex was dismissed later that morning and the Zunkers made their way home through streets flooded by more than seventeen inches of rain. Two blocks from their house, they had to park the car and wade to their front doorstep. Their house was high enough, however, so water had not gotten into it. And, fortunately, the waters had already begun to recede. Wreckage from the destructive winds lay everywhere.

After Alex had rested for an hour and eaten lunch, she and Paul returned to the car and headed across town to Memorial Hospital Northwest, close by the Houston Heights. The drive took over two hours as they were forced to make detours because of flooded conditions and debris littering the road. Also, they encountered the first evacuees returning home, although they weren't supposed to.

At the hospital, Alex gained entrance to the intensive care unit by telling a nurse that she was a first cousin. Inside, she was shocked to see Stephanie's condition. She had a chest tube and an NG tube, but she could still talk and she was awake.

Alex put her hand gently on Stephanie's head. "I talked with Mrs. Frank," she said quietly. "She told me what happened." Alex wouldn't mention her dream until later.

Stephanie looked up and tried to smile. "Johanna…Johanna tried to kill me," she said, slowly, painfully.

Paul, who had apparently sneaked in, moved up and put his hands on his sister's back. Alex turned to him and then back to her roommate.

"I know. Don't try to talk if it hurts you."

"If it hadn't been for Mrs. Frank," she continued, "she would have killed me."

Stephanie tried to smile again. "You look like shit. What happened to you?"

"So, you noticed." Alex grinned. "If it hadn't been for every cop in Southeast Texas, she would have killed me, too. She was all over me in the car and caused a wreck. The cops were right there. Thank God. They arrested me later, but I could have hugged every one of them."

"Oh, God." Stephanie glanced over at Paul who stood at the foot of her bed and then back at her roommate. "You, too? We wondered what had happened to you when we couldn't reach you on the phone." Stephanie began to breathe in and out deeply, but she continued. "She came out of that tall mirror by the front door in Mrs. Frank's house and hit me like a ton of bricks. She knocked me against the staircase so hard I thought I had been hit by a truck. I couldn't even see her. I was screaming…screaming as loud as I could. And I could hear Mrs. Frank screaming. I…I tried to get away from that thing but I couldn't. Finally, she threw me to the floor and hit me with what felt like her whole body, only it weighed a ton. She was crushing me when Mrs. Frank tried to pick me up. She was screaming…screaming 'get away from her, you monster. Goddamn you, you get away from that girl.' As hurt as I was, I was afraid she was going to have a heart attack."

"No. No," Alex interrupted, quietly. "She has a great heart."

"Finally, Mrs. Frank covered me with her whole body and that thing left. And what happened next, I don't know. When I came to my senses, I was here."

"We can consider ourselves lucky, I guess." Alex turned to her brother. "It's obvious she was out to kill both of us and she didn't." She paused. Then she bowed her head and said a prayer. She still hurt, but she knew her roommate hurt more. Hurt by a thing she did not understand. Alex wasn't sure she understood much about anything that had happened either. "She's gone now, Stephi,' she said, a tear rolling down her cheek. "I know it. I can feel it. She's gone."

Paul stepped over to the other side of Stephanie's bed and bent down and kissed her. "You need to get up from there. We've got a date for Sylvan Beach. Remember?"

Stephanie smiled again, as much as she could. "That's news to me, Junior," she said. "But when I get out of here, I'll give it some consideration."

Alex smiled, too. But then something else came to her mind and clouded it.

"I saw Stehle's Door," she said, looking from her brother to Stephanie. "For the first time in years, I saw Stehle's Door.

"What? Where?" Paul's eyes were saucers, but apparently, Stephanie either hadn't heard her or didn't understand.

"On the Gulf Freeway. It was there. I think Johanna brought it. I don't think it just happened to be there. She was leading me to it when I had the wreck."

"My God, Sis. Do you think she was trying to put you through that thing into… How…I mean how could she do that?"

"I don't know, Pauli, but it was there. I'm sure it was part of her plan for my death. I only saw it in an instant. I had my wreck and that's all I remember."

A nurse appeared at Stephanie's side. "Only one at a time," she admonished.

"I know. I'm sorry." Alex turned around to her brother and motioned to him. Then she bent down to Stephanie and kissed her on her forehead. "We were just leaving anyway."

Alex and Paul headed for the apartment. On the way, they talked about what had happened in the past few hours and then they talked about what had been happening over the past months. Although Alex knew everything was over, she was still apprehensive. They wouldn't find anything at the apartment or at Mrs. Frank's house, but what about the future? Would everything remain at peace? There were still unanswered questions.

For example, what about Billy? He had caused considerable damage, in Florida, Texas and Louisiana. The radio was calling him over and over again the worst hurricane on record, his two hundred and five mile an hour winds worse than even Wilma's one hundred seventy-five. He had almost destroyed a hurricane hunter. Was he the storm that had hit Galveston so many years ago? Was he a phantom, too?

Billy had brought the people of the storm months before. Now they were gone, their warnings heeded somewhat, at least by Alex, Stephanie and Mrs. Frank.

And Johanna Diehls? Her presence was also ended, after

more than a century of habitation in Mrs. Frank's house. But had she manipulated Stehle's Door and used it to try to kill Alex? And did Alex really go back through Stehle's Door and cause Johanna's death in the Galveston storm. Or was this just another trick? There was no way to tell now.

And what of Joseph Stehle's horrendous doorway into other dimensions? It was obvious it had been around in some form for quite some time. Could it be manipulated by the dead? And, if so, what about the living? After all, it wasn't gone. It couldn't be gone. It was as much a part of this world as night and day. And so it would remain, an everlasting presence, question mark and threat.

Acknowledgments

Thanks to the following for their support and advice for this novel:

~Mr. Newton Cole, instructor of Architecture and Engineering graphics

~Mr. David Bordelon, instructor of Biology and Physics

~Mr. Craig Hallmark, instructor of Law Enforcement and Criminal Justice

~Ms. Linda Lagrone, Head Librarian, for her support and help with both novels.

Enjoy an excerpt from

Stehle's Door

Also by William O'Brien

Stehle's Door

Prologue

St. Louis, 1925

The old man nervously stirred his coffee and glanced, annoyed, at the ceiling. Not again, tonight, he thought.

A heavy thump overhead shook the entire house.

"He's at it again, do you hear me? He's at it again!"

The angry voice on the stairs caused the man to spill some of his coffee when he put it down. He hurried into the hall, slamming the door behind him. This was the last warning. After this, he would send for the police.

"Go back to your room, Mrs. Dunbar," the man said, brushing past the agitated old woman who had reached the bottom of the stairs. "I'll speak with Mr. Stehle. We'll condone this behavior no further."

He climbed the stairs to the first landing and then hesitated before going any further. When he started again, he heard a curious sloshing sound directly above him. Alarmed, he bounded up the remainder of the stairs and turned to his right toward the first door off the hall.

Before he reached the door, however, it burst open and a large wave of vile smelling brown water rolled out, flooding the hall and spilling onto the stairwell.

"What in the name of God!" the man bellowed, groping his way through the open door. He waded through inch-deep water into the sitting room of a small apartment.

"Mr. Stehle? Mr. Stehle?" He called to no answer. Since the bedroom door was closed, he turned back toward the hall.

Abruptly, he stopped. He wanted to scream but somehow he couldn't. He just stared.

"What in the name of holy God?"

On the floor in front of him by the hall door lay a man, newly-drowned, water still pouring from his mouth and nose.

Chapter One

At two o'clock Sunday afternoon, the Zunker Aerostar pulled into the muddy, puddle-strewn parking lot of the Friendswood Flea Market, a malodorous, sprawling affair on the outskirts of a Houston suburb. The van jerked to a halt in a mud puddle and Alexandra and Paul spilled out to go their separate ways while Thomas, their father, cursed the mud and reminded his wife, Elizabeth, that he needed a gift for a distant relative. Then, he hollered through the window at the kids to remember to meet back at the van in two hours.

Paul wasn't thinking about the prearranged meeting, though. Thirty dollars of Christmas money rich, he would head straight to the large, central room where the itinerant dealers set up their tables. He knew anything could be found there. There he would find the new dealer his friend, Joey, had told him about. Or so he hoped.

Joey had said this guy had "neat stuff," particularly old military stuff. Paul wanted to repeat what Joey had done the week before — come away with something not only inexpensive, but "neat," like Joey's World War II German parachutist's badge. In Joey's words, something "awesome."

Fourteen-year-old Alex raced her brother to the outside door. When she got to the door, she turned and pressed her body tightly against it.

"To get in, you'll have to move me," she said, giggling and flipping a strawberry-blond wisp of hair out of her face.

"That'll be easy," her younger brother Paul replied. He grabbed the door handle with both hands and pulled.

Alex easily gave up and joined her brother inside. Together they broke into a hurried walk down a long hallway, Alex lagging behind.

"Wait, Pauli, I'll go with you." She caught up with her brother and matched him step for step.

They were a curious pair, for brother and sister. Alex was

tall, almost a head taller than her brother. At fourteen, she already had the body of a woman. Paul, however, one year younger, was small and slight. Physically, he was still a little boy.

"You know, you'll be lucky if this guy has anything," Alex said, out of breath, glancing at the shops on either side of the hallway. "Besides, Joey's Nazi badge is probably a fake, knowing him."

"How do you know?" Paul tilted his blond head upwards to his right, still walking. He didn't mind having to look up to talk to her but he did mind her treating him like a kid. She often told him that big sisters were supposed to be bossy but he still didn't buy it.

Alex spoke without turning her head. "Because Joey's full of bullshit. You know he never has half the stuff he says he has. And you believe everything he says." She turned her pretty head in her brother's direction.

Paul ignored her remarks and turned into another hallway fronting all of the antique shops. At the end of the hall were the massive doors to the main area.

"Come on, Alex, if you're coming." Paul began to jog toward the doors.

At the large, crowded, main vending area, both kids looked for the new dealer. Seeing only familiar faces among the sellers, they began to make their way through the crowd, all the time studying dealer's tables for a sign of anything new. Sunday crowds at the flea market were usually dense, but this one was worse than usual. Many people, it seemed, had come to the market because they couldn't do the usual Sunday afternoon outdoors things, like work in the yard. Others had just come out of the wet weather. The Zunkers were the former.

Paul felt uncomfortable in the big crowd and hoped he could find his seller and get out of this heavily crowded room. As long as he could remember, crowds had made him nervous.

Alex playfully bent down, grabbed the belt loop on the back of Paul's trousers and let him pull her through the crowd. Every now and then, she would lean back, causing Paul to stop in his tracks.

"Knock it off, will you. Help me find this guy." He twisted

out of his sister's grip. "He should be along the side. Joey said he had some stuff hanging up." Paul stood on his tiptoes in a futile attempt to see over or through the crowd.

"Won't find him that way, Shrimp." Alex grinned and stepped up into Paul's face. He turned away by reflex, feeling just a pinch of resentment. Everybody, it seemed, picked on him because he was short. His sixth grade teacher, almost as short as he was, had called him Dennis the Menace, mainly for his looks. And, of course, patted him on the head while she said it.

"Come on, follow me!" Paul made his way through the crowd toward the end of the building.

At the end of the large room, opposite the main snack bar, Paul sighted a large Turkish flag hanging on the wall behind a row of vendor's tables. The dense crowd obscured his view of the sellers behind the tables but since he had never seen the flag there before, he knew that its owner must be a new dealer. And flags usually meant military stuff.

"That's got to be him," he said, under his breath. Just like Joey said, he thought, stuff pinned up behind his table. Paul had thought that pinning stuff to the wall was illegal, but he guessed it wasn't. After all, it was a good way to attract curious people to your goods.

Alex had seen the flag, too. "Look, Pauli, Turkey," she said, and pointed. She began to outpace her brother again toward the flag. "You know," she said over her shoulder, "in World War I, the Turks were ..." In mid sentence, she stopped and pressed both hands against her stomach.

Directly behind her, Paul almost ran into her. Avoiding the collision, he placed both hands on the sides of her hips and maneuvered himself around her. Then, he noticed her bent-over position and expression.

"What's the matter, Sis, Papa's Liebfraumilch again?" He laughed. "You know, some gas might clear this place out pretty good.

"Pauli, I don't want to go over there."

"What?"

"I said I don't want to go over there." She turned toward him, her usual smile replaced by a wrinkled-up expression. "You go on. I'm going over to the snack bar and sit. I think the crowd has thinned out over there."

"Okay, but you're going to miss some interesting stuff."

"Just go, Squirt." She gave her brother a weak smile.

But Paul wanted to head her off. "Sis, just lay the fart. Don't wait until we get into the van or meet Mama and Papa."

"Well, you're probably right for once, Little Brother." She straightened up and pulled her jeans up at the belt loops. "I'm going over to the snack bar and get something that might dilute the acid."

"Okay, Sis, sure. I'll be with you in a minute and we'll look at some of the other stuff." He turned toward the vendor with the flag and began to walk slowly in his direction, a bit sorry that Alex wasn't with him. After all, she got excited about oddities and antiques almost as much as he did.

When he reached the row of tables against the wall, he noticed that two people stood in front of his dealer who sat back in his chair and examined the two customers before him. His head almost reached the bottom of the Turkish flag hanging immediately behind him. He was a slight man with a moustache, wearing slovenly clothes. And to Paul, he was a new dealer for sure, for he was a perfect stranger.

He walked up to the table and began to scan the merchandise before him. On the table was a small collection of bottles, all old, some obviously dug up. Also, there was a small case of foreign military insignias, some of which appeared old. Next to this was a larger case of Nazi artifacts, the source of Joey's famous badge, no doubt. Various other artifacts lay about the dealer's two tables, some military, but most antique tools and jewelry. A sign in front of the dealer stated that he bought antique and modern militaria. Paul picked up a piece near him and began to turn it over in his hand.

"That's a buckle for a shoulder belt, fella. I don't know how old it is." The new dealer's voice startled Paul. It was a little too high pitched.

He looked up from the article into the man's pale blue eyes, encased in wrinkles. He noticed the man sat completely still when he talked. Not even a twitch. A bit unnerved, Paul gently laid the shiny brass buckle down on the table. "It's not marked, is it?" he asked in an uneven voice.

"Doesn't need to be. It's some military academy, I think." Finally, the man wrinkled his nose and looked away. "Probably came off a drum strap," he said toward the crowd milling nearby.

Paul noticed that the man never completely closed his mouth when he talked. And his eyes darted nervously back and forth between Paul and the other two customers before him.

Nodding, the two earlier clients put down the pieces they were looking at and walked off. Paul stepped to the front of the table where they had been.

"Anything you looking for, fella? Anything special?" The dealer shifted in his chair so suddenly that he surprised Paul.

"Yeah — Yeah. I was looking for military stuff that's a little earlier than this, like..."

"How early?" The man settled back in his chair again and became perfectly still. "

That belt buckle's pretty old, isn't it?" Paul pointed across the table at a piece that showed obvious signs of rust.

"Don't know. Could be." The man moved his hands behind his head and leaned back in his chair again. "It came out of an estate full of old stuff."

"Could it be as late as World War I?" Paul began to be excited. Here was a guy who obviously had some neat stuff. Glancing around the table, he began to spot things he hadn't seen before, things that looked interesting. The cluttered table offered a veritable treasure hunt.

"World War I. Spanish American. Indian War. Anything in there." The man watched Paul even though other customers had moved up to his tables. "It's kind of a common buckle."

"Uh, do you happen to have anything from the Civil War?" Paul began to scan the table even closer. "Like maybe those buttons over there." He visualized, in the back of his mind, himself with an artifact much better than anything Joey had.

"Those are pre-World War I. They're aught two's'" The dealer moved his hands into his pockets, still leaning back in his chair. "Don't get much Civil War stuff. Goes pretty fast. You know? Everyone wants it. Can't keep it."

"Yeah, I know. I sure don't see it. In fact, I've seen it only in museums." Paul continued to scrutinize the table, talking absent-mindedly. "I've seen a lot there."

"Let's see, Civil War." The dealer aimed two pale blue marbles at the ceiling. "Nope, not now. That stuff goes real quick, like I said." The man twitched his nose and sniffed, loudly, reminding Paul of a rabbit. "Wait a minute." He sat straight up and reached down into a small case by his chair. "Guy came by and sold me these before lunch. Took the first bid I gave him and left soon's he got the money." He plopped down a packet of letters bound with what Paul thought looked like kite twine.

"You wouldn't believe how cheap I got these." The vendor put four chair legs on the floor and looked at Paul. "They're kind of military, written by a military man. I got a good deal on them so I'm going to do the same for you. Gimme twenty dollars." The dealer again leaned back in his chair and folded his hands across his chest.

"Are — Are they real?" Paul couldn't believe his eyes or his ears. Civil War letters for twenty dollars? It was too good to be true. He picked them up and began to examine them.

"Look real to me." The man at last began to eye the other customers near his tables.

Turning the letters over in his hands, Paul noticed that much of the writing he could see was faded. Also, the envelope on top of the stack was torn so badly that a portion of it dangled loosely out of the side of the packet. The dangling portion had a blue stamp with a picture of Jefferson Davis in profile. Paul brought the stamp up close and looked at it.

"God! These are Confederate." Paul's wide-eyed face turned to the dealer who said nothing. "Sure, I'll give you twenty dollars for these."

He fumbled for his wallet, not daring to say any more and somewhat sorry for what he had said already. He did not want the dealer to go back on his price because he found out what the letters really were. After all, he might not have noticed the stamp. His heart beating rapidly, he grabbed two tens from his billfold and laid them on the table.

"Twenty dollars," he said, barely able to conceal his excitement.

The dealer again said nothing but grabbed the money and

dropped it into the metal box behind his table.

Turning and walking away, the letters clutched tightly in both hands, Paul began to search the crowd for Alex. Then he remembered she had gone to the snack bar to sit down. He made his way through the still-growing crowd toward the large soft drink sign blinking over the far end of the main room. In his excitement he hadn't noticed that the crowd had grown so much that there was barely room to walk, something that had always annoyed him on earlier visits to the market. Now, however, he was walking on air. He still couldn't believe his luck, finding a Civil War artifact for only twenty dollars. He couldn't wait to tell Alex. And he couldn't wait to tell Joey.

His sister was not in the snack bar. Instead, she was sitting in a chair near the corner of the building, next to the restrooms.

She sat, motionless, looking straight at him with a wide-eyed stare that seemed not to see him at all. As a matter of fact, Paul thought momentarily that she looked plain scared.

"What the hell is the matter with you?" He asked under his breath, wondering where Alex's usual smile had gone. Although he knew that everything was all right, he couldn't help but feel just a bit uneasy.

He walked toward her, skirting tables and wedging himself between occupied chairs. Alex's face did not change expression until he was right in front of her.

"Well, what'd I miss?" Her face screwed up in a smirk that started to break out in open laughter.

Any apprehension Paul had felt vanished. Same old Alex.

"Is our boy Joey right for the first time in his life?"

"You wouldn't believe it, Sis. Civil War stuff. Mexican War stuff. Even Revolution and Napoleon stuff." Paul gestured furiously, while his voice rose and his eyes grew wider. "World War I. Spanish American War. All the neat pieces. You wouldn't believe it. You would have peed all over yourself you would of been so excited to see it."

Alex just crossed her arms in her sitting position and looked up into his face. "Yeah? And little-bitty sawed off liars are the worst of all," she said, softly, in a mocking voice.

"Seriously, Sis. He did have some neat pieces." Paul came quickly down to earth. "I got one."

"What did you get from that guy, Pauli?" She clasped her hands together, stood up and absentmindedly scanned the crowd. Then, she tilted her head downward, her blue eyes studying Paul's like an approving teacher, the smirk not altogether gone from her face.

"A bunch of letters, Dearie." Paul rose on his tiptoes, hands on his hips.

"Oh, boy. Letters, Pauli?" She turned to the side in feigned bewilderment. "They're probably fakes."

"Not these, Sis." He brought the packet out and turned the stamped fragment toward her. "There. That's a real stamp." He was annoyed, partly because his sister had pricked his balloon and partly because she had cast doubts on his treasure.

Alex took the letters and studied them. "You know, Pauli, they do look old."

"Sure they're old. Look at this stamp." Paul shoved the stamped portion toward his sister's face. "This, my dear, is Jefferson Davis, the Confederate president."

"Yep, that's him, all right." Her smirk had become more pronounced. She handed the letters back to Paul and turned away, giggling into her hand.

Brother, dear, you can buy an old stamp and put it on anything," she said. "And I wouldn't be surprised if the stamp was a fake."

"Fake, huh. I don't think so." He put the letters carefully into his jacket pocket. "You don't know anything about these."

"Sure I do." Alex crossed her arms over her chest and stared downwards into Paul's face, fixing him in his tracks, this time she was a teacher with an unruly student. "I know that creeps set up out here to sell junk to the naive and the unknowing, namely you and that knucklehead, Joey." She raised up on her tiptoes, momentarily, to look about the room. "I'll see you in a moment, Pauli. I need to visit the little girl's room." She turned and walked toward a crowd standing around a water fountain between the restroom doors.

"Fake?" Paul asked after her, almost in tears. "You don't know what fake is. I'll bet the pot you're going to sit on is fake." He walked over and sat down against a wall. Feeling real disappointment welling up within him, he choked back a sob and then was angry with himself for letting his sister get to him.

He took the letters out of his jacket pocket and began to turn them over and over in his hand. Somehow, now they didn't seem to be what they had been just a few minutes ago. Their glow had indeed been lessened, their heat cooled by the giggling cynicism of a big sister. When he turned the letters over again in his hand, perhaps too abruptly, a worn corner of a page flaked off and fell to the ground.

"How could these be fake?" Paul asked himself. The more he studied the letter, gently turning them in his hand, the more his doubts began to pass away. Fragility and faded writing certainly testified to their authenticity. And was that not a real Jefferson Davis stamp? Carefully, he took one letter out and read a few legible lines from it. That did it. The writing, obviously done with a quill pen, convinced him even more that they were genuine.

But there was something else, something that stirred in the back of his mind. It was something about these letters that he couldn't quite put his finger on. And it had nothing to do with a sister's sneers or even the letters dubious authenticity. Indeed, this certainty in the genuineness of his prize suggested something else, a strange insinuation that he couldn't identify.

Paul was glad that now he felt his treasure was, after all, real. But again there was that apprehension, a slight fear that suggested that even though the letters were the neatest thing he'd ever seen outside of a museum, he really shouldn't have bought them.

Chapter Two

Five o'clock found the Zunkers assembled at the van for the trip home. Since Thomas stressed punctuality, everyone had been a few minutes early, but Paul had wandered through the dealer's tables one last time and had been the last to arrive. He had separated from his sister — no longer wanting to hear her mouth — and had gone searching for something to spend his last ten dollars on. His search had not been successful since, after his bout with his sister, he had been more sensitive than ever to fake artifacts. Everything he saw seemed to him to be fake.

Curiously, the man who had sold Paul the letters was gone. Much too early, Paul had thought. He had wanted to look again at the other stuff the man had. Maybe even talk to him some more about the letters. But when he had found the man's two tables, they were bare. Everything, including the flag, was gone. At this discovery, the apprehension Paul had felt earlier returned. Now he wished the vanished dealer had been one of the usual bunch; someone he could catch out here next Sunday. Paul wondered if he would ever see him again.

He had felt again for the letters in his jacket pocket. Irked and just a little afraid, he had questions; questions he knew now would probably never be answered.

"Did you tell Mama and Papa about my letters?" Paul asked his sister as soon as he arrived at the van.

"No, I'm going to let you do that," she replied. She worked on a piece of gum that Paul thought gave her a flippancy that irritated him more than ever. "Papa'll probably give you a lecture about throwing twenty dollars down a rat hole."

Just then, Thomas came around the van and opened the sliding door to the back seats. "Well, did you find anything interesting in the market?" he asked, looking from Paul to Alex.

"Yes — Yes," Paul replied, remembering what his sister had just told him.

"Pauli bought some old letters, Papa," Alex said, matter-of-factly, and then climbed into the van.

"Some letters, Paul?" Thomas looked at his son in a curious manner. He was a tall, middle-aged man, hiding just a bit of gray in a full head of blond hair.

"Yes, Papa." Paul looked at the ground and then at his father. "Some old letters. From the Civil War."

"The Civil War?"

"Yes, Sir, the Civil War." Then Paul perked up a bit. "They're Confederate. I think they were written by a Confederate soldier."

"Let's see, Confederate." Thomas touched his finger to his face. "They were the people of the South, yes?"

"That's right, Papa, from the Southern states."

"You know, I remember reading about the American Civil War as a child in Germany. MutiZunker had plenty of books and I had plenty of time on my hands to read." He put his hands on his hips. "Well, very good, Paul. I should like to read some of your letters with you. By the way, your mother and I have decided to go to J.B. Juniors for hamburgers. That ought to please you, Paul." He smiled at Paul and winked at Alex who had turned her head toward her father.

"That ought to fill up a little of the world's smallest bottomless pit," she said.

"A bacon cheeseburger for me," Paul said to his father. "Oh, and Sis, I'm glad you remembered. I got the window this time." He leaped into the van, sat down in the second seat and immediately opened the window.

"Close that, Pauli, it's cold." Alex hugged herself.

"It's stuffy in here. I'll just keep it open for a few minutes."

"On second thought, keeping it open wouldn't be a bad idea." Alex turned in her seat toward her brother. "I can smell that junk you bought all over the van."

"What are you talking about?"

"That musty crud you bought from that guy." Alex faced him, sitting erect, matter-of-factly. "It stinks!" Tickled by her brother's agitated reaction, Alex turned back toward the front, relaxed, and began to pop her gum, loudly.

Paul, trying to control his irritation, replied, "For your information, I don't smell a thing. It must be your upper lip."

"Nope. It's that junk, all right." Alex grinned, widely, the gum behind her teeth. "It smells like a combination of old book room and open John."

Paul turned to her and scowled. "In case you'd like to know, Papa wants to read my smelly old junk, as you call it."

Alex put her hand to her mouth and giggled, staring straight ahead. "I know. I heard. I'll tell him to take a vacuum cleaner or a gas mask."

Still trying to control his temper, Paul turned toward the window to ignore her.

Twenty minutes later, Thomas turned the van into the crowded parking lot of J.B. Juniors. The restaurant, always crowded, had plenty of parking. They found a place, entered and stood in line to place their order. After studying the menu on the wall behind the main counter, Paul realized that he had left his letters in the van. He wondered why it would occur to him to bring the letters into the restaurant, but the thought that his new treasure was still in the van bothered him. Unconsciously scratching his ear, he began to maneuver through the crowd in order to see the van through the front window.

"What are you doing, Half Pint? Scratching fleas?" Unseen, Alex had come up behind him.

"I left those letters in the van." Paul re-searched his jacket pockets. "They must have fallen out of my pocket while I was sitting."

"Oh, wow. I wondered why people in here weren't bailing out through the windows while others hid under tables and held their noses." Alex's smirk glowed worse than ever. She started to say something else, but Paul cut her off.

"Listen to your mouth, wide open and saying nothing at …" He stared, in mid-sentence, through the window at the van.

Inside their Aerostar was a heavy, light colored smoke, so thick it made the vehicle seem likely to explode any minute.

Alex turned to see what Paul was staring at. "What is going on with the van?" she exclaimed, in disbelief. "Oh, my God! It's on fire!" Frantically, she looked around the crowded restaurant. "Papa? Pauli, where'd Papa go?"

"He's up by the front counter." Paul couldn't take his eyes

off the van. Fascinated, he couldn't move.

Alex grabbed her brother's arm and they hurried to their father who was in the process of placing their order.

"Papa, something's wrong with the van." The urgency in her voice made her father stare in disbelief. She grabbed his elbow and shook it to and fro, causing him to drop his wallet on the floor in front of the counter.

"What is it, Alexandra?" Giving his daughter an angry look, he retrieved his wallet from the floor and jammed it into his hip pocket.

"The van! It's on fire!"

Paul stood behind his sister's left elbow, eyes wide with terror.

Thomas studied both kids, a frown still on his face. Then he hurried over to the window. There, the three of them stared at their Ford Aerostar, sitting in the parking place where they had left it, not disturbed in any way.

"What about our van, Alexandra?" Thomas turned and addressed his daughter, the frown still on his face.

"Papa, a minute ago it was full of smoke, or something." Alex didn't wait for her father's reply, but stalked out through the door and straight to the van. Thomas and Paul followed close behind.

After he had unlocked the door, Thomas found everything just as they had left it. The windows were clear and the seats were clean. And there, on the back seat, were Paul's letters where they had fallen out of his pocket.

"Pauli and I both saw this van full of smoke, Papa." Alex turned to her father.

"Full of smoke?" Thomas asked. He unlocked the other doors and looked through the van carefully. Then he pulled the hood release and examined the engine. It was warm, but certainly not burning up. Next, he started the engine to check its temperature.

"What's going on out here?" Elizabeth, missing her family inside, had hurried to the parking lot and now stood next to her daughter. She was tall but Alex was almost as tall as she was. As a matter of fact, Alex was a younger edition of her mother.

"The children said they saw the van full of smoke."

Thomas had seated himself in the van and was turning on the ignition to see if the heat needle would rise quicker than normal. It didn't. "I don't know what it was. Probably some trick of the light in this parking lot. Anyway, there's no sign of any smoke." He chuckled and switched off the key.

"Papa, Pauli and I both saw it."

"Let's go get our supper and get home before it gets late, Alexandra," said Thomas, changing the subject and shaking his head.

Later, while they ate, Paul kept looking at the van through the front window. With the vehicle parked there, undisturbed, he began to think that maybe he and his sister had seen something that wasn't there; that maybe there was something to the "mass illusion" thing. He also wondered what Alex thought about it.

After supper the smoke-filled vehicle incident was forgotten. The family began the drive home, five miles across sparsely populated country. Paul gazed into the darkness while Elizabeth chatted with Alex, first about Paul's adventure at the new dealer's table and then about some clothes they had seen at the market that afternoon.

The two suburbs of Friendswood and Lake City are separated by a stretch of road about three miles running from east to west. The road, an old highway, is not lighted except for old farmhouses and an occasional icehouse or filling station. The area is rough gulf coast bottomland with here and there a small housing development or isolated house. There were former cultivated fields where cotton and other crops were grown at one time. The entire area looked about the same as it did sixty years ago when the highway was first built. On moonless nights, long stretches of blackness were common, and even with a moon, the darkness along the lonely road was thick, broken only slightly by occasional lights from buildings far off the road.

The Zunkers traveled this road often. They went to their favorite shopping mall over it; they went to the beach over part of it — to the main highway — and, of course, the flea market lay at the end of it. Tonight, Thomas was driving a bit slower than usual because a mist had begun shortly after they had left the restaurant. Working the wipers intermittently, he chatted softly with Elizabeth and Alex in the back seat.

Paul had replaced his letters in his jacket pocket and resumed looking out the window, trying to recognize familiar landmarks through the mist and darkness. Although he was half listening to what his family was saying, he was still thinking about his letters.

What little of them he had read so far fascinated him and he looked forward to reading them all through thoroughly. To read through them, he figured, would be like exploring an unknown country. He didn't know what he would find nor what he could expect. The experience would be altogether new and exciting, a history lesson written by someone who was there. Pleasantly excited, he began to speculate on what he might find.

Alex suddenly turned to her brother, a movement that broke his reverie.

"Pauli, turn the vent on, would you," she said, in a soft tone that made Paul wonder if she was going to go to sleep. "It's stuffy in here."

Automatically, he reached for the vent switch on the back seat climate control panel at the base of the window. He flipped the switch on and looked up through the glass. When he did, a large, dark object emerged from the blackness at the side of the road and darted for the road in front of the van.

"Thomas, seeing the thing flash in front of him, swerved the Aerostar to the left. The van had only begun its leftward movement when the right front bumper struck the streaking figure a glancing blow and the van skidded off the road and onto the shoulder.

"My God, what was that?" Thomas sat fully erect in the driver's seat and stared straight ahead. "It looked — It looked like someone's livestock."

"It wasn't a cow, Papa. It was moving too fast. I saw it before it ran onto the road." Paul, from the back seat, had already begun to search the road through the windows to the side and out the back for whatever they had hit.

Quickly, Thomas got out, walked around to the front and, by the light of the headlights, examined the front bumper. Even in this dim light, he could see nothing but a slight scrape; one that he knew had been there before. Whatever the van had hit had made no impression on their vehicle.

"Just a glancing blow, no damage," he muttered to himself. He ran his hand over the bumper and fender just to be sure.

Alex and Paul spilled out onto the road, leaving Elizabeth in the van.

"Papa, I think I see something in the brush on the other side of the road," said Paul. He turned and pointed to a dark area about fifty feet from the van. "Is the van okay?"

"Yes, Paul, not even a mark." Looking around in all directions, Thomas walked to the middle of the highway. "I don't see how, though. Whatever we ran into looked pretty big to me." He walked to the other side of the road and stared into the brush where Paul had pointed. "I think we better have a look over here, at least along the road," he said. "Whatever we hit might just be hurt enough to require some kind of care."

"I saw something move through those bushes just a minute ago, Papa." Paul looked right and left, and then crossed the highway to his father, leaving Alex by the van. He walked quickly to his father, across a small ditch by the road and toward the dark brush. "There was something here; I'm sure there was."

"Stay where I can see you, Paul," Thomas said. He stepped down into the ditch to follow his son. "Whatever that was, son, looked plenty big enough to make at least some noise in these bushes and trees." Thomas bent down and peered into the dark foliage, trying to see, in the limited light from the van, either something moving through the brush or some way through it.

They moved about ten yards down the highway and found a large, cleared-off area where a path left the road and led up to a gate about fifty yards away. There, Thomas and Paul stopped.

"Paul, go back to the van and get the flashlight," said Thomas, turning back to the highway and again looking right and left for any traffic.

Paul didn't need to go to the van. Alex met him in the middle of the road, flashlight in her hand.

"Thought you might need this," she said, with a grin. "Well, what did you find, anything?"

"Nothing, yet," Paul answered. Somehow, he thought his

sister's grin and flippant manner seemed out of place. "We found a clearing, though, by the road. There might be something nearby."

He grabbed the light from her and hurried back to his father, who, by this time, had started to walk the path up to the gate. While walking toward his father, Paul shined the light beam all around the clearing. He lit up the entire area in front of the gate. Then, he examined the path, deeply pitted and rough, along with the gate, which was old and had no lock. Thick bushes lined the open area and trash from the road mingled with scrub and wild ivy vines.

Paul and his father examined the densely packed bushes carefully. Nothing on either side of the path. Nothing along the highway. Once again, they swept the area with their light and then turned to walk toward the van.

They had almost reached the highway when something moved in the bushes to their right.

"What's that?" Paul threw his hand out to stop his father's progress.

Both of them stood perfectly still.

"I think it came from the bushes over there." Paul flashed the light into dense shrubbery ten feet from where they stood. The noise had stopped but they began to walk back into the clearing toward the source of the noise.

When they reached the little path to the gate, the noise began again.

Paul shined the light into the brush nearest the path, at the place where he thought he heard the rustling. Then, he saw it. A large animal ambled out of the thick undergrowth into the clearing but stopped before its entire body had cleared the brush.

A horse, dark and very large, stood watching them, about twenty feet away.

"That must be what we hit," said Thomas. He shoved his hands into his pockets and stared at the animal, an incredulous look on his face.

"It's got to be." Paul began to walk slowly toward it.

"Wait, Paul." Thomas put his hand on his son's shoulder. "It might be dangerous. A hurt animal can cause you harm."

“Let’s both go, Papa. Let’s get closer.” Together, they began to walk slowly toward the animal, which had not moved since coming out of the brush.

When they got within ten feet of the horse, both father and son stared, agape. Running from the base of the animal’s neck, three quarters of the way to its head, was a jagged and bloody gash.

Something had torn the animal’s body open so deep that, with the aid of the flashlight, Paul and Thomas could see well into its body cavity.

“Good God,” said Thomas. “We couldn’t have possibly done that. Not our front bumper. We struck it only a glancing blow.”

“Something did, Papa.” Running the light slowly all over the horse, Paul looked for other wounds. The animal was saddled but where was the rider? A glimmer across the saddle caught Paul’s eye and he stepped closer. Thomas followed, wary.

Suddenly the animal snorted and shuffled into the clearing. When it moved out of the bushes, Paul thought he heard a hollow “clank” from the area of the saddle.

Thomas stepped around his son and carefully put his hand on the saddle, while his other hand felt up and down the neck.

“This animal doesn’t seem to be in any pain, Paul,” said Thomas, his eyes wide, unbelieving.

“But look at that neck, Papa.”

Thomas moved his hand from the pommel to the seat of the saddle. He felt something wet. Immediately, he pulled his hand back, like something had bitten it. For less than a minute, he smeared the sticky liquid in his palm with his fingers and then stared, in disbelief.

Blood. Thick blood covered the tips of his fingers and the palm of his hand. Then, he looked closer at the saddle where his hand had been. It was covered with blood, from the seat downwards toward the stirrups.

“What in the name of God is this, now?” Thomas studied his hand and then the saddle, each in turn.

Paul saw the blood, too. “Was somebody riding this horse, Papa? I mean when you hit it.”

"I — I couldn't tell," he replied, in a strange, far-off voice. He took out his handkerchief and wiped the blood from his hand. "All I saw was a dark, hazy mass in front of the van. We struck whatever it was a glancing blow; nothing to do this." Again, he looked at the wounded animal. "There is no way it could have—have produced this." He indicated the bloody saddle and huge neck gash with a sweep of his hand.

Suddenly, the horse moved again, this time back toward the bushes. Paul heard the clanking noise again. Alarmed by the blood, he had momentarily forgotten about the mysterious "clank" on the saddle. However, now he stepped toward the animal to discover its cause.

He moved around to the other side of the horse, shining the light around the saddle as he went. When he reached the opposite side, he directed the light at the horse's side and froze.

There, dangling from the left side of the saddle was an empty saber scabbard. Since it had no blade to weight it down, it rattled every time the animal moved.

"Papa, whoever rode this horse had a sword!" He stared at the saddle area, not taking his eyes from the direct field of the light beam.

His father walked around the horse, his left hand extended toward the animal in an effort to steady it. "What on earth for?" he asked in a whisper.

"I don't know — I don't know." Paul answered his father's question although no reply was expected.

The horse shook its head and began to back further into the dense brush. Paul wanted to stop it but at the same time, he did not want to put his hand on the creature again. The sight of his father's bloody hand was enough for him.

When the horse backed up more, he stepped toward it, close enough to see the animal in what little light there was on the edge of the flashlight beam.

Suddenly, it turned its head directly toward Paul. He looked, momentarily, directly into the creature's face, and then felt like he was going to faint.

Where the left eye should have been, there was nothing but a jagged hole. They had paid all their attention to the neck and saddle and ignored its head. But now, this aberration was the ghastly piece de resistance to the animal's other injury as well as the blood. In the entire area of the left eye, there was only a black, empty hole, no organ residue or blood.

"My God, Papa, look!" Paul shouted and pointed. Startled by Paul's elevated voice, the horse quickly moved the rest of the way into the darkness of the bushes beside the clearing. In a flash, it was gone.

An attempt to find the horse with the flashlight failed; likewise, a brief search of the area.

After the search, Paul wasn't sure what he had seen. Nothing had made much sense. What had they seen in these dark bushes? A horse that should be dead? Some farmer's gravely wounded livestock? A specter out of nowhere? And the saddle with the empty saber scabbard, what was that all about? All of it certainly seemed real; it was real. But where did it go? He remembered hearing nothing after the animal left the range of their flashlight. And this silence was one more odd circumstance. After all, weren't horses supposed to be noisy?

Father and son walked somberly back to the van. "I think we had better call the animal shelter and report this as soon as we can," Thomas said. He fished deep into his pocket for the ignition key and then remembered that he had left it in the van.

"Papa, I know we had nothing to do with that horse's injuries," Paul said while they both crossed the road. "Something worse than the van made those injuries. Something horrible."

In silence, Paul seated himself in the van by his sister, now by the window.

"What happened out there, you guys," she asked, suddenly serious. She looked from Paul to her father. Her mother, seated in the front seat, was silent but had a concerned look on her face.

"We found a badly injured animal, Alexandra," Thomas replied, without turning around.

"Yeah, but we had nothing to do with the critter's hurts," Paul added, sensing his sister's next question.

"Anyway, I think we should phone the police. The animal control people won't be open this time of night." Thomas turned the ignition and the van's engine came to life. "There's an ice house down the road about a mile."

From the back seat, Paul filled in Alex and his mother all of the details about the encounter with the strange horse. They sat and listened in silence, Alex's mouth partially open in disbelief. Elizabeth just studied Paul closely as she listened.

When he was finished with his testimony, Alex blew a breath out of her mouth and turned abruptly toward her brother. "I can't believe you two let that animal get away," she said. "The poor thing was probably in pain. Or worse."

The sound of his sister's voice didn't convince Paul that she was really concerned about any pain the animal might have had. Given the circumstances as Paul had explained them, she knew better than to question them. So what was this concern bit?

They phoned the township police from an icehouse almost a mile from where they saw the horse. Thomas had no trouble relating significant details of the encounter and their location. Ten minutes later, their call was answered by an amiable, somewhat talkative, patrol sergeant from the Friendswood Police Force.

The Zunkers, busying themselves at the magazine rack, saw the sergeant as soon as he arrived. Thomas and Paul met him in the parking lot and introduced themselves.

"I'm afraid we have a badly injured animal on our hands," Thomas said to the officer still seated in his car. "And maybe an injured rider as well."

The Sergeant wrote something on a clipboard. Suddenly, he looked up into Thomas' face. "Go ahead and get in and show me where this animal is." He leaned over and opened the door on the passenger side. Thomas let Paul in the back seat.

"You know, these people out here are farmers in reputation only," continued the Sergeant, his head swiveling to scan both sides of the road while driving. "Nobody plants anything larger than a vegetable garden. Nobody has any livestock out here either. A few chickens, maybe. Biggest animal they might have out here is a large dog, for security reasons." He reached for his radio below the dash, and radioed his location to his dispatcher.

"I don't know where a horse would come from," he continued. "Unless someone brought it in recently. This township has never established an ordinance against such beasts. There just never has been any."

They arrived at the dark place along the road where Thomas and Paul recognized the clearing and the gate. All three got out of the car at the same time.

Thomas told the Sergeant where the horse had stood and the officer swiveled a large light attached to the car in the general direction and switched it on. The entire area lit up brilliantly, even the darkened gate so much that Paul, from the road, could tell that few of its boards were missing.

"Now, where did you say that animal was, Mr. Zunker?" The Sergeant reached into his unit and got his flashlight.

The officer was a big man, Paul noticed. He was the kind of man that would have six kids and want the boys to grow up to be football players. Also, he had a natural friendliness about him that Paul didn't think a typical cop should have, a good-naturedness that really belonged to a veterinarian or a children's doctor. Paul wondered what he would do if he ever ran up against a really desperate crook.

"Right there, next to those bushes, is where we last saw him." Thomas pointed toward the darkened mass of vegetation ten feet from the path leading up to the gate.

"You know, the little Donner girl down the road has a pony. Was this a pony, you saw?" The Sergeant flicked on his light and aimed the beam where Thomas had pointed.

"No." Thomas and Paul answered in unison. "This was a full grown horse," said Thomas, walking up next to the Sergeant and examining the lighted area with him.

"And he had a saddle," Paul added. "A saddle with blood on it."

"With blood on it?" The Sergeant turned in Paul's direction.

"Yes, blood. In the seat and down the sides."

The Sergeant turned back around and stood motionless, momentarily thinking. Then, he looked again at Thomas.

"Mr. Zunker, where, exactly, was this horse?"

"There, by that bush." Thomas started to walk toward the place he pointed at. "We should see his tracks or broken branches or something over here."

The policeman walked behind Thomas over to the indicated area. Both men then examined the ground, Thomas studying it like he would a map.

Finally, the Sergeant spoke. "Mr. Zunker, if that animal was as big as you seem to think it was, don't you think he'd leave some tracks?"

"What the —?" Thomas acted like he hadn't heard the question. "I can't believe this," he said. "Why the hell aren't there any tracks?"

"The ground's still wet. It has been raining." The Sergeant shined his light all over the indicated area. "No tracks!"

"My God, I didn't think of that." Thomas put his hand to his mouth in amazement. "But how did he not leave tracks?" He looked at his son.

But Paul stood next to his father and said nothing.

"It seems your horse was either standing somewhere where he wouldn't leave tracks, like on rocks or leaves, or —"

"... Or he wasn't here at all?" Thomas concluded.

"Well, Mr. Zunker, I was going to say he wasn't as close to you as you thought he was." The Sergeant continued to shine the light around the immediate area. "Mr. Zunker, I believe you. I believe you and your son saw something. And I'm going to keep an eye out for it." Placing his flashlight steadily under his arm, he took out a small pad and began to write. "Jack Finley from DPS runs a speed trap along here in the morning. I'm going to have his dispatcher tell him to keep his eyes open."

Thomas, bewildered, watched the policeman write in the tiny pad. Paul continued to search the ground, as much as he could see, for footprints, or something to testify that the horse had been there and had not been some optical illusion.

"This is a heck of a note for someone trying to be a good Samaritan," Thomas mumbled, while the Sergeant put away his pad.

"Well, Mr. Zunker, we can't solve the problems unless good folks like you tell us about them." The officer took one more look around the area and then turned toward the car. Thomas and Paul followed.

Thomas seemed in better spirits a little while later but Paul was worried.

“No prints, for God’s sake,” Paul said from the back seat on the way back to the icehouse. “No prints!”

“Shhh,” Thomas said over the seat. “Neither one of us should be cursing about this, Paul.”

“I know, Papa,” Paul said, in subdued tone. “But still, no prints,” he mumbled to himself. “Why?”

Suddenly, he remembered his father’s handkerchief, which he had used to wipe blood from his hand.

“Papa! Papa! Your handkerchief. You remember? You used it to wipe that blood off your hand. Get it!”

Thomas reached into his front pocket. Finding nothing there he searched through all other pockets he had but the handkerchief was, as Paul had somehow suspected, gone.

Stehle's Door

About the Author

William M. O'Brien, Jr. lives in San Antonio, Texas with his wife, two dogs, and a growing number of cats. His wide range of interests, activities and experiences is generally reflected in the writing he does. An avid reader of both fiction and non-fiction, he chooses fiction as the area in which to write, combining horror, history, and the occult in his novels STEHLE'S DOOR and I ALEXANDRA. The latter work is a semi sequel of the former. Both novels are very intense and can stand by themselves.

Mr. O'Brien is also a prolific writer of short fiction. Currently is compiling and writing an anthology of short stories entitled "Tales Written in Hell," which includes horror stories, satires, dark fantasies (many of which are experimental), conflict tales as well as others. His favorite type of short story is the ghost story. Many of his stories have appeared on line.

visit the author's website:
www.WilliamMObrien.com

find him on FaceBook:
www.facebook.com/pages/William-M-OBrien-Jr-Author/131890196907875

read his blog:
www.goodreads.com/author/show/5253597.William_M_O_Brien_Jr_

www.ingramcontent.com/pod-product-compliance
Lightning Source LLC
LaVergne TN
LVHW020523100826
845148LV00010B/1321

* 9 7 8 1 6 1 7 5 2 1 5 0 8 *